Steve has always been shy and lacking in confidence to the point where he has never dated. College was never an option. Expected to pay his way at the age of 16, Steve left school and went to work as an insurance clerk. Steve only started writing in 2017, just before his father passed away, and his mother passed away before the book was published.

I would like to dedicate this book to my parents, for without them I would not be the man I am today.

Steve Pretlove

PRINCE OLIVER AND THE WINTER QUEEN

AUSTIN MACAULEY PUBLISHERS™

LONDON * CAMBRIDGE * NEW YORK * SHARJAH

Copyright © Steve Pretlove 2022

The right of Steve Pretlove to be identified as author of this work has been asserted by the author in accordance with section 77 and 78 of the Copyright, Designs and Patents Act 1988.

All rights reserved. No part of this publication may be reproduced, stored in a retrieval system or transmitted in any form or by any means, electronic, mechanical, photocopying, recording or otherwise, without the prior permission of the publishers.

Any person who commits any unauthorised act in relation to this publication may be liable to criminal prosecution and civil claims for damages.

This is a work of fiction. Names, characters, businesses, places, events, locales, and incidents are either the products of the author's imagination or used in a fictitious manner. Any resemblance to actual persons, living or dead, or actual events is purely coincidental.

A CIP catalogue record for this title is available from the British Library.

ISBN 9781528999489 (Paperback)
ISBN 9781528999496 (ePub e-book)

www.austinmacauley.com

First Published 2022
Austin Macauley Publishers Ltd®
1 Canada Square
Canary Wharf
London
E14 5AA

I would like to thank everyone at Austin Macauley Publishers for all their help and support, I could not have done this without you.

Chapter 1
Richard's Torment

The river boundary between human and fairy kingdoms had closed and would remain closed for the next ten years. This was the one thought that ran through King Richard's mind constantly, accompanied by the image of Nicholas being carried away by a giant white eagle, and the leering faces of Dante and Cressida, smiling their sickly smile as their images slowly faded away. Richard's subconscious mind wondered. Had this been their plan all along?

King Richard tossed and turned in bed with this nightmare running through his mind every time he closed his eyes to sleep. He awoke with a start, screaming no, the images from his nightmare appeared to him as ghostly spirits floating around his room briefly before slowly evaporating. As the giant white eagle slowly faded, Richard realised he was sitting upright in bed, in a cold sweat. It was just past midnight. He had been asleep for less than an hour, yet his bedsheets were soaked. He closed his eyes and lay down. As his breathing calmed, he opened them once more, half-expecting to see the images again, half hoping not to, but they had gone. The dying embers of the fire provided just enough light to see what he was doing but little warmth, and so he climbed out of bed and removed his sleeping robe. The sweat made it cling to his body as he peeled it off. There was a cold sensation he felt all over his body and he shivered. Looking around for something to dry himself, he removed the top layer blanket from his bed which was dry and rubbed himself down. Then he got dressed in the clothes he had worn the day before that had been discarded and were lying on the floor, not bothering to put anything on his feet. He quietly left his bedroom, having picked up a candlestick with a solitary candle which he had lit using the fire.

As Richard walked barefoot down the hallway, the flame flickered and swayed with each step, casting dancing shadows on the walls and ceiling. Almost in a trance like state, he took no notice of the shadows.

Moving through the castle as quietly as possible trying not to disturb any of his children, Richard then descended the stairs. Stumbling halfway down, he grabbed hold of the banisters to prevent himself from falling and steadied himself. The candle sat firmly in the candlestick. Slowly, he continued down. Having reached the bottom of the staircase, Richard made his way across to the front door of the castle. He had a master key within his pocket that unlocked any door within the castle. As he quietly opened the door, the candles flame was extinguished by a sudden gust of cold air. Of no further use, he let the candlestick fall from his hand onto the floor by the door. The small candlestick bounced on the narrow strip of carpet, rolled across the stone floor and settled against the wall. The candle, having been dislodged from the candlestick, lay in the middle of the carpet. Richard stepped outside. There was a cooling breeze drifting across the gardens from the lake. Richard paused briefly. A veiled moon covered in wispy cloud provided a faint glow. He left the warmth of the castle behind, as he stepped into the cool night air. The stone steps beneath his bare feet were freezing cold to his touch. It was as if the soles of his feet absorbed the cold and it sent a shiver than ran from his feet up his legs and into the rest of his body. Stumbling through sheer exhaustion, he then made his way into the garden. Stepping from the pathway onto the grass, it was wet underfoot, not that he noticed, his feet already frozen. He found a seat and sat down feeling tired beyond belief. He tilted his head so he could gaze upon the stars in the heaven above. They twinkled down on him for a brief moment and then disappeared behind the thin cloud which lazily drifted across the black sky. "What have I done to deserve this?" he asked.

"You have done nothing to deserve this," answered a female voice. Richard looked around wearily for who had spoken, but with eyes half closed, there was no one he could see in the dim moonlight. Richard thought he must have imagined it, then he sneezed, his head forcefully falling forward. "Bless you," said the female voice. On hearing the voice the second time, he recognised it as belonging to Elizabeth, his wife, but he was too tired to stand up and look for her, and so he lowered his eyelids in an attempt to sleep once more, but, even in this exhausted state, his mind was too troubled to allow him the comfort of sleep.

When a hand rested upon his right shoulder unexpectedly, he barely flinched with surprise. His eyelids flickered as he attempted to open his eyes once more, but the small matter of opening his eyes required more effort than he could find, as the voice spoke to him once more. "Hello, Father." His mind confused he sat without moving, struggling to place the voice that he thought belonged to his wife Elizabeth, and then it dawned on him, he did recognise the voice, it belonged to his daughter Dorothy, who was so like her mother. "Father, please come back inside," she pleaded.

"What is the point?" said Richard. "I cannot sleep."

Unable to persuade him to return inside, she sat beside him and asked, "What's the matter, Father?" He looked at her with a deep sadness in his eyes.

"I am just so tired," he said.

"Right," said Dorothy resolutely, "I am taking you back inside. It is too cold to stay out here all night." She stood up and attempted to help her father to his feet, but he was so tired and had no strength to stand. For Dorothy, it was like trying to lift a dead weight. She struggled in her effort trying to get him to stand up, but he was just too heavy and she had to admit defeat. There was no way she could manage on her own. Then as she sat down beside her father, she saw a light floating in the darkness. Moving from the lake towards the castle, a disembodied hand carrying a candle was all she could see. Struck with fear that coursed its way through her body, she froze. As she recovered from the initial shock, *Who would be walking in the garden at night carrying a candle*, she wondered. As the flame from the candle flickered, the rest of the body was shrouded in darkness. For some reason, it sent a chill down her spine; she tried reasoning with herself. It wasn't like she had never seen anyone walking in the dark with a candle before, but for some reason, outside in the blackened garden, she couldn't help feeling disturbed by this strange sight. She was frightened enough to put her hand over her father's mouth, to keep him quiet, she had no idea who would be skulking around the palace gardens at night. Desperate for assistance in getting Richard back inside the castle, she wanted to cry for help more than anything, but fear of the unknown candleholder kept her quiet.

Richard was too tired and too weak to worry about the hand covering his mouth. With his eyes half closed and breathing through his nose, he was totally unaware of the approaching light. Dorothy on the other hand was extremely scared. Her thoughts running wild, what if it was somebody hoping to break into the castle, maybe even try to kill the king. In the cold chill of night, she sat perfectly still. Wanting to protect her father, she sat silently, watching. Her body began to tremble with fear. As the floating candle drew nearer, she held her breath. The moon and stars had completely disappeared, which she was grateful for, veiled behind dark clouds. If she had been on her own, she would have fled the first moment she had seen the candlelight, but there was no way she was going to leave her father alone. Even though she was terrified, she was determined they would face whatever this was together, but hoping it would pass them by undetected, and so she sat silently watching, the cloud covering the moon began to thin. She glanced up at the night sky. "No, not now," she said to herself, praying for the cloud to cover the moon once more. For the first time in her life, she felt she would be safer in the dark, but no, the clouds had parted at just the wrong moment, and a beam of moonlight illuminated the exact spot where Dorothy and King Richard were hiding. Even though she was wearing a dark-blue dressing gown which meant she was perfectly camouflaged in the shadows, she had been spotted. The floating light had changed direction and was heading straight towards them at a fast pace. With the light from the moon shining in her eyes, all Dorothy could make out was the candle and the silhouette of whoever was carrying it. Shadows seemed to dance around the figure as it approached. Dorothy's pulse was racing and her heart felt as though it would jump out of her chest. She wanted to hide, trying to shield her father and make herself as small as possible, but she knew they had been spotted. She was about to scream when a familiar male voice said, "Hello, Dorothy, are you all right?" Then he realised she was not alone but in fact cradling their father.

"Oliver." She sighed. "Thank God, you nearly scared me to death. Come and help me get father back inside, will you?" Oliver dropped his candle which had been the source of the floating light. He too was wearing a dark-blue dressing gown which was why he had appeared so mysteriously black in the candles flame. The candle expired as it hit the damp ground. Now they only had the moonlight to show the way as it peered from behind the drifting clouds. It took a great deal of effort but between the two of them, they managed to stagger their way back towards the castle. The door was wide open and as they stepped inside, Oliver trod on the candle which lay in the middle of the carpet, the candle which Richard had dropped earlier. It snapped in two and moved beneath Oliver's foot. Oliver stumbled sideways pulling Richard and Dorothy with him. They landed in a heap on the floor, with Oliver stuck beneath his father and sister. Dorothy had let out a small cry of surprise, as they had toppled sideways. Now she was getting to her feet once more. "Are you all right?" she asked Oliver. Oliver used all his strength to roll his father's body off himself, so he could stand once more.

"Yes, I'm fine," said Oliver, gasping for breath, "how about you?" he asked.

"I'm fine," she replied. Oliver walked over and closed the door. Now inside the castle with no candle and only the moonlight shining through the windows, their eyes slowly adjusted to the darkness. Both of them took hold of their father by his arms and between them, they lifted him off the floor. He was now unconscious and offered no assistance whatsoever, so, with his feet dragging across the floor, they stumbled their way to the nearest sitting room. Twice, they bumped into a piece of furniture hidden in the dark, but eventually they found what they were searching for and dropped Richard onto the sofa to rest. They managed to lay their father so his head was raised, resting upon a cushion, and Dorothy lifted her father's feet onto the sofa trying to make him as comfortable as possible. Only then did she realise his feet were bare, and wet. She rubbed them dry with the bottom of her dressing gown.

Dorothy and Oliver slumped into the armchairs at opposite ends of the sofa, breathing heavily after the exertion of getting their father inside. Dorothy asked Oliver, "What were you doing outside?"

Oliver answered, "I was having trouble sleeping and decided to go for a walk, that's all, seems to me you and father were having the same problem."

"Yes, I guess we were," said Dorothy. Richard had finally fallen asleep. Although his breathing was erratic and his body was making strange jerking movements, they both knew this signalled yet another nightmare. Dorothy and Oliver decided to stay and keep watch over their father, just in case Richard decided to go for another walk.

Dorothy with arms outstretched feeling her way across the room had decided to open the curtains that covered the large windows. As she pulled the curtains back, moonlight flooded the room just enough, so Dorothy and Oliver could see each other more clearly. As Dorothy made her way back to where Oliver was sitting, she asked in a whisper, "What was it like, the fairy kingdom?" They had been back a week and Richard refused to talk about it, and forbade anyone else, to talk of it. Oliver didn't like to disobey his father, but he had been dying for one of his sisters to ask him, now he felt was his chance.

He moved to a chair that was closer to Dorothy's and sat down. "It really is a kingdom like no other," said Oliver. "For a start, it has three suns, one yellow, one blue and one pink." Dorothy shifted in her chair to get more comfortable. She had been waiting to hear this long enough.

"Go on," she said, in a whisper, all excited, "tell me more."

"Well," said Oliver, "when clouds pass over the three suns, the clouds light up like a rainbow, and if it rains from a rainbow cloud, you get multi-coloured rain."

Dorothy's face was animated with excitement. "Oh, it sounds wonderful," she said.

Oliver was enjoying himself, finally being able to tell someone what he had seen, and so he continued, "At night, the three suns merge together to create a purple moon."

"Oh, marvellous," said Dorothy, "imagine a purple moon."

Oliver continued, "Then there is the rainbow forest, where all the trees have multi-coloured leaves like a rainbow."

"Quiet," raged Richard, neither of them had noticed their father waking up. "I forbid you to say another word."

In the light that shone through the window, he stood towering above them both, a ghostly figure in the moonlight, turning first to face Oliver and then he turned on Dorothy. She sat cowering with fear as he took a step closer. She had never seen her father like this before, so angry, his blood-red eyes glowed in his ghostly white face. She screamed and jumped from her chair, pushing Richard to one side as she raced from the room. He spun around stunned, as he watched Dorothy disappear down the hallway. He was calm once more. Turning to face his son, he asked Oliver, "What just happened?"

Richard, looking at his son, asked, "Why are you looking at me like that?" With fear etched across his face, Oliver explained to his father what had just occurred. Richard collapsed onto the sofa and began to sob. "I don't remember any of that," cried Richard, "the last thing I remember is you and your sister lying me down on the sofa, and just then, Dorothy pushing past me in tears screaming as she left the room." With his head in his hands, he asked, "What is happening to me?"

The noise Dorothy had made as she raced through the castle crying had awoke the palace guards. In sleeping robes, they raced from their beds down the hallway in search of the disturbance, each carrying a sword. The castle had fallen quiet once more. The guards separated to search the castle. There were no fires lit in any of the fireplaces. All candles on the walls had long been extinguished.

The only light available to them was the moonlight, which kept fading as clouds passed by. One of the guards stubbed his big toe on the leg of the solid oak dining table. He cried out in pain. Another guard who heard him cry out called, "Are you all right?"

"Yes," answered the guard who was stumbling around barefooted. They continued their search. By the time Richard and Oliver were discovered, it was Oliver who had fallen asleep whilst Richard watched over him. "Is everything all right, Your Majesty?" enquired one of the guards.

"Yes, everything is fine," said Richard, "goodnight." Satisfied the king was safe, the guards all returned to their quarters.

The next day found Richard talking with the court physician, sat in front of the fire in the sitting room with the portrait of Elizabeth on the wall above the mantelpiece. Oliver sat on a seat by the window. Richard and the physician were talking about what had occurred the night before. "And you don't remember screaming at Dorothy and Oliver?" the physician asked.

"No," said Richard, "I only know what Oliver told me." Feeling ashamed for frightening his own children, Richard sat with his head held in his hands.

"I think you need to sit down and talk to your children about what happened to Nicholas," said the physician, after a short silence.

"Who is Nicholas?" asked Richard, raising his head to look at the physician.

"Why, he is your youngest son, Your Majesty," said the court physician.

"What do you mean?" said Richard in surprise, "I have four children, I have three daughters Alice, Dorothy and Mary and I have one son, Oliver."

"But Your Majesty, you have a second son called Nicholas." Richard looked at the physician bewildered.

"No, you are lying," said Richard, "and where is Elizabeth?"

As Richard got more and more agitated, he started to pace the room. "Where is my wife?" he demanded. "Where is Elizabeth?"

Oliver was sat silently in his chair by the window. His thoughts had taken him back to happier times when his mother was still alive. Looking out into the garden, he smiled briefly. Then remembering the birth of his younger brother, Nicholas, and the death of his mother three days later, bought a tear to his eyes. He was brought back from his reverie as his father had slammed his fist onto a table. Oliver gave his head a shake as if trying to empty his mind. The court physician persuaded King Richard to have a drink, adding a little pill to calm his nerves without King Richard knowing. As Richard emptied the glass, the physician spoke again. "Keeping it to yourself and refusing to talk about what happened is only doing you harm, and in the long run, not allowing Oliver to talk about his experience will also have an adverse effect on his health."

As Oliver and the court physician watched, the pill had the desired effect and Richard calmed down. Seated once more, his breathing returned to normal, but Richard didn't like what he was hearing, for he didn't understand. He kept asking for Elizabeth, and refused to believe that he had a son called Nicholas. He was not feeling well and the physician asked a guard who was standing outside the sitting room to help King Richard to his chambers. Oliver wanted to follow, but the physician stopped him. Speaking to the guard, the physician said, "Make sure he gets some rest, and do not leave him on his own, I will be along shortly." The guard escorted King Richard from the sitting room. The physician wanted to talk to the four royal children. Oliver had already reassumed his seat by the window. A guard was sent to escort the princesses to the sitting room. When they arrived a few minutes later, they nervously entered the room not knowing what to expect. Sat on a sofa, so they were seated facing the physician. He stood with his back to the fireplace. The portrait of Elizabeth, their mother, visible over his shoulder. His hands were in front of his chest and he was wringing them, as he shifted uncomfortably.

"I am sorry to tell you this, but your father has fallen gravely ill, he seems to have no memory of Nicholas, and keeps asking for Elizabeth."

"But why would he do that?" asked Oliver.

"I can only guess that the trauma of what has happened has affected him badly. His mind has shut out those painful memories of losing Nicholas, and he only remembers what happened before Nicholas was born."

"You mean to say he has lost five years of memory?" said Dorothy.

"It would seem so," said the physician.

Alice began to cry, as Mary asked, "Are you saying our father has gone mad?"

"No, he hasn't gone mad, as such, it's just that it's such a painful memory to have lost Nicholas the way he did that his mind—"

"So he has gone mad," interrupted Mary.

"Oh, Mary, shut up," said Alice between sobs, "let the physician finish."

"Will he get his memory back?" asked Oliver.

"I'm afraid only time will tell," said the physician, "I will treat him as best I can. He needs plenty of rest, and don't try and convince him he has a son called

Nicholas. The more pressure you put on your father to remember, the more confused he may become, and this may slow his recovery."

"And what do we tell him if he asks for our mother?" said Dorothy.

"At this present time, I would suggest you tell him that she has gone to visit his sister. If you tell him she has died, the grief may be too much and he may never recover."

Alice burst into tears once more. Dorothy comforted her and put an arm around her shoulders. Mary was now sitting in stunned silence, and Oliver left the room. Dorothy called out to Oliver, "Where are you going?"

"I need to be alone," said Oliver.

Chapter 2
Nicholas at the Ball

Having been snatched from his father's shoulders by a giant white eagle, Nicholas at first had been scared. He turned his head to see the boundary between the two kingdoms close, separating him from his friends and family. He struggled against the giant bird's talons, as they gripped his shoulders, but as the giant bird had flown over the rainbow forest and beyond, Nicholas realised that resistance was futile. At this great height if the bird had released him, it would have meant certain death. Having given up his struggles, Nicholas had settled down to enjoy the bird's eye-view. Leaving the rainbow forest behind, they had crossed a barren land, followed by the tall green trees which Dante called home. Flying further north, the landscape had changed one last time. Flying low over ice-blue coloured lakes, Nicholas marvelled at his reflection, held gently but firmly in the talons of the giant white eagle. The air was cool as they sped over the lakes, and Nicholas could feel the cold invading his body with every breath, the cold air spreading like a rampant disease throughout his limbs. Nicholas was grateful he wasn't holding on for as he looked at his hands, they had turned blue with the cold and he had no feeling in them. They were completely numb.

Having been excited by his reflection in the water, Nicholas raised his head once more to look straight ahead. He had never seen a lake as big before, and as they flew over the first, it was quickly followed by two more, each as big as the first.

In the distance, Nicholas could see two smaller birds that looked as though they were fighting in the air. As they flew closer, two smaller golden eagles were squabbling over a carcass, and they were right in the flight path of the giant white eagle carrying Nicholas. Almost upon them, the giant white eagle carrying Nicholas let out a piercing scream. Startled, the two smaller eagles parted, dropping the carcass to the ground. As one flew off, the other seized the opportunity and dropped to the ground to retrieve its prize.

As they left the lakes behind, they continued to fly further north. The ground was covered with a sprinkling of snow, pine forests spread before them and herds of reindeer scattered as the giant white eagle soared overhead, casting a giant shadow. Then in the distance stood a solitary mountain that rose high in the sky. With its snow-capped peak, it stood like a beacon against the pale-blue sky. Nicholas looked down the snow-covered slopes of the mountain. At its base was a small village, surrounded by tall trees, all covered in snow. As excitement swelled inside his body, he forgot how cold he was feeling. Then as the eagle made a sweeping turn to the left, on an elevated position just to the left of the village, stood a castle. Shrouded in snow, it sparkled like a diamond, with more turrets and windows than on any castle Nicholas had ever seen. It reminded him of a picture he had once seen in a storybook that had belonged to his mother, covered in snow a vision of serenity and beauty.

The white eagle circled the castle once. It seemed this was their destination. Nicholas looked down into an empty courtyard. As the eagle landed, the snow that covered the ground became disturbed and raised into the air. Then having released Nicholas safely onto the ground, unharmed, with one flap of his giant wings, the eagle was airborne once more. The snow lying on the ground was disturbed again as the giant eagle took to flight. Momentarily, Nicholas could not see a thing as the snow swirled around him. Then as the snow settled once more allowing Nicholas to look around, he could see he was alone.

Nicholas might have only been five, but he was not scared. After the initial shock of being grabbed by the giant white eagle, he had enjoyed flying, so now he stood alone, but he was excited and wondered what was going to happen next. And so he waited, and he waited, but as time passed by and nothing happened, his excitement waned, and he began to feel the cold once more. With his arms folded across his chest to try and keep warm, he stood shivering. As he looked around the empty courtyard, hoping for some sign of life, he called out, "Hello, is anyone there?" But the only sound he heard was the echo of his own voice. He could not believe after being carried all this way, he was to be left alone. Surely, he had been bought here for a reason. Becoming bored of waiting, he started kicking the snow, and then bent down to grab a handful of snow and formed it into a snowball. In frustration, he threw it against a wall where it splattered on impact. On the windowsill just above where the snowball hit the wall, snow cascaded down and landed in a small heap at Nicholas' feet. He shivered once more. It seemed to Nicholas he had been waiting for hours. He called out again, "Hello, is anyone there?" Still no answer. He crossed the courtyard to the nearest door and tried to open it. It was locked. He knocked on the door and called out, "Hello, is anyone there?" Still no answer. It had only been twenty minutes, but he started to feel desperate, wondering why the white eagle had bought him to this seemingly abandoned castle. All the while, unknown to Nicholas, he was being observed from above. As Nicholas made his way to the centre of the courtyard once more, without warning, the gates to the castle opened and a carriage being drawn by four pure white horses entered the courtyard at great speed. Nicholas stepped to one side quickly to avoid being run over. As the carriage stopped at the stairs that led to the castle's main entrance, two women dressed in white stepped down from the carriage, helped by two footmen who had appeared from nowhere, followed by two men dressed in black who escorted the women, as they climbed the stairs. They were talking and laughing. Then as they reached the top of the stairs, the doors opened by themselves. It allowed the most fabulous music to escape. Nicholas was about to race up the stairs when a second carriage arrived. This carriage was even closer to knocking him over than the first one. He stumbled backwards upon the stairs. Two more women dressed in white stepped down from their carriage. They briefly stopped to look at Nicholas, giggling, but without offering to help him to his feet, they continued up the stairs. Two men dressed in black descended from the carriage and raced up the stairs after their dates for the evening without even noticing Nicholas. Nicholas decided it was safer to stay out of the way for now, moving away from the carriages higher up the stairs, and so he watched as eight, ten, twelve, twenty or so carriages in total arrived. As the last carriage left, Nicholas waited to see if any more were coming. After waiting a considerable amount of time, Nicholas dared to climb the stairs. He only intended to sneak a peek through a window at the ball that was taking place inside, but as he reached the top of the stairs, the doors opened, and he was ushered inside.

 He was led to the top of the stairs by a tall, thin man with a long, pointed chin. His hair was white and hung down over his shoulders ending halfway down his back. With deep-blue eyes and pale skin, he was attractive in an unusual way, dressed from head to toe in a blood-red outfit, except for his black shoes he stood out from the crowd. Standing at the top of the blue marble staircase, he looked down upon the guests gathered in the ballroom. The music stopped. "Your

Majesty," he announced, "your guest of honour has arrived." All faces were now turned in his direction, and so he took one step aside to reveal Nicholas.

Nicholas felt right at home. He had attended balls before at his father's castle and the fact everyone was looking at him didn't make him feel at all nervous. It made him feel special. Among the many faces, looking up at Nicholas as he stood at the top of the blue marble staircase, was one face that seemed familiar, and yet something was different. He recognised Eleanor. She was smiling at him. With her flaming-red hair, she stood out from everyone else. He returned her smile, then his gaze fell upon the most beautiful lady he had ever seen. With blonde hair, sapphire blue eyes and a pale complexion, her ruby red lips broke into a smile revealing perfect white teeth. She wore a crown of yellow, blue and pink diamonds, and her white dress was decorated with the purest of clear, cut diamonds. As she glided across the floor towards the blue marble staircase, she sparkled beneath the candle chandeliers. Eleanor walked alongside this vision of beauty. She was no longer wearing the blue patterned dress he was used to, instead the dress Eleanor wore was decorated with sapphires, emeralds and rubies. As the jewels reflected the candlelight, she reminded Nicholas of a beautiful peacock.

As the two women stopped at the bottom of the staircase, Nicholas descended. "Prince Nicholas," said Eleanor, "I would like to introduce you to my mother, Queen Elvira, also known as the Winter Queen." As Nicholas bowed before Queen Elvira, she reached out a hand which caressed the side of his face. As her fingers gently touched his bare skin, her body tingled with excitement.

"It is a pleasure to meet you, Your Majesty," said Nicholas.

"The pleasure is all mine," said Elvira. One of the guests started to laugh. Elvira shot a quick angry glance in the direction of the laughter, which ceased instantly. As Nicholas looked upon the two women standing before him, it was hard to believe they were mother and daughter. Eleanor herself didn't seem very old, but Elvira looked even younger than her daughter.

The music started up once more and all the beautiful people took to the dance floor and danced. Elvira offered Nicholas her hand. "I don't know how to dance," said Nicholas.

"Just follow me," said Elvira. Nicholas took hold of Elvira's hand and allowed himself to be led to the centre of the ballroom. Dancing couples either stepped aside or stopped dancing altogether. Elvira danced and Nicholas as if by magic was able to follow all the steps. They glided across the ballroom floor.

First spinning one way and then the other. Nicholas was having the time of his life. Once Elvira had danced enough, she left the dance floor and returned to her throne. It was Eleanor who replaced her mother on the dance floor. Queen Elvira watched with a huge smile upon her face and a mischievous glint in her eyes. She felt more youthful and alive than she had in years.

"You look different," said Nicholas to Eleanor, as they spun around.

"It's the ears," said Eleanor, and then he realised, they were no longer laying horizontally, but standing upright at the side of her head.

"I like them better like this," said Nicholas. Eleanor just smiled, as they continued to dance the night away.

Chapter 3
Oliver Tells All

It was morning and the sky was blue with small, white, fluffy clouds dotted here and there across an ocean of sky. Oliver was lying on the grass looking at the sky lazily. Reif was lying on the grass next to him. "It seems strange only having one sun," said Oliver.

"You forget," said Reif, "I haven't seen any sun for ten years." They both laughed. Despite the age difference, they had formed a close bond.

At the time Arec and Reif had been trapped in the black mountain, Reif had been a young boy of fourteen. Although he had grown, and his body had developed into that of an adult, at heart he was still a young boy, who in the ensuing years had had to learn how to fight.

The two boys had been swimming in the lake, something Reif hadn't been able to do in the last ten years. It had felt fantastic from the very moment they waded into the water, and he felt the cool water on his legs, and how his feet sank into the silt that sat covering the bottom of the lake. It oozed between his toes. Then he had dived beneath the surface and reappeared ten feet behind Oliver, and splashed him, and as Oliver turned to face Reif, they were using both hands to send water flying in all directions. Then Reif remembered the last time he had swam. It had been recently, when he had to swim beneath the surface of the moat, to escape Eleanor's castle. He remembered the large yellow eye of the giant fish, as it swam past him. The fins as they brushed against his legs and the flick of the powerful tail which had created a current which had briefly caused him some difficulty. His whole body shuddered, but he also remembered how Nicholas had helped distract the monster fish, which enabled him to get out of the water.

Oliver and Reif had removed their shoes, socks and shirts to go swimming. At last, Reif was able to enjoy the feel of the warm sun on his pale, naked skin.

As they lazed by the lake, they were joined by Alice, Dorothy and Mary. Mary sat a little too close for Reif's liking and it made him feel uncomfortable. He immediately sat up and put his shirt back on. Mary watched his every move. Then unexpectedly Mary asked Reif, "How old are you?"

Reif looked puzzled as he thought, *I haven't had a birthday in ten years, and I was fourteen when Arec and I got trapped in the black mountain.* He shrugged his shoulders. "So I guess that makes me, twenty-four," said Reif.

"Oh," said Mary, feeling disappointed.

Dorothy and Alice exchanged glances. Dorothy quickly changed the subject. "Tell us more about the rainbow forest?"

"Oh yes, please," said Alice, "please do."

"Only if you promise to keep it to yourselves," said Oliver. As his three sisters all agreed, Oliver started off by telling them about the rainbow-coloured forest and Samuel, the tree goblin, who was so brightly coloured that when sitting on a rainbow-coloured tree, he became invisible. Alice, Dorothy and Mary sat captivated wanting to hear more. Oliver then told them all about the encounter by the river with the mermaids and mermen. This part of the story got a lot of oohs and ahs.

Mary asked, "Are they handsome, the mermen?" Alice and Dorothy both giggled. Mary looked at her sister's indignantly. Oliver ignored Mary and continued with his story. He told them of the temptress in the river who tried to lure the five brothers to their death, only to be rescued by Eleanor.

"Who is Eleanor?" asked Alice.

"I'll come to her later," said Oliver, then he went on to tell them about the ogres, trolls, fawns and centaurs, explaining in detail what they all looked like.

Finally, he told them all about Cressida, the rainbow fairy princess, and her crystal palace, and when he had finished telling all, they had lots of questions they wanted to ask, but Oliver was famished and he realised it was time for lunch. "Let's go eat, and afterwards I will answer all your questions as best I can." The three princesses headed back to the castle while Oliver and Reif finished getting dressed.

Henry had been helping Stephen with his drawings, and paintings. Stephen had drawn everything they had experienced. His personal favourite was the archway created by the rainbow-coloured trees that led down the long pathway to the crystal palace. Henry's favourite picture was of the fawns, specially Langton, the fawn king, the horns on his head, his crowning glory, was as magnificent as any royal crown he had ever seen. Stephen was an exceptional artist and Henry had a memory like no one else, right down to the smallest detail. Between them, they had created a series of paintings and drawings that were extremely life like. When they joined Oliver, Reif and the three princesses for lunch, they left the paintings on display in the sitting room Prince Oliver had allocated for their use.

While they were at lunch, King Richard had risen from his bed. He had managed to slip past the guard who was supposed to be keeping watch over him and he was now wandering around the castle aimlessly. Confused in his own castle, even though surrounded by his own possessions, he staggered from room to room, when he stumbled across the sitting room where the paintings were on display.

Walking amongst the paintings, Richard had flashes of memory, which he didn't understand, feeling stressed and confused. *What were all these weird creatures,* he thought, as he looked from one painting to another. He spun around in the room totally confused and disorientated. His head felt as though it would explode. Then one painting stood out to Richard above all others. It was one with a giant white eagle carrying off what looked like a small child, carrying it off into the distance. As Richard stared at the painting, an image entered his brain and the painting seemed to come to life. Richard collapsed into the chair facing this painting. He sat staring at it blankly. Further images flashed into his brain; it was painful to see. He screwed up his eyes to try and shut the images out; it didn't help. Repeatedly, the image of the giant white eagle appeared. He felt a great sorrow, but couldn't understand why.

Voices were approaching the sitting room where Richard sat. He was bought back to his senses, as he recognised the voices of his three daughters. He rose quickly out of the armchair and stumbled his way across the room to the glass doors that opened onto the garden, knocking over a painting on the way. Normally, he would have stopped and picked it up, but he didn't want to get caught in this room, even though he didn't understand why, not today, not now. He was feeling extremely fragile once again, and totally confused. He had just closed the glass doors and stepped to one side, with his back against the wall, out of sight from those within, when they entered, he listened.

Mary commented on the painting of the centaurs and turning to Stephen, she asked, "Is this really what they look like?"

"Yes," said Stephen.

Mary then turned to Oliver and said, "Your description did not do them justice, dear brother." Alice's voice was the next Richard heard. She was looking at the picture of Cressida the rainbow fairy. She was in the air with her wings fully open.

"She looks like a giant butterfly," said Alice, only the most beautiful butterfly she had ever seen, Stephen agreed.

Then Richard heard Oliver talking with Reif, who had started to cry. They were looking at the painting of Reif's brother, Arec. Except in the painting he was depicted as an ogre, for this was the only form Stephen had seen of him before he died. Standing listening outside, Richard felt guilty even though he didn't know why, his heart sank, and weighed heavy in his chest, the last voice he heard was that of Dorothy. She had discovered the painting Richard had knocked to the floor. It was the painting of the giant white eagle flying away with Nicholas. "He looks so small," she said, as she placed the painting back on its stand. The room had gone quiet as everyone gathered around Dorothy to look at the painting. "I wonder what he's doing now," she said, trying to keep her voice light and cheerful. It was too much for Richard to bare. the name Nicholas meant nothing to him, and yet, each time it was mentioned, it caused him great pain. With his back against the wall, he slid down until he was a crumpled heap on the floor and began to cry. His crying was heard from inside and all those present raced across the room. Dorothy got to the glass doors that opened onto the garden first. As she pushed the doors open, they all poured out. The sight of King Richard lying on the ground crying was the last thing any of them were expecting. It was the three princesses who knelt beside their father to offer comfort. He tried to push them away, but they were having none of it.

They asked Oliver and Reif, "Can you help him back to his room?"

"Of course," they said. They stood either side and helped Richard to his feet. Oliver stumbled.

"Let me," said Reif. He bent down, lay Richard over one shoulder and stood up. "You lead the way and open the doors, I will follow."

"Are you sure you can manage?" asked Mary, impressed with how strong Reif was.

"Yes, of course," said Reif, "now mind out of the way." Up the stairs and along the hallway to Richard's bedroom, Reif carried him with ease. Oliver opened the bedroom door and Dorothy followed after Reif. She quickly turned, closed the door and locked it, preventing anyone else from entering. She could hear Mary outside complaining about being shut out, but Alice understood why Dorothy had locked the door.

"Do you really think father needs to be embarrassed anymore?" Without answering, Mary did her usual thing, and stomped off.

Stephen apologised to Alice. "I didn't mean for my pictures to upset anyone," he said.

"I know," said Alice. "We asked you to paint the pictures for us, so we could see what you had experienced; no one could know how upsetting they were going to be for father."

Henry who had been standing quietly alongside Stephen was feeling uncomfortable about the whole situation. He felt like an intruder into a family's private affairs. He turned away from Alice and walked back down the hallway. Stephen watched him go. Alice put a hand on Stephen's arm. "Go after him, there is nothing you can do here."

All alone outside Richard's bedroom, Alice gently knocked on the door. "I'm all alone," she said. The soft clicking sound told Alice the door had been unlocked. She turned the handle and slowly pushed open the door.

Dorothy quietly said, "Come in." Alice was pleasantly surprised to see her father sitting up in bed, chatting with Oliver and Reif. He said that he was fine. He felt more embarrassed than anything, being slung over Reif's shoulder like a sack of potatoes. They all laughed.

Dorothy explained to Alice, "He doesn't even remember seeing the paintings. He thinks he must have fallen over and that is why Reif carried him to his bed." The two sisters exchanged worried looks of concern for their father, but then smiled when he burst out laughing at something Oliver had said. He seemed happy sitting with Oliver and Reif.

Chapter 4
Nicholas the Ball and the Brooch

Nicholas having danced with Eleanor, now danced with Elvira, who had taken to the dance floor once more. Just the simple touch of his tiny hand in hers made her body tingle with youthful excitement for the second time. Now that Nicholas had been introduced as the guest of honour, all the beautiful women who had completely ignored him before now preened themselves in order to gain his attention. No longer was he seen as the small boy they had passed by on the steps on their way into the ball, for he was the guest of honour.

Elvira had taken to her throne next to her daughter Eleanor. She smiled gleefully, as the women started to fight over Nicholas. All the women were beautiful, but each one that danced with Nicholas somehow seemed younger than they had before, and as they danced with Nicholas, Elvira watched, her gleeful smile became more menacing, until, eventually she grew bored. She stood and raised her right hand above her head. The music stopped. "Enough," she said, as all the guests turned to look at Elvira, "I think it's time to liven up the entertainment." She walked down onto the dance floor and all the women fled, along with their male partners, leaving Nicholas standing alone, and bemused, Elvira unclipped a small brooch from her dress, that Nicholas had not noticed before. It was of a three-headed dog, multi-coloured as though it belonged in the rainbow forest. She placed it in the centre of the dance floor, and took Nicholas' hand as she led him back to her throne. She sat down with Nicholas on her lap. "Now watch this," she whispered into Nicholas' ear.

Everyone in the ballroom had fallen silent, and every single pair of eyes was locked onto the tiny brooch. No one could make out what it was Elvira had placed on the floor and so they waited, some excitedly and some nervously. With no audible sound in the room, it was as if everyone present were holding their breath. Then it happened, first a faint glow, an echoed gasp travelled around the room, then as the glow pulsed and the light grew stronger, the brooch grew larger. The more it pulsed, the larger the brooch became, palpable excitement now filled the room, only it was no longer a tiny brooch. The glow finally got so bright everyone had to look away. Slowly, the glow subsided, and there in place of the brooch, was a large multi-coloured three-headed dog, that sparkled beneath the candle chandeliers, with a long, thin tail that reminded Nicholas of a whip. It prowled around the dance floor, looking at all the guests, snarling and baring its teeth. Breathing had resumed, although to Nicholas it seemed faster than before. All the beautiful people now looked scared, which made them look ugly. As Nicholas wondered what was going to happen next, Elvira had risen from her throne. She called out to her guests, "Would anyone like to stroke my pet?" She looked around the room at the terrified faces of her guests. "What, no one?" she asked. "What about you, Sir Roger, you claim to have slain many a dragon, surely you are not afraid of a simple dog. Would you like to stroke my pet?" All the people standing beside Sir Roger had moved away so that he stood alone. He was a tall man with a thin face. Nicholas recognised him as one of those who passed him when he had fallen on the stairs. He shook his head vigorously without saying a word. "No," said Elvira, as she watched Sir Roger slip back into the shadows. She continued to look around the room. "What about you, Sir Cuthbert, he who has wrestled yetis and claimed to have killed them with your bare hands. Surely, you will come and stroke my pet?" Sir Cuthbert was a bear of a man, well over six feet tall, wide shouldered, and barrel chested with shoulder length flaming red hair and beard, but, again, he declined Elvira's invitation. Menacingly, she continued to survey the room. Nicholas also looked around the room and noticed everyone was trying to avoid Elvira's gaze. "Surely someone wants to stoke my pet?" asked Elvira.

"I do," said Nicholas.

"Do you hear that, ladies and gentleman, a mere child of five, braver than any of you." And with that, Nicholas jumped from Elvira's throne. She had not expected it, and before she could react, Nicholas had approached the dance floor and sat down. Collectively, the whole room gasped. The three-headed dog had been facing the other way when Nicholas had made his way onto the dance floor. Now it had turned and was facing Nicholas from across the ballroom. The whip like tail twitched from side to side, slapping down hard on the marble floor. The sound echoed around the room, as the three headed dog slowly, stealthily moved across the dance floor ever closer. His nails scraping on the marble floor sent a shiver down the spine of many a guest. Nicholas remained unfazed. Some of the male guests winced in pain, not because of what was happening on the dance floor, but because their female partners were gripping their arms so tightly circulation to their hands was being cut off. Elvira and her daughter Eleanor watched as the dog took its final steps to reach Nicholas. Elvira felt elated, more alive than she had in ages. Her body tingled with excitement. More than one of the female guests screamed, and a couple fainted, even some of the male guests had to turn away from what was happening on the dance floor, finding the scene unfolding before them unbearable. The sickening feeling in their stomachs made it impossible to watch, whilst others gripped with fear could not tear their eyes away.

Unexpectedly, Elvira suddenly burst out laughing, as the three heads of the giant dog all nuzzled up against Nicholas, knocking him to the floor. Nicholas lay on the floor as three giant tongues licked his face and body. He was laughing as each lick tickled. Those guests that hadn't fainted or looked away joined in the laughter. Some who had turned away dared to sneak a peek, while others still couldn't dare to look. Elvira eventually stood up from her throne and walked down to the dance floor. As she did, all the laughter stopped, except for Nicholas. Elvira's dress sparkled as she walked onto the dance floor beneath the candle chandeliers. She approached and then patted the giant dog on its back. It stopped licking Nicholas and stepped away, leaving Nicholas lying on the floor, with the three-headed dog sat beside her. Elvira helped Nicholas to his feet, his face and body covered in saliva. She magically brushed it away with the wave of her hand. Someone in the shadows started to laugh, and as a few more joined in around the room, Elvira stood motionless waiting for the laughter to cease. "Enough," called Elvira, "so you think that was funny, do you?" Everyone now looked on in terrified silence, recognising the anger in Elvira's voice. Elvira was surveying the room. She broke the silence as she looked upon her guests cowering in the shadows. "And you call yourselves men," she said, sneeringly, "all of you who claim to have killed single handed a monstrous beast of some kind." She paraded Nicholas around the dance floor like a champion Gladiator. The three-headed dog sat motionless. "The party's over." Snapped Elvira. She stood in the middle of the dance floor as the guests fled the ballroom, tripping over themselves in their desire to flee, terrified in case Elvira changed her mind and commanded one of them to approach her dog. She looked down at Nicholas and smiled. "Don't worry, they will be back for the ball next week."

Chapter 5
Percival Arrives Home

Percival had fallen into the river as the boundary between the two kingdoms had closed, carried away by the current which had increased as the mountain reappeared, Cressida and Dante had watched Percival drifting away down the river, and did nothing to help. Day was turning to night once more as he was carried away downstream, as the three suns began to merge to create the purple moon, there was a dazzling display of colours reflected on the water's surface, as it crashed against rocks, sending spray into the air, like a million coloured fire flies being released, dancing above the water's surface. Percival had managed to grab hold of a large piece of wood that had been drifting by and was able to stay afloat in the churning waters. As he coursed his way down stream clinging to the large piece of wood, it was constantly being bounced off rocks that sat within the river. Percival swallowed a mouthful of water, and was coughing, when the river fell away. It dropped a couple of feet over a mini waterfall. Percival struggled to maintain his grip on the large piece of wood. A whirlpool sat in Percival's path. There was not a lot of room to manoeuvre. As the water swirled in its circular motion and Percival felt himself being drawn towards the deadly swirl, he kicked his legs desperately trying to stay out of reach, but to no avail. He was being spun around as the powerful current of water circled, drawn ever closer, clinging onto the piece of wood for dear life and praying for a miracle. Percival finally lost his grip. The branch being ripped from his grasp. Beneath the water's surface he sank, spinning ever faster caught in the current. His first instinct was to fight against the turbulent water, but with no hope of escaping, he eventually stopped struggling against the current and allowed himself to be carried along. He held his breath, turning over and over as he was carried downstream. Beneath the surface, he could see light from above. The current had eased and he resurfaced gasping for air. As if by magic, the same piece of wood that Percival had clung to before reappeared. He grasped hold with his remaining strength. A sharp bend in the river appeared which forced the water to slow. The large piece of wood that Percival had used to stay afloat became wedged between two rocks on the bend. The river on this section was shallow but wide. Percival managed to get to his feet and scramble ashore. Then as he looked down river, he watched as the large piece of wood which had been his saviour had become dislodged and floated away. Percival watched as the piece of wood was smashed against rocks that stood proudly in the water, shattering it into small pieces. The river had narrowed once more and become progressively more violent.

Percival was exhausted and lay on the riverbank to catch his breath. As he lay there looking up at the changing sky, his thoughts were of what had just occurred. A smile spread across Percival's face, hard to believe he had just survived that ordeal. He was soaking wet and needed to dry off. From lying on his back, he rolled over onto his knees and struggled to his feet, standing at the bottom of a steep hill he began to climb, somehow, he knew this was where he was meant to be. The climb was slow going and the light was fading fast. A breeze had started to blow across the hill. He shivered in his wet clothes as they clung to his body. The extra weight he carried was exhausting, which made the climb ever more difficult, huffing and puffing his way to the top. Percival finally saw a solitary cabin. As he got closer to the cabin, the door opened allowing light to escape and a delicate voice said, "Welcome home, my son."

Percival's mother Saki stood in the doorway, with the light coming from behind her. He could only see her silhouette, just a faceless figure, but on hearing his mother's voice, it gave him the renewed energy he needed to complete the climb. He was exhausted.

"Hello, mother," said Percival, as she quickly ushered him inside and bolted the door.

"Well," she said, "let me have a good look at you then." She stood with her left hand resting on her hip and her right hand cupping the right side of her face, her fingers tapping away gently. She looked him up and down, told him to turn around and finally, said, "Yes, you look exactly as I knew you would, now get out of those wet clothes before you catch a death cold."

Wrapped in a blanket handed to him by his mother, while she placed his clothes to dry by the fire. "You look exactly as I remember," said Percival. Saki was slightly taller than her son. She looked very old; her skin was shrivelled and tanned with deep creases. The deep creases in her face reminded Percival of an old walnut, while the wrinkled neck resembled that of an old tortoise, the hands with their short stubby fingers were also deeply tanned, covered with warts. She moved slowly as if time itself had slowed. Her long hair once a rich auburn colour was now various shades of grey. It hung down either side of her face like an iron curtain, but the eyes, emerald green and sparkling; they were alive and youthful.

The light that had shone through the open door belonged to the roaring fire that owned the fireplace. The cabin looked much bigger from inside than it first appeared, with the roaring fire on the wall opposite the door, to the right of the fire on the end wall was a panoramic window, next to the window a rocking chair, where Saki would sit and watch the world around her. In winter, she would sit for hours watching the snow falling transforming the hills into a winter wonderland, with fantastic views of the surrounding mountains, and valley below. Although Saki lived alone these days, she had a large oak dining table that was big enough to seat twelve people. In front of the fire stood two large sofas that faced each other, so friends could sit across from each other and talk face to face, but that hadn't happened in a long time, as Saki had outlived all her friends. To the left of the fireplace two bedrooms and a washroom and toilet. Hanging above the large table were all the copper pots and pans Saki used for cooking. Gleaming, they reflected the light from the fire as it danced around the room. The walls were covered with shelves supporting glass jars filled with all sorts of odd things. Percival read the labels, Eye of Frog, Tongue of Toad, Shell of Snail, Slime of slug and Powdered weeping willow. Percival reached up and removed one of the jars. The label read, Powdered weeping willow, Saki chuckled. "Remember what that does?" she asked. As Percival struggled to remember, Saki reminded him. "Tip a tiny amount of powder into a drink of your intended victim and wait, it will put multi-coloured hairs on their chest, and everywhere else," she said. They both laughed. "Of course it is only temporary," said Saki. "But the more powder you use, the longer the effect, great fun at parties," she said.

Saki then reached up and removed another jar. The label read, Slime of Slug. "This can be very useful," she said. Percival didn't remember this one at all.

"So what does it do?" he asked.

"Add a small amount of this to any drink of someone you wish to follow, and even if they turn invisible, they will still leave visible footprints that can be followed." Saki handed both jars to Percival. "I think you should take these with you, they may prove to be useful."

"Thank you," said Percival.

"Oh, but wait, I almost forgot," said Saki. She opened the lid of a small chest that stood in the corner of the room. "You will need this," she said.

"What is it?" asked Percival. Wrapped in a silk cloth Saki handed Percival what looked like a small spyglass.

"This is no ordinary spy glass; it contains the eye of a barn owl. Only the person with this spy glass can see the footprints created by the slug slime." Again, Percival thanked his mother. He wrapped the tiny spyglass in the silk cloth once more and placed it into one of his many pockets, along with the two potion jars.

Percival made his way over to one of the sofas in front of the fire, and asked his mother to join him. As she sat down, she said, "I know what you are going to ask, for I know everything, but can divulge nothing, all I will say is, enjoy the adventure." And with that, she stood and walked slowly to her bedroom. "Goodnight, Percival," she said, as she closed her door.

"Goodnight, mother," replied Percival. He remained seated in front of the fire for hours as it slowly died, pondering what might happen next, finally falling asleep on one of the sofas.

Chapter 6
An Unexpected Visitor

The five brothers who had joined with King Richard when their mother had died were being trained to be palace guards. The four eldest took to training like a duckling takes to water, doing whatever asked of them. Joshua the youngest brother, however, was easily distracted. At fifteen, he was only three years older than the princesses, and he liked Alice. Every time she was around, he would do something foolish. Like the time he rode into a low hanging branch, got knocked off his horse and was unconscious in bed for three days, or the time when he climbed a tree trying to rescue a kitten, only for the kitten to retreat to safety as the branch snapped and plunged into the lake, from where Joshua needed rescuing.

    The guards were out hunting, along with the five brothers and Joshua was determined to make up for his mistake last time, when he caused Robert the head guard to miss out on an impressive stag. They hadn't been in the forest very long when Joshua found a set of tracks that were definitely those of a large stag. He signalled silently to his brothers who signalled the guards. Robert was not sure if he trusted Joshua's tracking skills, after his previous catastrophes, but decided it couldn't do any harm just to check it out. Robert gently guided his horse through the forest, making his way towards Joshua, when suddenly out of nowhere, a giant flash of white crashed its way through the forest, in pursuit of the stag. Joshua's horse reared and sent him flying through the air, only to land at the feet of Robert's horse. Robert was enraged. "What the hell are you playing at?" he barked. Robert was not amused as Joshua tried to explain what had happened, but it turned out no one else had seen anything large or white crashing through the forest. As Joshua's horse had run off, they left him to walk back to the castle, punishment for ruining another day's hunting.

Joshua walked back through the forest knowing full well that something large and white had scared off that stag. He was sure of it. With sword in hand, he was aware of every single noise around him. Feeling nervous and excited at the same time, he was determined to find out what had scared off that stag. Trying to move through the forest as quietly as possible, he was distracted by a noise above his head, and as he looked up, he placed his left foot into the entrance of a rabbit burrow which caused him to stumble. "Damn it," he said, louder than he had intended. Steadying himself, he turned his head to see what had caused the noise, only to see a couple of squirrels racing along a branch. He had to be careful he said to himself. Not only were there rabbit burrows to avoid but tree roots that sat above ground were just waiting to trip him up, and the brambles kept grabbing at his clothes. With scratches on his arms and legs, he kept searching. Finally, there was his evidence. As he walked along the pathway brambles lined up either side, and on the brambles clumps of white fur had been ensnared, to one side of the pathway, the brambles had been flattened, and more white fur lay on the ground. Joshua gripped his sword firmly and followed the trail. His heart began to race. For the brambles to be completely flattened, he had to be following something huge. Then as he listened, he became aware the forest sounded empty. No bird song could be heard, no squirrels chasing about in the treetops overhead. This was not normal, and he listened carefully. Only a gnawing sound could be heard. He began to doubt whether this was a good idea or not. He held his sword shoulder high with great difficulty, ready to swing if attacked. His arms trembled with the weight of the sword. It felt twice as heavy as usual. He crept forward slowly, trying to pinpoint where the sound was coming from. Along with the gnawing, a deep rumbling sound reverberated through the forest. *This was not a good idea,* thought Joshua, but he had come too far now to turn back. The light in the forest was beginning to fade. Then it happened. He stumbled over a fallen tree. He crashed through some tall ferns only to find himself landing at the feet of something, large, white and furry. His sword had flown through the air out of reach as he fell, and he landed face down. He dare not move, hoping that if he played dead, the beast would leave him alone. As Joshua lay still, two giant white feet appeared either side of Joshua's head. He trembled with fear as he tried to calm his breathing, but then, hot breath on the back of his neck told him his life was over. It was his own fault. He should never have gone looking for this beast by himself. He felt a cold, wet nose against the back of his neck. This was it. Then suddenly, he was being lifted into the air.

Expecting to be tossed around like some piece of meat, Joshua started to flail his arms and legs hoping to be released. The giant white bear had grabbed hold of Joshua by the collar and stood upright. Now he released Joshua who landed on his feet standing upright. The bear now dropped onto all fours. Still Joshua was facing away from the bear, not understanding what had just happened. He was still shaking but slowly turned around, only to receive a big wet lick right across the face. "Berwyn," he cried with relief, as tears of joy streamed down his face. The giant white bear nuzzled against Joshua almost knocking him off his feet once more. "Boy am I glad it's you," said Joshua wiping away the tears. He gave the giant white bear a hug, and rubbed behind his ears. Berwyn stood contentedly by Joshua's side.

"How did you find your way here?" asked Joshua, obviously not expecting a reply. "I think we should be getting back," said Joshua. Berwyn seemed to understand because he stopped nuzzling Joshua and headed off in the direction of the castle. Berwyn didn't need to follow a pathway through the forest, he created his own, much to the amusement of Joshua. Before long, they were on the edge of the forest, and the castle was in view. Two of the castle gardeners had their heads down digging over the dirt, pulling up vegetables, sweating profusely. They were too busy to notice anything as Joshua and Berwyn passed them by. Then Joshua could hear Oliver, Reif and Henry splashing in the lake although they were out of sight. As Joshua and Berwyn got closer to the castle, Joshua could hear the guards practising their sword skills in the courtyard, so that was where they headed. Joshua triumphantly rode Berwyn all the way across the lawn and passed beneath the entrance into the courtyard. He rang the bell that hung in the courtyard exclaiming, "Look who I found."

Annoyed by Joshua's interruption, the guards stopped fighting. "What now?" one of them asked, but they were all stunned into silence when they realised he was sat on the back of Berwyn. Then they all rushed forward.

"I told you I saw something, large and white," said Joshua, as they gathered around, patting Berwyn. One of the guards once more rang the bell vigorously. As the sound carried across the castle grounds, the two sweating gardeners exclaimed, what now. As they loaded all their tools into the wheel barrow along with the vegetables, they trudged their way wearily back to the castle. The sound of the bell ringing had also spread as far as the lake. On hearing the bell, Oliver scrambled out of the water picked up his clothes and raced bare footed across the lawn, followed closely by Reif and lastly Henry. They overtook the two gardeners with their heavy laden wheel barrows, and as they reached the courtyard, Reif passed Oliver to win the race, only to find himself face to face with the biggest bear he had ever seen. He came to a halt, instantly. As Oliver arrived in the courtyard seconds later, Reif put out an arm to prevent him from running straight into what would be certain death.

Reif was looking for a weapon. He was so fixated on the bear he hadn't noticed all the guards calmly standing around watching. Finally, he laid eyes on a sword. Oliver then realised what was happening. He had to intervene. As Reif bent down to pick up the sword, Oliver pushed him from behind, and he ended up sprawled on the ground at the feet of the giant white bear. Reif didn't understand why Oliver had pushed him over. For surely, it meant certain death. He lay still on the ground hoping the end would be quick. He turned his head away from the bear and closed his eyes, nothing happened, his pulse was racing. *Why doesn't he just finish it*, he thought. The waiting for the inevitable was surely more painful than the end. He couldn't take it any longer. He jumped to his feet, flung his arms open wide and said, "Come on then, kill me."

There were cheers, whistles and laughter, not what Reif had expected at all. Reif opened his eyes to see Oliver standing next to the bear who was lying down enjoying a good rub behind the ear. "This is Berwyn," said Oliver, "he is Percival's companion." Reif felt extremely foolish in front of all the guards, but also extremely happy. He crossed the courtyard to where Oliver was standing with Berwyn.

"You never told me anything about a giant bear," said Reif.

"I honestly didn't think we would ever see him again. He couldn't enter the fairy kingdom with my father and Percival because the mountain entrance was too steep, but the fact he has found his way back to the castle gives me hope of finding the kingdom once more," said Oliver. Alice, Dorothy and Mary had also heard the bell ringing vigorously from their bedroom where they had been talking about their father. They had come to investigate why the bell had been rung.

They passed Oliver who was on his way to see their father, and asked, "Why was the bell being rung?"

"Go and have a look," said Oliver excitedly, as he sprinted up the stairs to his father's bedroom. The three princesses arrived at the courtyard, and squealed with delight on seeing Berwyn. They all raced forward to hug the giant bear who was enjoying all the attention and affection he was receiving.

In his excitement, Oliver burst into his father's bedroom to tell him the good news, but at exactly the same time, Richard was having another nightmare. Oliver stood in shocked silence, as he watched his father writhe from side to side, screaming incoherently. For five minutes, he watched, unable to move. He was terrified, not for himself, but for what it was doing to his father. Then the screaming ceased. His father was lying perfectly still, covered in sweat. At first, Oliver was not sure if his father had died, but then he snorted, and Oliver realised he was sleeping. Oliver had been sweating with panic. He wiped his brow with the sleeve of his shirt, and decided it was best to let his father sleep, and so backed out of the bedroom and silently closed the doors. He re-joined the others who were still in the courtyard. "Where is father?" asked Mary, excitedly.

"He is sleeping so I decided not to wake him," said Oliver. For he didn't want to tell them what he had just witnessed, but Dorothy knew something was wrong, for Oliver was in a buoyant mood when they passed on the stairs, and now he was subdued. She decided to talk to him later, when they were alone.

Chapter 7
The Favonius Ball

A week had passed. It was now time for Elvira's next ball. Nicholas had spent the week with Eleanor, exploring the castle and the surrounding countryside. One thing Nicholas had realised since his arrival at the white castle was, it snowed every single night, so that each day when you awoke and looked out of your window, you had pristine white snow covering the ground.

The evening of the ball had arrived, and all the guests were present. Nicholas recognised Sir Cuthbert from the week before, with his flaming red hair and beard. He was the one who claims to have wrestled and killed a yeti with his bare hands, not that Nicholas knew what a yeti was. Nicholas was seated with Eleanor while her mother, Elvira, mingled with her guests on the ballroom floor. Resplendent in her crown of yellow, blue and pink diamonds, she wore a different dress from the week before, still purest white with the top half decorated with clear, clean-cut diamonds, but the bottom half of the dress was made of pure white feathers. She appeared to float as she moved across the dance floor.

The tall, thin man who had introduced Oliver the week before as the guest of honour stood at the top of the blue marble staircase, wearing the same blood-red outfit, as always. Elvira floated across the dance floor and made her way up to her throne, where she took her place besides Eleanor. Once seated, the tall, thin man announced, "Everyone is present, Your Majesty."

"Excellent," said Elvira, "let the music begin."

The ball started off pretty much the same as the week before. Elvira watched her guests dancing for a while before taking Nicholas by the hand and leading him to the dance floor, and so, Elvira danced with Nicholas first, enjoying the feeling of youth she received every time she held his hand. Only when Elvira felt fully rejuvenated did she leave the dance floor. It was Eleanor's turn to dance with Nicholas next. She wore the same dress as the week before. Covered in emeralds, sapphires and rubies, the dress sparkled beneath the candle chandeliers. She really did look like the most beautiful peacock Nicholas had ever seen.

When Eleanor finally retired to her throne besides her mother, Nicholas felt as though he was caught up in a feeding frenzy of a pack of wolves, surrounded by beautiful women, all who wanted to dance with him. He was pulled first one way and then the other. Elvira and Eleanor seated on their thrones watched the spectacle below with great delight. Eventually, Elvira came to Nicholas' rescue. She left her throne and glided onto the dance floor, all but two women had spotted her coming and stepped away from Nicholas. She placed a hand on the shoulder of each woman still squabbling, and they instantly turned to ice. Nicholas looked at Elvira alarmed at what she had done. "Do not worry," said Elvira, "it is only temporary, they are unharmed." Nicholas then danced continuously without tiring as he waltzed his way around the two ice figures, dancing with one beautiful woman after another. Some of the male guests looked on with envy, whilst others were quite nonchalant about the whole ball.

Elvira had grown bored; the time had arrived for some new entertainment. Elvira stood up from her throne and raised her hands above her head. The music stopped. Everyone turned to face Elvira, wondering what she had planned for a surprise this week. "Ladies and gentlemen, if you would be so kind to vacate the dance floor." Everyone quickly obeyed, nobody wanted to be last to leave the floor. The two frozen women had returned to normal, feeling embarrassed and humiliated at being turned into frozen statues. They quickly hurried off the dance floor disappearing into the shadows. Nicholas raced up the stairs to sit with Elvira and Eleanor, eagerly waiting for what was about to take place.

The tall, thin man in the blood-red suit stood at the top of the blue marble staircase. "Ladies and gentlemen, it gives me great pleasure to introduce to you, Priscilla Queen of the silk and her husband Ivan." A muscular young man descended the blue marble staircase and walked to the centre of the dance floor, with a length of pink silk draped over one shoulder. Some of the guests were heard asking, "Where is Priscilla?" He stopped and casually removed the silk from his shoulder and rolled it into a tight ball, keeping hold of one end of the silk, he threw the ball into the air. It unfurled as it rose high into the air above their heads, everyone looked up, as the ball of silk unfurled, Priscilla was revealed. Gasps of wonder and applause echoed around the ballroom. The ball of silk remained upright, like a column of marble with Priscilla at the top. All eyes were on Priscilla as Ivan gave a gentle tug on the silk. It collapsed instantly wrapping itself around Priscilla as she fell. Ivan caught Priscilla with ease; more gasps filled the room. Ivan paraded around the dance floor with Priscilla in his arms, he stopped suddenly, and this time, Ivan threw the silk across the dancefloor. It remained a foot above the floor, as it unfurled revealing Priscilla once more; applause broke out amongst the party guests. Priscilla stood on the end of the silk and wrapped it around one leg. When she was ready, Ivan pulled on the silk, not towards him this time however, but in a circle above his head, Ivan's feet and lower body remained stationary, but his upper torso moved slightly side to side with each rotation, but the arms and shoulders were where the effort showed with each muscle straining. Faster and faster, Ivan rotated the silk above his head, and as he got faster, Priscilla rose higher and higher. Once more, gasps and applause filled the ballroom as she flew above their heads. When the silk was fully upright once more, and Priscilla was spinning like a top, Ivan stopped. This time, the silk fell straight to the ground and landed in a crumpled heap, a single scream was heard as Priscilla fell through the air to be caught in the muscular arms of her husband Ivan. Their act finished, they bowed to Elvira and her guests to tumultuous applause and left the dance floor. Elvira congratulated them on a magnificent performance. "Bravo," she shouted.

As the noise subsided, she then glided her way down to the dance floor, everyone watched in anticipation. Just like the week before, she removed a tiny brooch from her dress, one of the female guests screamed before Elvira had even placed the brooch on the floor. She looked around at her guests with a knowing smile on her face. Half of them seemed excited, while the other half seemed terrified of what was to come. She stepped away from the brooch and made her way back to her throne. The brooch began to pulse just like before. With each pulse, it grew larger. The blinding light made everyone look away or shield their eyes, and when the light faded, it revealed a winged horse, coloured in shades of pink, green and white, it looked extremely delicate.

This was not what Elvira's guests had expected, which is why she had chosen that particular brooch. A sigh of relief travelled around the room. Elvira smiled triumphantly. "Always try to surprise," she whispered to Nicholas, there was some nervous laughter, as she called to her guests. "Would anyone like to ride my horse?" Elvira had made her way down to the dance floor and was standing alongside the winged horse. Looking around the ballroom, she seemed to be searching for one of her guests in particular. She eventually spotted him. "Sir

Horace, would you like to ride my horse, after all, you claim you can tame and ride any horse?"

"Sorry, Elvira," blustered Sir Horace "but I'm afraid I've hurt my back."

"Afraid yes," said Elvira, with a stinging sarcasm to her voice, "what a pity, does no one want to ride him?"

"I do," said Nicholas, "may I?"

"Of course, Nicholas, come down." As Nicholas made his way down to Elvira and the winged horse, guests all around the ballroom began to whisper.

Nicholas heard one say, "I hope he breaks his neck." Nicholas didn't know if she was referring to him or the horse, either way he wasn't deterred.

Elvira called Ivan over. "Can you please lift Nicholas onto my horse?"

"Of course, Your Majesty." Ivan picked Nicholas up with ease and placed him onto the winged horse and then returned to Priscilla to watch. Elvira whispered to Nicholas not to worry. "You can't fall," she said, as she silently cast a spell that would prevent him from falling, she then stepped away. With a clap of her hands, a whole wall of windows disappeared.

"What's his name?" asked Nicholas.

"Favonius," said Elvira.

Everyone followed as Favonius stepped into the courtyard. For the first time, he was able to unfold his giant wings. He rose onto his hind legs, a scream from one of the female guests. Nicholas sat firm. Favonius beat his wings, disturbing the snow on the ground sending it flying into the air, and then they were airborne. Favonius hovered above the courtyard and as the disturbed snow settled once more. With wings fully extended, Favonius looked radiant like a giant angel. Gasps of wonder echoed around the courtyard. Favonius beat his wings faster, turned and they were off. They disappeared into the sky flying over the walls of the castle. Nicholas felt exhilarated, leaving the castle behind flying low over the nearby village had people screaming, running for cover, not knowing what terror this was coming from the sky. Way beyond the village, they flew, passing over the snow-covered trees, and out across the frozen lakes. This was a winter wonderland, of beauty. Favonius flew faster than the harpy or the white eagle, and higher, it seemed like, all the way to the top of the mountain. Nicholas felt a strange lightheaded sensation as his ears popped because of the altitude. Favonius soared. The air was cold, and the cold was drawn into Nicholas' body. As he breathed in through his nose, he could feel the cold air as it dropped into his chest and from there, the cold spread throughout his body to the extremities of his limbs. Without warning, Favonius folded back his wings and went into a steep dive. Nicholas was feeling sick as if he had left his stomach at the top of the mountain. Favonius sped ever faster towards the ground, Nicholas clung on for his life, the magic spell to stop him falling held him firm as the wind battered against his small body. He had to close his eyes, for it was impossible to keep them open. He prayed that everything would be all right. They were above the castle once more. As they hurtled ever closer to the ground, several of the female guests screamed. Not that Nicholas could hear them above the roar of the wind in his ears. Elvira wasn't even watching Favonius take Nicholas for a ride. She was more interested watching the faces of her guests. The sheer terror they were experiencing was far more enjoyable to Elvira than a flying horse. Nicholas dared to open his eyes as Favonius neared the ground to even louder screams. He bought his wings forward and fully extended them to the sides. This slowed their descent, as he swooped over the heads of everyone standing in the courtyard, many of whom ended up on the ground having dived out of the way believing they were going to crash into the snow-covered ground. Elvira, Eleanor and the tall, thin man in the blood-red suit remained standing, along with Ivan and Priscilla. Favonius circled over the white castle once, and then landed in the courtyard, once again sending snow flying into the air. Some of the guests were still on the ground as the snow settled. Ivan walked forward and lifted Nicholas from the back of Favonius.

"Well done, lad," said Ivan, giving Nicholas a slap on the back as a way of congratulations.

"Thanks," said Nicholas, and then he passed out. Ivan picked Nicholas' limp body up from the snow-covered ground and followed Eleanor as she led the way to Nicholas' bedroom.

Elvira berated her guests once more. "Not one of you was brave enough to take the challenge and ride Favonius," she said, as she glared at them all with a loathing. Under her gaze, each party guest either looked away or lowered their gaze to the floor. "You disappoint me," she said with a venom, "once more, a child has shown more bravery and courage than any of you. Leave before I really lose my temper," she said, "party's over." They fled the courtyard to where their carriages were lined up outside the castle, Elvira had mounted Favonius and was hovering above the white castle watching her guests flee, knowing full well they would be back for the next ball.

Chapter 8
Oliver Makes a Decision

King Richard and his men had been back at the castle for a week, but it had taken a few weeks to get there after leaving the enchanted kingdom of the rainbow fairy, and in that time, King Richard's health had deteriorated. Oliver had already spoken with the head guard Robert about going back to search for Nicholas, but Robert had insisted on waiting until King Richard was feeling better. Oliver had argued, "What if he never gets better?"

Now that Berwyn had returned, Oliver made his plea once more, to go in search of his younger brother, Nicholas, and once more Robert declined to help. "My priority is the safety and wellbeing of the king," said Robert.

Oliver was down by the lake with Reif and Henry, watching Berwyn enjoying the water. As the giant white bear climbed out onto the bank right next to where they were sat, he shook his massive body, masses of water was sent flying in all directions, and the three of them ended up soaked. "Berwyn," cried Oliver, "we might as well have joined him in the lake in the first place." Laughed Reif. Berwyn walked a short distance away and lay down in the sun to dry off. Brushing his hair out of his eyes as water trickled down his face and neck, Oliver was lying on the ground raised up on one elbow.

He looked across at Reif and Henry and said, "I'm going to take Berwyn and try to find the entrance into the magical kingdom and search for Nicholas."

"Do you want some company?" asked Reif.

"Are you two mad?" said Henry.

"No," they replied in unison.

"I can't just sit around doing nothing, knowing Nicholas is trapped there," said Oliver.

"But where would you even begin to look?" asked Henry.

"I've been thinking about this since Berwyn's return," said Oliver, "I'm hoping that Berwyn can find his way back to the mountain where Percival and my father entered, and maybe we can find the same entrance. After all, he did manage to find his way back here."

"But what if he does find his way back to the same mountain, you won't know if it's the same mountain or not," said Henry.

"But I will," said Joshua, catching everyone by surprise, as he stepped out from behind some giant bull rushes, that grew on that side of the lake.

"So, you are willing to come with us?" asked Oliver.

"When do we leave?" said Joshua excitedly, Oliver looked across to Henry.

"Are you in or not?"

Reluctantly, Henry said, "Yes, but if I die, I'm going to come back as a ghost and haunt the lot of you." To which they all laughed. So, they had decided they were going to go. It was now a matter of deciding when, and what provisions could they get together without raising suspicion.

Oliver said, "If I tell Robert the head guard I want to teach Henry and Joshua how to use a bow and arrow, I know he will let me without question, for I'm the best archer at the castle."

"What about if I offer to train them with the sword?" said Reif.

"He might just go for that," said Oliver, "with us training the two youngest, it will allow Robert to concentrate on the four older brothers."

"So, that sounds like you have the weapons sorted," said Henry, "what about food and water?"

"Well, we can't take a wagon," said Oliver, "that would be far too obvious. We'll have to catch our own food and collect water as and when we find it."

"This is sounding better all the time," said Henry sarcastically. Joshua gave him a slap on the back, which made Henry jump.

"What's wrong with you," said Joshua jovially, "it's an adventure." Henry wished he'd said no, but felt he couldn't back out now.

The next question was, when. "I don't want to waste any more time," said Oliver, "but it's too late today for it will be getting dark soon."

"So, why not tomorrow?" asked Joshua.

"If we speak with Robert tonight about training Joshua and Henry and he agrees, we can make an early start tomorrow," said Oliver.

"Sounds good to me," said Reif. Henry's stomach sank. He'd only just agreed to go, against his better judgement, and now it was happening tomorrow. Joshua saw the look of worry in Henry's eyes.

"No need to worry," said Joshua, "I'll look after you." The thought of being looked after by Joshua didn't fill Henry with any great confidence. The one reassuring thing about this whole adventure was knowing that they would have Berwyn for company.

It all went to plan. Oliver had spoken with Robert who agreed it was a good idea. At least the four older brothers could get some proper training, without the constant distraction of Joshua.

Because Oliver had spoken with Robert who had agreed, there was no need for secrecy, so when he joined the others in the sitting room, he confidently announced. "It's all been agreed." Joshua and Reif who were playing a game of chess were delighted, Henry not so, as he watched waiting to challenge the winner.

Alice, Dorothy and Mary who were playing a game of cards asked, "What's been agreed?"

"Robert just agreed that I can train Henry and Joshua how to use a bow and arrow, and Reif can train them in how to use a sword."

"Oh, is that all?" said Mary, as she placed her winning hand of cards on the table.

Oliver, Joshua and Reif looked at each other knowingly. Henry just looked sick. What had he got himself into, he thought. After their first venture into the magical kingdom of the rainbow fairy, Henry was hardly excited about returning. Although he wouldn't mind seeing Langton and the fawns once more and the centaurs were pretty awesome, even if they were scary.

The following morning arrived with a glorious sunrise, Oliver, Reif and Joshua all felt rested and ready to start their adventure. Henry had hardly slept a wink of sleep all night. When he joined the others for breakfast, he looked tired, dishevelled and ready to collapse. None of the three boys had noticed how tired Henry looked. It was only when Dorothy appeared at the breakfast table unexpectedly. "Oh my god," she said to Henry, "you look awful." Only now did Oliver stop eating and look up at Henry.

"Are you feeling all right?" asked Oliver.

"Of course, he isn't," said Dorothy, "look at the state of him."

"I didn't sleep well last night," said Henry, "had a bad dream about ogres and trolls." Oliver was worried, he didn't want to put his plans on hold another minute.

"Will you be able to train with us today?" asked Oliver, with an urgency in his voice.

"Oliver," said Dorothy, "just look at him, he is in no state to do anything."

But Henry replied, "Yes." Oliver was delighted with Henry's answer, but Dorothy was annoyed with Oliver. She felt he was putting pressure on Henry.

"Why can't he miss today and start tomorrow?" she asked.

"No," said Oliver, a bit too aggressively, quickly realising this. "I'm sorry Dorothy," said Oliver, "I didn't mean to shout, it's just that everything has already been arranged." Dorothy accepted Oliver's apology, but knew something was not quite right. He had never before shouted at her or her sisters, and what exactly had been arranged.

Leaving Dorothy to finish her breakfast, the four boys made their way to the stables. Having collected their bows, arrows and swords, they led their horses from the stables into the courtyard and mounted them. They were surprised to see Dorothy crossing the courtyard towards them. "Come to see us off, have you?" asked Reif, jokingly.

"No, I'm coming to watch," said Dorothy.

Reif smiled weakly and looked over to Oliver. The look of horror on Oliver's face prompted Reif to try and put Dorothy off. "Surely you don't really want to come and watch," he said, "it will get dead boring just sitting there."

"And when I get bored, I will leave," said Dorothy, she disappeared into the stables to saddle up her horse. While she was inside, the four boys gathered around.

"I guess we will have to pretend to practice and make it as boring as possible so she quickly gets bored and leaves," said Oliver. They were all in agreement.

So that was the plan, to make it as boring as possible. Once Dorothy had mounted her horse, they set off across the lawn. They were joined by Berwyn who had been let out earlier, after sleeping in Oliver's bedroom. The six of them were heading for the far side of the lake. This was where the targets were set up for archery practice. It was quite a ride, but it was the safest place to practice with a bow and arrow. No one usually came here unless they were practising archery.

When they arrived and dismounted, Dorothy sat on a grass slope just behind where the boys were standing. Oliver picked up his bow and arrow, took aim and fired, bullseye. Reif took his turn next, fired and his arrow nestled in the target right alongside Oliver's, who was duly impressed. "Right, who's next?" asked Oliver, Joshua was eager to have his turn, and raced forward. Oliver reminded Joshua, whispering in his ear, "We need to make this boring." So, before he allowed Joshua to pick up a bow, he showed him how to correctly place his feet for perfect balance. As Oliver took a step back to observe the way Joshua was standing, Joshua deliberately did it wrong so Oliver showed him again. After four attempts at placing his feet correctly and getting into the correct stance did Oliver hand Joshua a bow and arrow. Now Oliver took his time showing Joshua how to correctly hold the bow. "Place the arrow here like this and pull back, keep the elbow up," said Oliver, "and release." The arrow dropped to the floor at Joshua's feet, like a dead twig falling from a tree. Dorothy laughed. Oliver looked over his shoulder at his sister annoyed. She was still there. She thought he was angry because she had laughed, and so she apologised.

"Again," said Oliver, each time giving lengthy instructions, but with the same result. Joshua himself was getting bored and finally fired an arrow that sat just a few inches away from the arrow's shot by Oliver and Reif that occupied the bullseye. Oliver gave Joshua a look of disappointment, but Dorothy was clapping encouragingly.

"Well done," she said, as Joshua went and sat alongside Dorothy on the slope.

"That was fun," he said, "do you shoot?"

"Sometimes," said Dorothy.

Now it was Henry's turn, and it quickly became apparent that Henry had never held a bow before in his life. Oliver had gone through the same routine as he had with Joshua. First get the stance correct, then the bow and arrow. Henry was so bad, Oliver really did want to give up. Finally, he said, "I think we should have a rest." Sat on the grass slope behind them, Joshua and Reif were sitting either side of Dorothy. Oliver and Henry joined them on the slope. Oliver was now fed up, Henry was exhausted and Dorothy had words of encouragement for Henry.

"Don't worry," she said, "you will get there in the end." Oliver glared across at his sister angrily, but she didn't notice, for she was looking at Henry, but Reif had noticed.

"Are you not bored yet?" asked Reif.

"Oh no," said Dorothy, "it makes a nice change to get away from the castle for a while." Reif looked at Oliver and shrugged his shoulders. Oliver would have to think of a way of getting Dorothy to leave. Judging by the sun in the sky, it was midday. If they didn't leave soon, it would be too late and another day wasted. He was not about to let that happen.

Oliver lay down on the grass thinking. After a short while, he sat upright. He knew how to get rid of Dorothy. He launched straight into an attack without any warning. With real venom in his voice, he asked, "Why are you still here?" It was such a sudden outburst of anger it took everyone by surprise. Dorothy was stunned by Oliver's outburst, and momentarily didn't respond. She looked at the other three and then back at Oliver, then emotions took over and she burst into tears. She raced over to her horse and climbed into the saddle. She looked at Oliver one last time, with tears streaming down her face, confused not knowing what she had done wrong, and then she turned her horse away and rode off.

"That was a bit harsh," said Reif.

"I know," said Oliver, "I didn't want to do it, but I just had to get her to leave." Now that Dorothy had left, they gathered up all their belongings and mounted their horses. Berwyn had been lazing in the sun and slowly got to his feet when Oliver called.

Unbeknown to the four boys, but Dorothy had been wearing a bracelet which had fallen from her wrist. She hadn't gone far before realising it was missing, and she knew she was wearing it while they had been firing arrows at the target, for she had been admiring it in the sunlight. After the way Oliver had spoken to her, Dorothy didn't really want to see him again so soon, but she wasn't about to lose this bracelet, it was the last thing her mother had given her before she had died.

She turned her horse around and galloped back to where she had left the four boys. She was expecting Oliver to be annoyed with her on seeing her return, but she didn't care what he said, she had to find her bracelet. What a surprise Dorothy got. She arrived at the targets but there was no one there. *What a relief*, she thought. She quickly dismounted her horse and searched the area where she had been sitting. There it was, nestled amongst the daisies she had been using to make a daisy chain. She was glad Oliver was nowhere to be seen, but now she had found her bracelet, she wondered where on earth had they gone. They hadn't gone back to the castle because she would have passed them. Dorothy was in two minds what to do, return to the castle and forget today ever happened, or try to find out where they had gone. Not normally the adventurous type, she was intrigued and decided to find out what they were up to. After all, they couldn't have gone far. She was only gone a couple of minutes before she had returned. She decided they must have gone into the forest. For if they were riding across the open fields, surely she would be able to see them. She hesitated. What if she went into the forest and couldn't find them. It would be dark in a couple of hours and then she would be alone in the dark. Dorothy quickly put these thoughts out of her mind and set off. She reasoned with herself, if she hadn't found them by the time it started to get dark, she would turn around and go back to the castle.

Berwyn was leading the way through the forest, followed by Oliver and Reif, then Joshua and Henry, riding side by side. Joshua called out to Oliver, "I think Henry needs to rest."

Oliver shouted over his shoulder without looking back, "No, I can't afford to lose any more time." Just at the same time, Henry toppled from his horse and crashed onto the forest floor. Joshua pulled his horse to halt, and jumped to the ground. Oliver and Reif had heard the crash and rode back to see what had happened.

"I told you he needed to rest," said Joshua. Oliver was fuming, thanks to Dorothy they had been delayed for hours, and now this had happened.

"Maybe we should go back," suggested Joshua.

"Or you could take him back," said Oliver, "and allow Reif and I to go on alone."

"But without my help," said Joshua, "you won't know when you're at the right mountain or not." It was late afternoon and they had a couple of hours of sunlight before it got dark. It was decided Oliver and Reif would try and catch something to eat, while Joshua stayed with Henry.

Henry had some bruising to his face after his fall, but apart from that, seemed uninjured, and was sleeping at last. Berwyn had gone off by himself, which meant Joshua sat alone listening to Henry breathing and the sounds of the forest. In the dappled forest sunlight as the rays penetrated the canopy above, the forest was alive. Joshua sat watching a hairy green caterpillar munching away on a leaf one minute, only to become dinner to a forest bird the next. Then something on the forest floor caught his eye, combat between a large brown beetle and a gang of red ants, even though the beetle was much bigger than the ants, it was soon over powered by sheer numbers. The body of the beetle was dissected into smaller pieces and carried off back to the ants nest.

"Ouch." Someone was nearby. Joshua got to his feet, but crouched low. He moved amongst the tall ferns, trying to make as little noise as possible. He could hear someone cursing. They sounded female. Slowly, he crept closer to where the voice was coming from. He could hear a horse snorting, as the rider struggled to keep control of the horse and free herself from a thorn bush which had got tangled in her hair. "Ouch," she screamed again, the thorns stabbing her fingers as she tried to free herself. From behind a tree, Joshua watched as Dorothy struggled.

Oliver and Reif had returned having killed a couple of rabbits. Henry was still asleep, but Joshua was nowhere to be seen. Wondering what could possibly have happened to Joshua, they started to call his name. He returned shortly, but was not alone. Oliver was furious. Joshua returned and was leading a horse, a horse being ridden by Dorothy.

"What are you doing here?" asked Oliver.

"Following you," said Dorothy, defiantly. "What are you up to?"

"It's nothing to do with you," said Oliver.

"I think you're leaving to go in search of Nicholas," said Dorothy. Oliver, Reif and Joshua all looked at each other. "I knew it," said Dorothy.

"So, I suppose you're going to try and stop us," said Oliver.

"Why would I want to stop you?" said Dorothy.

"You mean you're not going to try and talk us out of it?" asked Oliver.

"No," said Dorothy.

"Then why are you here?" he asked. But before she could answer it dawned on Oliver. "Oh, you must be joking," said Oliver.

"No," said Dorothy. Reif had realised what was happening, but Joshua was still in the dark.

"Would someone please tell me what is going on?" Oliver was shaking his head in disbelief.

"I'll tell you what's going on, she," he said pointing at Dorothy, "wants to come with us." Joshua laughed, thinking Oliver was joking, but as he looked at each of them, he realised this was no joke.

"But she can't come with us," said Joshua.

"Why, because I'm a girl?" said Dorothy.

"Yes," said Oliver. Berwyn came crashing through the brambles at this point, which caused Dorothy to scream in fright.

"See," said Oliver, "you're frightened of the smallest of things."

"Berwyn is hardly the smallest of things," said Dorothy, "anyway I can ride a horse as well as any one of you, and I'm better with a bow and arrow than either Joshua or Henry."

"But it's too dangerous," said Oliver.

"Well, I'm afraid you have no choice but to take me with you," said Dorothy. "If you send me back, I will tell Robert what you are up to." As frustrated as Oliver was, he had to concede Dorothy was right.

"But someone will have to return to the castle," said Dorothy.

"Why is that?" asked Oliver.

"Because if I don't return, Alice and Mary will want to know where I am and start asking questions," said Dorothy. "And then Robert will come looking for me. One of you will have to go back," she said. Oliver looked at Joshua and Henry.

"Well, I'm not going back," said Joshua, "anyway, you need me," he said. This was true for he was the only one in the group that had been through the mountain his father had taken. He looked across at Henry, who had woken up with all the shouting.

"I'll go back," he said.

"Good, that's settled," said Dorothy, "but when you go back, you will have to convince everyone that we have decided to stay overnight in the old gamekeeper's lodge."

"Do you think they will believe me?" asked Henry.

"What choice do we have?" said Oliver.

"It's up to you to convince them," said Dorothy. So, as the other four moved off further into the forest with Berwyn leading the way, Henry waited a while before setting off back to the castle.

Henry took his time returning to the castle, to give his four friends as much time as possible to get a head start. He was worried in case they didn't believe his story. When he got back to the castle, he needn't have worried however, both Alice and Mary seemed to accept what he told them. It was only after dark and Robert the head guard did his routine check on the horses in the stables that he realised that four of the horses were missing. He entered the castle looking for who had returned. Knowing that five had left earlier in the day, he found Henry in one of the sitting rooms playing cards with Alice and Mary.

"Where are the others?" demanded Robert.

"What do you mean the others?" said Henry, trying to remain calm.

"You know very well what I mean," said Robert, the vein in the side of Robert's neck began to twitch; both Alice and Mary knew this was not a good sign.

"They are staying the night in the old gamekeeper's lodge," said Mary. Robert was suspicious of Henry who seemed a little flushed, but as it was already dark, decided to give Henry the benefit of the doubt. He would check the old gamekeeper's lodge at first light.

Chapter 9
Elvira's Tale

Saki awoke in the morning and left her bedroom, only to find Percival asleep on one of the large sofas in front of the fire. The flames had died, and it was just the embers that glowed in the fireplace. They provided little warmth. As the cabin sat at the top of a large hill, surrounded by mountains, the early morning air was crisp and cold. Saki magically placed logs into the fireplace, and the fire ignited. She sat on the sofa opposite Percival fully clothed with a shawl wrapped around her shoulders, and she watched as the flames danced between the logs. It wasn't long before a roaring fire was burning bright once more, warming the large cabin.

Percival finally awoke as the smell of Saki cooking breakfast invaded his senses. Percival sat up on the sofa, yawned and stretched. "Good morning, Percival," said Saki.

"Good morning, mother," replied Percival.

"Did you sleep well?" she asked.

"I guess I must have, for I didn't hear you get up this morning," said Percival.

"Come and join me for breakfast, I've got fresh eggs, bread made from mountain corn, and mountain moss tea," said Saki, "it's bit of an acquired taste, but it's piping hot." Percival joined his mother as she sat at one end of the table that was built to seat twelve.

As they sat eating, Saki watched her son. "You know I cannot tell you what the future brings," she said.

"I know," said Percival.

"But I can tell you of the past." Percival looked at his mother and smiled. "You wish to know about the white eagle," she said knowingly.

"I do," said Percival, "does it belong to anyone?"

"Now let's not get ahead of ourselves," she said. "I'll tell you a story."

"Many years ago, two sisters were born, to a king and queen that lived far away in a cold land, covered in ice and snow." Percival placed his knife and fork on the table as he stopped eating to concentrate on what Saki was saying. She continued, "One of the princesses was blonde the other dark. They grew up using magic. The princess with the dark hair only used her magic to help others, while the blonde princess used magic to get whatever she wanted, and if that meant using it against someone for her own amusement, she would do so." Percival picked up his mug of tea and took a large gulp. It was hot as it passed down his throat and warmed his body from the inside, not quite the taste of tea he was used to, more flowery with a perfumed scent, but acceptable. After he placed his mug back on the table, Saki continued.

"The young princesses would often clash over the use of magic. Where the blonde princess gained enjoyment from tormenting others, her sister would always try and stop her." Percival reached for his mug of tea again but knocked it over and sent tea flying across the table top. Saki ignored the spilt tea and continued. "As the young princesses grew older, they drifted further apart, neither understanding the other, the blonde princess being the eldest grew tiresome of life at the white castle. Seeking adventure, she left the safety of their parents' castle to find love."

"And did she find love?" asked Percival.

"She did, she travelled far and wide and eventually meeting a handsome fairy prince. They fell deeply in love, but his parents were opposed to them getting married."

"Why was that?" asked Percival.

"Because she was not a fairy," said Saki.

"More importantly, however, the blonde princess had been observed using magic to inflict pain on others, something the fairy king and queen could not abide. They tried to tell the young prince what they had witnessed with their own eyes, but he would not believe them, saying it was just another excuse to break them apart."

"Unbeknown to the young prince and his parents, the blonde princess had used magic to ensnare the fairy prince, who was besotted with her. They had arranged to be married. The date was set and all the preparations were underway. Just two days before the marriage, however, the young princess was overheard preparing more of the potion to keep the prince under her control. This was reported to the fairy king and queen, who immediately cancelled all preparations for the royal wedding and banished her from their kingdom. At first, the young prince was furious. Why was his bride to be banished, but within two days, the potion had worn off and he realised he had been tricked into the marriage. Without delay, the prince was introduced to a young fairy princess, and they were married.

"Elvira didn't leave quietly however. A week after the prince had got married, she re-entered the palace to announce that she was with child. As the fairy king and queen sat in stunned silence, it was the fairy prince who this time banished her from the kingdom. She pleaded with him, this is your child I am carrying. I'll have nothing to do with a child of yours, he raged."

Percival started to eat once more as Saki took a gulp of tea, then she continued. "Turned away by the prince she had tricked into loving her, months later, the princess eventually returned home with her child to the far north, the land of snow and ice, the baby girl's name was Eleanor. On her return, Elvira was greeted with love and warmth, both from her parents and her sister, Elizabeth. They doted on Eleanor, for the first time in ages the two sisters got along, but as the years passed, Eleanor developed a taste for inflicting pain on others, just as her mother used to. The sisters clashed once more. Eventually, Elizabeth decided to leave, only she renounced magic, refusing ever to use it again. Her parents pleaded with her to stay, but as Elizabeth left, Elvira stood looking out of a window with Eleanor by her side, as her sister said goodbye to her parents for the last time."

"So, what happened to Elizabeth?" asked Percival.

"She left the magical kingdom behind and had a family of her own," said Saki, "she married a king and they had five children. Three princesses and two princes, but sadly she died after the second prince was born."

Percival sat looking at his mother in disbelief, then asked, "What were the names of the children?"

Saki smiled, as she answered, "The three princesses are Alice, Dorothy and Mary and the princes are Oliver and Nicholas." Then she paused as she observed Percival's reaction. The realisation that the Elizabeth he had known had been a witch and had travelled from this enchanted kingdom to the land of men, Percival's mind was in a spin.

Then he asked, "Does that mean that the five children have magic?"

Saki replied, "They are inextricably linked to this kingdom."

Chapter 10
Dorothy's Adventure Begins

The four young adventurers had spent the first night sleeping in the open. This was a first for Dorothy. Upon awakening, Oliver asked his sister, "How did you sleep?"

"Surprisingly well, thank you, once I got to sleep, I had no idea how noisy the forest is at night, how about you?"

"Oh, I've slept outside so many times it's nothing new to me," said Oliver.

Reif who was also awake said, "I think we should make a start because we have no way of knowing how convincing Henry was. The castle guards could be searching the forest for us this very minute." Joshua was still sleeping. Reif kicked the soles of his feet to wake him up. "Come on," said Reif, "it's time to leave." They gathered all their belongings, so they would leave no trace behind. Unfortunately, they couldn't remove all traces of Berwyn's white fur, they just didn't have enough time. As usual, Berwyn led the way, but instead of creating his own pathway, he followed the path that ran through the forest. They followed in single file leading their horses, Reif first, then Dorothy, Joshua and lastly Oliver, who had taken it upon himself to remove as much of Berwyn's fur as possible that got snagged on any bushes. The air was pleasantly warm in the early morning sun. As the dappled light penetrated through the canopy of trees, birds were singing their morning chorus.

Back at the castle, Alice and Mary were awake. "I wonder how Dorothy got on sleeping in the gamekeeper's lodge?" asked Mary.

"I'm sure she was fine," said Alice sleepily, "after all, she is with Oliver, Reif and Joshua."

"Oh, and don't forget Berwyn," said Mary. They were both still lying in their beds having only just woken up. "I can't imagine there was a comfortable bed for her to sleep in," said Mary.

"Oh, I'm sure she can cope for one night," said Alice.

"I can't help thinking of all the cobwebs and spiders, and all the bugs running all over you, as you are lying in some dusty old bed, sleeping," said Mary. Alice had closed her eyes once more and drifted off to sleep. Mary snuggled down in her warm bed and did the same.

With Berwyn leading the way the party of four were in a good mood, Oliver was no longer looking at Dorothy as though she had ruined everything. They covered a lot of ground on their first day, so Oliver was happy with the progress they had made. He had followed last in line behind Berwyn so that he could try and cover their tracks. He wasn't entirely confident he had done a good job, but he knew he had done the best he could, and that was all anyone could ask. They would have to remain vigilant. As evening approached, they stopped at a clearing and made camp for the night. Oliver and Reif skinned the two rabbits they had caught the day before, Joshua started a fire, while Dorothy collected fresh water from a nearby stream.

When they had finished eating, they settled down for their second night away from the castle. Dorothy didn't act at all like Oliver had expected. He thought she would complain all the time about wanting to stop riding and rest. He felt sure she would moan all the time about sleeping on the forest floor, but he was impressed with his sister for she hadn't complained once, then he reminded himself, this was only their second night. As he made himself comfortable on the ground, he said, "Goodnight."

To which they all replied, "Goodnight."

It had been a pleasant sunny day and a warm evening, but during the dark hours of night, rain had arrived. Joshua was the first to awaken, as a branch above his head sent a constant trickle of water that dripped down the back of his neck. He woke with a start, not sure what was happening. As he sat up the water raced down his back, sending a chill down his spine. It was cold and made him feel uncomfortable, then he realised that although the top half of his legs had been sheltered from the rain and were dry, the lower half of his legs and his feet were soaking wet. Joshua could barely make the others out in the dark, just shadowy figures laid out on the forest floor. "Hey, you lot," he shouted, "wake up, it's raining." Dorothy was the first to wake after hearing Joshua shouting.

"Oh, good heavens," said Dorothy when she realised how wet her clothes were. "Oliver," she called, "Oliver wake up." Reif was the next to wake and find himself half soaked and half dry, only when they finally managed to wake Oliver from his sleep, did they find out he was perfectly dry. "How did you manage that?" asked Dorothy.

"I covered myself with the largest leaves I could find, like I always do, in case it rains," said Oliver.

"Thanks for the tip," said Dorothy. They all laughed. Now in the dark of night, they had to find some sort of shelter from the continuing rain. Berwyn was nowhere in sight, but they knew he would find them the next day. Fumbling in the dark, Oliver had managed to find a dry piece of wood that had been protected from the rain by the same leaves he had used to cover himself. Using an old trick that Percival had once shown him, Oliver managed to set the piece of wood alight. Now they could see where they were going at least. In single file, Oliver now led the way. In places, puddles of water had collected on the ground, wading through the water ankle deep everyone now had wet feet, that squelched as they took each step. Finally, they found an abandoned old shack that was barely standing. In fact, the only thing holding it off the ground was a large tree it was leaning up against, but it provided some shelter from the ever increasing, now heavy rain. No one managed to get any more sleep that night, even Oliver had ended up wet through to his skin after walking through the forest in the pouring rain, and now they were cold, with no fire for warmth.

The rain finally eased off shortly before dawn. Everyone was feeling miserable, although no one said anything in complaint. Oliver and Reif went to fetch the horses; it wasn't long before they returned. Oliver helped Dorothy onto her horse, then the three boys mounted their own horses, Berwyn was still nowhere to be seen. "So, what do we do now?" asked Dorothy.

"We wait," said Oliver, "he'll find us." It wasn't long to wait before they heard a crashing sound heading their way. It was Berwyn once again creating his own pathway through the forest.

"He looks completely dry," said Dorothy.

"Yes, he does, doesn't he?" said Oliver laughing. "He must have found shelter from the rain." So now they had Berwyn leading the way once more, they exited from the forest into open countryside. The sun had risen above the surrounding hills. As their soaking wet clothes warmed in the sun, they began to send up plumes of steam, like a boiling pot of water on a camp fire.

They had no change of clothes with them, so they had no choice but to stay wearing their wet clothes while they dried off. It was an uncomfortable ride at first but as the warmth from the sun increased, it didn't take too long for their clothes to dry. The next problem was hunger. The only thing they had eaten the day before were the two rabbits that Oliver and Reif had caught.

While Reif and Joshua looked out over the open countryside for any sign of rabbits, Oliver turned his attention to the skies, and sure enough a flock of geese where heading their way. He quickly told both Joshua and Reif to get their bows ready. As they did, a small speck from high above the geese started a rapid descent. "Eagle," cried Oliver. The eagle had landed an attack on the lead bird. The others dispersed in different directions. Now only two were heading their way. "Wait," said Oliver, they watched as the birds drew nearer, "now," shouted Oliver. All three boys fired an arrow and missed both birds. As they were reloading a second arrow, a large goose fell from the sky and landed at their feet with a thud. Dorothy smiled triumphantly, as they looked at her in disbelief.

"Anyone can hit a stationary target," said Dorothy, "a moving target is completely different." The three boys all laughed.

"Let's eat," said Oliver. A couple of hours or so later with bellies full, they continued, on their way.

Back at the castle, Henry was being questioned by Robert. "Where did you last see Prince Oliver?" asked Robert.

"I told you," said Henry, "at the targets, they were still shooting arrows, when I felt ill and came back."

"And you came back alone, why didn't Dorothy come with you?" asked Robert.

"I told her she didn't need to. I was quite capable of making my way back alone."

"And you say they were going to spend the night in the gamekeeper's lodge?" said Robert.

"Yes," said Henry, but it was obvious to Henry that Robert didn't believe his story.

"How did you get that bruise on your face?" asked Robert. Henry had forgotten about that and had no answer. Robert made his way to the courtyard and rang the bell. There in the courtyard, the guards answered the call of the bell. Robert waited for all his men to gather around. He stood where they could all see him and he selected six to join him in the search for Oliver. "The rest of you," he said, "stay here and make sure nobody leaves, and I mean nobody." He was staring at Henry when he said this, which made Henry squirm, feeling uncomfortable, as all eyes were now upon him.

"We're leaving right now," said Robert, "if I'm right, we have some catching up to do." They dashed into the stables to collect their horses and within a couple of minutes, they were racing across the lawns towards the far side of the lake. Half an hour's ride and they reached the archery targets. They bypassed them and continued on to the gamekeeper's cabin which sat on the edge of the forest. As soon as they opened the door, it was evident no one had been there in ages. The deep dust that covered the floor sat undisturbed.

Robert was caught in two minds what to do, return to the castle or continue to search for the missing prince and princess. The problem was where to search. Out across the open fields or into the forest, he decided on the forest. It was muddy and slippery underfoot and leading into the forest was a small hill. The palace horses struggled in the conditions. It was like taking two steps forward and one step backwards, but eventually with persistence, they made it up the hill and into the forest.

They had no footprints to follow, after the heavy overnight rain, but Robert looked around searching. Then he found what he was looking for. "This way," he said. He had spotted where Berwyn had made a new trail for himself, a wide path of flattened ferns and brambles showed the way, as they followed the pathway, further evidence they were on the right track revealed itself in the clumps of white fur caught on thorn bushes.

They followed the signs for quite some time until they reached a stream that ran through the forest. Robert looked up and down stream but could find no trail to follow. "Wait here," he told his men. Robert rode his horse upstream looking for evidence of where Berwyn had crossed the stream and exited the other side. He had been gone for quite a while and the palace guards were talking amongst themselves when he returned.

"Did you find anything?" one of the guards asked.

"Nothing," replied Robert, "we will try this way." And so they headed off downstream, with Robert leading the way. They had been travelling for quite a distance and still no sign of anyone having crossed the stream. Robert was frustrated and beginning to think maybe he had missed something up stream and was thinking of turning back. Just as he was about to turn around, one of the guards had spotted something.

"What's that?" he shouted, pointing to something the other side of the stream. There were no flattened bushes to follow, and no clumps of fur. This part of the bank was bare rock, but what the guard had spotted was a piece of material, pink silk, to be exact, frayed and laying on the ground almost completely covered in mud.

"Wasn't Dorothy wearing a pink dress?" the guard asked.

"Yes, she was," said Robert.

Having crossed the stream, they were certain they were on the right trail, but there were no flattened bushes to follow, and no sign of white fur. They continued searching until it started to get dark, then they had to stop. They lit a camp fire and settled for the night. Storm clouds rolled in once more, jet black against a fading moon. They crept over the forest like a plague, then a flash of lightning, followed by a clap of thunder, but no rain, not yet, but within seconds, another flash of lightning along with a clap of thunder directly overhead that shook the forest. The heavens opened up and torrential rain pelted down. Now they were running looking for shelter. They found an old shack leaning against a tree. The tree was the only thing stopping the shack from falling over completely.

For the second night, Oliver and his companions had to find shelter from the rain. Having left the forest behind, they had been crossing open countryside. Tonight, however, luck was on their side. An old abandoned barn stood next to the shell of a burnt-out cottage. Inside the barn, it was dry and even though the wind had picked up and was howling outside, the barn was fairly draft free. Berwyn lay in one corner of the barn. Oliver and Reif started a small fire for warmth. As they all settled for the night, they lay listening to the storm raging outside. One loud thunderclap after another, as the lightning lit up the sky. Slowly, one by one, they fell asleep.

Chapter 11
Choosing the Brooch

Two days had passed since the last ball. Nicholas had asked if he could ride Favonius again. His request met with a resounding 'no'.

Elvira too was busy, and Eleanor who usually kept Nicholas entertained was nowhere to be found. Nicholas was bored being stuck inside. He was already dressed in his own clothes but put on a fur coat and hat that Elvira had provided. His hands buried deep inside a pair of fur gloves. He had decided he was going to go exploring, as no one was available to go with him Nicholas decided he would go alone. The castle seemed empty. As he passed along the hallway from his bedroom to the top of the stairs, he saw no one, even the tall, thin man in the blood-red suit was nowhere to be found and so Nicholas was able to leave the white castle via the main entrance. A blast of icy cold wind smacked him in the face as he stepped outside. He shivered as the shock of cold air on his face made his eyes water. He pulled the collar of his fur coat tighter to his neck. The steps leading down from the castle were covered in fresh snow, which had fallen throughout the night. It looked beautifully clean and was silent in the courtyard. Nicholas carefully descended the steps, but soon realised that beneath the layer of fresh snow was a covering of ice, with his feet slipping from under him with every step he took, and yet he somehow managed to get to the bottom of the steps without falling over.

Leaving behind a trail of tiny footprints, Nicholas made his way down to the nearby village. Apart from flying over the village twice, first being held in the talons of the giant white eagle, and second riding on the back of Favonius the flying horse, this was Nicholas' first visit by foot.

The small village seemed empty of people, but evidence of their existence showed on the ground by the many footprints in the snow. As Nicholas looked around for any further sign of life, he realised that all the footprints seemed to be heading in the same direction, which he decided to follow. As he turned a corner, the wind howled as it raced down the street towards him. As it swept over him, the sound ringing in his ears sounded like a wounded animal howling in pain. Snow from the rooftops kept blowing down upon him, and the snow and ice crunched under foot as he walked along. A row of identical small houses lined each side of the street. The only thing different between them was the gold number on the door. It dawned on Nicholas that he hadn't seen a single shop.

With snow swirling around, being blown from the rooftops by the strong wind and inhibiting his vision, Nicholas finally came to the end of the street. Standing alone was what looked like a large barn. All the footprints on the ground led towards a set of double doors. Nicholas eagerly approached. He pulled on the door handle and stepped inside. As he entered through the double doors, his ears were assaulted with a cacophony of sound and his eyes lit up. He had found the village shops. As he approached the first shop, his sense of smell told him this was a baker's. An assortment of different breads and pastries were on display, as two shop assistants one male and one female were being kept busy by a constant flow of customers. He stood staring through the shop window at all the delights on display before moving on, square cakes covered in pink icing, with a thin strip of green icing that wrapped around with a bow on top, which made them resemble a Christmas present. Then there was a flat cake, shaped like a Christmas tree covered in green icing with tiny icing candles them seemed to glow, and lastly, a round cake covered in white icing called a snow bomb. Nicholas had no idea what this meant, but was intrigued. As he stood admiring the cakes, he found himself unceremoniously bustled along. As more people started to queue outside the shop, he moved on.

The next shop that caught his eye was a butcher's. Large slabs of meat hung in the window suspended on giant hooks, blood dripped from the meat onto the floor. Nicholas peered through the window beneath the slabs of meat. A large woman held a meat cleaver that she was using to chop the meat into smaller pieces. Her white butcher's apron was splattered with blood, as were the white tiles that covered the walls of the back room where she was working. Two male shop assistants were serving the customers.

Nicholas felt slightly sick at the sight of all the blood and so moved on once more. It was getting warmer inside the giant barn, so much so that Nicholas removed his fur hat, unbuttoned his fur coat and took his gloves off and put them in the pockets of his coat. Nicholas came to a halt outside a shop selling glass, as he entered a bell above the door rang, and a great warmth washed over him. The shop was empty of any assistants. Nicholas began to look around at the objects on display. Large glass bowls in various colours sat on shelves behind a glass counter, beautiful glasses sat neatly in rows, some with long thin stems, some with no stem at all. Then a voice called from the back of the shop. "I'll be with you in a minute." Nicholas went to investigate. As he stepped through a doorway at the back of the shop, he understood why it felt so hot. He found himself standing in a glass blowing foundry. Half a dozen men and two women were doing various tasks. Boy was it hot.

Each person was wearing a face shield to protect their eyes from the intense heat, and protective clothing covered their bodies. When one of them spotted Nicholas just standing there, they immediately put down what they were doing and raced over to him. Removing her facemask, one of the women said, "You can't be back here, it's not safe." She took Nicholas by the hand and led him back into the shop. Nicholas was looking at her with a puzzled expression on his face, "What?" she asked.

"I know you from somewhere," said Nicholas.

"Been sneaking around the foundry before, have you?" she asked, "no," said Nicholas. Just then, a bear of a man over six feet tall with flaming red hair and beard appeared.

"Why aren't you at your workstation?" he bellowed.

"I know you," said Nicholas, "you're Sir Cuthbert."

Caught completely by surprise, Sir Cuthbert said, "Oh my goodness, it's Prince Nicholas," as the woman looked at him oddly, "Elvira's guest of honour," said Sir Cuthbert.

"That's where I've seen you before," said Nicholas to the woman standing by his side, "at the ball."

"What are you doing here?" asked Sir Cuthbert.

"Just looking around the shop," said Nicholas innocently.

"Surely you're not alone?" said Sir Cuthbert.

"Yes, I am," answered Nicholas casually. Something tiny had caught Nicholas' eye, as he looked around the shop once more. He crossed the shop floor to a glass cabinet and was surprised to find dozens of tiny brooches.

He turned to face Sir Cuthbert but before Nicholas said anything, Sir Cuthbert said, "Yes, I make the glass brooches for Elvira, but she is the one who enchants them."

The bell rang violently as the door to the shop was quickly opened. A frantic Eleanor entered. Upon seeing Nicholas, she said, "Thank God I found you."

"We have only just discovered him ourselves," said Sir Cuthbert. "I was just about to bring him back to the castle."

"Thank you," said Eleanor, dismissively.

As she led Nicholas from the shop, he called out to Sir Cuthbert, "I really like your shop." Sir Cuthbert smiled and waved Nicholas goodbye.

As they walked past the shops, Nicholas tried to button up his coat. It was impossible using one hand. Eleanor had a firm grip on the other. She was not about to let him go. As they reached the double doors, Eleanor stopped abruptly. Nicholas stumbled forwards but remained on his feet because Eleanor still held his hand. "What were you thinking going off like that?" she scolded.

"I didn't think anyone would mind," said Nicholas, innocently. Eleanor could not help but smile at Nicholas.

She buttoned his coat, put his hat on and asked, "Where are your gloves?" Nicholas put his hands in his pockets and pulled his gloves out. "You're going to need them," said Eleanor.

From the warmth of the giant barn, Eleanor opened the door and stepped outside. The freezing cold air that greeted them was in complete contrast to the warmth inside the barn. Once more, she had a firm grip of Nicholas' hand, and with good reason, a blizzard had started. The strong wind was blowing the heavily falling snow horizontally down the street into the faces of Eleanor and Nicholas. it was almost impossible to see where they were going. Eleanor used one hand to try and shield her eyes from the snow, whilst keeping a firm grip on Nicholas with the other hand. As they struggled through the snow, Nicholas had closed his eyes against the chill, allowing himself to be guided by Eleanor. In places, the strong winds had blown the snow into deep drifts, leaving parts of the street with barely any snow. Walking suddenly became easier, but only for a few paces. Unable to see more than a few feet ahead, progress back to the castle was slow. With the wind howling in their ears, they were unable to communicate. It was exhausting battling against the strong winds and knee-deep snow, but finally, having fought their way through the blizzard, they eventually made it back to the castle, only to be greeted by the thin man with long, white hair wearing the blood-red suit.

"Elvira is waiting for you," he said. As they entered the castle, he quickly closed the doors behind them.

Eleanor removed her fur coat and hat, then she helped Nicholas remove his fur coat, before they went off to find Elvira, leaving behind a heap of snow on the marble floor. The tall, thin man in the blood-red suit cleared away the snow with a wave of his hand. Eleanor knew where to find her mother. Candle chandeliers hung from the ceiling lit the way. Nicholas peered out the windows on the way to see Elvira. The snow was falling heavier than he had ever experienced before. His eyes opened wide with excitement and he could not help but smile, for he loved to play in the snow. Eleanor was dreading appearing before her mother. She knew she would be blamed for Nicholas leaving the castle alone, but she could not put it off. *Best get it over with,* thought Eleanor.

Elvira was sat in her favourite sitting room waiting on a large chair close to the fireplace. The fire roared as huge flames danced over the coals. The upholstery on Elvira's chair was sky blue, with ornate gold feet and arms. As always, Elvira's dress was purest white. Elvira smiled at Nicholas and Eleanor as they entered the room, not what Eleanor had expected. "Did you enjoy your trip to the village, Nicholas?" asked Elvira.

"Yes, thank you," said Nicholas eagerly, "it was great fun in the glass shop. I met Sir Cuthbert in there."

"Yes, I know," said Elvira. Eleanor watched her mother closely, waiting for Elvira to say something to her, but for now, she addressed Nicholas once more. "Did you see all the brooches in the glass shop?" asked Elvira.

"Yes, I did," said Nicholas.

"Would you like to choose the one for this week's ball?" asked Elvira.

"Can I?" said Nicholas excitedly.

"Of course you can," said Elvira, as a huge smile spread across her face.

Eleanor dared a quick glance out of the window, the snow was falling so heavily you could not make out individual flakes of snow. It was just a sheet of snow falling past the windows. As Eleanor turned from the window to face Elvira once more, Elvira asked, "Is everything all right, Eleanor?"

"Yes, mother," she said, as she tried to sound confident, but knowing that she had failed miserably. Eleanor was confused, why hadn't Elvira had a go at her about Nicholas leaving the castle alone. She knew her mother was in a rage because of the storm that continued outside. Eleanor knew full well that the angrier Elvira got, so the storm got worse, and Eleanor hadn't seen a storm like this in years. In fact, the more she thought about it, she realised she had never seen a snowstorm quite like this before.

Eleanor looked hesitantly at her mother, "I'm sorry Nicholas left the castle alone," said Eleanor, "only I was busy arranging something for this week's ball."

"Oh, did Nicholas leave the castle alone? I had no idea," said Elvira. Eleanor still confused by her mother's actions, knew this must be a lie, for the storm outside continued to rage unabated.

Elvira turned her attention back to Nicholas. "Tomorrow, Nicholas, I promise I will take you to the glass shop where you can choose the brooch for this week's ball." Nicholas needed to visit the bathroom and asked to be excused. As he left the room, he cast his mind back to the brooches he had seen. He already knew which one he wanted. Elvira spoke softly to Eleanor so that no one else could hear. "I hold you responsible for Nicholas," said Elvira, "if anything should happen to the child, you would feel my wrath," she said.

"Yes, mother, I understand," said Eleanor, it was no more than Eleanor had been expecting, but now it had been said, the storm outside seemed to ease off slightly.

The following day as promised, Elvira took Nicholas to the glass shop. It had stopped snowing, but Nicholas had never seen such deep snow before. They had to wear special shoes that allowed them to walk across the surface of the snow without sinking up to their knees, and in some places up to their waist. All around them, the villagers struggled as they sank into the deep drifts of snow. Some seemed completely stuck, waving their arms frantically for someone to help them. Nicholas wanted to help all of them, but Elvira said 'no'. It reminded Nicholas of how he felt when he first arrived at the castle, when he had fallen on the castle steps, and no one offered to help. Elvira walked past without giving anyone a second glance. Nicholas offered his hand to a young girl in order to try and pull her free from the snow's icy grip on her legs, but Elvira holding Nicholas' other hand pulled him away.

"Sorry," he called, to the young girl, as she pleaded to be rescued. Nicholas looked to the sky. The clouds were gathering again, dark grey with the promise of yet more snow to come.

As they approached the barn, the doors opened. The warm air that escaped carried with it the scent of the bakery. "I love that smell," said Elvira. Nicholas made no comment. He couldn't stop thinking of the young girl he wanted to help. "Are you all right, Nicholas?" asked Elvira.

"Why couldn't we help those people?" he asked. Elvira looked at him with a puzzled expression.

"Why should I?" she asked.

"We could have helped, but you just left them stuck in the snow," he said. Elvira still had hold of Nicholas by the hand. Without another word spoken by either of them, she proceeded to the glass shop at a fast pace. Nicholas was practically running to keep up. As the door opened, the bell above the door announced their arrival. It was Sir Cuthbert who came into the shop from the foundry out back. Carrying his protective facemask in his hands, he placed it on the glass counter.

"Good morning, how can I help?" asked Sir Cuthbert.

Elvira and Nicholas had their backs to Sir Cuthbert, as they bent down and looked at the brooches. Again, Sir Cuthbert asked, "Can I help you?"

Still Elvira didn't respond to Sir Cuthbert, but instead spoke to Nicholas. "Have you made your choice?" she asked.

"Yes," said Nicholas, "can we have that one?" He was pointing to a brooch that sat right in the middle of the display.

"I'm sorry," said Sir Cuthbert, "but those are not for sale, they are for our Queen Elvira."

Elvira who had bent down besides Nicholas to look at the brooches stood up and turned to face Sir Cuthbert. "Your Majesty, forgive me, I did not know it was you," said Sir Cuthbert apologetically.

"That's quite all right," said Elvira, "Nicholas has made his choice for this week's ball." She pointed to the brooch that sat in the middle of the display. Sir Cuthbert opened the glass door and reached in for the brooch. His hand trembled as he reached towards the brooch indicated. "Come, come," said Elvira, "it's only a brooch." Beads of sweat had appeared on Sir Cuthbert's face. Elvira's presence always made him nervous. He gently grasped the brooch in his enormous right hand and removed it from the display.

Carefully wrapped in tissue paper and placed in a small box, Sir Cuthbert handed over the brooch to Elvira. "And remember," she said, "not a word to anyone."

"Yes, Your majesty," said Sir Cuthbert. The bell rang once more as they opened the shop door to leave.

Nicholas then asked, "Why must Sir Cuthbert not say a word?"

"Because the brooch needs to be a surprise," said Elvira.

Chapter 12
Return to Deadman's Lake

Oliver, Reif, Joshua and Dorothy being led by Berwyn had reached a large lake. The sun glistened on the surface of the water. Lily pads spread out across half the lake. Lilies with white flowers and yellow centres dominated, but there were a few pink flowers also with yellow centres that grew in small clumps close to the water's edge. Dragon flies hovered over the surface of the lake, then quickly darted from view. Water boatmen, strange looking animals that looked like spiders with their long thin legs skated across the water's surface.

They had stopped for a welcome drink of water. Having dismounted their horses, Oliver bent down and cupped his hands to quench his thirst. The others had done the same. Now satisfied, Oliver stood up and stretched. They were all feeling stiff after hours of horse riding. Reif stood beside Oliver. "Something about this place seems familiar," said Oliver. He started to wander around the perimeter of the lake. Berwyn had laid down and Dorothy and Joshua were seated on the ground resting. Reif was walking with Oliver. A group of sparrows were bathing at the water's edge.

"It is so tranquil," said Reif.

"Something feels wrong," said Oliver.

"What do you mean?" asked Reif.

"I feel as though I've been here before," said Oliver. As they continued walking around the lake, he stumbled on a piece of wood hidden in some long grass. He bent down and picked up the offending piece of wood. "Oh my god," said Oliver. "I know where we are," he exclaimed. "This is dead man's lake," said Oliver.

"How do you know?" asked Reif.

"Look," said Oliver, he turned and showed Reif the piece of wood he had just found in the long grass, "it bares my father's crest," said Oliver, "it's part of the wagon Stephen was driving. This must be the spot where the guards fell through the ice," said Oliver. He looked out over the lake once more, and although it was a beautiful scene, he suddenly felt sick to his stomach. A cold chill ran down his spine with the memory of what had happened there.

"We need to leave," said Oliver.

"But the others are resting," said Reif, "what do we tell them?"

"Nothing," said Oliver, "I don't want Dorothy to know."

Oliver walked quickly back to where Joshua was sitting with Dorothy. "We're leaving," said Oliver. With no explanation, he walked straight over to his horse and mounted. Reif followed. "Are you coming or not?" asked Oliver, Dorothy went to say something but saw Reif shaking his head no, so instead said, "Yes, of course I'm coming."

Robert and the guards who were still searching for Oliver and Dorothy had found the barn where they had rested from the stormy night which had cleared away by morning. With no further rain, they finally had a decent set of Berwyn's footprints to follow in the soft ground. Robert could see that Oliver had tried to hide the tracks by riding the horses behind Berwyn, but it had not been completely successful. The footprints led them all the way to the lake, and they arrived at the lake as the sun was setting. "This is a good spot to rest for the night," said Robert. They dismounted and set up camp. A fire was lit. Rabbit was on the menu. After they had eaten, they settled under the stars for it was a cloudless sky, and so to sleep.

Bird song announced the arrival of dawn at the lake. Robert was the first to wake and lay listening to the beginning of a new day. A rustling in the long grass disturbed his thoughts. He took hold of his sword which lay on the ground beside his body. The noise was approaching from behind Robert. Swiftly, Robert rolled over and thrust his sword towards the intruder. The old woman screamed, "Agh." The tip of Robert's sword was no more than an inch from the old woman's throat, as she had bent forward.

The scream had awoken all the guards. The old woman had straightened up, clutching at her throat. "What did you do that for?" she screamed at Robert.

"It's your own fault," said Robert, "creeping up on a man whilst he sleeps. How was I to know you weren't an outlaw out to rob us?"

"I wasn't creeping, as you put it, I was just trying not to disturb you from your slumber," said the old woman, angrily.

"Then why were you bending over me?" questioned Robert. The old woman was feeling flustered, but quickly composed herself.

"I was checking you were sleeping and not dead," she said.

"Well as you can see, we are very much alive," said Robert, as a huge grin spread across his face, and all the guards laughed.

"I expect you are all hungry as well," said the old woman, "my farmhouse is just the other side of the lake. That's how I knew you were here. I saw your fire last night. Breakfast is already cooked if you are interested." Robert looked at his men. They were all smiling, hoping he would accept the old woman's offer of breakfast.

"Thank you, we accept," said Robert.

The smell of bacon and eggs, and freshly baked bread welcomed them as the old woman opened the door to her farmhouse, where upon they entered straight into the kitchen. "Please take a seat," said the old woman, indicating the large dining table.

As they all sat around the table, the old woman served up plates of bacon and eggs for one and all. Freshly baked bread along with a dish of butter sat at the centre of the table, there for them to help themselves. She poured each a mug of tea. "Are you not eating?" asked Robert.

"Oh I had my breakfast more than an hour ago," said the old woman. She had positioned herself at the head of the table and sat with her elbow's resting on the table. One hand was closed into a fist the other lay on top. Her chin resting on them both. She watched silently as they ate.

Sat in the old woman's kitchen, Robert noticed for the first time just how old she looked. Her hair was grey and thin, her pale blue eyes seemed to bulge out of sunken eye sockets, her hands covered in liver spots, warts on at least three of her fingers and a large boil sat on the end of her nose. He could not help but think she looked like a witch. Looking down the table at Robert as he was eating, she smiled revealing broken yellow teeth. Robert felt uncomfortable under her gaze. He lowered his eyes, as he cleared his plate.

After they had finished eating, Robert thanked the old woman for her hospitality and apologised for nearly taking her life. She waved her hand as if brushing away an annoying fly. "No need for apologies," she said, "it was my own fault."

Robert then asked, "Have you seen three boys and a girl recently?"

"I haven't seen anyone for the past month," said the old woman. "Should I be worried?" she asked. "Are they dangerous?"

"No, nothing like that," said Robert. But he didn't elaborate any further, for he didn't want anyone to know that Prince Oliver and Princess Dorothy were missing, as they would be easy targets for outlaws.

Robert looked down the table. "Are we all finished?" he asked.

All his men replied, "Yes." Thanking the old woman one last time for her generous meal, they were about to leave when George spotted a shield with his family crest.

"How do you happen to have this shield?" asked George, enquiringly.

"What's the matter?" asked Robert.

"Look," said George, becoming more agitated, "it's Arthur's shield." Robert turned to face the old woman.

"Well," said Robert. With all eyes upon her, she remained calm.

"I found it by the edge of the lake after the snow had melted. Why, what are you accusing me of now?" she asked.

"Sorry," said George apologetically, "I overreacted, it used to belong to my brother, but I know he died at dead man's lake."

"Oh, I'm sorry to hear that," said the old woman, "take it, it belongs to you," she said. Annoyed with herself for bringing them to her farmhouse. *That was a good quality shield; it would have sold for a high price,* she thought.

George picked up his brother's shield, apologised again and left the farmhouse. One by one, the guards followed, with Robert the last to leave. "Thank you," he said. He placed five gold coins onto the table. *Not such a bad idea giving them breakfast after all,* she thought. They mounted their horses and rode back around the lake to find Berwyn's footprints, so they could continue their search for Oliver and Dorothy.

Chapter 13
Percival Leaves Home

Percival had found out from his mother, Saki, that the deceased Queen Elizabeth he knew was in fact a witch. This news had come as quite a shock, and it meant that her five children were in fact inextricably linked to this magical world. *Surely, they must possess magic themselves,* he thought, but not one had shown any signs of magic. Percival had to leave his mother to go in search of Prince Nicholas, Saki knew this, and understood why, but she was still sad to see her only son leave again so soon. "Do you remember when you left home the first time, how you managed it?" she asked.

"No," said Percival, "I seem to have no memory of that." Saki nodded.

"As I expected, but I can assure you this, the longer you remain in this enchanted kingdom, your memory will return," she said, "you need to find the one-eyed hag's wishing well. It can transport you to anywhere you want to go, but heed this, the well can only be reached by giving the one-eyed hag an offering, a hot drink made of honey. She cannot resist the sweetest of drinks known to man, but be careful or you will end up facing your worst fears. Do not allow the one-eyed hag to look you in the eyes. She will search inside your soul for your deepest fears and bring them to life."

"But, how do I find the one-eyed hag?" asked Percival.

"Follow the cobra-headed snakebird, it will take you to the one-eyed hag," said Saki.

"But what does this snakebird look like?" asked Percival.

"You will know it when you see it," said Saki, "good bye my son and good luck." Percival kissed his mother on the cheek and bid her farewell.

"I will be back," he said.

"I know you will," said Saki.

A giant horn lay on the ground resting against the side of Saki's cabin. Percival raised it off the floor and placed one end against his lips and blew. The deep booming sound created by the horn echoed around the mountains and sank into the valley below, and so Percival waited, but he didn't have to wait long before a giant mountain goat appeared, with massive horns that sat upon a broad head and a long shaggy coat to cope with the cold mountain weather. The massive goat had answered the call of the horn. "He will take you to the bottom of the mountain," said Saki, "but that is as far as he can go."

"Thank you, mother," said Percival. Saki placed a stool beside the mountain goat to enable Percival to climb onto its back. Just then, Percival remembered he wanted to ask about the giant white eagle. But before he could ask, the goat was off. From the top of Saki's hill, the goat raced higher into the mountains. Saki watched as Percival's image finally disappeared against the backdrop of the grey mountain. Having reached its peak at great speed, the goat skilfully made its way down the side of the mountain, picking out a path that no other creature would dare. The sure-footed goat jumped from rock to rock, crevices in the mountain that looked impossible to pass were no match for the giant goat's agility, and before he knew it, Percival was at the bottom of the mountain. The goat came to a halt. Percival knew this was as far as the goat could take him and so slipped from its back, but before Percival's feet had even touched the ground, the goat had started to climb the mountain once more, and within seconds, was out of view.

All alone, Percival felt very small in front of the tall mountain, and the vast open space that spread out before him didn't help. Still, he had a journey to undertake and there was no time like the present to get started, and so he decided in which direction to walk and off he set. At first, Percival thought he was alone, but for the occasional bird soaring high in the sky overhead. He looked into the sky to see if it was the cobra-headed snakebird, but then a noise on the ground caught his attention, and as he turned to the right, he saw a group of burrowing animals heading down a large hole in the ground. Suddenly, a dark shadow appeared on the ground from behind Percival. Travelling at great speed, the shadow plunged towards the ground and at the last second, a large bird appeared. It plucked the last of the animals from the ground before it could escape down its bolt hole. The large bird beat its wings and gracefully soared back into the sky carrying its feast for the day in its talons. Still alive, the captive animal squealed with legs flailing as it struggled to escape. Percival watched, as they disappeared into the distance.

Percival felt thirsty. His mother had given him a container with water and so he stopped to have a drink. She had also provided a supply of food, but he was not hungry yet, and so after taking a sip of water, he returned the bottle into the bag which was slung over one shoulder and carried on.

Percival continued, on foot for quite a while, covering a fair distance, where the air up on the hill had been cool and refreshing down on the ground it was hot and dry, his thirst had returned. The mountains had shrunk behind Percival, and the ground beneath Percival's feet was dry and cracked. It was hard to believe that this was all part of the enchanted kingdom that contained the rainbow forest. Percival stopped to rest, seated on a large boulder he took another sip of water from the container, now he was feeling hungry and took out a pie that his mother Saki had prepared for him. With a small knife, he cut away a small piece of pie and placed the rest back into his bag.

As Percival sat eating, he was contemplating about visiting the one-eyed hag, and how he could overcome the problem of her staring into his soul. He was bought back from his reverie suddenly, as something appeared on the horizon that caught his attention. Holding the piece of pie in one hand, he shielded his eyes with the other hand to block out the sun. Whatever it was, it was heading straight for Percival. Instinct told Percival to seek cover. A group of large rocks sat close to where Percival was resting. He made his way over to the rocks and climbed in between them. As Percival sat and waited, a thunderous noise approached, the ground began to tremble, as the rocks swayed ominously. If they toppled inward, Percival could easily be crushed.

As blinding dust filled the air, Percival realised it was a stampede, but what had caused the animals to stampede in the first place. Holding his handkerchief over his mouth, as he tried not to breath in any dust, he waited with eyes closed tightly, waiting for the dust to settle. All he could do was listen; the thunderous noise caused by many animals seemed to go on forever blocking out all other sound. The ground continued to tremble as the stampeding animals passed by. Then suddenly, it stopped. The ground was no longer shaking as the pounding of many hooves had ceased. The deafening sound had abated, to be replaced by voices. As Percival sat safely between the rocks able to breathe properly once more, he suddenly thought, voices, people. Percival clambered out of his hiding place amongst the rocks only to be confronted by not people but centaurs.

Aegeus spotted Percival as soon as he had arisen from his hiding place between the rocks. "What are you doing there?" called Aegeus.

"Hiding safely from the stampede," said Percival. Aegeus galloped across to where Percival had appeared and came to a halt.

"I know you," said Aegeus, "you were with that human king."

"You mean King Richard," said Percival, "yes, I was."

"But I thought you fell in the river," said Aegeus.

"I did," said Percival.

"So how did you survive?" asked Aegeus.

"With a great deal of luck," answered Percival.

Changing the subject, Percival asked, "What's going on here?"

"It's the annual stampede," said Aegeus, "every year before breeding season begins, we stampede the buffalo, any that cannot keep up, such as the old, weak or injured will be culled to be eaten. This way, only the strong and healthy go on to breed which keeps the herd healthy."

While Aegeus and Percival had been talking, another ten or so centaurs had rounded up all the buffalos that failed to remain with the herd. "We have them all, Aegeus," called another of the centaurs.

"You had better come with us," said Aegeus.

"That was my intention," said Percival.

Aegeus then surprised Percival as he knelt. "Climb aboard," he said.

"I didn't think centaurs liked to be ridden," said Percival.

"We don't," said Aegeus, "but this is my choice."

"Thank you," said Percival.

"How else were you going to keep up?" asked Aegeus, with a smile, as he cantered along. Percival was extremely grateful for the ride. Even though they were not travelling at full speed, because of the old, injured and weak buffalo, he still would have struggled to keep up, if on foot.

As the rainbow forest came into view, Percival wondered what sort of reception his reappearance would receive. It was as if Aegeus had read his thoughts because the next thing he said was "Cressida will be pleasantly surprised to see you again."

Percival was in no doubt she would be surprised to see him again, considering she and her brother Dante had stood and watched him being carried away down river without making any effort to rescue him, but Percival doubted very much, it would be a pleasant surprise.

As the crystal palace came into view, Percival realised they were approaching from the rear. No rainbow coloured archway leading down a long straight path, nothing but holding pens for the buffalo lay before them, and the smell was over powering. Aegeus left the other centaurs to put the buffalo into the pens. He and Percival quickly moved on past, leaving the smell behind them. As they approached the crystal palace, they came upon the most fragrant flower garden Percival had ever come across. The reason for this was obvious, not only was it beautiful to look at but it also blocked the stench of the buffalo.

Aegeus came to a halt next to a large rose bush with multi-coloured roses. "Wait here," he said to Percival, as he dismounted. Percival was happy to wait in the garden. He paced around admiring the beautiful flowers and the highly fragrant scent they provided.

Aegeus had entered the crystal palace via double doors that led into the garden. His hooved feet tapped away on the glass floor as he made his entrance. As the sound carried throughout the crystal palace, it announced his arrival.

Cressida was sat waiting on her throne for Aegeus. When he entered, he bowed. "Your Majesty," he said.

"How many?" she asked.

"A good cull this year," said Aegeus, "ninety-seven."

"That is good," said Cressida. "Well done, Aegeus."

"Thank you, Your Majesty." He paused.

"Is there something else?" asked Cressida.

"There is something else we found I believe you will be interested in," said Aegeus.

"Well, where is it then?" asked Cressida.

"He is waiting for you in the garden, Your Majesty," said Aegeus.

Cressida stood up from her throne, opened her rainbow-coloured wings and glided down to the floor effortlessly. Once landed, she drew her wings in close to her body. "Lead the way," she commanded. As she was about to enter the garden, Dante her brother appeared. "Join me," said Cressida, "Aegeus says he has found someone of interest." They both followed Aegeus into the garden, and stopped abruptly. The look of surprise on their faces made Percival smile. He bowed.

"Your Majesty," he said.

Trying to conceal his shock, Dante replied, "Why, Percival, what a pleasant surprise."

"I thought we had lost you forever," said Cressida.

"Yes, I was rather fortunate to survive," said Percival. "Now I am back, I was hoping you could help me with something."

"Ask me anything," said Dante.

"I was hoping you could tell me about the giant white eagle that snatched Prince Nicholas from King Richard's shoulders."

"Ah yes, the giant white eagle," said Dante, "most unfortunate, but I'm afraid I cannot help you, for I have never seen the giant bird before." Percival turned to look at Cressida.

"No, sorry, Percival, but like my brother, I have never laid eyes on such a bird."

"Oh well," said Percival, "I knew it would be unlikely that you would know anything, but I had to ask just in case."

"So, what will you do now, go home?" asked Cressida.

"Oh no," said Percival, "I will continue my search for the giant white eagle and Prince Nicholas."

"Where will you look?" asked Cressida.

"Well, I remember when I fell into the river and saw the two of you standing there, that the white eagle disappeared in the distance to the left of where you were standing. As that is all I have to go on, that's the direction I will be heading," said Percival.

Cressida glanced over to Dante. They both realised that Percival knew they had stood and did nothing to help him as he had been carried away by the river. *But so what*, thought Cressida, *what could he do about it.*

"When will you leave?" asked Cressida.

"Oh, I think I'm ready to go right now," said Percival, "no time like the present."

"But how will you travel," asked Dante, with mocking concern, "surely not on foot."

"I always seem to find a way," answered Percival.

"You must have something to eat before you leave," suggested Cressida.

"Thank you," said Percival, "but I've already eaten quite enough for one day."

"Can we offer you any assistance?" asked Dante, still mocking Percival.

"No, no," said Percival, "well if you will excuse me, I will be on my way." He bowed first to Cressida and then to Dante, then he turned and left the garden through the same gate he had entered. Percival had wanted to see their reaction to his reappearance, but he had no intention of telling them about the one-eyed hag that he sought, or the cobra-headed snakebird. Cressida moved closer to Dante as they both stood watching Percival leave.

"What do you make of that?" asked Cressida.

"I don't know," said Dante, "but I think we should keep an eye on him, don't you agree?"

"Who do we know that can keep an eye on him without being seen?" Then after a moment's pause, looking at each other, they both said Samuel. Samuel the tree goblin who could disappear when sitting in a rainbow-coloured tree because he was also multi-coloured was summoned. They explained what they wanted him to do and he was sent on his way.

Chapter 14
Dorothy's Dress

Having left dead man's lake, Oliver was glad they had managed to avoid the old woman who lived there. The old woman who lived besides the lake and claimed she drained it every year so she could rob from the dead, who had perished in the frozen lake in winter. Dorothy would have appreciated a bit more time to rest but the last thing she wanted was to prove Oliver was right, that this adventure was no place for a girl.

Berwyn had led them across open countryside for a couple of weeks without any incidence, now looming before them was a massive hill, littered with boulders of various sizes Berwyn picked a pathway which they all followed. They had climbed about half way up the hill on horseback, but as it got steeper towards the top, they were forced to dismount and lead their horses by their reigns. The climb was not easy for any of them, but it was especially hard for Dorothy, because of her long dress, trying to hold it off the floor to stop herself from tripping and holding onto her horse was proving almost impossible, finally she said, "I can't go on," and collapsed against a large boulder. Reif was the first to respond. He tethered his horse to a small bush and made his way to where Dorothy was resting. When she had collapsed, she had released the reins of her horse which was now carefully making its way back down the mountain.

Reif had rushed to Dorothy's side, as she gasped for breath. Kneeling beside her, he cradled her head in his lap and opened his water container, encouraging Dorothy to take a sip. Oliver was now by his sister's side. "Is she all right?" he asked Reif. Dorothy was barely conscious and groaned a reply.

"I am fine," she said, not wanting to be a burden, with sweat pouring down her face from her forehead.

"I think the problem is this dress," said Reif.

"What do you mean?" asked Oliver.

"Well look at her," said Reif, "she's burning up."

"So, what can we do?" asked Oliver.

"This," said Reif. He grabbed hold of one of Dorothy's long sleeves and tore it free from the dress.

"What do you think you're doing?" asked Oliver.

"Saving your sister's life," said Reif, he proceeded to rip off the second sleeve, then the neckline, buttoned high under her chin, Reif pulled this apart, buttons flying everywhere, but who cared about buttons when trying to save a life.

Finally, he took hold of the hem of the dress in both hands and ripped it apart. Oliver watched horrified at what Reif had done, the once floor length dress now barely reached Dorothy's knees. "What the hell did you do that for?" shouted Oliver.

"I told you, I did it so save her life," said Reif.

"What, by ripping her clothes off?" said Oliver. Reif could not believe what he was hearing. He felt sure it had been the right thing to do, and here was Oliver accusing him of just ripping Dorothy's clothes off.

In disbelief, hurt and stunned by Oliver's accusation, Reif moved away. Oliver's first instinct was to follow, but instead returned to where Joshua was now comforting Dorothy. "What was all the shouting about?" asked Dorothy, who was barely conscious.

Oliver avoided answering her question and asked, "How are you feeling?"

"I'm feeling better," said Dorothy.

"What happened?" asked Oliver.

"I don't know," said Dorothy, "one minute I was feeling fine and then I became so hot I couldn't breathe."

"How do you feel now?" asked Oliver.

"I feel so much better," said Dorothy, and she went to stand up, but as she did, her head was spinning and she felt faint once more. She quickly sat down again aided by Joshua who was holding her hands.

"Right, that's it," said Oliver, "we will camp here for the night." Reif stayed away from the others and started a small fire for himself. Oliver, Joshua and Dorothy had a larger fire to sit around, but no one ate. As the dark blanket of night spread across the sky, it descended upon them as the stars came out to shine, the moon shone brightly. Berwyn disappeared in search for food; nothing was going to upset his appetite.

A new day dawned on the hillside. Dorothy was the first to awaken and the first thing she felt was a chill on her bare arms. Then as she sat up, she realised her legs were also bare, she had no idea what had happened to her dress, and as she looked around for answers, she could see Oliver and Joshua were still sleeping. *But where is Reif,* she wondered.

The sun was just rising above the top of the hill and as Dorothy stood, she could feel the gentle warmth of the early morning sun on her bare arms, a golden glow of warmth spread, enveloping her body like a warm blanket. As she looked around, she spotted Reif lying alone on the ground about twenty feet away. She couldn't think of why he was lying on his own. Just then he stirred, rolled over facing Dorothy and he was awake. He smiled upon seeing Dorothy standing there, and so she quietly approached, not wanting to wake Oliver or Joshua.

"Why are you over here by yourself?" whispered Dorothy.

"Oliver and I had a falling out last night," said Reif.

"What about?" asked Dorothy.

"You," said Reif. Dorothy didn't understand.

"Me?" she asked.

"Yes, you," said Reif.

"But why?" Dorothy was anxious to know why her brother and his friend had fallen out over her.

"Have you noticed anything about your dress?" asked Reif.

"Yes, of course I have," said Dorothy, "why what happened?" But, before Reif could answer, a thought suddenly entered Dorothy's head, had Reif attacked her, and Oliver had come to her rescue. She backed away from Reif. She was no longer smiling and looked quite fearful. Reif thought something must have appeared over his shoulder. He slowly moved his right hand to grasp the handle of his sword, which was always by his side when he slept, an old trick Robert had taught him. Dorothy saw Reif move his hand towards his sword. She could not believe what was happening. Dorothy's eyes were open wide. She began to sweat on her forehead which ran down the side of her face and neck, and her body began to shake with fear. Without warning, in one single movement, Reif had jumped to his feet and spun around with sword in hand to face the unseen assailant. To his surprise, there was no one there, but Dorothy had screamed. Now it was Reif's turn to be confused. When he turned back to face Dorothy, she screamed once more, almost hysterical.

"It's all right," said Reif, as he took a step towards Dorothy.

"Don't come any closer," she screamed. At this point, Joshua and Oliver arrived.

"What's going on?" asked Oliver.

"I don't know," said Reif.

"He attacked me," said Dorothy, pointing at Reif.

"What?" said Reif in disbelief.

"Give me your sword," said Oliver. Without argument, Reif handed his sword to Joshua as Oliver stood holding his sword against Reif's chest. "What happened?" asked Oliver.

"He attacked me," said Dorothy, "he tore my dress off." Dorothy then grabbed Reif's sword from Joshua as she pushed Joshua to the ground. Reif stood motionless. It had all happened so fast, one minute he had Oliver holding a sword against his chest, and now it was Dorothy's turn to keep Reif at bay with a sword, but this was more terrifying, for where Oliver had been reasonably calm, Dorothy was hysterical. "Why did you lower your sword?" Dorothy screamed at Oliver.

"This is all a big misunderstanding," said Oliver. But Dorothy wasn't listening. She had convinced herself because of the state of her dress, and the fact Reif was sleeping alone, he must have attacked her. Reif tried again to plead his innocence. Dorothy made a wild swing with Reif's sword. He took a step back and the cut across his chest only ripped apart his jacket. Joshua was back on his feet and grabbed Dorothy from behind, holding both her arms close to her body she was no longer able to wield the sword. She was screaming at Joshua to let her go.

"You idiot, what are you doing?"

Oliver placed his hand on Dorothy's and calmly said, "It's all right." As Dorothy looked into Oliver's eyes, she loosened her grip on the hilt of the sword and allowed Oliver to remove it from her grasp.

In floods of tears, Dorothy collapsed to the ground. Reif made a move forward to console Dorothy, but she screamed at him again to leave her alone. Oliver placed a hand on Reif's shoulder. "Let me," he said, as he handed Reif his sword.

Oliver sat on the ground beside Dorothy as Joshua and Reif walked away. Oliver explained to Dorothy what had happened to her dress, and how he had overreacted, which was why Reif had slept apart from the group. "The fact is," said Oliver, "Reif saved your life yesterday." Knowing this only made Dorothy feel worse for the way she had behaved.

"I must apologise," she said. She stood up to look for Reif, Oliver stood also.

"I need to do this on my own," said Dorothy.

Reif and Joshua were standing a short distance away looking out over the mountains that lay ahead. As Dorothy approached, Joshua and Reif turned around. "May I speak with you alone?" she asked Reif. Joshua walked away and left the two of them to talk. "I am so sorry," said Dorothy. "I don't know what came over me, can you ever forgive me?" she asked. Reif smiled.

"You know you could have killed me with that sword," he said.

"Please don't make fun of me?" she asked.

Trying not to smile, Reif said, "I don't blame you for the way you reacted."

"But I know now that what you did saved my life," said Dorothy.

"It's a life worth saving," said Reif. Dorothy blushed as Reif raised a hand to brush the hair away from her face.

"You know I care for you deeply, I could never do anything to hurt you." Dorothy moved closer and lay her head against Reif's chest. He embraced her in his strong arms and she felt safer than ever before.

Berwyn, who had been nowhere in sight when they awoke made his return, he walked over and gave Oliver a gentle nudge, which nearly sent Oliver flying down the hillside. As he stumbled, Berwyn stopped. As Oliver regained his balance, Berwyn began to walk off. Oliver did not follow straight away. Berwyn looked back, all four were now watching as Berwyn raised up onto his back legs and roared. Then he fell back onto all fours and carried on walking away. "I guess it's time to go," said Oliver. Quickly, they gathered their belongings, with only three horses remaining after Dorothy's had escaped when she had fainted, they led them up the hillside. Berwyn had reached the top of the hill and stopped, he looked back again. As Oliver, Reif, Dorothy and Joshua joined him at the top of the hillside, the spectacular view took their breath away.

A large lake as blue as the sky above sat nestled between snow peaked mountains, the reflection of the mountains so clear on the lakes surface made it look like a mirror.

Chapter 15
Nicholas' Choice of Brooch

At Elvira's winter palace, the day had arrived for the next ball. Nicholas had chosen the brooch and even Eleanor, Elvira's daughter, had no idea what brooch he had chosen. She had asked her mother once about what brooch Nicholas had chosen. Elvira, still unhappy with Eleanor over allowing Nicholas to go to the village alone, gave no answer, but the look she had given her daughter had served as a warning not to ask again.

The blizzard conditions from earlier in the week had finally ceased, but the deep snow on the ground made the use of carriages impossible. "Will the guests be able to get here?" asked Nicholas, as he stood looking out of the window at the deep blanket of snow that covered the ground.

"Do not worry about the guests," said Elvira, "they will be here." And sure enough as the afternoon wore on, the guests started to arrive.

Whereas before the carriages arrived one after the other in quick succession, arriving on foot however made the whole process a lot slower. The tall man with long, white hair and wearing his blood-red outfit was on hand to greet the guests as they arrived as usual. Each male and female guest arrived wearing a fur coat to protect them from the cold winter air as they made their way on foot. They stomped their feet to remove the snow from their shoes before entering the castle. As each guest removed their coat and handed them to the tall, thin man, he placed them onto coat hangers. As each coat was hung, he inserted a small gold pin with the name of the owner, so as to make sure everyone got back their own coat.

After arrival, each guest made their way down the blue marble staircase onto the dance floor where they all mingled while they waited. Neither Elvira nor Eleanor was there to greet them, as it was such a long process waiting for all the guests to arrive. Some of the female guests started to complain about how long they had been kept waiting for the ball to start, their male companions urged them to be quiet.

"I am not afraid of Elvira," said one of the female guests, "I am so glad to hear that," said Elvira, who had appeared suddenly and caught everyone off guard.

"You can be the one to face the brooch later on," said Elvira, "Nicholas chose it." She smiled knowingly as she walked away.

The female guest so brazenly outspoken only moments before said nothing, as she watched Elvira walk away, but she turned crimson with embarrassment, as Elvira left the dance floor a wicked grin illuminated her face. She headed up the stairs to join Eleanor and Nicholas who were now seated on their throne. The woman feted to face the brooch later on which had been chosen by Nicholas, needed help to leave the dance floor as the realisation of what she had gotten herself into sank in. All courage and bravado seemed to have left her body and her legs were incapable of supporting her weight. From crimson red, she had turned ghostly white.

As the music started to play, as always Elvira danced with Nicholas first, and then Eleanor. When Eleanor returned to her throne beside her mother, she led Nicholas by the hand. The female guests on the dance floor eagerly awaited their chance to dance with Nicholas.

Elvira spoke softly to Nicholas, before allowing him to take to the dance floor once more. "They will all ask about the brooch you have chosen, but no one can know, is that understood?" she said.

"Yes, Your Majesty," said Nicholas.

"Now go and have some fun," she said, as she sat back on her throne to watch.

Indeed every single partner that Nicholas danced with asked the same question, some were more forth coming than others and asked outright, which brooch have you chosen. Nicholas just smiled and shook his head without saying a word. Some played it more casual, talking about how bad the blizzard of a couple of days ago had been, and how joyous the music made them feel, before slipping in, so what brooch have you chosen for tonight. But either way, Nicholas' response had been the same, to just smile and shake his head. As each woman failed in their attempt to find out about the brooch, they returned to their friends disappointed. Elvira was laughing with Eleanor at their failed attempts to discover the identity of the brooch.

Elvira decided the time had come for the identity of the brooch to be revealed. She raised a hand and the music ceased. All couples quickly left the dance floor, some looked extremely nervous, whilst others seemed excited. There was an electric atmosphere that seemed to buzz around the room. Nicholas had left the dance floor and joined Eleanor, while Elvira made her way down to the dance floor, people were whispering as she passed them by. "Do you think she will make Emily face the brooch?" asked one female guest of another.

"Probably, after all she did say she wasn't scared of Elvira," said the second female guest.

As expected, once Elvira had made her way to the centre of the dance floor, she called Emily forth. "Come take a look at my brooch," she said. There was a lot of shuffling of feet as the guests moved aside to make way for Emily. Where before she had stood tall and proud and was brazenly outspoken, Emily now seemed a completely different woman. All her confidence and bravado seemed to have disappeared. She now appeared small and timid. She stumbled from the last step onto the dance floor, but no one offered assistance as she regained her balance. She shuffled across the dance floor towards Elvira, looking at the floor, not daring to look Elvira in the eye. "Ladies and gentlemen," said Elvira, "please put your hands together and give a warm welcome to our willing volunteer, Emily." Whispers spread around the room as everyone looked on.

"You can do it, Emily," shouted an unknown male voice, Emily raised her head, as she took the final steps and approached Elvira. She smiled weakly, but the fear was there in her eyes. Elvira's smile and eyes were full of menace. She was enjoying every second of Emily's discomfort.

"Ready," said Elvira, as Emily came to a halt in front of her, but Elvira didn't wait for a reply. She bent down and placed a tiny black and white brooch on the floor. Emily gave a small squeak, and began to ring her hands. Elvira stepped away slowly. Emily looked at Elvira hoping for forgiveness as tears began to form in her eyes. Elvira watched gleefully. Emily shaking with fear watched as Elvira turned away and finally left Emily standing alone in the middle of the dance floor. Everyone's attention was now focussed on Emily and the brooch.

As Emily stood trembling, in the centre of the dance floor she had never felt more alone, totally exposed and helpless. Emily stood shaking with uncontrollable fear, waiting for something to happen. It seemed like time itself had frozen. For ages, she had waited, and nothing had happened to the brooch. She was staring at it completely transfixed, but because of its diminutive size, she could not make out what it was. A call went up from amongst the guests. "What's happening?" asked a male voice.

"Nothing at the moment," answered another.

Then a female guest asked, "What is it, it's so tiny I can't make out what it is?"

Murmurs and whispers travelled around the room as they waited in expectation. "What do you think a young boy would have chosen?" asked one male voice.

"I bet he's gone for a dragon," answered another.

"What about the flying horse?" suggested a high-pitched, female voice. Just then, it started to glow and Emily screamed. She put her hands to her face, wanting to cover her tear-stained eyes, scared of what was about to appear, and yet she found herself wanting to see what was happening, all at the same time. As with all the other brooches before, the glow pulsed as the brooch grew. Fearful of what was about to happen, Emily finally turned away, unable to watch any longer. There was the flash of bright light. Emily said to herself, it must have finished growing, and so she waited, too scared to face her fate, she dropped to the floor on her knees, her body shook as she cried great howling sobs, then she flinched as something touched her foot and she screamed her loudest scream.

Everyone present was laughing at Emily and the scene on the dance floor as it unfolded. Each time the creature touched Emily, she jumped a couple of inches into the air emitting a piercing scream, and each time the audience laughed harder. Emily was totally unaware of what was going on as she was so terrified. Fear had a hold of her body and tightened its grip. Elvira hadn't laughed so much in years. She had a stitch in her side where she had laughed so much, it ached.

The spectacle of Emily and her unseen tormentor had lasted for fifteen minutes, and proved to be highly entertaining for everyone present, everyone except Emily that is. Finally, Elvira descended from her throne to the dance floor, wearing white as always she glided across the floor to Emily and without saying a word, she touched Emily on the shoulder. Emily jumped higher into the air and screamed louder still. The raucous laughter that flooded the room suddenly penetrated through Emily's fear. She dared to raise her head and open her eyes. To her horror, all she could see were her friends and fellow guests in rapturous laughter. So hard were they laughing, they were in tears. Disgusted by their actions, Emily completely forgot her fears. She found her inner strength and stood. "How dare you laugh at me?" she said. "With my life in mortal danger."

But if she had hoped to quell the laughter, she was in for a shock, for the laughter continued unabated. Emily stamped her feet on the marble floor and demanded quiet, but the more she tried to quieten the guests, the louder they laughed, some of the guests were unable to stand, having laughed so hard for so long, and had collapsed in a heap on the floor.

As Emily spun around on the dance floor, she finally realised she was not alone. Elvira, having at last stopped laughing herself called, "Quiet." Slowly, the laughter died.

"Would you care to see what the brooch became?" asked Elvira sweetly. Emily who had briefly regained her courage suddenly seemed very small once more.

"Nicholas, come here, bring your friend," said Elvira. Nicholas was sat at the edge of the dance floor, but Emily couldn't see anything else. Nicholas got to his feet and approached Emily. Her eyes showing fear once more as Nicholas got closer, and her body started to shake uncontrollably but still she couldn't see anything. She looked beyond Nicholas searching for some large beast, but could see nothing. *Was it lurking way back in the shadows,* she wondered. Elvira called for quiet and the room fell deadly silent. All Emily could hear was her heart pounding crazily fast as her blood coursed through her veins. The room held its breath.

"Would you like to hold my kitten?" asked Nicholas.

The whole room burst into uncontrolled laughter once more, as Nicholas stood before Emily holding out in cupped hands a tiny black and white kitten. Emily burst into tears, took the kitten from Nicholas and kissed its head, held it aloft and turned full circle to show everyone in the room.

Emily herself began to laugh as tears of joy streamed down her face, having been so terrified the overwhelming emotions caused Emily to faint. It happened in slow motion as everyone watched, like a snowman slowly dying in the warm sun. Emily's legs seemed to melt away as she collapsed onto the floor. Nicholas retrieved the kitten, and Elvira took hold of Nicholas by the hand as she led him from the dance floor. The tall, thin man with long, white hair and wearing the blood-red outfit picked Emily's limp body off the floor and carried her away.

Seated back on her throne, Elvira watched as the music started up once more. At first, her guests seemed reluctant to return to the dance floor. She then turned to Eleanor. "So what surprise did you get for me?" Eleanor had completely forgotten the lie she had told her mother. She had to quickly think of something.

"Sorry mother," she said, "I wasn't able to get what I wanted."

"Never mind," said Elvira. The ball continued for another hour. Eventually, Elvira grew tired. She stood up from her throne and all eyes were on her wondering in anticipation what was going to happen next. Elvira simply announced, "Party's over."

Chapter 16
The Mountain Search

Having stopped briefly at the sky-blue lake to wash and refill their water containers, with Berwyn leading the way, they had finally reached the mountains. "I'm sure this is the one," said Joshua, as they stood at the bottom of a mountain and looked up. The top of the mountain was totally obscured by the heavy mist that sat like a halo, but Berwyn having stopped briefly moved on. "Hey, where is he going?" shouted Joshua. They had all been staring at the daunting climb that lay ahead, but now they were watching as Berwyn moved away. "Hey, come back," called Joshua.

"Are you sure this is the right mountain?" asked Oliver.

"I'm sure it is," said Joshua, but doubt had crept into his mind the further Berwyn moved away. "All right," he said, "I can't be sure."

The frustration was evident on all their faces, but no one commented apart from Oliver. "Let's follow Berwyn," he said.

The terrain became more rugged and perilous. As the winds raced down the side of the mountain, boulders were loosened by the gale force winds, which sent them tumbling down the mountain. As they crashed into ever larger boulders on the way down, an avalanche was born. The roar of the wind and the falling boulders created a deafening sound, as the boulders, some as large as a horse crashed into the ground and shattered. The terrifying scene had happened a hundred feet or so in front of them, but the sound had totally enveloped them as the ground beneath their feet had shook, dust and debris filled the air. Dorothy had clung to Reif for reassurance, two more of the horses had broken free, Berwyn stood motionless.

Slowly, everything settled down once more, and as the dust cleared, Oliver asked, "Is everyone all right?"

Reif, who still had Dorothy clinging around his neck, said, "We're fine."

"But where's Joshua?" asked Oliver. Oliver began to search for Joshua. Although the larger boulders had fallen quite a distance ahead of where they were standing, the dust and debris that had been kicked into the air had swamped over them. Reif, Dorothy and Oliver had a light covering of dust on their clothes which was easily brushed away. As Reif and Dorothy joined Oliver in his search for Joshua, Dorothy stopped.

"Did you hear that?" she asked.

"Hear what?" asked Oliver.

"I thought I heard Joshua groaning," said Dorothy.

Berwyn had been leading the way and his white fur was now grey covered in thick dust. Joshua had been standing closer to the impact alongside Berwyn. They all listened without moving. It was Berwyn who eventually discovered Joshua. Buried under a pile of dust, Joshua was lying on the ground. Berwyn gave Joshua a nudge with his powerful head, and rolled him onto his back. Covered in grey dust from head to toe, he looked as though he was made of stone. He coughed as he got to his feet which dislodged a heap of dust from the top of his head. Oliver, Reif and Dorothy could not help themselves and all burst out laughing. "Oh, very funny," said Joshua, as he tried to brush himself down.

"Come here," said Dorothy, "let me help." As he walked towards her, she couldn't help but laugh again. "I'm sorry," said Dorothy, "if only you could see yourself."

She mimicked the way Joshua was moving and explained how even the slightest movement dislodged more dust. In the end, Joshua was laughing as much as the others. "Stand back," said Joshua. He placed both hands on his hair, closed his eyes and mouth and vigorously moved his hands back and forth. He looked like a dust monster as his head and body was engulfed in dust once more. They cheered and clapped and laughed again, and when the dust settled, they all approached Joshua.

"Keep your eyes closed," said Dorothy, a heavy layer of dust had settled on Joshua's eyelashes. She blew hard and removed the dust from his lashes.

"That's better," she said.

"Thanks," said Joshua.

"We need to find some water," said Oliver, "you need to bathe."

Oliver decided to set free the last remaining horse, as the terrain ahead was clearly more treacherous. Berwyn leading the way took them to a mountain stream, where he plunged straight in. "There you go," said Oliver to Joshua, "jump in." Without stopping to think, Joshua leapt straight in.

"Oh my God, oh my God," screamed Joshua, as he scrambled out of the water dust free, "that is freezing," he said.

"Well, what did you expect," said Reif, "it's come down from the top of the mountain; you need to get out of those wet clothes." Joshua struggled to undo the buttons of his shirt, as his fingers had turned numb with the cold. When he finally removed all his wet clothes, "Here, take these blankets," said Reif. So while Joshua wrapped himself in the blankets, Reif had passed him. The others searched for anything to burn. There was no wood from trees they could use to start a fire, but there were plenty of small shrubs with woody stems. Oliver, Reif and Dorothy gathered great armfuls of twigs and moved into a more sheltered position. Berwyn meanwhile had reappeared from the stream as white as ever, shook his body vigorously to remove as much water as possible and then wandered off. Oliver and Dorothy started a fire whilst Reif continued to gather more woody shrubs to keep the fire going all night. As the fire grew stronger, Joshua sat as close as possible to get warm, wrapped in just the blankets Reif had given him, his clothes had been placed in a position by the fire to dry out. As the fire burned bright, day slowly turned to night, and the temperature plummeted, all four huddled together around the fire. Dorothy with bare arms and legs was feeling cold. She cuddled up against Reif. He felt cosy and warm. Oliver realised they were all feeling the cold and called Berwyn over. Berwyn had returned just before dark and his coat had dried in the afternoon sun. He lay on the ground behind them and as they leant back, they could feel the warmth of his body through his fur coat, as one by one, they drifted off to sleep.

Joshua was the first to wake. The embers of the fire glowed faintly. It was still night time for the moon was high in the cloudless sky. He reached for his clothes. They were dry. Without disturbing any of the others, Joshua got dressed. As he pulled on his boots, something had moved in the shadowy distance. He was sure of it, then as Joshua peered out into the dark, there again something had moved amongst the shadows. It was time to wake the others.

He moved around the fire and gave Oliver a shake to wake him up. Deep in sleep, Oliver gave a little moan at being disturbed and adjusted his position. Joshua shook Oliver more vigorously. Oliver reluctantly opened his eyes. In the dim light, all Oliver could see was a shadowy figure looming over him. Still half asleep, he had been dreaming of his nice, warm bed, tucked in, all cosy and warm. Suddenly, the dream was shattered. "Intruders," shouted Joshua, in an instant Oliver and Reif were awake and by Joshua's side, both with sword in hand. Dorothy stayed sat on the ground, Berwyn slept on.

"What did you see?" asked Oliver.

"Something moved over there," said Joshua, pointing out in the blackness of night.

"What did it look like?" asked Reif.

"I don't know," said Joshua, "I couldn't make it out." All three stood motionless and alert, scanning the dark shadows for any further sign of movement. Joshua's nerves were getting the better of him. He was convinced something was lurking in the shadows. Oliver and Reif had seen nothing.

"We can't go searching in the dark," said Oliver, as he placed more twigs onto the fire.

"The safest place for us is here by the fire," said Reif, "we can search in the morning, when it's daylight."

Both Oliver and Reif sat down once more, keeping hold of their swords, not totally convinced it was safe, but trying to put on a brave front for Dorothy, who moved closer to Reif.

Joshua remained standing alone. Doubt was now flooding his mind. He could have sworn he had seen movement in the shadows, but maybe it was his imagination after all. He turned his back on the shadowy dark night and went to resume his position by the fire.

"It's not wise to turn your back on the dark," said an unseen voice. A cold, spine-tingling chill ran down Joshua's back. Oliver and Reif had both heard the strangely familiar voice.

"Who's there?" shouted Oliver. "Reveal yourself, step into the light." Oliver, Reif and Joshua who had spun around stood side by side, each holding their sword ready to repel an attack.

"No need for swords," said Robert, as he stepped out of the shadows into the fire light, followed by his fellow guards. Oliver raced forwards and embraced Robert.

"It's so good to see you," said Oliver. "How did you find us?" he asked.

"It's not hard to follow footprints made by a giant bear." Laughed Robert.

"So, you've come to join us in our search for Nicholas," said Oliver, "what changed your mind?" Before Robert answered however, Dorothy spoke.

"He hasn't come to help look for Nicholas, he's come to take us back," she said.

The smile on Oliver's face disappeared instantly to be replaced by a determined frown. "Is that true?" asked Oliver. "If you think I'm going back after coming this far, you are mistaken," said Oliver.

"What makes you think you have a choice?" said Robert. Only now did Oliver realise, in his haste to greet Robert and the other guards, he had dropped his sword onto the ground, as had Reif, which had been retrieved by one of the guards. Joshua was the only one left holding his sword, but what could he do. When Robert asked him to lay down his sword, he did so without question.

Berwyn had still not stirred from his slumber as Robert and the palace guards sat on the opposite side of the fire to Oliver, Dorothy, Reif and Joshua. With nobody speaking, they all sat in an uncomfortable silence, as they waited for daylight.

Chapter 17
Percival Seeks the One-Eyed Hag

As Percival headed away from the crystal palace out into the rainbow forest, he was pursued by Samuel, the tree goblin, who was perfectly camouflaged against the rainbow-coloured trees. Percival knew he was being followed not because he could see Samuel, but he felt his presence, as his mother Saki had said, he was remembering things he had long forgotten, and the ability to sense the presence of others when unseen, seemed to be one of those things. As day turned to night, the three suns merged to form the purple moon. Percival had found himself a safe place to sleep overnight, a small cave with no rear entrance. He made a fire both for warmth and protection against any night time visitors. Samuel made himself comfortable in a tree that sat just outside the entrance to Percival's cave.

As Percival dozed off to sleep, he was unaware of an unseen danger that lurked in the shadows above him. From the cavernous ceiling, multiple eyes no bigger than a pinhead reflected the glow from the fire. Each tiny spider began to descend on its own silvery thread towards the unsuspecting Percival. Like snowflakes gently falling from the sky, the tiny spiders on their silk threads gently swayed as a breeze from outside entered the cave. Percival stirred as the cool breeze swept across the fire causing the flames to dance wildly. Bleary eyed, Percival looked at the ceiling. Had he seen something. He wasn't sure. Rubbing his eyes to wake himself, he looked again at the ceiling, and spotted the hundreds of eyes twinkling as they abseiled from out of the shadows. Realising what they were, Percival picked up a piece of burning wood and held it aloft. The tiny spiders, feeling the heat from the flames quickly ascended once more, back to safety on the cave ceiling. Percival moved closer to the fire knowing the heat would keep the spiders at bay, but he struggled to sleep for the rest of the night. His mind was troubled, full of thoughts of what lay ahead. Finally when it was daylight, he left the cave. Outside, just one set of tiny footprints, showed that one small animal had passed by during the night, nothing more. Sitting in the tree outside the cave, Samuel waited for Percival to leave. Percival sensed Samuel's presence. He was tempted to say good morning, but in the end decided against it. He would let Samuel think he was being followed unnoticed.

The yellow, pink and blue suns sat in an early morning sky of the palest blue, completely cloud free, birds were singing their morning song, and rabbits with tiny antlers scurried about on the ground amongst the trees. As Percival followed a small stream winding its way through the rainbow forest, Samuel followed. Splashing and sounds of joyous laughter spread throughout the forest and reached out to Percival. He went to investigate. The King Fawn Langton and his sons Darius and Ferdinand were frolicking in the stream. As Percival approached, he was spotted by Langton. "Good morning," he called to Percival, "I thought you and King Richard had left this kingdom."

"We were leaving," said Percival, "but I fell into the river and got swept away." Langton laughed with his deep booming voice.

"So what are you doing now?" he asked, as he stepped out of the stream and approached.

Percival explained the rest of what had happened. "As the barrier between our two kingdoms closed, a giant white eagle snatched Prince Nicholas from the shoulders of King Richard." Langton was no longer laughing.

"So, where is King Richard now?" asked Langton.

"King Richard made it across the river, just before the boundary closed, but it won't open for another ten years, he is stuck on the other side."

"But you found a way in before," said Langton, "surely King Richard can find a way in."

"I fear without my help, all is lost for King Richard." Langton looked across at his two sons as the news of what had happened to King Richard sank in. He knew what it was like to be separated from ones children, having only recently been reunited with his own sons. Percival interrupted Langton's thoughts by asking, "Do you know where I can find a cobra-headed snakebird?"

"We do," said Darius and Ferdinand excitedly, as they joined their father and Percival, wanting to help. Langton smiled at his two sons.

"Yes, I know where you can find such a bird, you will need to cross the border into the land of the ogres, but why do you need to find one?" he asked.

Samuel the tree goblin sat in the rainbow-coloured tree, beneath which Percival and Langton were talking. To hear them better, Samuel had wrapped his oversized feet around the branch and hung upside down, still hidden amongst the rainbow-coloured leaves. Percival, knowing full well that Samuel was listening to every word, said, "I understand they make an excellent stew." Langton laughed with his deep booming voice.

"You want to go to all the trouble of finding a cobra-headed snakebird, to make a stew." As he continued to laugh, Darius and Ferdinand joined in the laughter with their father. Samuel raised himself back onto his branch frustrated and annoyed. *What a complete waste of my time,* he thought. He sat pondering for a while. Was it really worth shadowing Percival's every move if he was only looking to make a stew? He decided he had had enough. He would go back and report to Cressida what he had found out, and that would be the end of it, and so Samuel set off for Cressida's crystal palace. Percival felt Samuel's presence fade away. Once he was convinced he had gone, he asked Langton a second time. "Do you know where I might find a cobra-headed snakebird?"

"You're serious," asked Langton.

"I am," said Percival. Realising this was no joke, Langton walked from beneath the rainbow-coloured tree and pointed to the west.

"You do realise when you leave the rainbow forest, you cross the border into what is the land of ogres," said Langton.

"I do," said Percival.

"Why are you really seeking the cobra-headed snakebird?" asked Langton.

"I believe it can lead me to the lair of the one-eyed hag," said Percival. Just the mention of the name made Langton and his son's recoil.

"You're not serious about finding the one-eyed hag?" asked Langton anxiously.

"I am," said Percival, "I believe she can help me find Prince Nicholas." Langton looked at Percival with a puzzled expression.

"Very well," said Langton, "I can escort you to the edge of the rainbow forest, but after that, I'm afraid you are on your own."

"I understand," said Percival.

Samuel had returned to the crystal palace. As he approached the glass doors, he was completely exposed, for he had to leave the rainbow-coloured trees behind and approach on the green grass, with his oversized feet that were excellent for climbing trees, on the ground moving around he was cumbersome. As the glass doors opened, Samuel was greeted by two centaur guards. "Follow us," one of the guards said.

Their hooves tapped away on the glass floor which echoed throughout the palace, as they led Samuel to meet Cressida. Up a wide staircase, they went. Samuel remained at the bottom watching as they ascended all the way to the top. When they reached the top of the stairs, they turned around expecting Samuel to be right behind them.

"Where is he?" said one guard to the other.

"I'm down here," called a faint voice.

"What are you waiting for?" shouted one of the centaurs. Samuel smiled, and gave a little laugh.

"There is no way I can make it up those stairs," he said, pointing at his oversized feet.

In a bad temper, one of the centaurs said, "Why didn't you say something, instead of letting us get all the way to the top?" He started down the stairs once more.

"Stop," called a new voice. Dante appeared behind Samuel. "No need to come all the way down, I will bring him to my sister, you may announce our arrival."

Although not much bigger than a child himself, Dante picked up Samuel and opened his transparent wings, then soared effortlessly to the top of the stairs. Although Samuel lived in the trees and had no fear of heights, the sensation of flying was new to him, one that he didn't enjoy. Once on the floor again, Samuel felt safer. Even if it was difficult for him to walk, Dante now led the way. Samuel had been inside the crystal palace before, but never upstairs. The crystal sculptures that lined the hallway depicted scenes of beauty and violence. Fairy mothers with their children flying overhead was the first to cause Samuel to stop. The detail was incredible. He would not have been at all surprised if they had come to life. Dante beckoned Samuel to follow. Then just a few paces further along the hallway, a battle scene, with fairies standing victorious on the bodies of slain ogres, a shudder slid down Samuels spine, Dante called, "This way."

Crystal chandeliers hung from the ceiling. The only light they provided was reflected from the three suns, yellow, pink and blue. Dante led Samuel into a large room where they found Cressida waiting. She was sat behind a large oak table, seated on a high backed oak chair. This was the only piece of furniture made of wood Samuel had ever seen in the crystal palace, and yet somehow it didn't feel out of place. With its ornately carved legs and side panels, it was an impressive piece of furniture, sprawled across the table in front of Cressida was a large map showing all of the kingdom. "Ah, Samuel," she said greeting him like a long lost friend, "how did you get on, what news do you have for me?"

"Your Majesty," said Samuel, he told of how Percival met Langton and asked if he knew where to find a cobra-headed snakebird.

"Now, why would he wish to find a cobra-headed snakebird," said Cressida.

"He said he wanted to make a stew," said Samuel. Cressida laughed.

"And you believed him, how stupid are you?" she said. She was pacing around the table looking down onto the map. "What are you up to?" she said to herself. "You need to go back and follow him some more," said Cressida.

"I'm afraid I must decline, Your Majesty," said Samuel. Cressida spread her wings and rose high above the table menacingly.

"You dare to defy me, goblin," she said.

With a hint of fear in his voice, Samuel answered, "Your Majesty, I will be of no further use to you once they leave the rainbow forest and enter into the land of the ogres."

Although angry, Cressida realised what Samuel was saying was true. Without rainbow-coloured trees, he could no longer follow invisibly. "We will have to find another way of keeping an eye on Percival," she said.

"My dear sister," said Dante, "the answer is staring you right in the face. I can turn invisible and follow him anywhere he goes."

Cressida smiled. "Yes, of course, I keep forgetting you can turn invisible." Turning to face Samuel. "Be gone, goblin," said Cressida. In the blink of an eye, Samuel found himself transported back to his beloved rainbow forest, happy to be of no further use.

Turning to Dante, Cressida said, "I want you to find out exactly what Percival is up to."

"Of course, dear sister," replied Dante, "I shall leave immediately." As he turned and walked out of the room, he faded into invisibility. She smiled as her brother went on his way, trusting that he would not fail.

Langton had taken Percival as far as he dare. "Are you sure you want to do this?" he asked.

Percival simply answered, "It is my destiny." They said farewell and Langton and his sons Darius and Ferdinand watched as Percival crossed into the land of the ogres until he disappeared.

As the three suns began to merge and night time approached, Percival found himself once more searching for a safe place to rest overnight. He found a hole in the ground. Looking at the entrance, there was no sign of footprints leading into the hole. He took this as a sign that no animals were present. He reached into one of his many pockets and found a glass orb that his mother Saki had given him. Inside it contained a candle which burst into flame at the touch of bare skin on glass. He entered the tunnel. On all fours, Percival crawled into the tunnel, with the orb held in his right hand. He slowly made his way deeper underground towards the end of the tunnel. He stopped suddenly, something ahead was moving, moving slowly in his direction. Percival could not see what was ahead but could feel its presence. He started to retreat out of the tunnel as fast as he could, followed all the while by the unknown inhabitant, it was much harder moving backwards through such a small space but keeping the flaming candle contained within the orb held in front of his face the tunnel was brightly illuminated. The predator that followed was out of sight way back in the shadows. Finally, Percival had managed it. He felt the cool night air on his legs as he backed out of the tunnel into the night. Then he quickly stood upright and stepped to one side. Placing the orb back into a pocket, the candle expired. Under the moonlight, he moved away from the entrance and climbed into a nearby tree to watch. Before he saw what had followed him down the tunnel, he heard a sound that sent a shiver down his spine. The unmistakable sound of a large bodied snake slithering across the dirt earthen ground. The first sight Percival saw was that of a large forked tongue, flicking, testing the air, then the head, with large, opaque eyes. Percival knew this meant the snake was blind and therefore he could not be seen. Percival watched from the safety of the tree as the snake slithered past on its way for its nightly hunt.

So focussed on the snake, Percival was unaware of Dante's presence, who watched on silently. He had found the spot where Samuel had left Percival and Langton. Following the footprints made by three unsuspecting fawns and Percival had been easy. Even after Percival had parted from Langton and crossed into the land of the ogres, the trail had been easy to follow, Percival had made no attempt to conceal his tracks.

The snake slithered on by under the cover of dark. For with no sight, it was too vulnerable to hunt during daylight. Percival watched, as the sinewy body seemed to glide across the ground. Suddenly, it stopped. Something had moved in the shadows. The snake having detected its presence, flicked its tongue testing the air. It recoiled its body and lay in a striking pose. Out of the shadows, strutted a long legged bird, with scaled legs to protect it from snakebites, and large feet with huge talons, perfect for gripping such a large snake's body. The powerful looking body of the bird supported large wings, a thick neck and finally the cobra head. Percival could not believe his luck. This was exactly what he was looking for. He stood motionless watching from the branch of his tree. The large bird took no notice of Percival. It was as if he was not present. All focus was on the large snake which lunged forward. The bird skipped sideways. The snake recoiled its body once more. Hissing an angry warning, the giant bird tilted its head to one side but stayed focussed on the snake. Again and again, the snake struck forwards missing each time. Finally, the snake struck forward and the huge bird attacked, grasping the snake behind its head with one clawed foot. As the snake's body began to writhe on the ground, the bird grasped the snake with its second foot. With talons firmly grasped around the snake's body, the large bird opened its wings. With ease, the bird took to the air. Percival reacted quickly without thinking, and as the bird passed within reach, he grasped hold of the snake's tail. He felt his feet leave the branch behind and he was airborne, flying through the air holding the tail of the large snake, being carried away by the large cobra-headed snakebird. Dante who had been watching whilst invisible took to the air to follow.

All through the night, they flew with the cobra-headed bird carrying the large snake, whilst Percival held tightly to the snake's tail. The added weight of Percival seemed to make no difference to the powerful bird, Dante followed. It was dawn. The suns were parting and a group of mountains lay ahead, below swampland spread far and wide. As they cleared the swamp, lush green plants and trees grew in abundance. They were descending towards the ground. The large bird was heading for an opening in one of the mountains. As they got close to the ground, Percival released his grip on the snake's tail. He landed on his feet but the momentum of his fall caused him to roll over a couple of times before he stopped. He ended up lying on his back, gasping for breath as the fall had knocked the breath out of him. As he recovered, he raised his head and watched as the large bird disappeared into the mountain. Dante landed a short distance away from Percival, still invisible, still watching, undetected, or so he thought, but for the first time, Percival felt his presence.

Dante had heard of this place as a child but had never believed it to be true, imagining it to be just a story told by his mother. The large opening in the mountain looked like a giant mouth. Two smaller openings above resembled eye sockets. A glow emanated from within, creating an eerie atmosphere. A chill ran down Dante's spine and he shivered. Dante felt as though he was being watched, a feeling he couldn't shake off. If his mother's story was true, this was the lair of the one-eyed hag.

Dante watched curiously, as Percival gathered wood and started a fire. Percival then suspended a small pot over the fire and poured in a small amount of water. Then reaching into another of his many pockets, he removed a small container of honey. He slowly poured the honey into the water to warm through. As the honey warmed, the sweet fragrant scent rose into the air. It was ready. Percival added some powdered weeping willow and gave it a stir. He removed the pot of warm honey from above the fire and poured it into a cup. He then approached the entrance to the mountain. "Who are you and what do you want?" called a female voice from within.

"My name is Percival and I seek an audience with the one-eyed hag known as Helga." There was no reply. As Percival stood waiting, the scent of warm honey drifted towards the mountain entrance.

"I have an offering for you," called Percival. He knew the one-eyed hag could not resist the temptation of warm honey and so he placed the cup on the ground and stepped away. He knew it was disastrous to look the one-eyed hag in the eye. For anyone who did so would have their deepest, darkest fears become their reality. The one-eyed hag drawn by the sweetest of smells appeared at the entrance. She looked around cautiously. Dante could not believe his eyes. He was expecting her to be old and withered. For when his mother had told him the story as a young fairy, she had said Helga was ancient, and yet as she stood at the entrance of the mountain, she had the body of a youthful young woman, with long, blonde hair and full shapely lips. Then his gaze rose higher up her face, to a delicate nose and finally towards the eye, piercing blue. It sat in the centre of her forehead. Unblinking, she bent down and picked the cup of warm honey from the ground. The smell was irresistible. She drank the contents of the cup in one go and the warm honey was like an elixir. She revelled in the sensation, but something was wrong. She felt a strange sensation spread throughout her limbs, and suddenly multi-coloured hair sprouted all over her body, from her head to her toes. It grew right down over her eye.

She screamed, "What is happening to me?"

Only then did Percival speak. "My name is Percival," he said, "I needed a way to speak with you."

"What enchantment is this?" she bellowed.

"I will give you the antidote if you help me first," said Percival. Unable to see Percival, she could not look into his soul, for the long multi-coloured hair blinded her one eye. The one-eyed hag was not used to being tricked so easily and was extremely angry, but she had no choice.

"What is it you need of me?" she asked.

"I need to find someone, I need to use your wishing well," said Percival. The one-eyed hag didn't answer straight away, but eventually agreed.

"So, I allow you to use my wishing well and you give me the antidote?" she said.

"Yes," said Percival.

"How do I know I can trust you?"

"You don't," said Percival, "but what choice do you have?" The one-eyed hag reluctantly led the way into the mountain where the cobra-headed snakebird was sat upon a large flat stone eating the large snake. Having lived in the cave all her life, Helga didn't need to see to know where she was going.

They arrived at the wishing well. "Do you know how this works?" asked the one-eyed hag. But before Percival replied, she said, "Repeatedly say the name of the person you wish to find, step up onto the wall of the well and as the water starts to swirl, jump in, it will take you to whoever you seek." Percival stepped forward. All along, he had thought he would say Nicholas, but now beside the well, the name that sang inside his head was Berwyn. He hesitated. "Is everything all right?" asked Helga.

"Yes," said Percival. He started to repeat over and over again the name, Berwyn. He then stepped up onto the wall of the wishing well, the water within began to swirl.

"What about the antidote?" asked the one-eyed hag.

"Time is the antidote," shouted Percival, as he leapt into the water and disappeared. Instantly, the surface of the water calmed. Dante who had witnessed everything was still invisible. The one-eyed hag felt cheated having been given no antidote. She hadn't understood what Percival had said. Then a strange sensation gripped her body once more and all the hair fell from her body. She screamed in frustration at how easily she had been deceived. Then a noise caught her attention, another intruder. She turned and looked in the direction from where the noise had come. Dante stood still having knocked over a goblet which had fallen onto the dirt floor, and rolled up against the rock wall. He was intrigued to look closer at the one-eyed hag, believing himself to be safe because of his invisibility. Although the one-eyed hag could not see anything, her stare had the same effect as always. As Dante looked at her piercing blue eye, his greatest fear began to surface. He was being transformed from a fairy to a human. He tried to tell himself this was only his fears and not reality, but he had succumbed to the power of the one-eyed hag. He fell to his knees in despair, becoming visible at the same time, and she revelled in his misery, as he knelt before her.

Percival's journey as he passed through the swirling waters of the well to find Berwyn, had taken him to the entrance of a mountain cave. Below was a group of humans all sleeping.

Chapter 18
The Ice Caves, and Dorothy's Coming of Age

Oliver was the first to wake and was well aware of the predicament they were in. Caught by the guards who wanted to take them home to the castle where King Richard was gravely ill, Oliver knew he had to quietly try and wake his friends and sister Dorothy. All the guards seemed to be sleeping. As he moved stealthily around the camp, firstly he managed to wake Reif, then Joshua and finally Dorothy. They began to take their first steps towards leaving when they were startled, as a loud voice said, "Good morning." It was Robert, the head guard.

"Leaving so soon?" asked Robert.

"You cannot stop us," said Oliver defiantly.

"Oh, but I think I can," said Robert, "you see, while you were sleeping, I confiscated all your food and water." Oliver looking horrified quickly checked his bag, as did the others. "You see," said Robert, "you really don't have a choice."

"Yes, they do," said a familiar voice. They all turned their heads towards where the voice had come from. Above them on the mountain, as they all looked up, they were blinded by the early morning sun. The silhouette of a small but strangely familiar figure stood with the sun behind its back.

Berwyn, who had disappeared before Oliver was awake, had returned. He rushed past everyone towards the small figure. As they watched, Berwyn climbed higher up the mountain. It suddenly dawned on Oliver. "Is that you, Percival?" he called.

"Yes, it is," said Percival. A huge smile appeared across the faces of everyone. Dorothy and Oliver embraced with new hope of finding their brother Nicholas, only Robert was not smiling. For him, nothing had changed. He was determined to return to the castle with Prince Oliver and Princess Dorothy.

Percival carefully made his way down the mountain accompanied by Berwyn. Oliver and Dorothy greeted Percival enthusiastically. Filled with excitement, they were bursting with questions they wanted to ask. Robert came to Percival's rescue. "Give the man a chance to breathe," he said. "How are you Percival?" asked Robert, as he escorted him back to the camp where they sat down.

"I am very well, thank you, but I am surprised by what I just heard," said Percival.

"And what did you hear exactly?" asked Robert.

"That you have given up on Nicholas," said Percival.

"It's not so much that I have given up on Nicholas," said Robert, "but the boundary between the two kingdoms will not open for another ten years."

"What if I have found another way into the kingdom," said Percival.

"What do you mean?" asked Oliver.

"I'm here, am I not?" said Percival.

Percival explained everything that had happened to him since the last time they had seen each other, including meeting his mother. Everyone listened in silence. "So, how do we get into the kingdom of the rainbow fairy?" asked Oliver. "Can we use the wishing well?"

"There is no wishing well here," said Percival, "I believe we need to use the same entrance from which I have just emerged and enter into the mountain." Robert had misgivings about entering yet another mountain.

"We need to get back to King Richard," said Robert.

"How is His Majesty?" asked Percival.

"He is not well," said Robert.

"My father has lost his memory," interrupted Dorothy angrily, "he has lost five years of his life, he has no memory of Nicholas and doesn't realise that our mother has died." With tears filling her eyes as she spoke, Dorothy said, "We must go on and find Nicholas. We need to bring him home to save our father."

Robert had a difficult decision to make. After hearing Dorothy's heartfelt plea to go on, and with the reappearance of Percival, he needed time to think, and so walked a short distance away and sat down. Dorothy wanted to go after him but Oliver grabbed hold of her arm and stopped her. Dorothy turned to face Oliver. "He needs time to think," said Oliver.

"But what if he still decides to go back," said Dorothy, "what do we do then?"

"I don't know," said Oliver. While everyone waited for Robert to make his decision, Berwyn was getting reacquainted with Percival.

Robert sat alone. Fully aware everyone was waiting for his decision. If he took Prince Oliver and Princess Dorothy back to the castle and King Richard, nothing would have changed. King Richard would no doubt still have no memory of his youngest son or the fact that his wife had died after giving birth to Nicholas, but, as they were already at the mountain with Percival and Berwyn to lead the way, Robert got to his feet. Everyone waited anxiously for Robert's decision. "As we are already here," said Robert, "I think we should continue the search for Nicholas." Instantly, Dorothy had jumped to her feet and flung her arms around Robert's neck.

"Thank you," she said, as tears of joy flooded her eyes and overflowed down her cheeks. Dorothy then stepped back from Robert and hugged Oliver. Both were filled with joy that Robert had made the right decision.

"So, what are we waiting for?" said Robert. Looking at Percival, he said, "Lead the way."

With Percival and Berwyn leading the way, they climbed from where they were at the foot of the mountain. With only a rope to help them, with the rope tied around Berwyn's powerful neck, each person wrapped the rope around their waist, it was by no means the smallest mountain in the range, but the climb was gradual rather than steep. Even so, eventually they had to release all the horses, for the ground under foot was littered with broken pieces of rock and stones which moved under foot, making it unstable to walk on, impossible for the horses. Having unloaded the provisions from the horses' backs and carrying as much as they could themselves, they continued the climb taking frequent breaks. From where they had started their climb, there was no opening visible, but as they climbed higher, an opening gaped before them.

"I think we can remove the rope for now," said Percival. Making sure everyone was present before entering the mountain, Percival reached into a pocket and produced a glass orb that his mother Saki had given him. Holding it in cupped hands, the warmth of his hands caused a flame inside the orb to appear. "This will light our way," said Percival, and so they took their first tentative steps into the unknown.

Inside the mountain, they had only one tunnel to follow, high enough for even the tallest of them to stand upright, and just wide enough for Berwyn. The walls of the tunnel were completely smooth and reflected the glow from the orb

Percival was carrying. This meant there was no problem with visibility. It seemed for hours they had walked, and they had no idea how far they had to go. But as they walked through the tunnel, one thing was evident, the temperature was dropping. The tunnel had been rising steadily all the while. Dorothy was beginning to feel the cold on her bare legs and arms. Oliver pulled his blanket from the bag he carried and wrapped it around Dorothy's shoulders.

"Thank you," she said. They pressed on, but as they did, the rock walls of the tunnel began to emanate a coldness that filled the air. Their breath becoming visible. Still walking in single file, they eventually made it to a cavernous space within the mountain. "I'm not sure I can go much further," said Dorothy, as her teeth chattered with the cold. Oliver agreed.

"This is getting really cold, how are we supposed to carry on?"

"We have to," said Percival, "I have something to help protect us against the cold. It is a potion that my mother gave me." He took the container of powdered weeping willow from one of his many pockets, and then rummaged in his bag for the container of water. He emptied all the powdered weeping willow into the water container and gave it a good shake. "This will help to keep you alive," said Percival, "but there is one thing, you will have to remove all your clothes."

"You are joking," said Oliver.

"How can you expect me to remove all my clothes?" asked Dorothy.

"I'm afraid it is a case of remove your clothes and drink the potion, or die," said Percival. Dorothy looked at Oliver for reassurance.

"If we are to do this, Dorothy will need some privacy," said Oliver.

"When you drink the potion you can step behind Berwyn, no one will be able to see you get undressed," said Percival. Dorothy was not sure she wanted to get undressed with so many people present, but she trusted Percival and so nodded in agreement. "Who would like to drink first?" asked Percival. They all looked at each other uncertain whether or not to take the drink.

"Oh, come on," said Oliver, "we trust Percival, don't we?"

"It doesn't have much flavour but you will feel a strange sensation," warned Percival.

"Swallow three mouthfuls," suggested Percival, as he handed the potion to Oliver, "that should be enough." And so, Oliver took the potion and swallowed three mouthfuls as instructed and then started to disrobe. As he removed his jacket and then his shirt, multi-coloured hair started to appear all over his body. Everyone in the group watched in amazement. The hair grew thick and long and by the time Oliver had removed all his clothes, he was completely covered in hair. Having watched what had happened to her brother, Dorothy took the container and did as instructed, drinking down three mouthfuls and then passed the container to Reif. She disappeared behind Berwyn for privacy. At first, she didn't feel any different and wondered if it had worked. Then as she started to undress, she felt the strange sensation just as Oliver had previously. She felt it coursing throughout her body. She looked over her shoulder at Percival with a terrified expression on her face, scared of what was happening. Percival reassured her that what she was feeling was correct. Then as she looked at her arms, hair started to sprout all over her body. She didn't know whether to laugh or cry. She continued looking at her arms as long multi-coloured hair appeared from her head to her toes. It grew so fast and was so thick that she felt instantly warm.

"And this is what's supposed to happen?" she asked.

"Yes," said Percival. Just then, Reif was transformed. They looked at each other and burst out laughing. One by one everyone drank and swallowed three mouthfuls. "I know this is a weird sensation," said Percival, "but it will keep us alive, for I believe it is going to get much colder than this." Once everyone had had a drink, Percival placed the container of water into his bag. They had used just over half.

"How long will the effect last?" asked Oliver.

"Oh I reckon it will last about four days," lied Percival. For he had no way on knowing how long the effect would last. All he had to go by was the knowledge that the more you used of the weeping willow powder, the longer the effect lasted. "We've only used half the potion, so I'm sure we will be fine," said Percival.

"Right then," said Robert, "gather up all your clothes. I think we have rested long enough, don't you? Let's go."

With only one tunnel leading away from the cave, it rose still higher within the mountain. The air pressure caused their ears to pop, which caught everyone by surprise. Percival explained what had caused the strange sensation, but Reif and two of the guards had felt no such sensation. Instead, they felt light headed, dizzy and sick deep in their stomach. They could barely walk and as the tunnel rose even higher, their pain and suffering only increased. They felt the need to rest, but, as they collapsed one by one against the tunnel wall, they received no relief.

"It is the pressure on their ears that causes the pain," said Percival, "the only way to relieve the problem is to descend."

"But how can we do that," said Robert, "they can't even walk."

"Then they will have to be carried," said Percival, "it is that, or leave them behind." Robert and Oliver took hold of Reif. Oliver grasped Reif by the shoulders while Robert took hold of his legs. The remaining guards picked up the two guards who had also collapsed. As the tunnel led them even higher, Reif and the two guards moaned. They writhed in agony which made carrying them even more difficult. Dorothy could not help but shed a tear as their pitiful cries filled the tunnel. Everyone was grateful when Reif and the two guards eventually passed out. Percival had been right. As this strange group of long-haired, multi-coloured humans made their way along the tunnel the air had turned distinctively colder, every breath they took made them look as if they were breathing smoke, but with their long shaggy coats, they no longer felt the cold. The glass orb Percival held continued to glow, where the walls of the tunnel had emanated cold before, they were now covered in a layer of ice, as was the ground, on which they walked. This meant the light from the orb shone brighter than ever, reflected off all the ice. Berwyn who was in front of Percival stopped abruptly. No one was expecting it, and they all stumbled into each other. "Ouch," cried Joshua, as one of the guards pushed into him from behind and knocked him to the floor. He dropped the legs of the guard he was carrying, but he remained unconscious. The sound of Joshua's cry echoed throughout the tunnel. Helping Joshua back onto his feet, the guard asked, "Why have we stopped, is everything all right?"

Up front, Berwyn was sniffing the air. It seemed he had picked up on a scent with his superior sense of smell. After a short pause, he slowly began to walk forward once more. Robert sensing danger alerted the others to be vigilant. Dorothy and Percival were at the front, but they had the protection of Berwyn leading the way. He was confident they were safe. Carrying the three bodies of their stricken friends made progress much more difficult, but eventually the tunnel started to descend.

Passing over them, down the tunnel, a blast of icy air travelled, carrying with it a howling sound that caused them all to pause. "What was that?" Dorothy asked Percival. "Was it the wind?" she asked hopefully.

"I cannot be sure," said Percival. After pausing briefly, they continued. Berwyn constantly sniffed the air. He seemed to be getting more and more agitated. A second blast of icy cold air entered their tunnel, once more carrying a howling cry. Dorothy was convinced this sounded more like an animal than just the wind. Her bow and arrows were slung over one shoulder. She removed her bow and placed an arrow ready to fire if necessary. Oliver standing behind Dorothy carrying Reif by his shoulders could not help but smile at her bravery. If only he knew, Dorothy didn't feel very brave even though she was standing behind Percival and Berwyn.

The narrow tunnel they had been following continued to descend, and at last, it opened into an expansive cave. Reif and the two guards who had suffered with altitude sickness were placed on the ground, while everyone rested. Reif was the first to awake. "How are you feeling?" asked Percival.

"A lot better than before," said Reif. Just then, the two guards stirred. One of the guards tried to stand as soon as he woke up, but soon found he was still feeling light headed and collapsed back onto the ground as his legs buckled. As the second guard stirred, Dorothy went to him.

"Do not try to stand," she said, "you need to rest."

The guard smiled at her and said, "Thank you."

Now all three men were awake. Robert who was eager to press on asked them all, "How are you feeling?" They all gave the same reply, they were feeling better than before, but they still felt light headed.

"That should improve the more we descend," said Percival.

After having rested for a while longer, Robert asked, "Do you think you are ready to carry on, are you able to walk?"

"I believe so," said Reif. As he stood up without feeling any dizziness, the two guards nodded in agreement.

"We will take it slowly," said Percival.

The tunnel continued to descend. Gradually, Reif and the two guards began to feel better. By the time they had reached yet another cave, all three were feeling back to normal, which was just as well, for there was a problem. There was no floor to this cave. On the opposite side to where they were standing was the entrance to another tunnel, the only way across was a narrow slither of ice.

"You can't expect us to walk across that," said one of the guards.

Percival replied, "We have no choice, there was no other tunnel to choose." Berwyn began to walk across the ice bridge. Everyone held their breath. If this thin slither of ice could support Berwyn's weight, then surely it would be safe for them to cross. After a tense few minutes, Berwyn had made it to the other side. With a sigh of relief, Percival felt able to breath once more.

"Who would like to go next?" he asked. Oliver stepped forward. Percival placed a hand on Oliver's chest to stop him. "Once you start to cross, do not look down," said Percival, "understand?"

"Yes," said Oliver. Percival removed his hand and allowed Oliver to step forward onto the ice bridge. At first, Oliver was doing fine, making steady progress. He was looking straight ahead at Berwyn who was waiting on the other side. As he reached just beyond halfway, a blast of freezing cold air filled the cavernous space. Oliver stumbled slightly, but regained his balance, back where he had started out Dorothy could not bear to watch. Everyone had gasped. Oliver called out, "I'm fine." Then he slowly made his way across the bridge inch by inch, and was greeted by Berwyn when he was clear of the ice bridge.

"Right, who's next?" called Oliver. Percival went next, and once again, Dorothy found herself unable to watch/ Percival however made it across with no problems. As one after another, they all safely made it across. Finally, there was only five left to make the crossing. Robert, the two guards, who had felt sick earlier, Reif and Dorothy.

Dorothy, knowing that she would have to cross the ice bridge at some time, decided it was time to face her fears. She let go of Reif's hand, as she stepped tentatively onto the ice bridge. Oliver called to his sister, "Remember, don't look down." She wished he hadn't said that, for now, the one thing she felt compelled to do, was, look down.

Composing herself and taking a deep breath, she started off making steady progress. Then the one thing she knew she shouldn't have done, but with the words ringing in her ears, look down, look down, the temptation was too great to resist, instead of looking straight ahead, she lowered her gaze. The ice path she was walking across suddenly began to sway. Below the ice pathway, nothing, just a huge empty blackness. Her legs began to feel weak, and her eyes started to roll. She felt dizzy and was close to fainting, when suddenly from behind, Reif caught her as she was about to collapse. She passed out in his arms, as he steadily carried her to the other side. As Reif stepped away from the bridge and placed Dorothy safely on the ground, Oliver bent down to check on his sister. Within seconds, she had regained consciousness.

"Are you all right?" asked Oliver.

"I'm fine," replied Dorothy, feeling slightly dazed, "but what happened?"

"You fainted," said Oliver.

"So, how did I get to this side?" asked Dorothy. Before answering his sister, Oliver then turned to face Reif.

"How are you feeling?" he asked. At that precise moment, Reif stumbled backwards into the wall and had to place his hand against the wall to stop himself from falling.

"Just felt a bit dizzy, that's all," said Reif, "but I will be fine."

One of the guards who had felt unwell had followed after Reif and had safely made it across. Only one guard was left behind with Robert. "You go next," said Robert, "and I will follow." And so the guard stepped forward. He looked back at Robert, fearful, not wanting to take another step. Robert encouraged the guard. "You can do this," he said, and so the guard turned towards the ice bridge and began the slow walk to the other side. He was clearly nervous. His whole body was shaking with every step he took. From behind, Robert spoke words of encouragement, from the other side those who had already crossed safely were calmly talking to him. He had made it three quarters of the way across the bridge, when a blast of freezing cold air shot through the tunnel. He swayed as the air caught him face on. He froze with fear.

"I can't make it," he cried, "I can't move."

From behind, Robert called, "Stay there, I will come and get you." And so, Robert started to cross the bridge. He moved quickly and had almost reached the guard who stood petrified just a few steps ahead. As the guard waited to be rescued, he couldn't resist the temptation to look down. This was his undoing. A sickness churned in his stomach at the sight of nothing below his feet. His body gripped by fear. His head spinning. He fell from the bridge just as Robert reached out to him. A loud scream echoed throughout the chamber and seemed to go on forever, as he fell into darkness. Dorothy had screamed also at the sight of the guard falling from the bridge. She had instinctively reached out a hand. All his colleagues who had successfully crossed and were waiting on the other side gasped as he disappeared from view, some shed a tear, some turned away. Robert was dumbstruck by what had just happened right in front of him. He momentarily stood rooted to the spot, as if frozen in time. Then something miraculous happened. The guard reappeared from the depths of darkness, floating in the air. Percival stood with a hand resting on Dorothy's shoulder. That's right, concentrate on what you are doing, bring him to us. Everyone had fallen silent, watching in disbelief. The fallen guard's body floated all the way to Dorothy's feet and landed gently on the ice. Dorothy then passed out. It had taken all her strength for what she had just achieved. Robert composed himself and continued across the bridge, finally reaching the other side. Only now having completed the crossing did he allow his emotions to show. He fell to his knees and sobbed. "I knew he was nervous, I should never have let him cross alone, we should have crossed together."

"It's all right," said Percival, "he is safe."

Dumfounded by what he had just witnessed, Oliver asked Percival, "What just happened?"

"Your sister has come of age," said Percival.

"What does that mean?" asked Oliver.

"It means she can perform magic," answered Percival.

Chapter 19
Nicholas' Night-time Sleigh Ride

A couple of days had passed since Emily's humiliation at the ball. Nicholas had wanted to keep the kitten but Elvira would not allow it. She had taken the kitten away from Nicholas the moment everyone had left the castle, returning it to its former glass brooch status and placed in into the cabinet with her vast collection. Even though Nicholas had pleaded with Elvira to allow him to keep the kitten, she had refused to change her mind.

Nicholas was no longer happy at the winter castle. He had wanted to go outside and play in the snow, but was never allowed outside on his own. He missed his brother, Oliver, and his sisters, Alice, Dorothy and Mary. All he wanted now was to go home. As he lay in bed remembering fun times he had shared in the past with his siblings, Nicholas remembered how he used to sneak out of the castle at night with Oliver and visit the forest with all its nocturnal animals, or that time when he and Mary went for a ride all alone. He suddenly felt very sad and lonely. Finally, his reverie led him to his father, King Richard, remembering how he had been snatched from his father's shoulders by the giant white eagle. A knock on his bedroom door bought him back from his reverie. As the door opened, it was Eleanor's voice who asked, "Are you all right, Nicholas?" But as Nicholas didn't answer, she assumed he was sleeping, and so she quietly left him to rest.

It was dark outside. They had eaten their evening meal and Nicholas was now sitting alone in his bedroom looking out at the gently falling snow. Having just been paid a visit by Eleanor who thought he was sleeping, he knew no one else would bother to check on him again, believing he had gone to bed. He quietly got dressed in his winter coat and hat, not forgetting his scarf and gloves. He carried in his arms his special shoes that allowed him to walk on the surface of the snow without sinking. Quietly, he opened his bedroom door. He could hear voices talking downstairs. He moved to the top of the stairs to listen. He recognised Elvira and Eleanor's voices, as they were talking. Every now and then, an unknown male voice interjected.

Knowing Elvira and Eleanor were together in the same room gave Nicholas confidence he would succeed. Light from below lit the galleried landing allowing Nicholas to walk freely to the second staircase that was hidden behind a wall panel which the servants used. Elvira's servants were blinks, strange looking creatures with no mouth to speak, and no ears to listen. They only communicated what they saw, so, as long as Nicholas stayed out of sight, he would remain undetected.

Nicholas hurried down the stairs that were lit by a single candle. The blinks were all together in one room sleeping, standing up. He had witnessed this before at Eleanor's castle. Even though he knew they couldn't hear, he stealthily walked on passed this room. Down into the vast kitchen he went, a giant table dominated the centre of the room. Suspended over the table were hundreds of copper pots and pans of various sizes, all gleaming brightly in the moonlight, a large sink sat beneath a panoramic window that overlooked the castle gardens, and on the opposite wall to the window were all the cooking utensils and knives. Also on this wall was the set of keys needed to unlock the door that led into the garden. Nicholas had to stretch onto tiptoe in order to reach the keys. Using his fingertips, he managed to dislodge the keys from the hook where they were hanging, but they slipped through his fingers onto the tiled floor. The chunky metal keys crashing onto the tiled floor echoed around the large kitchen. Scared someone may have heard, he raced towards the kitchen door, but then he remembered that blinks cannot hear, and Elvira and Eleanor were in the front of the castle. He slowed his breathing and calmed himself. There were three locks on the heavy wooden door and a dozen keys to choose from. He tried the first key in all three locks, but it did not fit, the same result with the second and third keys. He removed each key from the large ring to which they were attached and lay it on the floor. Finally, the fourth key opened the second lock, then the fifth key opened the first lock. His hands were shaking with excitement. He was nearly there. Just one more key to find, with seven to choose from. One after the other, he tried all the keys, but none of them fit. Nicholas didn't understand. He tried all the discarded keys again, thinking he must have missed the right one in his excitement, but no, none of the keys that now lay strewn across the floor fitted.

Nicholas was beginning to feel anxious. This was proving to be more difficult than he had expected.

As he sat in silence trying to think, he could hear footsteps approaching the kitchen, and as he listened, he realised it must be the blinks coming down the stairs. He thought of looking for another key, but there wasn't time. Then he thought, *What about the two keys already in the locks?* He removed the key that had opened the first lock and tried it in the third lock. To his shock and surprise, the key fit. He turned the key in the lock and opened the door. He quickly gathered the keys off the floor and removed the two keys from the locks, closing the door behind him just as the blinks arrived in the kitchen. Leaving the keys on the stone step outside the kitchen door, Nicholas stepped into the garden, quickly placing his feet into his special shoes which allowed him to walk on the surface of the snow without sinking.

This was Nicholas' first time outside at night. The air was considerably colder than what he had experienced before, during the day. He pulled the collar of his coat tight around his neck and lowered his fur hat so that it covered his ears. Snow was gently falling. The light from within the castle illuminated each flake as it passed by the windows on its descent towards the ground. Nicholas looked up at the sky. Snow tickled his nose and eyelashes. Free at last to do something fun, he decided he was going to build a snowman. He made a snowball with his hands and placed it on the ground and rolled it along. It grew in size. When he could no longer move it, Nicholas decided that it was big enough. He then placed handfuls of snow on top of the ball, building it up to make a head. When he was happy with his work, he decided it needed some arms. He searched the garden and selected a couple of twigs, poking them into the snow on opposite sides of the body, he stepped back to admire his work. It needed a hat. He again searched the garden for something suitable. Eventually finding half buried beneath the snow an old wooden bucket, he placed it onto the snowman's head. It sat slightly lopsided. It looked great, thought Nicholas, but still, something was missing. He then realised he hadn't given it any eyes or nose. Once more, he began to search the garden. Then as he was bending over searching through a woodpile, someone tapped him on the shoulder. Expecting it to be Elvira, he turned with a glum expression on his face. He started to apologise, but stopped instantly upon seeing who was stood before him, for it was not Elvira as he had expected, neither was it Eleanor. A huge grin spread across Nicholas' face. The snowman stood before Nicholas with eyes of sapphire blue, and a ruby red nose and a row of sparkling diamonds sat where its mouth should be, and then it spoke. "Good evening," said the snowman, as he gave a little bow.

"Good evening," replied Nicholas, as he giggled, with excitement.

"Would you like to go for a ride with me?" asked the snowman.

"Yes, please," said Nicholas all excited by the prospect of having fun with the snowman.

"Hop aboard then," said the snowman, and magically a sleigh of ice appeared, with four ice reindeers to pull the sleigh. Nicholas climbed aboard excitedly and sat next to the snowman who held a set of reigns. "Away we go," shouted the snowman. As he gave the reigns a gentle flick, the four ice reindeer sprang to life and effortlessly, they were pulling the sleigh across the snow-covered gardens.

Elvira and Eleanor stood watching from one of the many upstairs windows. "Thank you, mother," said Eleanor. Elvira smiled at her daughter without reply and then turned to gaze upon the happy scene below, as mother and daughter watched from a third floor window, the reindeer sped ever faster around the garden. Nicholas was enjoying every minute of the ride. Although at one point, he thought he was going to be thrown from the sleigh when the reindeer made an incredibly sharp turn and the sleigh tilted to one side, but the snowman reached across Nicholas with his twig arm to prevent him from falling out. When the sleigh was upright once more, it was Elvira who was taken by surprise when the snowman suddenly headed straight for the wrought iron gate which sprang open just in time to allow them to pass through.

Beyond the village and out into open wilderness, the reindeers dashed. The gently falling snow had ceased and the moon shone brightly. On they sped through a pine tree forest. Nicholas and the snowman found themselves having to duck beneath snow-laden branches, as the sleigh weaved its way between the trees as it followed behind the reindeer. On they sped towards the top of a hill, picking up speed all the while, and then they were launched from the top of the hill, and for a second, it felt as though they were flying. As they touched down again, turning to Nicholas, the snowman asked, "Having fun?"

Just as Nicholas replied yes, they hit a rock buried beneath the snow. The ice reindeers and sleigh were launched through the air. As Nicholas and the snowman were both thrown clear, the reindeers and sleigh crashed into another rock and shattered on impact, leaving the snowman and Nicholas alone in the wilderness at night.

As the snowman had fallen onto the ground, he had rolled over and over, collecting more snow. When he finally came to a stop, he was twice the size he had been. Nicholas clambered to his feet, unhurt, brushing the excess snow from his coat and legs. He looked across at the snowman and burst out laughing.

"What are you laughing at?" asked the snowman, as he looked at Nicholas quizzically.

"Have you seen how fat you are?" said Nicholas.

"I am not fat," said the snowman indignantly, "I am rotund." Nicholas didn't know what this word meant, but it sounded funny, just the same, he continued to laugh.

"Where are we?" asked Nicholas, as he looked around.

"How should I know," said the snowman, "you've only just made me." In the bright moonlight, the snow sparkled as if it were covered in diamonds, and as Nicholas looked around, he could see nothing but an open expanse of snow. As he turned full circle, there was nothing to see to indicate where they were. He decided all they could do was follow the tracks the sleigh had made and head back to the castle, and hope it didn't start snowing.

As they started out over the snowfields following the tracks made by their sleigh, a howling crept across the snow towards them. Nicholas couldn't determine whether it was the wind or a wild animal, but he suddenly felt very small, and exposed. Nicholas was wearing his special snowshoes, that allowed him to walk across the snow without sinking. The snowman simply glided along at his side. More howling spread across the wilderness. The hairs stood up on the back of Nicholas' head. He was convinced this time the howling was made by an animal. He stopped momentarily looking out over the open snowfields. A group of small black dots appeared in the distance. As Nicholas watched, he realised they were heading his way. He turned away and tried to run. Although the snowshoes he wore stopped him from sinking into the snow, they were a hindrance when it came to running. Nicholas looked over his shoulder again. The small dots were now much larger and gaining rapidly. He counted eight. His fear grew as he realised they were being chased by a pack of wolves. He knew there was no way he could outrun them, and so stopped. Out of breath and feeling as though there was no hope, he slumped to the ground. He prayed for a miracle. The snowman stood by his side. The pack of wolves had stopped running and cautiously approached, baring sharp teeth and growling, hackles standing on end, they circled Nicholas and the snowman. Nicholas did the only thing he could and made a snowball compacted hard within in hands and launched it at one of the wolves. Catching it square in the face, it gave a small cry of discomfort, but in no way was it deterred. Following his lead, the snowman started to launch snowball's at the wolves himself. They were much larger and harder than the one Nicholas had made. Each strike made the wolves cry out in pain. At first, they backed away, uncertain of what was happening. Nicholas felt momentarily relieved as the wolves backed off, but his relief was short-lived. They were gathering again, moving ever closer. The largest of the pack howled a terrifying sound that sent shivers down Nicholas' back, and the pack attacked. The miracle that Nicholas had prayed for appeared in the shape of the snowman. As the snowman magically split into four and surrounded Nicholas, trapped behind a wall of snow, the four snowmen provided a shield to protect Nicholas. He could no longer see what was happening. The wolves sounded ferocious, with all the snarling and howling, but the snowmen stood firm.

Elvira had not meant for the snowman to leave the castle garden, when she had bought him to life. As soon as he had passed through the wrought iron gates, she had gone to her room and selected a brooch from her glass cabinet. She knew of the dangers that came with being out after dark. Standing in the courtyard, she placed a small brooch of a blue dragon on the ground. As it pulsed and grew, she stepped away. Once the blue dragon had finished growing, she climbed onto its back. Taking to flight, it soared through the air following the tracks of the sleigh, way beyond the village and above the pine tree forest, she flew. Before she saw anything, she heard the howling of the wolves. As she flew over the crest of the hill that led to the valley of the lakes, there in the depths of the valley were the snowmen fighting off the pack of hungry wolves. The wolves had started to claw away at the base of the snowmen, who were beginning to subside until finally Nicholas was revealed. As Nicholas stood perfectly still, the wolves closed in. The first wolf to make the final leap to reach Nicholas was in for a shock. As it flew through the air with teeth bared, a spear shaped piece of ice thrust by the snowman lying on the ground lodged itself into the wolf's side. With one last howl, it collapsed onto the snow dead. The remaining wolves became ever more wary. Realising there was no time to waste, Elvira guided her escort to launch an attack. Focussed on Nicholas, none of the wolves had seen Elvira's approach. So swift and unexpected was the attack from the sky, the vulnerable wolves were caught completely off guard. Grasped within the talons of the giant blue dragon, two wolves were discarded, as they were lifted into the air, howling all the while, then dropped from a great height, dead.

Four of the five remaining wolves, attention was now fixated upon the blue dragon. No longer was food their priority. This was now a matter of survival. The blue dragon circled menacingly overhead as the wolves cowered and backed away. Then, as the blue dragon swooped out of the sky once more, four of the wolves fled, only the largest of the wolves stood its ground. Elvira was not interested in those that ran away, and so she guided her dragon to face the one remaining wolf. This one remaining wolf, the largest of the pack was not going to give up its prey so easily, but it was no match for the giant blue dragon. As the dragon descended towards the ground and flew over the top of the lone wolf, it breathed a blast of freezing cold air. Too late, the wolf tried to retreat. It was instantly turned to ice. The blue dragon then swooped down and plucked Nicholas from the snow and flew up into the air, back to Elvira's winter palace, leaving the broken snowmen behind. Nicholas was getting quite used to being plucked into the air, first by the harpy, then the giant white eagle and now to top the lot a giant blue dragon. On landing in the courtyard, the lying snow was displaced into the air by the blue dragon's powerful wings. With each beat of his wings, more snow flew into the air, making the courtyard look like a giant snow globe. Having released Nicholas safely onto the ground, Elvira slipped off of the blue dragon's back. It lowered its head, and Elvira stroked its neck three times with long sweeping strokes. It shrank in size, to become once more a brooch made of coloured glass. Elvira bent down and carefully picked the little blue dragon off the snow-covered ground.

Elvira said not a word but simply walked away. The tall, thin man in the blood-red suit appeared and escorted Nicholas to his bedroom where Eleanor was waiting. She hugged him and asked if he was all right, to which he replied yes. She then undressed him and tucked him into bed. He wanted to ask about the blue dragon, but Eleanor told him it would have to wait until the morning. It was late and it was time to go to sleep. The problem was, Nicholas was so excited by everything that had happened that night there was no way he felt at all sleepy. And so as Eleanor blew out the candle beside his bed and crossed the room to leave him to sleep, Nicholas lay with his eyes closed as images of the snowman and the sleigh ride danced inside his head. Even the wolves didn't seem scary anymore, knowing now that he would be saved by a blue dragon, he smiled to himself and sleep finally came.

Morning had arrived, and Nicholas lay awake. Still wrapped in warm blankets upon his bed, he stared out of the window. A small gap between the curtains allowed him to see it was snowing once more. As he lay in bed all cosy and warm, he tried to remember the dream he had last night. Visions of a snowman coming to life danced in his head, a sleigh with reindeer sculpted from ice, thrown from the sleigh as it crashed and shattered against the rocks, chased by wolves, only to be rescued by Elvira riding a giant blue dragon.

He sat bolt upright. Suddenly, he was fully awake. *Had this been a dream?* he asked himself. It all seemed so vivid and clear, but surely not. Then a gentle tapping on his window. At first Nicholas chose to ignore it, then thud, he climbed out of bed and pulled open the curtains, the remainder of a snowball was sliding down the window obscuring his vision, thud a second snowball splattered against the glass. Nicholas could not see through the snow who was attacking his window, and so he moved to another window and looked down into the garden. He could not believe his eyes. Wearing his lopsided wooden bucket for a hat, the snowman stood waving at Nicholas. Tears of joy filled Nicholas' eyes. He raced to get dressed so he could go and play once more with the snowman. Before leaving his bedroom, he glanced out of his window. His joy turned to despair as the snow had stopped and the clouds parted. As the sunlight crept across the garden, the snowman's fate was sealed. He removed his hat and gave a little bow. Then caught in the sunlight, he briefly sparkled, before he slowly sank into the snow that covered the ground, the only thing left, a wooden bucket, two blue sapphires, a ruby and a row of diamonds, all sat upon the snow forming a face. It was as if the snowman had simply laid down.

Nicholas collapsed onto the window seat crying. Eleanor who was coming to check on Nicholas heard his sobs from the hallway. She quietly opened the bedroom door and crossed the room. Doing her best to comfort Nicholas, she looked out of the window. Smiling up at her was the face of the snowman. Memories flooded Eleanor's head of long ago when she had been a child. With one hand rested on Nicholas' shoulder, she shed a silent tear. As Nicholas mourned the loss of a new friend, Eleanor remembered her loss of long ago. As the two of them looked down upon the snowman's smiling face, the sun became veiled behind snow clouds, and as the gently falling snow settled on the ground, the snowman's face slowly disappeared, finally laid to rest.

Chapter 20
Dorothy's Magic

Everyone was ecstatic to have their fallen friend back amongst them once more, as they all gathered around eagerly asking questions. How did it feel falling to certain death? How did it feel floating back up from the depths of darkness? But he heard nothing, his gaze was fixed upon Dorothy who had backed away from the group. Even though her actions had just saved a life, she was feeling terrified of what she had just achieved. With a million questions racing through her own mind. *How did this happen, why did this happen, why me,* she thought, how could she possibly, her thoughts were abruptly interrupted when Oliver grabbed hold of his sister and gave her a hug and asked, "Are you all right?" She looked at her brother as if he were a stranger, then blinking she shook her head and came back from her reverie.

"What?" asked Dorothy.

"Are you all right?" repeated Oliver.

"Honestly, I don't know," she said. Dorothy then looked beyond Oliver to where the guard was still seated on the ground. "Is he all right?" she asked.

"Yes," said Percival, "a bit shaken, obviously, but I'm more concerned about you, how are you feeling?"

"Oh, I'm fine," lied Dorothy. Percival knew this was not true, for no one could have experienced performing magic the way she had for the first time and not be affected, but he decided not to pressure Dorothy into revealing her true feelings, not just yet, but he would be watching her very closely.

The young guard who had fallen from the ice bridge had recovered from the shock and declared he was ready to carry on. As they all lined up once more to follow Berwyn, Dorothy avoided eye contact with anyone, choosing instead to look at the floor. She followed behind Percival as Oliver fell into line behind his sister, everyone else followed single file.

No one was speaking, which allowed Dorothy time to think. How is it possible she had used magic? She wasn't a witch, was she? But then, if she was, what about her brothers and sisters. She felt so confused by all the emotions that were in her head. She started to feel faint again. She stumbled sideways and ended up leaning against the ice wall. Oliver who was right behind his sister took her in his arms and carried her through the tunnel.

The ice tunnel twisted and turned as it continued to descend. Reif and the two guards who had suffered at altitude were now feeling back to normal. In single file, they followed Berwyn, until they found themselves in another cavernous space. As they spread out to sit down and rest, Oliver placed his sister Dorothy on the ground leaning against a large slab of ice. She came around within a couple of minutes. Seeing his sister open her eyes, Oliver asked, "Feeling better?" As she looked at him questioningly, he said, "You fainted again."

She heaved a big sigh and replied, "I don't know what's the matter with me, I've never fainted before."

"It's nothing to worry about," said Percival, "it's just the shock of everything that has happened."

With giant icicles suspended from the ceiling and columns of ice growing up from the floor, this cavernous space was quite unlike any other they had so far come across. They decided to rest a while longer making sure Dorothy felt fully recovered before moving on. This was the first opportunity for the fallen guard to approach Dorothy. She was talking to Oliver and Reif when she saw the guard. As he approached, she asked Oliver and Reif for some privacy. They moved away and joined the rest of the group, allowing Dorothy and the guard to talk alone. "I need to thank you," said the guard, "for saving my life."

"You don't need to thank me," said Dorothy.

They both felt slightly awkward, unsure of what to say to each other. Then unexpectedly the guard flung his arms around Dorothy and cried, letting all the emotions flood out of his body. Dorothy who had tried to contain her emotions could do so no longer, and they stood in the middle of the cave crying. Some members of the group felt uncomfortable watching and so looked away. Oliver went to join his sister, but, Percival placed a hand on his shoulder and said, "Give them a moment." Finally, Dorothy and the guard released each other and stepped back. Now they were laughing at how embarrassed they felt for crying in front of everyone. "Thank you," he said once more.

As they re-joined the group, Dorothy asked Percival, "How is it that I can do magic?" Percival had been waiting, expecting this question. All eyes were turned on him waiting to hear his reply. Then, just as he went to speak, a mournful cry entered their chamber. A spine-chilling echo that reverberated off the ice walls. They all stood in shocked silence, listening. Only now did Oliver notice there were many tunnels that led off from this chamber. He pointed this out to Reif who was standing next to him. Robert the head guard had also noticed the many openings, as he spun around in search of where the cry had come from. Another cry entered their chamber deeper in tone than the first, and louder. Because of the echo bouncing off the ice walls, they could not tell from which tunnel it came. With swords drawn, they huddled together in the centre of the chamber. Berwyn stood tall on his hind legs sniffing the air. Then unexpectedly, he dropped onto all fours and charged down the nearest tunnel, emitting a howl so loud that some of the icicles suspended from the chambers ceiling overhead vibrated. He disappeared down the tunnel. His howl answered by more cries that entered their space from all sides. As the echoes bounced off the walls and ceiling, a loud crack was heard overhead. Fragments of splintered ice crashed down on top of them and onto the ice-covered ground, where they shattered into smaller pieces on impact. As the howling increased in ferocity, the sound continued to echo through the tunnels and into their chamber. With the howling increasing in volume, the vibrating off the ice walls increased. With nowhere to hide, large pieces of stalactite crashed to the ground. Screams became mixed with howls as the cacophony of noises blended together, then silence.

Reif was the first to stand up after everything had settled down. He had been lucky, having only been partially buried beneath some small fragments of ice. He looked around at the devastation that surrounded him. Bodies were scattered everywhere. He started to search among the fragments of ice. He found Oliver first, for he had been standing closest to Reif. As he uncovered Oliver, he was startled to find that Oliver was lying on top of Dorothy, having flung her to the ground to shield her with his body. Oliver was coming to his senses again and Reif helped him to his feet. Then as Oliver looked around in a daze, Reif bent down to check on Dorothy. Other members of the group were coming around also. Robert was moving about the cave helping everyone to their feet once more. Percival and Joshua were both all right. Dorothy had been knocked unconscious. When she finally came around, the first thing she saw was Reif's smiling face, hidden beneath a mass of brightly coloured hair. She smiled.

"Are you all right?" asked Reif.

"I've been asked that a lot today," she said jokingly, as she got to her feet. Once standing, "Yes, I'm fine," said Dorothy.

Having moved around the ice cave checking everyone was all right, Robert was relieved at just how lucky they had been, just a few minor cuts and scrapes, then, as the rest of the group gathered around asking, if everyone was okay, Robert had stopped searching. He stood a lonely figure away from the main group with his head bowed. Percival was the first one to notice this. He separated himself from the rest of the group and crossed to where Robert was standing. Percival knew as he crossed the chamber to where Robert was stood alone, a life had been lost, blood stained the ice covered floor, however, he was shocked to find it was the young guard who had fallen from the ice bridge, saved by Dorothy only a short while before, his body lay crushed beneath a large piece of ice. Percival bent down to check. There was no sign of life. As Percival stood once more, Dorothy spotted the two men standing alone. She called across the ice cave. "Is everything all right?"

When neither answered, she became distressed. Knowing something was wrong, she started to make her way towards them. Stumbling her way between the shards of ice that lay shattered on the ground, Dorothy made her way across the cave. Fragments of clear ice littered the floor, but as she drew closer to Percival, she noticed some of the ice was stained red. Percival moved towards Dorothy and blocked her way. She could see the lower half of a leg and foot. "Who is it?" she screamed. The remainder of the group had heard Dorothy's cry and were now looking across the cave to where Robert was standing alone, beyond Percival and Dorothy. She struggled, trying to get past Percival and was becoming hysterical, but he was not about to let her past. Oliver reached his sister and spun her around. She threw her arms around Oliver's neck and began to cry in despair. Reif passed beyond the siblings to join Robert, realising a tragedy had occurred. He too was shocked to find it was the young guard who had so miraculously been saved by Dorothy only moments before.

"We cannot let her see this," said Reif.

"I know," said Robert, "but I cannot just leave him there like this, I need to cover him properly." Oliver looking over Dorothy's shoulder understood a signal from Reif to take Dorothy away, and so as Oliver led Dorothy away, Joshua and the other guards went to help Robert and Reif. They were all shocked to see the crumpled body of their friend lying half-buried beneath the ice. His blue eyes staring at the ceiling. A look of horror forever etched on his face. Joshua the youngest member of the group looked away as the tears formed in his eyes. Some of the other guards began to cry as well as they helped to lay their fellow guard flat on his back with his arms folded across his chest. They then buried his body beneath pieces of ice laying them carefully into position. When finished, the young man beneath the ice looked as though he could be restfully sleeping. Percival said a prayer, as Dorothy and Oliver watched silently from a distance.

Berwyn returned, as Oliver and Dorothy were stood alone, the others still standing beside the grave of the young guard. Berwyn gave Oliver's hand a gentle nudge to announce his presence. Oliver was relieved to see Berwyn had come back to them unscathed. He called across the cave to Percival that Berwyn had returned. This was perfect timing, for everyone was feeling emotionally exhausted. With Berwyn's arrival, Percival led the guards across the cave. Robert stayed behind. Being head guard, Robert felt responsible for all his men. He needed to be alone to say his final farewell.

Once Robert re-joined the group moments later, having said his final goodbye, Berwyn led them down the tunnel he had raced into. It looked no different to any of the tunnels they had already passed through, but there was an unpleasant smell that lingered on the air. The tunnel split by a column of ice branched off in two directions. Berwyn did not hesitate as he took the tunnel to the right. Percival followed unquestioningly. Some of the guards at the rear faltered.

"How do we know the bear is going the right way?" one called.

"We don't," said Percival, as he continued to follow Berwyn, "you are more than welcome to try the other tunnel if you wish," he called. The guards looked at each other in astonishment, to even suggest they try the other tunnel alone. They quickly fell back in line behind Robert who was smiling to himself. *Such bravery*, he thought.

The smell that lingered on the air grew stronger, as they entered yet another cave. The reason soon became apparent. In the centre of the cave lay a half, eaten carcass of some large animal, blood stained the ice that covered the ground and a trail of blood from where the animal had been dragged entered a tunnel opposite the one they had used to get this far. The guards alert and with swords drawn followed Berwyn. As they passed beyond the carcass and into the tunnel following the trail of blood, many eyes watched their progress, hidden away in the shadows of the cave. Then a sudden blast of freezing cold air penetrated their tunnel and they found themselves stepping out of the tunnel and into the open night air. Compared to the cold they had felt inside the ice mountain, the wind was blowing a gale, and the windchill made it feel much colder outside.

Standing on the side of the mountain, they looked out over a landscape like no other they had witnessed before. A forest of tall pine trees standing erect covered with snow. Their lower branches so heavily laden with snow, bent, touching the ground. Beyond the pine trees shimmering in the moonlight, a frozen lake. As they stood looking at the scenery in amazement, Oliver asked, "Where are we?"

"We have made it to the frozen north of the enchanted kingdom," said Percival.

"But why are we here?" asked Dorothy.

"It seems this is where we need to be if we are to find Nicholas," said Percival.

Dorothy turned to Oliver with a huge smile upon her face. The hope of finding Nicholas once more made Dorothy very happy. With everything that had happened inside the ice mountain, she had almost forgotten why they were here in the first place. As Oliver smiled back at his sister, his expression suddenly changed. Pain was etched across his face. He bent double holding his stomach, and without warning, all the hair that had kept him warm within the ice mountain suddenly fell out. He collapsed onto the snow-covered ground shaking uncontrollably. Dorothy called for Percival. As he turned and saw Oliver lying naked on the ice shaking, he reached into his bag for the container of water with the weeping willow potion. As he bent down to administer the drink, Oliver needed to stay alive. Two of the guards also collapsed. As Reif took hold of Oliver's head holding it still, Percival encouraged him to drink. As soon as the hair started to regrow, Oliver stopped convulsing. Percival was then able to turn his attention to the guards and treat them. Having drunk just over half the potion before, there was just enough to treat everyone. Percival drank last.

Fully covered in multi-coloured hair once more, they were ready to continue. Berwyn started on his descent down the mountain. The deep snow shifted beneath his feet, with every step. "We must remain quiet as we descend the mountain," said Percival, "any noise could cause an avalanche."

"What's an avalanche?" asked Dorothy in a whisper.

Oliver replied. "I don't know, so let's just stay quiet." As they moved away from the entrance to the tunnel, a large clawed hand appeared on the ice wall, covered in long white hair, then appeared a face. It had an almost human quality, with a broad nose and piercing blue eyes, but with purple skin. Long, white hair hung around its face, and with white facial hair growing from its chin, its appearance looked like that of a very old man, a very tall, very old man. Silently, the yeti observed as he watched the giant white bear lead this strange colourful group as they made their way down the mountain, away from his home.

Chapter 21
Cressida's Concern for Dante

Cressida was sat on her throne surrounded by fairies who tended her every need. She had everything she had ever desired. The rule over her magical kingdom was unchallenged. With the crystal egg in its rightful place in her crystal crown, she had no one to fear, and yet she was bored. Ever since Percival had reappeared, she had wondered, what had happened to Nicholas.

Cressida had lost count of how many days had passed since Dante had left the crystal palace in order to follow Percival. She had received no news from her brother and was growing concerned. As the fairies fluttered around her in attendance, she became more agitated by their presence. "Leave me," she said, with such authority that the fairies were blown across the room. She had risen from her throne wings fully extended looking down on those below. Aegeus the centaur entered, as the fairies were picking themselves off the floor and flying out of the room, leaving him alone with Cressida.

"Your Majesty," said Aegeus, as he entered further into the room, and bowed.

"What news have you?" she asked.

"We have found no trace of Dante," said Aegeus, "not since he crossed the border between the rainbow forest and entered into the land of the ogres."

With the crystal egg back where it belonged, mounted within the crystal crown, it provided Cressida with greater power than she had ever known. However, she was still learning how to enhance this power. "Follow me," she said to Aegeus. She spread her wings and floated from her throne high above and landed gracefully besides the centaur withdrawing her wings. Aegeus followed as ordered. Cressida led the way down three flights of stairs, into a labyrinth of corridors. Without Cressida leading the way, Aegeus knew he would easily get lost. With bare walls of glass, there was nothing to visually record to memory, and yet Cressida did not hesitate. She was lured by the powerful magic of the crystal crown. Only she was able to follow its trail. Finally, they reached the end of the corridor where a glass door stood, closed, carved into the glass door were square panels of yellow, pink and blue. Cressida stood before the door and closed her eyes. Aegeus stood silently watching. After pausing briefly, Cressida placed her hands onto the square panels. Each one she pressed then lit up. It was a sequence that had to be followed to gain entry into the room that housed the crystal crown. The sequence was different every time. That way, no one could memorise it and gain entry. The glass door swung open. These were new measures that Cressida herself had put in place, but there was still the floor to navigate. A sequence of steps upon the floor led to the crystal crown. One mistake and instant death, and there it sat upon its plinth, in the centre of the room, the fabled crystal crown.

Like the door, the floor was coloured in yellow, pink and blue squares. Once again, a different sequence had to be followed every time. Aegeus waited as Cressida slowly crossed the room. Placing the crown upon her head, she told Aegeus it was now safe to enter. She crossed the room and stood before a blank canvas. "Show me my brother," she commanded. A paint brush appeared and magically painted a picture of Dante.

"No, that's not what I wanted," she said impatiently. The picture showed Dante standing by her throne. She thought again. "Show me where Dante is this very minute." The brush quickly went to work. A dark cave appeared on the canvas. This didn't help either, for the cave was indistinctive and could have been anywhere. "How can I find my brother?" she said out loud in frustration.

"Your Majesty," said Aegeus, tentatively, uncertain of her response to any suggestion he might make, "may I suggest you try and be a bit more specific?" She looked at him thoughtfully, as she pondered his suggestion.

"Paint me the journey that my brother took, and show me where he now resides, and who he is with," said Cressida. "Is that specific enough for you, Aegeus?" she asked, as she turned to face the centaur. He gave Cressida a nod of approval without speaking. As the brush got to work, it first painted a picture of Dante leaving the rainbow forest. She recognised the stone bridge where he had crossed the border. Then this picture faded, only to be replaced by another, showing Percival coming out of the hole followed by the snake, as Dante watched in the background. Again, the picture faded. The next picture showed Percival holding the tail of the snake as they were flying through the air being carried away by the cobra-headed snakebird, with Dante following. Cressida's head was beginning to ache. She was struggling to make sense of what she was being shown. Then as the brush strokes created the next picture, the mountain cave appeared, with an opening that looked like a mouth and two small openings above that looked like eye sockets. Cressida recognised this place. She knew where this place was, and she knew who resided there before being shown by the paint brush. "Helga the one-eyed hag, but surely she cannot still be alive," said Cressida, "she must be over two hundred years old, and why is Percival going to see her," she said.

"Your Majesty," said Aegeus. She had forgotten he was there, lost in her own thoughts, she returned from her reverie. "Your Majesty, what do the paintings mean?" asked Aegeus.

"They mean we need to go visit Face Mountain and the lair of the one-eyed hag called Helga." The mere mention of her name caused Aegeus to take a step backwards, for he too had been told stories of her exploits, of how she could create fear within one's mind, so much so, that centaurs had been known to try and kill their own reflection before finally being driven completely mad. Cressida was standing facing the canvas still showing the last painting.

As the painting started to fade, Cressida started to feel the effects of wearing the crown. The effort used in creating such magic was taking its toll. She started to feel dizzy, and stumbled towards a seat and sat down. Showing concern, Aegeus asked, "Your Majesty, are you all right?"

"Gather twenty of your bravest centaurs," said Cressida, "we leave for Face Mountain immediately."

Having rested briefly, the dizziness had faded. Cressida eventually opened her eyes and raised her head. She was surprised to see Aegeus still standing there. "Well, what are you waiting for?" she asked.

"Your Majesty," said Aegeus, she looked at him quizzically.

"Yes?"

"Your Majesty," said Aegeus again, "the one-eyed hag." He faltered in what he was trying to say.

"Go on," said Cressida, who was showing signs of losing her patience with Aegeus, for she had started tapping her right foot on the floor. Aegeus recognised the sign, and so pressed on.

"Your Majesty," he said for the third time, "I'm not sure my centaur brothers and I can be of much use to you in this endeavour."

Cressida laughed, and Aegeus knew he was in trouble, as she moved closer. "You seem to be under the delusion that this was a request," said Cressida threateningly, "so let me make this quite clear, I command you to gather twenty Centaurs so we can leave immediately to go in search of my brother." Without uttering another word, Aegeus bowed and quickly left the room. Surprisingly, instead of finding himself confronted by a labyrinth of corridors he found himself at the foot of the stairs. He ascended quickly. Following Cressida's order, he gathered twenty centaurs. Once alone, Cressida removed the crystal crown. She felt faint. Every time she used the crown, she felt as though her energy was being drained from her body. The longer she wore the crown, the weaker she became. This was a secret burden she dared not tell anyone.

Cressida was back sitting on her throne moments later when Aegeus returned with twenty Centaurs. "We are ready, Your Majesty," he announced.

"We will leave the rainbow forest using the old troll bridge and cross into the land of the ogres," said Cressida. As she walked past the Centaurs leaving the room, they all bowed. Then following Aegeus, they followed Cressida outside.

Once outside the crystal palace walls, Cressida produced a crystal flute, which she began to play, a melodic tune drifted across the rainbow forest, unheard by all, but the one it was intended for. The great beast stirred as the music played on, and so the beast was lured all the way back to its source.

It was a matter of minutes before the great beast appeared, a giant, white stag stepped out of the rainbow-coloured forest, unusual, for the fact of it being completely white in a land of colour, but it displayed the most impressive set of antlers that sparkled like crystals in the sunlight.

"This is Oberon," said Cressida. The centaurs looked on in awe for they had heard his name, but always thought of him as myth.

"Your Majesty," said Oberon, as he lowered his head and knelt before Cressida.

"He will be my ride," said Cressida. She stepped forward and gracefully mounted the giant, white stag. As large as the centaurs body wise, but with his impressive antlers, he looked the dominant force of the group as they headed off on their journey to find Dante and the face mountain.

Travelling at great speed through the rainbow forest, Oberon led the centaurs to the old troll bridge. They slowed to a walk as they approached. On one side of the bridge, small, brightly coloured flowers grew amongst the cracks. On the far side towards the land of ogres, nothing grew.

The troll who used to guard the bridge no longer resided there, having been returned to human form. His name Frederick, a long-lost love of Cressida, but since being returned to human form, he had been unwell. Cressida had tried everything she knew to help him, but nothing had worked so far. He lay unconscious but alive back at the crystal palace.

Ogres had long been fearful of the Troll, for legend had decreed, that no ogre could stand against the Troll of the bridge and survive, knowing the Troll no longer protected the bridge between the land of the ogres and the rainbow forest, the centaurs were cautious in their approach. As Oberon led the way, the centaurs followed, with bow and arrows at hand. Cressida sat on the giant, white stag, watching for any sign of danger.

They were three quarters of the way across the old stone bridge before it happened. A large boulder flying through the air. The narrow bridge didn't afford much room for manoeuvre as the centaurs tried to avoid the impending impact. Using her magic, Cressida transformed the boulder into a mass of rainbow coloured petals, that showered down upon them harmlessly. She was not about to retreat. The order was given to move forward, and although they could be heard roaring defiance, no ogre showed itself on this occasion. "It seems, Your Majesty, that your magic has scared them off," said Aegeus.

"It would seem so," said Cressida, "but I don't expect it will be long before they regain their courage and attack again, we must remain alert at all times."

"Yes, Your Majesty," said Aegeus.

They left the bridge and crossed into the land of the ogres. Unlike the land where Cressida reigned supreme, in this land all the trees were green as were the bushes and grass, and there were swamps to be avoided at all cost. As the three suns began to merge and night time approached, Cressida created a fire dome to protect them while they slept. Nothing could penetrate through. It had taken a great deal of effort to perform such magic, even with the crown to enhance her power, but without the crown, she was exhausted and weak. Trying to hide this fact from the centaurs and Oberon, she lay down to sleep. The heat from the dome was on the outside, the air within was cool and fresh. Protected beneath the fire dome, the centaurs were able to relax and sleep also, whilst on the other side of the fire dome, many eyes filled with hatred watched.

Cressida's sleep was not comforting. She had visions of Dante suffering at the hands of Helga, the one-eyed hag. One question kept invading Cressida's subconscious. Why did Percival go to see Helga, when he was seeking Nicholas and the giant white eagle.

Oberon lay beside Cressida. Not needing to sleep, he watched as she tossed and turned, her arms moving involuntarily, her fingers twitched, emitting sparks, then a fireball shot into the night air and suddenly everyone was awake, everyone except Cressida.

Slowly, Cressida's nightmare visions ceased. She relaxed as Oberon hummed a tune, his voice a resonant baritone soothing to the soul. It was not long before everyone was able to settle down once more. When morning arrived, Cressida awoke feeling fully refreshed. She remembered nothing of the nightmares from the night before. Oberon was still by her side. The centaurs were already awake. She stood and stretched, fully extending her wings, the firewall still in place. Cressida clapped her hands and the firewall slowly lowered. As they ventured away from their camp into the land of the ogres, evidence showed that they had been surrounded during the night, but come the light of day, not one ogre was present.

Cressida sat high riding on the back of Oberon once again and led the way. It was a barren land compared to the rainbow forest they were used to, giant trees stood alone, with brown bark and green leaves. *Extremely dull and boring*, thought Cressida. Large boulders lay strewn across the land. "Shh," said Oberon who had come to a standstill. As he held his head high, he sniffed the air, the centaurs did the same.

"Ogre," exclaimed Aegeus.

"Yes," confirmed Oberon. Suddenly, they were being charged at. From behind a mound of rock and stones, three ogres appeared. With clubs raised above their heads, they charged towards Cressida and the centaurs yelling a terrifying scream. Oberon took a deep breath and exhaled, and as he did, the sound which he produced was directed at the ogres. They dropped to their knees clutching their hands over their ears. The smallest of the three ogres was blown off his feet and crashed to the ground. Cressida caused a dust cloud to blind the other two. As this was going on, to the right two more ogres had charged. These were briefly halted under a hail of arrows fired by the centaurs, but as the centaurs reloaded their bows, the two ogres continued their attack. Screaming defiance, they started to swing their clubs. Oberon turned to face this onslaught, and Cressida sent a fireball in their direction. A direct hit on one caused it to fall to the ground screaming in agony as it was engulfed in flame. The other faltered. A dozen more appeared. It was time to escape, as they realised they would not be able to fight them all off, without sustaining any loss, or injury.

Oberon took the lead as the ogres closed in. Lowering his antlers, he charged. The sunlight reflected from Oberon's antlers shone into the eyes of the ogres. As they were temporarily blinded, Oberon battered his way between them sending two of the ogres flying through the air. They crashed into the ground momentarily dazed. The centaurs followed through the large gap created by Oberon as quickly as possible. The ogres recovered and closed ranks and the last of the centaurs was trapped. As Oberon raced to safety with Cressida on his back, the centaurs followed. Nobody realised that one of their group had not made it clear. Only when they heard the screams of terror and agony did they halt their escape, but by then, it was too late. As they looked back, all they could see was the group of ogres repeatedly wielding their clubs, above their heads and forcefully smashing them towards the ground. As one of the centaurs attempted to race back to help his friend, Oberon blocked his way. "There is nothing you can do to save your friend," he said, as finally the screaming stopped. The only sound from the distance that could be heard was the triumphant roars of the ogres.

"We dare not linger in this place for more ogres may show up at any time," said Oberon. The centaur stood facing Oberon with anger in his eyes, but Oberon was not about to let him past.

Cressida spoke. "You knew of the dangers when asked to join us on this journey," she said.

"We were not asked," said the centaur, as his anger increased and his voice grew deeper, a loathing stirred within his chest, "you commanded us to join you." Cressida would not tolerate being spoken to in this manner without repercussions.

"And I warn you now, centaur," said Cressida, "move on with us, or face the ogres alone." As the centaur went to reply, Aegeus stepped between them.

He looked the centaur in the eyes and said, "I cannot bare to lose yet another, you must stay with us it is our only hope of survival. If we try to go alone, we are doomed." Giving Cressida one last glance of defiance, the centaur turned away from Oberon and joined with Aegeus. This time, they would lead the way.

Chapter 22
Nicholas Rebels

Having watched his snowman melt away, Nicholas was unhappy. He wanted to go home, and he let everyone know. He was barely eating his food and would talk to no one. The only time he spoke was when he demanded to be sent home. Elvira had allowed him three days to calm down before she finally snapped. "There is a ball this evening, you will attend," said Elvira. She was sat at one end of her dining table having breakfast. Eleanor sat at the opposite end, with Nicolas sitting to the right of her. Four of Elvira's servants, blinks, stood in a line with their backs to the wall awaiting further instructions.

"I will not come to the ball tonight," said Nicholas defiantly. He pushed away his bowl of porridge that had cinnamon sprinkled on top. The smell and taste reminded him of home. "I wish to go home," he demanded. Finally, Elvira had had enough. She arose from her seat with such anger her chair flew backwards across the room. She slammed her hands down hard on the table, sending a shockwave of anger that spread the length of the table. The two candle sticks that sat each end of the table had fallen over, shooting the ignited candles into the air. They had scorched the carpet where they fell. As the ripple of Elvira's anger reached the opposite end of the table, Nicholas' porridge had erupted, showering both himself and Eleanor.

"You will attend tonight's ball," said Elvira, then she turned and left the two of them covered in porridge sitting at the dining table. The blinks rushed forward to clear up the mess. With a wave of her hand, Eleanor and Nicholas were clean once more.

Nicholas left the table without saying a word. Eleanor called to him. He halted at the doorway without looking at Eleanor, but listened to what she said. "You would be wise not to upset my mother too much," she said, as a friendly warning. Nicholas lingered in the doorway briefly, then without uttering a single word, he left the room. He no longer cared for this place, but longed to be back home with his brother and sisters. As the blinks tidied the table, Eleanor ran a hand over the damaged carpet, instantly repaired.

Nicholas went straight to his room to put on his fur coat and hat. He was going to leave immediately, but as the door to his room closed, he heard the lock click into place. He turned around and grabbed hold of the door handle and tugged with all his strength, it would not budge. He then raced across the room to the windows; trying each one in turn, they would not open either. Outside a snow stormed had started. Nicholas had learnt from Eleanor that this was an indication of how angry Elvira was, and it was snowing heavily. It seemed Elvira would get her way. Nicholas would not be leaving today, but would be attending the ball.

As the day wore on, Nicholas lay on his bed gazing at the heavily falling snow. The fire in the fireplace was lit keeping the room warm and snug. He tried to imagine what his brother and sisters were up to. Little did he know that Oliver and Dorothy were part of a group along with Percival and Berwyn that were trying to find him. He couldn't remember ever feeling so alone before. He was pulled back from his reverie however, by a loud knocking on his door, as he rolled off the bed and approached the door. It opened. Three blinks entered. One carrying a tray of food, bread, cheese, meat, tomatoes and pickles. One carrying a tray with a hot drink, the third, just stood in the background. Nicholas guessed the third one was in case he tried to escape. But for now he had decided he would not try to leave. After all, there was a blizzard raging outside, so where would he go. The blinks crossed the room and placed the two trays on a bedside table, then left. As Nicholas watched them close the door, he heard the familiar sound of the lock as it clicked into place. He sat on his bed eating his food watching the snow falling. He smiled. A thought occurred to himself, *If it keeps snowing this hard, there won't be any guests to attend a ball.*

How wrong was he. The snow fell incessantly all day. As it piled up on his windowsill, his view of the garden below was blocked. Looking out of the top half of the window, he could see it still snowing unabated. Happy in the thought of there being no ball, Nicholas had enjoyed the hot drink and finished off the last of the food the blinks had brought earlier. Then he lay down and dozed off to sleep.

A rapping on his door awoke Nicholas, who had no idea how long he had been asleep. A quick glance through the top half of the window showed it was still snowing. The click of the door being unlocked heralded the entrance of Eleanor. "I am here to escort you to the ball," said Eleanor.

"But I didn't think there would be a ball tonight, what with all the snow," said Nicholas.

"You underestimate my mother," said Eleanor "you have no idea what my mother is capable of." She held out a hand which Nicholas grasped. For the first time since his arrival, he was a little afraid of what Elvira might do. Eleanor helped Nicholas to change into a royal blue outfit, with gold buttons on the jacket, his royal blue trousers had a line of gold that ran down the outside of his leg and his shiny black shoes had a gold buckle. As they reached the top of the blue marble staircase, they were greeted by the thin man in the blood-red suit. He announced their arrival. Nicholas was looking down at his feet as he descended the staircase. Only upon reaching the bottom of the stairs did he raise his head. He didn't understand. Apart from Elvira seated on her throne, and the orchestra playing a joyous tune, the ballroom was empty.

Eleanor led Nicholas, who was feeling a little bit uneasy. She led him by the hand as they crossed the dance floor. He glanced around wondering if there were more guests. He couldn't see hidden away in the shadows.

Elvira seated on her throne, dressed in white as always greeted them with a smile as they approached. Eleanor bowed her head as she greeted her mother. She sat on her throne besides Elvira. Nicholas sat upon her lap. Once seated, Elvira called, "Let them in." A door, way back in the shadows could be heard opening. Nicholas could see movement in the shadows. This he thought must be the rest of the guests, but then he heard crying. He looked up at Eleanor, for some reassurance, of what was going on. Eleanor stared across the dance floor towards the shadows without showing any emotion, avoiding Nicholas' gaze.

The music stopped as three blinks stepped onto the dance floor, each holding the hand of a young child, two girls and one boy. They all looked roughly the same age, about the same age as Nicholas' brother and sisters, but somehow, they seemed different, youthful in appearance at first glance, their movement across the floor made them look old, and weak, barely able to lift their feet as they shuffled their way across the floor. It was as if they had been drained of all energy. Nicholas tore his eyes away from this pitiful sight and looked up at Eleanor. She was crying, silent tears, but still avoided looking as Nicholas, who then looked across to Elvira, who in complete contrast to her daughter Eleanor. Elvira was smiling. She seemed to be revelling in the distress the young children were going through. Nicholas had seen this side of Elvira recently, when Emily was left alone on the dance floor, alone to face the brooch that he himself had chosen. "What is happening?" he asked. Elvira looked upon his face with menace in her eyes.

"These children are of no further use to me," she said.

She clapped her hands and the blinks released the hand of each child they held, as the blinks left the dance floor the three children struggled to even stand. "What do you mean, they are of no further use to you?" asked Nicholas.

"Why, I have you know," said Elvira, and she looked at Nicholas with a greedy glint of menace in her eyes and traced her finger across his forehead and down the side of his face, enjoying the tingle of youth that coursed through her body.

As Nicholas watched not understanding what was going on, Elvira descended the stairs that led to the dance floor. The three children recoiled in terror as she made her way towards them, the boy and one of the girls started to cry. "Why us?" they pleaded. Elvira looked at them unsympathetically.

"You have given me everything you had to give," she said.

"Yes, that's right," said the girl who wasn't crying, "you've taken our spirit, now take our bodies as well." Elvira glared at her menacingly, but without another word being spoken, the girl stood defiantly staring at Elvira as she placed a brooch on the floor. Then as Elvira stepped back, she turned and walked away across the dance floor, a sinister grin spread across her face. With menace in her eyes, she looked at Nicholas, as the other two children clung to her legs. The defiant young girl called to Elvira, "Do your worst."

As Elvira turned to face the defiant young girl, she said, "Oh, I intend to, my dear."

As the brooch began its familiar glow, Nicholas felt Eleanor's arms tighten around his body pulling him closer in her embrace. He then felt the tears from her eyes as they fell from her chin onto his cheek. He was scared. Not for himself but for the three children stranded on the dance floor. They watched in silent horror. The brooch glowed brighter as it grew bigger. The defiant girl tried to remain strong for the other two. Then a blinding flash of light, and as the light subsided, a giant scorpion was revealed. Nicholas gasped, and Eleanor's grip tightened. Nicholas hadn't thought that was possible, for he was already struggling to breath in Eleanor's embrace, while down on the dance floor, all three children were now huddled together on the floor.

The hard shell of the scorpion was black, revealing a hint of blue that flashed in the candlelight. With its many legs, it moved across the marble floor towards the three children, pincers held high in the air, stretched out in front of the scorpion's head, clicking constantly. The scorpion's body was long and narrow, with a segmented tail that curved upwards and forward ending in a sting of bright red that seemed to glow, menacingly suspended high in the air.

The young boy on the dance floor struggled to break free from the two girls as the scorpion approached. They tried to keep a hold of his arm but eventually he broke away. Stumbling, he fell to the floor. The scorpion attracted by the movement closed in on the boy, with pincers clicking away furiously. The boy screaming in terror tried to kick out at the scorpion, but with no way to defend himself, he was totally helpless. Nicholas pleaded with Elvira to stop it, but she ignored his plea. The scorpion grabbed one of the boy's legs as he tried in vain to keep the scorpion away, the boy cried in pain as the pincer crushed his leg. Hoisted into the air by his ankle, the boy's head hung perilously close to the scorpion's mouth. Nicholas again screamed to Elvira to put a stop to what was happening. "Stop this, please, stop this," he pleaded. She clapped her hands and the scorpion froze, leaving the boy suspended by his broken ankle, screaming in pain.

"You will not disobey me again," she said.

"No, no," cried Nicholas, as he looked at the young boy hanging upside down.

"Very well," said Elvira. She clapped her hands again. The scorpion flexed its tail and the bright red sting shot forward into the body of the young boy, who made not a sound as his life was extinguished forever. The two young girls screamed as the scorpion released the boy's ankle and let his small body crash onto the floor. As Nicholas sat with his mouth wide open in shock, stunned into silence, he watched as Elvira made her way down to the dance floor. The scorpion shrank back to being a harmless brooch as Elvira ran her hands along its back. Elvira then reached down and picked the brooch off the floor. All the time being watched by the two young girls. Elvira left the dance floor walking past the rigid body of the dead young boy without giving him a second glance. Instead of returning to her throne, she silently left the ballroom. Silence had befallen the ballroom. The three blinks reappeared. One picked up the body of the young boy, the other two each took a hand of one of the young girls and led them away. Nicholas observed them leave in silence. Still sat upon Eleanor's lap, as he wiped away the tears from his eyes and looked up at Eleanor, he asked, "Why?"

"Because my mother likes to get her own way," said Eleanor. She paused as she took a deep breath. "When you are no longer of any value to her, she simply disposes you of."

"What do you mean, no longer any value to her?" asked Nicholas. Eleanor paused before answering.

"Has it not occurred to you how my mother stays looking so young?"

"No," said Nicholas.

"What if I told you my mother is over 100 hundred years old?"

"That's not possible," said Nicholas.

"I'll let you in on a secret if you promise not to tell anyone," said Eleanor. As Nicholas agreed to keep the secret, Eleanor froze. The tall, thin man in the blood-red suit was crossing the dance floor towards them. "Queen Elvira is waiting for you in her chambers," he announced. Eleanor sat on her throne waiting for him to leave so she could tell Nicholas of her mother's secret, but leave he did not. He simply stood there staring at them both, under his watchful glare. Eleanor finally gave in. She lifted Nicholas from her lap, stood up and holding Nicholas' hand, they headed across the dance floor heading towards Queen Elvira's chambers. "I will tell you another time," she whispered to Nicholas.

As they entered Queen Elvira's chambers, she greeted them with a smile, as if nothing out of the ordinary had just taken place. Nicholas went to speak, but Eleanor gripped his hand tightly, squeezing it so hard he was not able to utter anything other than 'ouch'.

Looking concerned, Elvira asked, "Are you all right, Nicholas?"

As he looked into Eleanor's terrified eyes, Nicholas answered, "Sorry, stubbed my big toe." Eleanor beamed down at him, assuring him he had said the right thing.

"I am so sorry no one turned up for the ball," said Elvira, "that has never happened before."

"I guess it's because of the snow storm," said Eleanor, "I have never seen anything like it before."

"Neither have I," said Elvira, "let us hope it DIES, down before next weekend, I will make it up to you, Nicholas," said Elvira, "I will make sure the next ball is extra special to make up for this weekend's disappointment."

Eleanor had noticed the emphasis Elvira had placed on the word, DIES, and replied. "I am confident it will be a spectacular ball," said Eleanor, as she gazed upon her mother's face watching her reaction.

Elvira returned the gaze with a smile, and said, "I want no one leaving the castle without my permission, now leave me I need to rest."

"Yes, mother," said Eleanor.

Chapter 23
Avalanche

It was a struggle to descend the snow-covered mountain. It took far more effort than walking normally did when walking on solid ground. With each step, the shifting snow fell back into each footprint, as their feet sank into the deep powdery snow almost up to their knees.

Joshua scooped up a handful of snow and tried to make a snowball to throw at Reif, but the snow was so powdery it was impossible to make into a snowball, and as he tried to throw it, the snow just fell apart. He laughed and settled for scooping a handful of snow as if cupping his hands in water, and sprayed Reif with a shower of light fluffy snow. Reif replied with his own handful of snow. They both laughed. The long, multi-coloured hair that covered their bodies was a great insulator against the cold, but at the same time, it was a hindrance. The snow was building up on their legs sticking to the long hair, although the top layer of snow was powdery and dry beneath. It was cold and damp. Their legs were becoming heavier. Each step needed more effort than the last. Percival and Dorothy were following in the trail left by Berwyn, which made it much easier. Oliver was walking along side Reif and had strayed a couple of feet to the right of the trail Berwyn had made. "There's nothing quite like walking in freshly fallen snow, and being the first one to leave footprints," said Oliver. Suddenly without warning, Oliver sank up to his waist. Caught completely by surprise, he screamed. Reif being right next to Oliver stopped suddenly. Oliver was already waist deep in the snow but appeared to be slowly sinking. Reif had to react quickly, as he reached out a hand to pull his friend out of the deep snow.

Slowly, the snow around Oliver started to fall away. Sensing urgency, Reif pulled on Oliver's arm. With Reif pulling in one direction and the snow pulling in the other as it fell away, Oliver felt as though he was being stretched. At first as Reif pulled, there seemed to be no movement, but as more snow shifted from around Oliver's legs, he inched slowly clear of the hole. The guards moved towards Reif to help. "Stay back," shouted Reif, the guards all stopped, the reason Reif had shouted to them to stop became apparent within seconds, a loud cracking noise filled the air as the snow just beyond where Oliver and Reif were now standing fell away, a deep crevasse had opened.

"That was lucky," said Oliver. "Thank you," he said to Reif.

"You would have done the same for me," said Reif panting heavily.

Percival was looking beyond where Oliver and Reif were standing. His gaze was focussed on the top of the mountain. "Is everything all right?" asked Robert.

"I'm just checking," said Percival. Robert looked towards the top of the mountain following Percival's gaze.

"What are you checking for?" he asked.

"That," said Percival, as he pointed to the very top of the mountain. Robert watched in silence as a crack appeared in the snow. In slow motion, the snow started to shift. "Avalanche," shouted Percival. Luckily, Berwyn had not stopped ploughing his way through the snow when Oliver had sunk into the snow up to his waist. "Run," shouted Percival. Everyone was now racing single file in the trail left by Berwyn. The snow had started to move a couple of thousand feet above them but Percival knew it would pick up speed on its descent down from the top of the mountain and be upon them within a minute. He was right, as the snow cascaded down the mountain, all the while picking up speed, snow blasted into the air. As Oliver looked over his shoulder, it looked like a giant cloud skating across the landscape sweeping everything in its path along for the ride. On it raced down the mountain, the roar of the snow made it difficult to hear what was being said. "Head for the rocks," shouted Percival. Oliver only managed to make out the word rocks, but it was enough to understand what Percival wanted them to do. Grabbing Dorothy by the hand, he left the trail created by Berwyn and headed for a large group of rocks. With fear coursing through their veins, they found renewed energy to scramble their way through pristine snow. Oliver pulling Dorothy along, they made it to the rocks and hopefully safety, followed by Reif who was now carrying Percival. The roar of the avalanche became deafening. Sitting behind the mound of rocks huddled together, they waited, as one by one they were joined by all the guards. Robert being the last to join them, a blast of cold air passed over the rocks. The ground beneath their feet seemed to vibrate, as the snow appeared above their heads, shot into the air as it crashed against the rocks which they were hiding behind.

They were then showered down upon with snow, huddled together in fear. One of the guards who was sat just behind Oliver got swept away. His screams went unheard. As more and more snow piled down the mountain, uprooted trees were carried along, one tree crashed into the rocks they were hiding behind. Flipped into the air it came crashing down and became lodged in between the rocks, branches were ripped away from the trunk which held firm. This caused the snow to part as it continued to race on down the mountain, passing by on either side. All anyone could do was pray and wait for the seemingly endless snow to stop.

All huddled together anxiously waiting for the snow to pass, no screams could be heard. Eventually, the avalanche ceased, and as the roar of the snow dissipated into silence, a new sound could be heard, a wailing, mournful cry that echoed throughout the mountains, not a human cry for they were all buried beneath a layer of snow, but the cry of some animal they had yet to encounter. Those closest to the rocks had the least covering of snow and so were the first to recover. Brushing away the snow that covered his sister, Oliver was beaming at Dorothy as she lifted her head. Relieved they were both alive and unharmed, she returned his smile. As others around them began to stir, Oliver and Dorothy started using their hands to shift the snow and uncover their friends. Percival was uncovered next, coughing as he struggled to get his breath. Reif lay motionless by his side. Dorothy tried to wake Reif who was unresponsive. She screamed at Percival to do something. He leant over Reif's body. He could detect a faint breath.

"He is alive," said Percival, "help me sit him upright." And so as Dorothy helped Percival move the snow off of Reif and place him in an upright position, Oliver continued to unbury the others. Reif slowly came around, only to find himself flattened against the snow as Dorothy flung her arms around him and cried. So overcome with joy Dorothy forgot herself and kissed Reif, full on the lips, then as she realised what she had done, she pulled away feeling embarrassed. Reif gave her a smile which didn't help, and so, she turned away and started to help Oliver uncover everyone else who was buried beneath the snow.

They searched the area behind the rocks where they had sought refuge, having thought they would be safest there, but when they did a count of heads, there were three people missing, and one of them was Robert, the head guard. They widened their search, plunging their hands into the snow hoping to find a limb or something to grab hold of, but they could find no trace of their three missing companions. Oliver was frantic in his search, shouting at the top of his voice, calling for Robert. He dug deep into the snow with nothing to use but his hands, hoping to find someone. Those who had been lucky in surviving the avalanche continued to dig deep into the snow also, but it was tiring work, exhaustion came quickly. As one by one, his companions gave up their search, too tired to carry on. Percival approached Oliver. "There is nothing more you can do," said Percival. Oliver knew this to be true, but wasn't yet ready to accept it, not yet. He kept on digging deep into the snow, watched by everyone else who had survived. Oliver eventually fell to his knees in defeat, too exhausted to even cry out, silent tears ran down his cheeks.

Berwyn reappeared totally unscathed, for which they were all grateful. He approached Percival with his head held low. It was as if he understood there had been a great loss. Even with his superior sense of smell, he could detect nothing beneath the deep snow that had so dramatically changed the landscape of the mountain. With so many trees uprooted, looking back up the mountain, it looked entirely different from before. Gently, Berwyn nudged Percival who got to his feet. "I think it's time we moved on," said Percival. Slowly, one by one, each member of the remaining group got to their feet. Dorothy made her way over to join Oliver. She glanced back over her shoulder to look at Reif, who smiled at her, a pang of guilt and embarrassment for the kiss made Dorothy look away quickly. Reif smiled to himself. He understood how she felt, caught up in the emotion of the moment. He promised to himself, to save Dorothy from any further embarrassment, he wouldn't mention the kiss to anyone.

As Berwyn led the way, nobody spoke. In silence, they followed along in single file. Percival was first in line behind Berwyn. Reif had taken up position at the rear. A large shadow appeared on the snow-covered ground. It came from behind Reif. Therefore, he was the first one to spot it. As he looked towards the sky, a giant white eagle soared overhead. "Percival," shouted Reif, everyone stopped, "look up," called Reif. As all eyes turned towards the sky, a feeling of elation spread throughout.

"Could that possibly be the giant white eagle that took Nicholas?" asked Dorothy, hopefully. Percival remained calm however, as he gazed upon the giant white eagle as it soared overhead.

"It is possible," he said, "but we don't know how many giant white eagles exist in this land. There may be only one, or there may be a hundred. I wouldn't want to build your hopes up unnecessarily."

"Oh, but it must be the same bird," said Dorothy, "surely there can only be one giant white eagle?"

"It is promising," said Percival, "but only time will tell, if that is the same bird that took your brother." Dorothy was convinced it was the same bird. She didn't know how because she hadn't been there when Nicholas had been snatched from his father's shoulders, but for some reason, she couldn't explain, she was convinced it was the same bird. They all fell silent once more. The only sound that could be heard was the wailing mournful cry that haunted them as they made their way down the mountain towards the valley below, and the high pitched, screeching of the giant white eagle, that continued to soar overhead.

Berwyn came to an abrupt stop, and howled. To the right of Berwyn lying on top of the snow was a body, not a multi-coloured body, but a body covered completely in white hair. Oliver wanted to investigate but Percival stopped him. "Best we leave it be," said Percival.

"But why," said Oliver, "I want to see what it is, don't you?"

"It is not safe to linger on the mountain, best we keep moving," said Percival.

"It will only take a minute," said Oliver, he moved beyond Percival and made his way towards the white-haired body. Dorothy glanced at Percival with fear in her eyes. He understood her fears.

"Oliver, we must keep moving," he called.

"Almost there," shouted Oliver, just a couple of steps and he would be there. As he finally approached the body, it was much larger than he had first thought.

Percival called again, "Oliver, we really must be on our way." Oliver took one more step. The half-buried face of a creature Oliver had never seen before stared up out of the snow, with piercing blue eyes. Oliver was startled by how human it looked. He jumped as a hand rested on his shoulder. Reif had been sent by Percival to bring him back.

"Look," said Oliver, as he realised it was Reif who was behind him. As Reif looked beyond Oliver at the body that lay upon the snow-covered ground half buried, the wailing mournful cry that had haunted them since the avalanche grew louder.

"I think it's time we left," said Reif.

There was no argument from Oliver this time. His curiosity having been satisfied, he would talk to Percival later. As they re-joined the others, Dorothy asked, "What was it?"

"Turns out, it was just a sheep," lied Oliver, as he looked at Percival. Berwyn continued to lead the way. They had successfully moved beyond the mountain and were approaching the frozen lake that looked as though it covered almost two thirds of the valley. Oliver was reminded of 'dead man's lake'. He faltered. "Are you sure this is safe?" he asked Percival. Percival reassured them all.

"Berwyn will not step onto frozen water," he said. With Percival's reassurance, they followed Berwyn who continued to create a wide pathway through the snow.

Not unexpectedly but rather sooner than he had hoped, Percival started to feel a strange sensation within his body. As his muscles started to convulse, he knew what was about to happen. He just hadn't expected it to happen quite so soon. Percival had been the last one to take a drink of the weeping willow potion. He had only received one sip before the potion was all gone. He hadn't told anyone this for he didn't want anyone to panic, but there was no way of hiding it. His hair fell out within the blink of an eye. The sudden drop in temperature sent his body into shock and he collapsed onto the ground shaking. The one thing Percival had wanted to avoid was panic, but seeing Percival on the ground shaking uncontrollably, panic ensued.

The guard that had been closest to Percival when he fell screamed, which alerted everyone else that something had happened. "What do we do," shouted the guard, "what do we do?"

"For a start, we need to calm down," said Reif.

As Percival lay on the ground shivering with cold, his body started to turn blue. Keeping calm, Oliver had found a blanket in one of the bags they had with them. He covered Percival in the blanket and lifted him from the snow-covered ground.

"This will not be enough to keep him alive," shouted Oliver, "we need shelter and to start a fire." Berwyn began to howl, pining for Percival, sensing he was in danger. Reif suggested laying Percival on Berwyn's back.

"The warmth generated from Berwyn will hopefully give us time to find some suitable shelter."

Berwyn seemed to understand what Reif had said, for he lowered his body so that Oliver could place Percival onto his back, covered in the blanket that Oliver had found. One of the guards came forward with a second blanket. This was then wrapped around Percival who was still shaking uncontrollably.

All the while, Oliver and Reif had been tending to Percival, three of the guards had wandered off, each one in a different direction. In blind panic and fearing for their lives, they had done the one thing they should not have. They had separated from the group. Dorothy who had been standing praying for a miracle while Oliver and Reif had tended to Percival was the first to realise that three guards had wandered off. She called to them, "Come back." As she did, Oliver looked away from Percival and saw Dorothy's face. A look of sheer horror showed in her eyes. Oliver looked in the direction of Dorothy's gaze. There was nothing to see.

"What happened?" asked Oliver. Dorothy unable to speak just stood staring blankly. Oliver approached and grabbed Dorothy by both arms. Shaking her, he asked, "What just happened?" Unable to find any words to say, she was shaking but not with the cold, then she blurted out "he was there one minute, and then he just disappeared from sight." Oliver followed the footprints made by the guard. He stopped suddenly at the water's edge, realising the guard had stepped onto the frozen lake, but then he noticed a different set of prints, larger than those made by the guard, but they looked just as fresh. Oliver didn't know what had made the second set of prints but believed the guard must have fallen through the ice. Oliver returned to Dorothy knowing there was nothing they could do. "I'm sorry," said Oliver.

Another one of the guards who had wandered off suddenly called to Oliver. "This way, I've found a cabin." The third guard who had separated from the group heard the call and headed back to join the others. As Berwyn reached the cabin, the door opened, and a wrinkled old lady welcomed them inside.

The guard who had headed off by himself and heard the call, saw the door close after Berwyn entered carrying Percival on his back, followed by the others. It wasn't far, thought the guard, a few minutes walking and he would be back amongst his friends, in the warmth.

Then movement beyond a distant tree told the guard he was not alone. Hoping it was one of his friends who had gone missing in the avalanche, he was torn between investigating, and the warmth and safety that beckoned within the cabin. He chose to investigate. If it turned out to be nothing, he was still only a short distance from safety. As he rounded the tree that stood before him, he suddenly froze. There just a few feet away a grisly scene. Two large creatures covered in long, white hair were devouring the corpse of one of his fellow travellers. He only knew this because of the multi-coloured hair they were tearing away from flesh. He backed away slowly, the two creatures so engrossed in what they were eating hadn't noticed the guard. He walked backwards around the tree keeping them in sight. Only when he could no longer see them did he turn to face the cabin. How was it possible? When he had walked away from the cabin, it had seemed so near, now with his life in danger the cabin seemed twice the distance away. He tried to remain calm as he headed towards the cabin. The door unexpectedly opened and Oliver appeared. Looking out Oliver called to the guard he could see in the distance. The guard waved frantically trying to stop Oliver from shouting, but it was too late. The guard looked back over his shoulder. His heart sank as from behind the tree, two bloodstained creatures appeared. The guard tried to run through the deep snow, as Oliver watched from the doorway. At first, all he could see was the guard, but knew something was wrong. As the guard struggled to make his way through the deep snow, they appeared, covered in bloodstained, long, white fur, Oliver realised the guard was in terrible danger and called for Reif, who instantly joined him by the open door.

"What the hell are they?" said Reif.

"I don't know," said Oliver, "but something tells me they don't want to play." The guard was frantically trying to scramble his way through the deep snow. The two creatures had started to follow and were gaining. Reif ducked back inside the cabin to gather up two bows and some arrows.

Dorothy asked, "What's the matter?" But Reif didn't have time to explain and dashed back outside. Passing a bow and arrows to Oliver, they both took aim. Firing simultaneously, they shot their arrows above the guard who watched as they passed overhead. Each hit one of the creatures following the guard who had stopped to watch. His hopes of the two creatures being slain was short lived, the arrows seemed to have little impact. Dorothy had come to see what was happening.

"Oh my God," she said, "what are they?"

"We don't know," said Oliver.

"They are yetis," said the old woman, who had appeared without anyone realising she was present. "They would normally avoid human contact but because of your appearance, they are not scared," she said.

The guard was terrified, for he kept looking back and could see the two creatures were gaining. Saki standing next to Dorothy said, "You can save him, you know."

"How?" asked Dorothy.

"With magic, of course," said Saki.

"But I don't know how," said Dorothy.

"And yet you managed it in the ice cave," said Saki.

"How do you know about that?" asked Dorothy.

"I know many things," said Saki. She then went back inside the cabin, leaving Oliver, Reif and Dorothy alone. Oliver and Reif had both fired a second arrow, and still the creatures pursued the guard undeterred. Dorothy didn't know what she was doing but reached out her hands. It had worked when the guard had fallen from the ice bridge. Maybe it would work again. As she raised her arms, miraculously it did work. The guard was suddenly lifted into the air high above the snow, out of the reach of the two white-haired yetis who halted their charge. Then without knowing why he did it, Oliver took a deep breath and blew. His breath like a gale force wind raced across the surface of the snow, whipping it up likes waves of an ocean that grew taller the further they travelled. The two yetis had never seen anything like it before and grew terrified. As the snow wave grew twenty feet into the air, the two attacking yetis were forced to retreat. Berwyn appeared between Dorothy and Oliver. Seeing the two white-haired creatures, he rose onto his hind legs and roared. The two white-haired yetis already forced into retreat disappeared under the crushing wave of snow. As the last of the snow settled and the danger had cleared, Dorothy relaxed, but kept control. The young guard who had been carried up into the sky slowly descended towards the ground. He landed safely in front of Dorothy, who ushered him inside. Grateful to be back on the ground and safe, he thanked them all as he passed into the warm cabin.

"Don't ever go off by yourself again," scolded Dorothy, as if she was talking to Nicholas. The young guard feeling embarrassed, joined with his friends who were sat by the fire.

Dorothy sat next to Oliver in silence as they warmed themselves by the fire, stunned by what she and Oliver had just achieved. As the realisation sank in, looking surprised, she turned to her brother Oliver and asked, "How did you do that?"

"I don't know," said Oliver. "It just seemed like the right thing to do," he said.

As they all sat around the roaring fire, Percival was laid out on a couch nearest the warmth. He continued to shake with the cold. His breathing had become faint. Oliver believed he was near to death but didn't dare tell Dorothy.

Dorothy wanted to ask the old woman how she knew about her magic. Oliver now had questions of his own, for that was the first time he had done any magic. Like Dorothy, he didn't understand how he knew what to do to halt the two yetis, or how he did it, but their questions would have to wait. The old woman was busy collecting extra blankets to cover Percival. She then gave him something to drink. All the while, she was watched in silence. Only when she had finished fussing over Percival did she introduced herself.

"My name is Saki, I am Percival's mother."

As everyone sat momentarily stunned into silence by this revelation, it was Saki who spoke. "Your hair will start to fall out any minute. There are screens for you boys to go behind if you are modest, makes no difference to me. I've seen it all before." She then turned to Dorothy. "My dear, there is a bedroom for you to use."

"Thank you," said Dorothy. Dorothy took the bag that held her clothes and entered the bedroom. All the boys had hurried behind the screen. Within a matter of minutes, the boys all reappeared fully clothed and back to normal. They joined Saki by the fire.

"How is Percival?" asked Oliver.

"He will be fine," said Saki. Just then, the bedroom door clicked open and Dorothy reappeared. Saki took one look at Dorothy's ripped silk dress with its missing arms and torn hemline and said, "Oh my dear, that will never do, come with me." She led Dorothy back into the bedroom. A couple of minutes later, the door opened. Saki, and then Dorothy reappeared. Dorothy was wearing men's trousers, a shirt and jacket, on her feet a sturdy pair of boots. "Much more appropriate for these weather conditions," said Saki.

Oliver laughed at his sister's appearance. "Now you really look like one us," he said, Dorothy sat between Joshua and Reif. She knew he was only trying to wind her up.

"I guarantee one thing," said Dorothy.

"What's that?" asked Oliver.

"I look a lot better in your clothes, than you would in mine," she said, and everyone in the cabin burst into laughter, including Oliver.

Chapter 24
Nicholas Tests Elvira's Patience

Having witnessed the young boy being killed by the scorpion, Nicholas knew he wanted to go home, now more than ever, not because he was scared, but because he was horrified having seen what Elvira was capable of. Up until the death of the young boy, it had all seemed like fun, but now the fun seemed to have disappeared from this palace and Nicholas realised how much he missed his brother and sisters. He knew he would not be able to sneak out on his own again, not after the last time when he had managed to sneak outside and ended up having to be saved by Elvira riding a blue dragon. Now he was watched like a hawk, with one blink standing guard of each doorway that exited the palace. As he couldn't leave on his own, he would just have to get someone to take him outside. He knew his best bet would be to ask Eleanor. It was early morning and so Nicholas got dressed. He crossed his bedroom and tried the door. He was no longer locked in, for there was no need, now that a blink stood guard at each exit.

He wandered down the hallway, heading towards Eleanor's room. A heavy hand unexpectedly grabbed Nicholas' shoulder. He froze on the spot, startled by the interruption in his thoughts. He slowly turned his head to see who had crept up behind him and given him such a shock. The tall, thin man in the blood-red suit was glaring down at him. "Where do you think you are going, Prince Nicholas?" he asked. Nicholas gulped a deep breath before answering. For some reason, this man always made Nicholas feel uneasy when they were alone.

"I was just on my way to find Eleanor," said Nicholas.

"Then you are heading the wrong way," said the tall, thin man, "Eleanor is already downstairs having breakfast."

"That's odd," said Nicholas, "she never gets up this early, why is she up so early?" The tall, thin man said nothing, and after staring at each other for what seemed like a lifetime, it was Nicholas who turned around and walked away.

Back down the hallway, all the while watched by the tall, thin man in the blood-red suit.

As Nicholas reached the top of the stairs, he could hear Eleanor's voice, followed by a voice he didn't recognise. It was male. Nicholas raced down the stairs eager to see who Eleanor was having breakfast with. He started to head towards the dining room, but then realised the voices were not coming from the dining room after all. There was a smaller room to the left of the dining room which housed the library. Nicholas entered. Although smaller in size than the dining room, the library had the tallest ceiling of any room Nicholas had been in. Row upon row of books climbed the walls from the floor to the vaulted ceiling. He stood in awe as he looked upwards at the countless books. There was a ladder on runners attached to the wall so that even the books at the highest level could easily be reached.

He had followed the sound of voices and entered, as he lowered his gaze, seated opposite each other at a small table were Eleanor and a handsome, dark-haired man. Eleanor was surprised to see Nicholas and blushed. The handsome stranger stood and introduced himself. "My name is Prince Pierre Mathier." Dressed in black trousers with a gold stripe that ran down the outside of his legs, he wore a bright red jacket that had gold buttons down the front and on the cuff of his sleeve, gold braid decorated his shoulders and ran across his chest. He clicked his heels of his shoes together and gave a little bow. Nicholas introduced himself.

"I am Prince Nicholas," he said, returning the bow.

"Please join us," said Prince Pierre. He pulled out a chair and Nicholas sat down.

"Where do you come from?" asked Nicholas.

"I come from the neighbouring kingdom, my castle is a week's travelling from here," said Pierre, "but where do you come from?" asked Pierre. "I have never seen you before."

Nicholas looked away from Pierre towards Eleanor before answering. "I come from a distant kingdom," said Nicholas.

Before either of them could say anything more, Eleanor arose from her seat and said to Prince Pierre, "I think it is time we left." Pierre arose from his chair, bowed to Nicholas and bade him farewell. Nicholas watched them leave hand in hand. He had never seen Eleanor look so happy before. Moments later, however, she returned alone.

"Were is Pierre?" asked Nicholas.

"He had to leave urgently," said Eleanor. Nicholas noticed that Eleanor held something in her hand, something small and brightly coloured. A gift from Prince Pierre, no doubt.

With Pierre now out of the way, Nicholas asked Eleanor if she would take him to the village. "Why do you want to go to the village?" she asked.

"I wish to visit the shops," he lied. After giving it some thought, Eleanor agreed. It would do them both some good to get away from the castle for a while. Eleanor informed the tall, thin man that she was taking Nicholas to the village.

"Please let my mother know when she wakes where we have gone."

"Is it wise to take the boy without your mother's permission?" challenged the tall, thin man.

"Who are you to question my decisions?" snapped Eleanor, "I suggest you do as I ask."

"Yes, princess, my apologies."

Eleanor and Nicholas dressed for the cold weather that awaited outside, with a fur hat pulled down to cover his ears and a fur coat with its high collar pulled tight to stop the chill around his neck. His hands were placed into warm fur mittens. He was ready to step outside. With Eleanor dressed the same, they approached the castle door. The blink who was standing guard stepped to one side to let Eleanor pass, but blocked Nicholas' exit. "I am the daughter to Queen Elvira," Eleanor said, "you will let up pass." The blink turned to look at Eleanor. She stared straight at her for a moment, unblinking as if studying her, then lowering her arm, she allowed Nicholas to leave.

Nicholas requested that they take a carriage ride into the village and Eleanor agreed. "It would make a nice change from walking," said Eleanor, "and then afterwards maybe we could take a ride out into the countryside." Upon entering the stables, they found the master of the carriages who was busily working away, grooming the horses. "We require a carriage to take us to the village," said Eleanor.

"Right away, princess, if you would just follow me." He led them to the rear of the stables. There were five carriages to choose from, three were open carriages with no roof, two were enclosed, all gleaming white, some more elaborately decorated than others. "If I may suggest one," said the master of the carriages, "this one is the best considering how cold it is outside." He had pointed to the plainest one of the five. It had a roof, but was uninspiring. Nicholas had his eyes fixed on the most elaborately decorated open carriage in the collection.

"May we take this one?" he asked, looking up at Eleanor.

She smiled and said, "That one it is."

"I will get some blankets," said the master of the carriages. When he returned, he hitched the four white horses into position and then helped Nicholas into the carriage. Eleanor climbed into the carriage besides Nicholas and sat down, but as she did so, a small brightly coloured object fell from the pocket of her fur coat. Nicholas retrieved the object from the seat as Eleanor stretched forward to gather the blankets the carriage master had placed on the seat opposite. Nicholas held the brightly coloured glass object and inspected it closely without saying a word. Eleanor having unfolded the blankets started to spread them out over both of their legs. "It will be cold when we get into the countryside," said Eleanor. As Nicholas did not respond, Eleanor looked up from what she was doing. Nicholas had tears in his eyes, and then Eleanor realised what he was looking at.

"How did you get that?" she asked angrily.

"It fell from your pocket when you climbed into the carriage," said Nicholas. "Is this Prince Pierre?" he asked.

Embarrassed to admit it but, "Yes, it is Prince Pierre," replied Eleanor.

"But why?" asked Nicholas.

"He was meant as my mother's birthday gift," said Eleanor, "but then he made me so happy," she said, "everything he believes to be true about his background, is what I told him when my enchantment was placed upon him."

As the carriage master took his seat and gathered up the reigns, "Ready," he called. Without waiting for an answer, he drove the horses from the castle courtyard out through the gates.

Eleanor turned to Nicholas and said, "I have no friends, I am as much a prisoner here as you." Nicholas was taken by complete surprise by Eleanor's revelation. When they had first met Eleanor had her own castle, she had appeared confident and totally capable of looking after herself, with her magic staff she carried everywhere, then it dawned on Nicholas, ever since he had been at Elvira's castle, he hadn't seen Eleanor with her magic staff, not once.

"Where is your magic staff?" asked Nicholas.

"Ah, my magic staff," said Eleanor with a sigh, "it was not mine, it belongs to Elvira," she said.

Realising for the first time how unhappy Eleanor really was, Nicholas asked, "Why do you stay?"

After a long pause, "She is my mother," said Eleanor.

"But you left before, you had your own castle and everything."

"Only because I was doing her bidding, for she cannot leave this frozen land, and she desperately wanted the crystal egg."

"Why did she so desperately want the crystal egg?" asked Nicholas.

"Because with the power of the crystal egg, she believes she would finally be able to leave this frozen land once and for all, and rule over this kingdom," said Eleanor.

As they drove away from the castle, the blink who had been standing guard at the front entrance relayed the vision of Eleanor and Nicholas leaving the castle to Elvira who was sleeping. She awoke suddenly. As she got out of bed in her white silk nightdress, she wrapped herself in a white shawl, then she called for the tall, thin man in the blood-red suit. As she waited impatiently, her anger grew and it started to snow.

"What is the meaning of this?" she demanded, as he entered the room. Without waiting for an answer. "Why did you allow Eleanor to take the boy and leave the castle?" she ranted.

"I tried to tell her it was not a good idea, Your Majesty," he said weakly. Elvira pushed him to one side and he fell to the floor. She gave him a look of disgust. Losing the shawl and grabbing a fur coat instead, she left him sprawled on the floor.

As the wind grew stronger and the falling snow increased, Eleanor realised that her mother must be aware of them leaving the castle. Eleanor asked the driver to hurry, for she knew Elvira would soon be following, but had no idea by what means. As the master of the carriage drove the horses faster, the carriage slid from side to side. Then the carriage nearly toppled over when going around a bend. Instinctively, Eleanor grabbed hold of Nicholas to save him from being thrown from the carriage. The master of the carriage slowed the horses down. "What are you doing?" cried Eleanor.

"We nearly crashed on that last bend," said the master of the carriage.

"I don't care," said Eleanor frantically, "we need to keep moving."

Eleanor's fears were soon realised. As the carriage master drove the horses forward, the snow became heavier, visibility became poor and the going became tougher. Looking ahead through the heavily falling snow, the carriage master could see a shadow blocking their way, but visibility was so poor he could not make out what it was. "Something is blocking our way," shouted the carriage master.

"What is it?" called Eleanor.

"Something is standing in the middle of the road," he said. Eleanor's heart sank. She knew before looking that it must be Elvira. The carriage came to a standstill. Eleanor disembarked the carriage and walked past the horses who seemed agitated. She went to check what was blocking the road. She had been right. Elvira sat upon the back of the blue dragon, completely blocking their path.

"Mother, what is wrong?" asked Eleanor, "we were only going to the village."

"No, one, is allowed, to leave the castle without my permission," said Elvira, "I thought I had made myself perfectly clear on that," she said.

"I'm sorry, mother, I did not realise that applied to me," said Eleanor.

"Go back to the castle and we will say no more about it," said Elvira. Eleanor turned and walked back to the carriage. She was fuming. Still her mother treated her like a child.

"One of these days," she said to herself, only when she got back to the carriage and started to climb on board did she get the shock of her life. Nicholas was not there. "Where is Nicholas?" Eleanor demanded frantically.

The master of the carriage replied, "What do you mean?" As he turned in his seat to look behind him, "Blimey," he said, "the last time I looked, he was sitting right there on that seat."

"Well, he isn't there now," said Eleanor. Elvira had moved closer towards the carriage still riding the blue dragon. The horses were becoming more nervous.

"What is the problem," she called, "why haven't you turned around?" The blue dragon towered above the horses who were becoming very restless indeed. The carriage master held tightly onto the reigns trying to keep the horses under control. The front two horses were rearing up and kicking their legs at the blue dragon, neighing wildly. The two horses behind tossing their heads wildly from side to side. The blue dragon remained silent, but with a hungry look in his eyes.

Eleanor made her way back to speak to her mother. "He's gone," she said.

"What do you mean, he's gone?" asked Elvira angrily.

"He is not in the carriage," said Eleanor.

Elvira screamed, "You idiot, how can you do this to me?"

The blue dragon took to the air instantly. One effortless beat of its wings and he was airborne, circling the carriage. The terrified horses pulled even harder against the reigns, as the carriage master struggled to gain control. On the ground, Eleanor called for Nicholas. As the blue dragon circled overhead, Elvira looked for footprints. She had created her own problem. As her rage increased, so did the falling snow. Visibility was hindered and no footprints could she see. Elvira screamed in frustration ever louder. The winds roared as the blizzard gained in strength.

Nicholas had managed to sneak out of the carriage while Eleanor and Elvira were talking. Little did they know that he had been nearby listening. There was a rack underneath the carriage seats for carrying luggage, loaded from the back. Nicholas had slid in and lay perfectly still as the carriage turned to head back towards the castle.

"I will continue my search for Nicholas," he heard Elvira shout, as the blue dragon hovered above the carriage, disturbing the snow-covered ground, the displaced snow mixed with the heavily falling snow creating perfect cover from prying eyes above. "You will return to the castle and stay there until I return, is that understood?" she said.

"But, mother," said Eleanor, "I can help."

"You have done enough," said Elvira. Under Elvira's command, the blue dragon turned in the air. As it ascended higher into the snow-filled sky, Nicholas peered out from under the carriage as it slowly made its way back to the castle. He watched as the dark figure in the sky disappeared into the snowstorm.

Nicholas knew there was a nearby wood and decided to slip out from under the carriage when it came into view. He didn't have to wait long. He pushed himself backwards from the rack and fell silently onto the soft, powdery snow. As the carriage moved on down the road, he quickly got to his feet and headed into woods. The pine trees heavily laden with snow were the perfect hiding place. Nicholas managed to duck below the branches of the tallest tree without disturbing any snow that lay on its lower branches. Hidden beneath the snow-covered tree, Nicholas was glad to have found shelter from the howling winds and persistent snow that had instantly covered his tracks.

Elvira continued to soar through the air on the back of the blue dragon. Far and wide, she searched, much further than a small child could have travelled in a short space of time, but her rage drove her on. Out across the frozen lakes, she flew high above a cabin, a cabin that contained Prince Oliver and Princess

Dorothy. Knowing full well that Nicholas could not have got that far, the cabin was overlooked. Elvira's rage increased with every passing minute, but eventually she had to give up the search, for even she was blinded by the heavily falling snow. She had returned to the castle. The blue dragon once more sat within the cabinet that contained the glass brooches. At Elvira's command, Eleanor had been bought to her chambers by two blinks. "Why did you do it?" Elvira asked, trying to control her temper, but judging by the snow falling outside the window, failing miserably.

"We just wanted some time away from the castle," said Eleanor.

"How stupid can you be?" asked Elvira. "Allowing yourself to be manipulated by a child." She was losing control of her anger once more. Eleanor knew she had to be careful of what she said next.

"I'm sorry, mother," said Eleanor. Elvira approached her daughter who had lowered her gaze towards the floor. Elvira placed her hand beneath Eleanor's chin and gently raised her head so they could look into each other's eyes. Only now did Eleanor see the madness within her mother's eyes. She quickly looked away, saddened by what she saw.

"Take her away," commanded Elvira, "she is to remain locked in her room until further notice."

"Mother please," begged Eleanor, as the two blinks took hold of Eleanor by the arms and escorted her from her mother's chambers. Elvira turned her back on her daughter and her pleas for forgiveness, as she continued to look out into the ever-strengthening blizzard. It was to be a cold, stormy night.

Chapter 25
Cressida Defeats Helga

Cressida riding Oberon was leading the way once more. In the distance, they could see their destination. A range of snow peaked mountains that stood proud against the pale-blue sky. "We have a few more days travel before we reach the mountain," said Cressida, "and we have yet to encounter the valley of swamps."

One of the younger centaurs asked Aegeus, "What is the valley swamps?"

"I have never heard of such a place," answered Aegeus.

Oberon having overheard the two centaurs talking explained, and with his booming voice, he announced, "The valley of swamps is like no other, also known as the swamps of lost souls. In places the swamp waters are but a few inches deep and easily crossed, but without warning, one wrong step and you can find yourself in deep water, being pulled below the surface, by the souls of those who have already perished."

"How do we follow a safe path?" asked one of the younger centaurs.

"I will lead the way," said Oberon, "just follow me, tread where I tread, but beware, if you hear someone calling for help, do not go looking for them. The lost souls of the swamps will cry out for help, but their true intent is to have you join them." The younger less experienced centaurs looked nervous.

"Do not be afraid," said Aegeus, "do as Oberon says and we will make it through the swamp."

"One last thing," said Oberon, "the tall grass indicates a safer route through the swamp, but be warned, there are hidden dangers that lurk amongst the tall grasses."

Feeling more nervous than before, the younger centaurs followed behind Oberon, with Aegeus bringing up the rear, vultures soared overhead, black specks against a pale sky. Oberon had spotted the vultures, along with Aegeus, both knew this was a sign of death. As one by one, the vultures descended from the sky and landed a hundred feet or so to the left of where they were walking, the remains of a large carcass was visible. Only a few scraps of flesh were left. The vultures squabbled among themselves, as they picked the skeleton clean.

Onwards they marched, headed towards the mountains in the distance, and the swamps, vigilantly looking for signs of ogres or any other danger. Rustling amongst some bushes to their right alerted them to a possible threat. The centaurs removed their bows and placed an arrow ready to shoot. As they stood facing the bushes, the sound of branches being snapped was unmistakeable. They watched the bushes with baited breath. Suddenly, five wild pigs snorting and squealing wildly came into view, running out of the bushes at speed as if their lives depended on it. Then appeared a large cat. On seeing the centaurs, the cat stopped. The wild pigs would have made for a tasty snack, but the centaurs would make for a meal. From past experience, Aegeus knew that this species of cat hunted alone. It began to circle the centaurs looking for the weakest. All the centaurs kept facing the large cat. By stalking the centaurs face on, the cat provided a small target. The centaurs were nervous, one fired an arrow and missed, the cat snarled. "Oh, enough of this," said Cressida, who rode the back of Oberon and had gone unnoticed by the cat for she was leading the way, she sent a fireball that engulfed the large cat, it fell to the ground where its roars of agonising pain filled the air, as it writhed where it had fallen, the pitiful whimpering sound it made reminded the centaurs of the sound that had been made by one of their own as it had been bludgeoned to death by the ogres.

They left the charred body of the cat behind them, as Oberon said, "We must leave this place immediately, the cries from the cat would have been heard throughout the valley, and the scent of burning flesh will be carried on the breeze." How right he was, the vultures were airborne, circling the skies once more, the scent of burning flesh carried along on a stiff breeze. The real concern was that it was blowing in the direction they were heading, this was not good, for the scent of the dead cat would lead any predator right into their path. "We need to move fast," said Oberon.

With Cressida riding high on the back of Oberon, they were the first line of defence against any attack they might run into. The problem was, as they raced across the valley, the vultures soaring in the sky had alerted a pack of wolves to a possible meal. With the scent of burnt flesh carried along on the stiff breeze travelling in the same direction, they were in a head on collision with a small pack of wolves.

Oberon and the centaurs were aware of the possible danger, but unaware they had been spotted, the pack of wolves approaching from the right were now giving chase. As the lead wolf raised his head and howled towards the sky, his howl travelled across the valley, calling for more wolves to join the hunt. Now the centaurs were aware they had been spotted. As the centaurs raced across the valley, Cressida looked back, she shot a fireball which exploded on hitting the ground. "There are too many of them," she said to Oberon.

The wolves, although not as fast as the centaurs, were beginning to lose ground, but they knew they had the stamina to keep chasing, and that eventually the centaurs would tire and slow, Oberon knew this also. Feeling relieved for they had outrun the pack of wolves, the centaurs continued to race ahead. Their relief, however, was short lived. Suddenly, more wolves appeared right in their path, having answered the call of the lead wolf. Oberon came to a halt.

Faced with a dozen wolves blocking their path, the centaurs stood surrounded, as the pack of eight which had given chase finally caught up. With their hungry eyes and bared teeth, the ferocious snarling wolves were in no rush, for they believed they had their prey trapped.

Standing tall, Oberon could see that a short distance beyond the wolves lay the swamps and relative safety. "I cannot kill them all at the same time," said Cressida, "there are too many."

"Leave it to me," said Oberon. "Close your eyes," he shouted, "and listen to my command, when I say run; run." Without question, the centaurs closed their eyes, Oberon started to hum, a deep resonating hum that filled the air. The wolves seemed to become more agitated by the sound, but did not attack. Suddenly, and unexpectedly, the giant antlers that sat upon Oberon's head shone brighter than the three suns in the sky. The wolves staggered, blinded by the light. "Now," shouted Oberon. He lowered his giant antlers which were no longer glowing and crashed a pathway between the wolves that stood in his way. having opened their eyes, the centaurs followed through the gap.

Within a matter of seconds, the wolves had recovered from being blinded by the light. Two lay dead where Oberon had battered his way through their ranks. The chase was on once more, but ahead, the landscape had changed dramatically. The centaurs and Oberon slowed to a walk. No trees stood before them, only pools of water with short grass at the edges, and taller grass that spread out before them. "Remember," said Oberon, "follow where I step, and take no notice of voices calling for help. They are the lost souls, and they will try and entice you to step into the swamp before pulling you below the surface to become one of them."

As Cressida rode on Oberon's back into the swamp of lost souls, the pack of wolves had finally caught up. The centaurs disturbed the surface of the water with each step. A muddy cloud rose to the surface along with a dark swarm of flies that took to the skies, and hovered above the surface. A stench of decaying flesh filled the air. Able to taste the smell of death that lingered on the air, the wolves stopped. They watched as the last of the centaurs entered the swamp, disappearing amongst the tall grass. They chose not to follow, a meal had escaped them, but they would live to hunt another day.

Just as Oberon had warned moments after they had stepped into the swamp, the voices calling, pleading for help had started. It was unnerving. At times, a single voice could be heard. The voice sounded like that of a child, crying for help, begging to be saved, even though they had been forewarned, they were not prepared for the cacophony of voices that suddenly erupted from the swamp. So many voices all calling, screaming to be saved, pleading, "Help us." It became deafening. The millions of tiny flies that had buzzed around their feet were now swarming around their heads, an added irritant. As Oberon stepped tentatively through the swamp, some of the younger centaurs had difficulty in concentrating. Oberon sensed the danger.

"Keep focussed," he called. Aegeus looked back over his shoulder to check on the rest of the centaurs. In doing so, he stumbled. Creating a tremendous splash, he crashed into the pool. A hand shot out of the water instantly. Ghostly white with skin peeling away revealing bare bone. It tried to grasp Aegeus by the neck. As the centaur struggled to break free, more hands broke the surface of the water, all grabbing at his body trying to pull him beneath the surface, he fought off one, only for two more to appear. Struggling as he did, Cressida dared not use magic for fear of hurting Aegeus in the process. Oberon lowered his head so that his antlers were within reach of Aegeus, who grabbed hold. Now began a tug of war. With legs flailing in the water, lost souls were kicked and dispatched by Aegeus, only to return within seconds, but those few seconds counted. Oberon with all his strength had pulled Aegeus close enough to solid ground for more centaurs to assist in pulling him clear of the water. Still more hands were thrust out of the dark, murky waters grabbing at hooved feet. The stench was almost unbearable. Now Cressida used her magic. With Aegeus safely back on solid ground, she created a whirlpool and as the waters swirled the lost souls, ghostly white, with decaying flesh hanging from their limbs were drawn beneath the surface of the swamp water. As their cries faded away, everything went quiet. The only sound was made by Aegeus, as he struggled for breath. "We must keep moving," said Oberon, looking at Aegeus, having returned to normal breathing.

"I am ready to continue," said Aegeus.

The tall grasses before Oberon split into two separate paths. A decision had to be made. Cressida said, "I will take a look." As she unfolded her wings, she ascended from the back of Oberon into the sky. She began searching for a safe passage. She flew above the grasses. The pathway to the left only went about eighty feet before it encountered a giant pool. To the right, the pathway continued.

"We need to go right," said Cressida. Resuming her place sat upon the back of Oberon, they took the path to the right. The tall grass thinned to a narrow strip with pools either side. As the cries of lost souls had resumed once more, the centaurs struggled not to be affected. Oberon walked on relentlessly, unaffected by the mournful, wailing voices. Cressida looked concerned, not for herself, but for her centaur escorts. She could sense they were becoming more and more distressed. Then, at frightening speed, a giant snake launched an attack from amongst the grass on one of the smaller centaurs near the rear of the group, wrapping its giant body around the centaur's neck. The centaur collapsed to the ground under the sheer weight of its attacker. It all happened so fast, the centaurs who had been following the victim had no warning of an attack and no time to react. Right in front of their eyes, the snaked coiled its giant body around the young centaur as he fought. Once again, Cressida found herself with the dilemma. If she used magic, she could kill the centaur along with the snake, but if she did nothing, the snake would definitely kill the centaur. The rest of the centaurs were powerless to assist. Cressida cast her spell and the snake burst into flame. She had taken too long to make the decision for fear of injuring the centaur. As the snake and centaur fell into the water, they were dragged beneath the water's surface, fighting for survival but without a hope. The younger centaurs in the group panicked, fleeing into the pool on the opposite side of the narrow strip. They found themselves in a cauldron of grasping hands. Fighting the urge to flee, the remaining centaurs watched from their narrow strip of solid ground. "There is nothing to be done to save them," said Oberon, "they have ventured too far into the pool and cannot be reached." Aegeus stood watching as one after the other, the centaurs were dragged into the depths of the swamp waters. Their cries of help mingled with those of the lost souls. Cressida could do nothing to help the centaurs either, for she knew anything she did would also affect the centaurs so intertwined were their bodies with their attackers.

As the last hooved foot disappeared below the surface and the waters stilled, Aegeus fighting to hold back the tears turned away from the pool. "Let us keep moving," Oberon called, "there is no time for tears." With Cressida sat upon the back of Oberon and leading the way, it was only fifty paces and they were finally free of the swamp. They had been so close. Now all emotions that had been held in check whilst in the swamp burst forth, like an erupting volcano. Each one of the centaurs cried openly, falling to their knees, the grief robbing them of the ability to stand. It was a pitiful sight for Cressida and Oberon to behold. They watched in silence. It was late in the afternoon for the three suns had already passed overhead and were beginning to merge signalling night fall was on its way.

"We should move away from the swamp," said Oberon, "the lost souls will call again throughout the night. We are not safe from their calls yet."

"I know," said Cressida. "Aegeus," she called, Aegeus left the younger centaurs he was comforting and walked over to where Oberon was standing.

"Your Majesty," he said, looking up at Cressida with a deep sadness in his eyes, "what can I do for you?" he asked.

"We need to move further away from the swamp before we are safe," said Cressida. Aegeus turned away from Cressida and called to the centaurs.

"We must leave this place now, for we are still close enough to be affected by the call of the lost souls." The older battle-weary centaurs had regained their composure, but some of the younger centaurs still needed assistance to stand. Slowly, one by one, they were helped onto their hooved feet.

"We are ready," said Aegeus. As they left the swamp behind, Aegeus thought to himself, it had been a costly journey. Having lost one of his centaur brothers early on to the ogres, and now one to the giant snake and four more to the lost souls, Aegeus was down to fourteen, having started out with twenty.

They moved swiftly away from the swamp as night was approaching fast. Only when Oberon and Cressida decided they were a safe distance from the swamp did they stop. "We will rest here tonight," said Cressida. Thankful of a chance to finally rest, the centaurs lay together. Cressida and Oberon lay a short distance away from the centaurs allowing them some privacy to grieve for their lost friends. Cressida used her magic to create an invisible barrier to protect them whilst they slept, but sleep did not come easy that night, for any of them. Although far enough away from the swamp not to be affected, the faint cries of the lost souls drifted over them like a gentle breeze.

The arrival of morning was heralded by the parting of the three suns. Once the last of the centaurs was awake, they were ready to move on. Oberon had the ability to pass through the invisible barrier put in place by Cressida. Having already observed the landscape, he returned. As he passed through the barrier, his body shone a brilliant silver, returning to its original white once clear of the magical protective barrier. The centaurs looked on in awe. To them, Oberon was a living god to be obeyed; they bowed as he approached. "The mountain you seek is here," said Oberon, "about half a day's walk."

"Good," said Cressida, "we leave immediately." She mounted the back of Oberon, and removed the barrier so it was safe to leave. As Oberon turned to lead the way, the centaurs did not move.

"We are not coming," said Aegeus, "we have lost too many of our brothers to assist you anymore." Showing no sympathy, Cressida laughed.

"You do not have a choice. You cannot make it through the swamp alone; come with me, or die, trapped here forever."

Aegeus had to restrain two of the younger centaurs, who were angry at being used by Cressida. "Why is it we do her bidding?" they asked. "The fawns live free, why can't we?"

"Because we are not fawns," said Aegeus. "One day, you will understand," he said. The two young centaurs calmed down under the glare from Oberon. Although angry, Aegeus was their leader and they trusted his words.

On this side of the swamp, the land was green with lush plants and trees everywhere, fed by mountain streams that flowed, but with the swamp acting as an unpassable barrier they would be trapped. Knowing Cressida spoke the truth, Aegeus and the remaining centaurs reluctantly followed Oberon, who had been right. By midday, they were at the foot of the mountain. They could see the three openings that looked like a mouth and two eyes. Oberon stopped unexpectedly.

"This is as far as I go," said Oberon. As Cressida went to speak, Oberon reminded her. "You called upon me to bring you to the one-eyed hag, this I have done," he said, and in a flash of brilliant white light, he was gone. Cressida found herself standing on the ground, feeling quite vulnerable. Without the giant, white stag, she herself was now stranded with the centaurs between the mountains and the swamp, for although she could fly, she could not cover the whole distance of the swamp in one attempt.

"Very well," said Cressida, turning to face Aegeus, "we no longer need his help anyway." She started to climb the mountain. The opening was not high above where they stood, and the climb was easy. Cressida told Aegeus to wait for her return. This puzzled Aegeus, but the rest of the centaurs were happy to let her visit the one-eyed hag alone. Cressida tentatively approached the entrance looking all around as she moved ever closer. She froze as a voice called from within.

"Who are you, and what do you want?"

"My name is Cressida, and I come seeking my brother, Dante."

"Ah, so the fairy princess herself has come for her brother. I had not expected that," said Helga, "step into my home," she said. As Cressida entered into Helga's cave, she produced a magical mirror and held it in front of her face. This allowed Cressida to see where she was going but would not allow Helga to look into her eyes.

"I see you have come prepared," said Helga, upon seeing her reflection in the mirror. "Clever girl," she said, as she turned away.

"I know my magic cannot harm you, but I know how to protect myself," said Cressida.

"Indeed," said Helga, "so you have come to rescue your brother, but if I release him, what do I get in return?" she asked.

"I have fourteen centaurs with me to trade for my brother," said Cressida.

"Fourteen centaurs," said Helga, gleefully, without hesitation, "done," she said. "But how do we make the trade?" asked Helga.

"I will return and tell the centaurs that I have killed you and need their help in searching for Dante. Once the centaurs are trapped, you release Dante to me, and allow us to use your well to return home."

"Agreed," said Helga.

So, overjoyed with the thought of fourteen centaurs to torment, Helga had not picked up on the deception. Cressida made her way back down to where Aegeus and the centaurs were waiting. She told Aegeus of her plan. "Helga is expecting fourteen centaurs, once they are trapped, she will release Dante," said Cressida.

"But there are fifteen of us," said Aegeus.

"But Helga does not know that," said Cressida, "my magic cannot harm her, but a single arrow into the eye and she will have no power to torment anyone ever again."

It took some convincing to get the fourteen centaurs to agree to enter Helga's cave, but in the end, they were persuaded to do so with the promise of safe passage home. It was Aegeus who would remain hidden from Helga when the fourteen centaurs entered the cave. It was his responsibility to shoot the arrow, to blind the eye, and so led by Cressida using her mirror for protection, the fourteen centaurs entered the cave. Helga greeted them eagerly, but it was Cressida who cast the spell to capture them. As promised, Helga released Dante. He had been chained to a wall hidden in the shadows. The sound of the chains falling to the ground echoed off the cave walls and was followed by a hushed silence. Then as she listened, a faint sound like something being dragged across the floor could be heard. "You will find your brother much changed," said Helga, with an unbridled joy to her voice. As Dante appeared out of the shadows, crawling towards Cressida, whimpering, unable to stand, with sores on his wrists, the hatred Cressida felt for Helga was immeasurable. At the precise moment, Cressida knelt down to help her brother. An arrow fired by one of the captive centaurs flew towards Helga. She caught it in her hand inches from her eye. "Did you really think it was that easy to deceive me?" she asked. Then as she laughed, a second arrow fired by Aegeus pierced the eye. Helga stumbled backwards, as she screamed in agony.

"No, I didn't expect it to be that easy," said Cressida.

"What shall we do with her?" asked Aegeus.

"Kill her, kill her," chanted the centaurs.

"No," said Cressida, "killing her would be too merciful. It is her time now to suffer as others have suffered at her hands."

Helga screamed, "Show mercy, please I beg of you."

"Why should I show you any mercy," asked Cressida, "when have you shown mercy to anyone who pleaded their innocence?" With the loss of her eye, all Helga's powers were gone. She would never again be able to cause anyone to suffer.

Cressida removed her spell which had held the centaurs captive. Then she helped her brother Dante to his feet. She could not imagine what torment Helga had put him through. His face was blank and expressionless, but the fear showed in his eyes as they darted back and forth between Cressida and the gathering centaurs. Aegeus approached Cressida, and Dante pulled to get away. Aegeus stopped. All the centaurs watched on silently, as Cressida spoke softly to her brother. He eventually stopped struggling to get away and calmed down.

"We need to find the well," said Cressida, "it is our only way of getting home from this place." As the centaurs paired off to search the cave and its many tunnels, Dante struggling under the effort slowly lifted his left arm and pointed. Nobody at first noticed. Only when Dante tried to speak did anyone finally take notice of him.

"Look," said one of the centaurs. Cressida who had been speaking with Aegeus turned to look at her brother.

"This way," she called. Aegeus went first down the tunnel indicated by Dante, followed by the rest of the centaurs. It was only a short tunnel that opened into another cave. Sat in the middle of the cave was a large stone well. Having searched the cave for any hidden dangers, they called Cressida. She duly arrived supporting Dante. "We need to repeat where we want to go and then jump into the well as the waters swirl," said Cressida, "I will go first with Dante." And so Cressida climbed onto the wall of the well and repeated, "The crystal palace, the crystal palace." The waters began to swirl as she knew they would and taking a leap of faith, holding both of Dante's hands, she jumped into the well taking her brother with her. It didn't feel like jumping into water however for it was not wet, but it was a strange sensation of falling through the air. They were in total darkness, spinning, a faint light appeared beneath them, when suddenly there was a flash of bright light and they came to a halt. As their eyes got used to being in the light once more, Cressida could see they were back where they wanted to be, standing inside the great hall of the crystal palace.

Dante's legs buckled and he fell to the floor. Cressida knelt beside him, no longer interested in what Percival was up to, her only concern was in looking after her brother. Fairies that had at first fled the room when Cressida and Dante reappeared in a flash of light, now came flooding back as they realised who had entered the palace. Helping Cressida to get Dante back to his feet, the fairies were shocked to see the terrified look on Dante's face. He raised his hands and cowered away, only allowing Cressida's touch.

Back at the well, the centaurs were in discussion. "Why should we return to the crystal palace?" asked one of the younger centaurs. "Why can't we take this opportunity to escape into the rainbow forest?"

"Because there is no escape," said Aegeus.

Three of the younger centaurs disagreed, and said, "We are not going back to the crystal palace."

"And I cannot make you," said Aegeus, "but I would advise against it," he said. As he repeated the words, the crystal palace, over and over, Aegeus and all but the three young centaurs jumped into the well. One after the other, soon to reappear in the great hall where Cressida and Dante had returned. The remaining three young centaurs climbed onto the wall surrounding the well. Instead of chanting the crystal palace, they chanted, the rainbow forest, repeatedly, as before the water began to swirl, then one after the other they jumped into the swirling water and were transported off to their new destination.

Chapter 26
Lizard Licks and Lovebird Eyes

Saki had informed Oliver and Dorothy that Percival would be ready to travel within a couple of days' time. They were anxious to continue their journey as soon as possible, but knew they could not find Nicholas without Percival's help. Both had questions they wanted to ask Saki about their magical powers, and if she knew how to use them, but Saki denied any knowledge of such things. They were not sure that they believed her, but they were not about to call her a liar. After all, her cabin had provided the shelter and warmth they had needed to survive, and she was Percival's mother.

The day was bright with no wind. Oliver and Reif stepped out into the cold, crisp air. Although the sun was shining, it provided little warmth; it was absolutely freezing. They quickly ducked back into the cabin. "I don't suppose you have anything to wear for going outside?" Oliver asked Saki.

"Yes, of course," she said, "in that cupboard over there." Oliver looked behind him. Standing in the corner indicated by Saki was a tall cupboard made out of dark wood.

"I don't remember seeing this before," Oliver said to Reif.

"That's because it wasn't here before," said Reif, "I should know, that is where I slept last night, up against that wall."

They approached the cupboard with its double doors and each taking hold of a handle slowly pulled the doors open. Inside was nothing but selection of fur coats. They looked at each other in amazement. "There are enough for all of you," called Saki, as she tended Percival. "Any one will fit," she said. They both reached forward and chose a dark fur coat. Saki was right. Although Oliver and Reif were a different build, the coat that each of them had selected fit them perfectly.

As Oliver and Reif walked towards the door now dressed for the cold weather that awaited them outside, Dorothy called, "Wait for me." She quickly dashed across the room and chose a light-grey fur coat. It had a high collar and a matching fur hat. Having put on the fur coat, Dorothy followed after Oliver and Reif who had stepped outside. Their breath revealed how cold it was, billowing out of their mouths, like steam from a pot of boiling water. Dorothy placed the fur hat upon her head and pulled it down over her ears.

As they stood looking out over the snowy landscape, a large shadow appeared on the ground, but Oliver and Reif hadn't noticed because their attention was taken by movement just beyond the nearest tree. Dorothy however looked towards the sky. "Look," she shouted, "it's the white eagle again." Whatever it was, lurking beside the tree, as soon as Dorothy spoke, it made a hasty retreat. Now all three of them watched as the white eagle soared overhead and disappeared into the distance. "I know that's the eagle that took Nicholas," said Dorothy.

"What makes you say that?" asked Oliver.

"I don't know," said Dorothy, "it's just a feeling I have."

At that moment, Saki opened the door. "Percival is awake," she said. As Dorothy and Reif stepped back inside the cabin, Oliver took one last glance towards the trees. "It would have run off when hearing Dorothy's voice," said Saki.

"What would?" asked Oliver.

"The yeti," said Saki.

Not only was Percival awake but he was sitting up. Berwyn lay next to Percival with his large head resting on Percival's knee. "How are you feeling?" asked Dorothy.

"Warm," said Percival, as he caressed the top of Berwyn's head. Having removed his fur coat, Oliver sat next to Dorothy.

"You had us scared there for a while," said Oliver, seated opposite Percival. He smiled broadly at his friend. Cupped in his hands, Percival held a large mug of homemade soup.

"How is everyone?" asked Percival. The smile left Oliver's face instantly.

"We have lost five, one of them was Robert," said Oliver.

"I am sorry to hear that," said Percival. After having taken another sip from his mug of soup, Percival said, "So you have met my mother, what has she told you?"

"She hasn't told us anything," said Dorothy.

As Percival continued to sip his mug of soup, Dorothy glanced furtively in Saki's direction, who seemed not to have noticed the slight tone of annoyance in Dorothy's voice. "Let me explain," said Percival, "my mother can see the future and remembers all of the past."

"So, if she can see the future, she can help us find Nicholas?" asked Oliver, getting excited.

"I have not finished," said Percival.

"Sorry," replied Oliver.

"Although my mother can see the future, she cannot tell you what the future brings."

"Why not?" asked Dorothy.

"Because as soon as I tell the future, it would change," said Saki, "and I would be of no use to anyone."

"So, can you tell us of the past?" asked Dorothy.

"What would you like to know?" asked Saki. Dorothy looked at Oliver, not sure what his reaction might be to the question she had in mind.

"Can you tell us about our mother?" asked Dorothy.

"Why would you ask that?" said Oliver.

"I would like to know more about where she came from," said Dorothy.

Saki sat down on a seat next to Percival. Looking directly at Dorothy and Oliver, she asked, "What do you know of your mother's past?"

Dorothy answered, "We don't know anything about our mother's life before she married our father." Dorothy then looked over at Oliver. He was watching Saki with a puzzled expression on his face. Dorothy suddenly felt rather perplexed herself, as she waited for Saki to reply.

"Your mother's past has everything to do with your ability to do magic," said Saki.

Dorothy took hold of Oliver's hand as they looked at each other again. Both now shared an expression of utter bewilderment, not knowing what to say next. They sat staring at each other. Oliver finally turned back to Saki and asked, "Please, tell us all you can about our mother."

"I will," said Saki, "but you are in for a surprise." Dorothy's grip on Oliver's hand tightened. Percival seated alongside his mother gave them both a reassuring smile, as Berwyn stretched full length across the floor, causing Reif and Joshua to quickly move out of the way or risk getting squashed against the wall.

Without any warning or pretence, Saki said to Dorothy and Oliver, "Your mother Elizabeth was born into this magical kingdom, and she has a sister."

"Now wait a minute," said Oliver, interrupting Saki, "sorry, you said our mother was born here, in this kingdom."

"That is correct," said Saki.

"And that she has a sister," said Dorothy. For the third time in quick succession, Dorothy and Oliver exchanged glances. "This can't be true, can it?" Dorothy asked of her brother.

"I assure you it is quite true," said Saki, "but if you prefer, I will not say another word."

"No sorry, please go on," said Dorothy, and so, Saki continued with her tale about two sisters born to magical parents who reigned over a frozen kingdom. She told them of how the two princesses were completely different in their attitude towards magic. Whilst the one called Elvira who was the eldest would frequently use magic to inflict pain on other's for her own enjoyment, the younger sister called Elizabeth, only ever used her magic to help anyone in real need.

Dorothy swelled with pride knowing that her mother had only used magic to help others. Oliver sat watching and listening to Saki without saying a word. As they both listened to Saki talk about their mother, as a young girl it saddened Dorothy as she realised how little they knew of her. Silent tears streamed down Dorothy's face, as Saki continued. Until now, she hadn't realised how much she missed her mother. Taking a glance sideways to look at her brother, Oliver, Dorothy was surprised to see that he was also crying. She gently squeezed his hand, but Oliver's gaze was fixed on Saki. He sat motionless. Only when Saki reached the end of Elizabeth's life story and the birth of Nicholas did Oliver move. He quickly got to his feet, releasing Dorothy's hand. He made his way to the cabin door and opened it. The freezing cold air that greeted him as he stepped outside and quickly shut the door behind him was a welcome relief. The numbness of the cold seemed to freeze his thoughts and aid him in bringing his emotions under control.

When Oliver eventually stepped back inside, he asked Saki, "If she had magic, why didn't she save herself?"

"Because Elizabeth had already renounced her magic," said Saki.

"But why would she do that?" asked Oliver.

"Let me explain," said Saki, "please come and sit down." Oliver resumed his seat next to Dorothy, who reached out her hand but he did not take it.

"There are good witches and wizards and there are bad witches and wizards," said Saki, "sometimes a good witch can be forced into using magic in a way they wouldn't normally."

"What do you mean?" asked Dorothy.

"It has been known for a good witch to be forced into performing magic for the gain of another."

"But how?" asked Oliver.

"Usually if there is a loved one who is being threatened," said Saki, "your mother renouncing her magic meant that she could never be controlled in that way by her sister." Dorothy looked at Oliver who was staring at Saki. She could imagine all sorts of thoughts racing around in his head for that was exactly how she felt.

When Oliver spoke, he asked, "What happened to Elizabeth's sister?"

"Queen Elvira is still very much alive," said Saki, "having taken over the reign of the frozen kingdom when her parents' died, she is also known as THE WINTER QUEEN."

It was Dorothy's turn to stand up and walk away. She went and stood by a window. Oliver went to follow but Percival stopped him and said, "Let me have a word with your sister." And so, Oliver sat down once more and watched as Percival crossed the room and stood besides Dorothy. "It's beautiful, isn't it?" said Percival. Dorothy continued to stare out of the window at the snow-covered wilderness, without acknowledging his presence, but Percival was right, snow always delivered a majestic beauty quite unlike anything else, but she did not care how beautiful it looked. Her mind was reeling from the revelation Saki had just imparted.

Without looking at Percival, as she struggled to keep her emotion's under control, Dorothy quietly asked, "Are all my brothers and sisters capable of performing magic?"

"I would assume so," said Percival calmly, "although your mother renounced her magic, it did not stop her gift being passed on to you, her children." As Dorothy kept her eyes averted from Percival's gaze, he knew she was in turmoil, struggling to comprehend everything that had happened.

"It's snowing," said Dorothy, in an emotionless voice which caught Percival by surprise. He had expected there to be more questions.

It seemed that within the blink of an eye, the gentle snow that had begun to fall had turned into a raging storm. The wind had picked up and the snow-covered trees that had appeared so stately before now swayed violently against the battering gale force winds. The cabin itself seemed to quake as Dorothy continued to stand at the window. All thoughts of magic pushed to the back of her mind. Oliver had joined his sister by the window. As he placed an arm around her shoulders, he tried to turn her away from the storm outside, but she would not move. "I wonder what Nicholas is doing right now?" she asked.

Unbeknown to those inside the cabin, the blizzard that raged outside was the same storm caused by Elvira whose anger continued to grow having lost Nicholas. The giant white eagle that Dorothy had spotted earlier had been sent by Elvira to search for Nicholas, it had since returned to its mistress' side, with no sighting of Nicholas, and so her anger continued to grow.

Within twenty minutes of it starting to snow, two inches of snow had fallen. Dorothy and Oliver stood silently watching as it piled up outside the window. Then, as if in slow motion, they stood rooted to the spot, as a large, dark shadow appeared to be heading their way. Unable to make out what it was because of the heavily falling snow, they stood motionless. Then thud, and they both screamed, their whole dwelling shook as a large branch stripped away from its trunk had collided into the side of their cabin, everyone inside jumped with fright, everyone except for Percival, Saki and Berwyn, who was fast asleep. "Do not worry," said Saki, "the cabin will hold."

As the storm raged on relentlessly, the sky darkened signalling nightfall. Now only the light from within the cabin lit up the snowflakes that were hurled against the window by the strong winds. Eventually, Dorothy and Oliver moved away from the window. As she looked around the cabin, it was as if she was seeing it properly for the first time. The walls of the cabin were covered in shelves and upon these shelves sat glass jars.

"What are these?" she asked, pointing to the many jars.

"Potions and poisons, my dear," said Saki, as Dorothy reached up to remove one of the glass jars. "Be careful of that one," said Saki, "it's poisonous." Wanting to know more, Dorothy carefully lifted the jar from the shelf. The label on the jar read, LIZARD LICKS—POISONOUS. Inside the jar was a dark liquid revealing nothing. Dorothy placed the jar on the table and looked into it. The only thing she could see was her own reflection, staring back at her. Thinking the jar empty apart from the liquid, Dorothy went to put the jar back on the shelf.

Only then did a tongue suddenly appear on the inside of the glass and start licking at the point where Dorothy's fingers were wrapped around the jar. She screamed and stumbled backwards falling to the floor. She inadvertently knocked the jar over and it was spinning in the centre of the table. The impact of the jar falling over had caused the lid to fall off. As the jar spun, it sprayed its contents across the surface of the table. Amongst the thick, black liquid, two tongues were slopping about. Saki moved swiftly for the first time in ages defying her ageing limbs. She retrieved a set of wooden tongs and picked up the two tongues. "There were three," she shouted, "where is the third?" As panic ensued all around her, Dorothy sat motionless on the floor. She dared not move, and found herself unable to speak. Beads of sweat had appeared on her forehead. Her breathing was fast and shallow. The missing tongue had landed on Dorothy's jacket and was inching its way up her sleeve like a giant slug. As everyone else was frantically searching for the missing tongue, it was Percival who noticed Dorothy stationary on the floor. Try as she might to stay still, she had begun to tremble. Unblinking eyes stared as the tongue moved towards her shoulder, as the mayhem continued around her.

"Mother, quick, it's on Dorothy's sleeve," shouted Percival. Oliver made a move to retrieve the slimy looking tongue from Dorothy's jacket.

"No, don't touch it," shrieked Saki, "its poisonous." Oliver stopped in his tracks, with his outstretched right hand just inches from the tongue. A look of horror on his face as Dorothy continued to shake uncontrollably. Saki calmly but swiftly crossed to where Dorothy was sprawled on the floor. All eyes were now on Dorothy and the poisonous tongue. All sound seemed to have ceased and the silence was deafening. With tongs in hand, Saki gently picked the tongue from Dorothy's sleeve and placed it back into the jar. Only then did Dorothy let out a huge sigh of relief as tears streamed down her face. Using a magic sponge, Saki mopped the trail of saliva from Dorothy's sleeve. Then she turned her attention to the black liquid spread across table. Mopping it up using the same sponge, once the table was clear, Saki then squeezed the sponge to remove the liquid and let it drip, into the jar once more.

Oliver and Reif bent down and helped Dorothy back to her feet. "Are you all right?" asked Oliver.

"Yes, I'm fine," lied Dorothy still feeling shaken. She approached Saki who was at the table snapping the lid back into place. Dorothy asked, "Why is it called LIZARD LICKS?"

"I would have thought that obvious," said Saki, as the tongues continued to lick at the exact spot where Dorothy's finger prints showed on the glass. "It's called lizard licks because as you can see that is what is does, one lick from that tongue and you would have died the most excruciating of deaths," said Saki.

"So why do you have it then?" asked Dorothy.

"You never know when it might come in handy," said Saki, with a wicked grin, "besides, remove a small amount of saliva from the tongue and it counteracts against any known poison."

"Oh," said Dorothy feeling relieved, and slightly disgusted, at the same time.

Oliver tried to persuade Dorothy to leave the jars on the shelf and come away, but Dorothy insisted she was fine. Her curiosity aroused, she left the jar of lizard licks poison on the table and moved along the shelf reading more of the labels. The next one that caught her eye read, LOVEBIRD EYES. "What is this one?" Dorothy asked.

Saki who had placed the LIZARD LICKS—POISON jar back on the shelf out of harm's way was standing right besides Dorothy and said, "You can lift that one down it is quite safe." And so, Dorothy lifted the LOVEBIRD EYES jar from the shelf. As she did, so a pair of eyes blinked at her from within the jar. She quickly placed the jar on the table and stepped back startled. "It's quite all right," said Saki, "this one isn't poisonous."

As Dorothy moved closed to the table once more, she bent down to have a closer look. The pair of eyes that sat within the clear liquid were a pale blue, and Dorothy felt as though they were watching her every move, studying her. Whilst Dorothy's attention had been taken by the pair of eyes, Saki had removed from the shelf an empty glass bowl and filled it with water. As she placed the bowl onto the table next to the jar containing the LOVEBIRD EYES, Dorothy asked, "What are these for?"

"Remove the eyes from the jar and place your lips against them," instructed Saki, Dorothy looked at Saki horrified, "I'm not going to put my hand in there and pick up a pair of eyes."

"oh well," said Saki, "if you don't want to see your one true love, we will just put them back on the shelf."

"Wait a minute," said Dorothy, as Saki reached up to place the LOVEBIRD EYES back on the shelf, "what do they do, these eyes?" asked Dorothy.

"Place your lips against the eyes and float them in the bowl of water," said Saki, "then they will reveal the identity of your one true love. At the exact moment, you realise they are the love of your life, of course if you'd rather not know." Dorothy was tempted. Tentatively, she reached forward and placed her hand into the jar containing the LOVEBIRD EYES. The eyes closed as Dorothy placed her fingers around them and gently lifted them from the jar. Closing her own eyes, Dorothy then placed the LOVEBIRD EYES against her lips for a second. For some reason, she had expected them to be slimy to touch, but they were not. Opening her eyes, Dorothy reached forward. As she placed the LOVEBIRD EYES into the glass bowl of water where they opened once more, Dorothy and Saki sat watching. The water in the bowl slowly became misty and as Dorothy waited patiently, a figure began to form. Transfixed by what was happening in the bowl, Dorothy was unaware that Reif and Oliver were now standing right behind her looking over her shoulder. Then as the misty water cleared, a man covered head to toe in mud stood before Dorothy.

"But who is it?" she asked Saki.

"I cannot tell," said Saki, "but at this particular moment in time, you will realise this man is your one true love." Disappointed, Dorothy turned away from the bowl, only to come face to face with her brother Oliver and Reif who were both grinning and laughing at her.

"So, who is your one true love?" teased Oliver. Feeling embarrassed, Dorothy pushed passed them both and bade them goodnight. As she closed the door to the bedroom she shared with Saki, she could see Oliver laughing. As Reif stood by his side looking embarrassed.

The one candle that was alight in the room allowed Dorothy to see what she was doing. She turned down the blankets on her bed and got undressed. As she climbed into bed and pulled the covers up around her neck, she forgot about Oliver and his teasing. She laid staring up at the candle lit ceiling as the flame flickered and danced, which allowed her thoughts to wander, eventually drifting off to sleep, to dream of her one true love. All thoughts of the raging storm outside, and Oliver's teasing, having long been forgotten.

Chapter 27
Silver Wings

As night had fallen on the cabin where Oliver and Dorothy were asleep, the blizzard winds raged on. So the night had darkened for Nicholas also. Cocooned from the blizzard under the heavy, snow-laden branches of the pine tree he sat. Wrapped in his fur coat, he was comfortably warm. He had thought of seeking shelter elsewhere, but as the storm had shown no sign of abating, he had decided to stay where he was and hope the weather had improved by morning. Feeling drowsy, he sat with his back resting against the rough bark of the tree trunk. Tired, his head fell forward, the sudden jolt awoke Nicholas with a start. For a brief second, he forgot where he was. Then the realisation dawned on him once more. Sat beneath the pine tree, grateful for the fur coat for he was lovely and warm, he closed his eyes once more in an attempt to sleep, when a faint rustling noise from above made Nicholas open his eyes again. As he sat in the dark, he wondered what could be causing this noise, for he could see nothing. As he listened, a soft buzzing noise permeated the blackness. He continued to listen without making a sound. Yes he thought, the soft buzzing was definitely getting louder. Then he felt the air brush against the side of his face. Was that a breeze or was it something else disturbing the air? As he tried to imagine what might have caused the sudden airflow, it increased tenfold. The only thing that Nicholas could think of was a flock of tiny birds as their wings beat, but surely, that was not possible.

Sitting silently in the dark, Nicholas could just about make out a dark mass against the white snow as the tiny birds flew below the lowest branches out into the storm. He sat worried for their safety. How could they possibly survive in those blizzard conditions. He didn't have to worry long, for as quickly as they departed, they returned. Only this time, they didn't seek refuge in the tree above Nicholas. The first one to return dropped into Nicholas' lap and he could feel it crawling up his coat. Its tiny feet gripping at the fur, then a second, third, fourth and so on. Each one landing in his lap and then crawling up his coat, right up to the collar, where they stopped. They made a soft buzzing sound as they settled down. It wasn't long before Nicholas felt his body completely covered by this strange, little bird, and as the storm continued to rage outside, Nicholas felt warmer than ever, and slowly as the soft buzzing sound set an even rhythm, he drifted off to sleep.

At the white castle, Eleanor could not sleep, held captive by her own mother, she could not rest for fear of what had happened to Nicholas. How could he possibly survive the night outside on his own. A knock at the door, and as the door opened, Elvira entered. She looked older than she had done in a long time. She marched across the room to stand face to face with Eleanor. She could see her daughter had been crying. Eleanor straightened up defiantly expectant of another argument.

"Why did you leave the castle with Nicholas?" asked Elvira. Taken aback by the softness in her mother's voice Eleanor answered rather more abruptly than she meant to.

"We just wanted to visit the village and go for a ride in the country," said Eleanor, who immediately regretted the harshness of her tone. Elvira had turned away from her daughter and went to leave the room. "I'm sorry," called Eleanor. Elvira stopped, without turning to face her daughter.

"So am I," she said. As she swept from the room, the door shut behind Elvira and the locks clicked in place.

When Nicholas awoke the next morning and before his eyes had fully adjusted to the dim light that was penetrating from beneath the lowest branches, he realised that the gale force winds from the day before had ceased. The only sound was the soft rhythmic buzzing that radiated from all over his body, then he remembered the tiny birds that had settled on his coat. Wanting to investigate what was happening with the weather, Nicholas tried to move. Only now did he fully appreciate how many tiny birds must have settled onto his coat, for he was unable to move under their combined weight. Unable to free himself, he started to think of how he could get the birds to move. He felt guilty about disturbing them from their sleep, but he needed to go to the toilet. First of all, Nicholas tried humming as he didn't want to startle them, but all this did was cause a few to shift around. One of them on his collar brushed up against his cheek, as it repositioned itself. Funnily, it felt different from what Nicholas had expected. It didn't feel like feathers at all. It felt more like velvet.

Nicholas then tried to move his legs and found he could sway them side to side. This had the desired effect, as slowly one by one, the small birds left the warmth of Nicholas' coat and flew up into the branches above. One actually crawled over Nicholas' face, only then did he realise that it was not a bird at all but in fact a tiny bat. As Nicholas looked into its black eyes, he could see his own reflection looking back, with wings as soft as velvet that shone silver in the dim light. Nicholas smiled to himself. The tiny bat continued to crawl over Nicholas' face and then fly off into the branches overhead.

As he felt the last of the bats leave his coat, Nicholas moved towards the lowest branches in search of the opening they had used the night before. Only now, there was no opening, just a wall of white snow. The dim light that enabled Nicholas to see, was seeping, in from above. He started to use his hands to dig his way out, but it was cold and it wasn't long before his fingers started to go numb and he had to stop. He put his hands in his pockets and found his gloves. Once his hands were inside his gloves, they started to warm. The tips of his fingers tingled as life came back into his hands.

With his hands warm inside his gloves, Nicholas began to dig away at the snow, which had compacted into a wall of ice. It was tiring work and Nicholas seemed to be making little progress. Exhausted, he sat with his back against the tree trunk to rest. Trying to think of how he could get out of this mess he had found himself in, he wondered if he could climb the tree and find an opening above. As he looked up in the dim light at the branches overhead, he dismissed the idea straight away. The branches were so close together and intertwined, he could not see how it would be possible for himself to climb his way out.

Leaning back against the tree and closing his eyes, Nicholas knew the bats had gone to rest. Thinking to himself, *I wish you could show me a way out*. Almost straight away, the tiny bats started to drop down from the branches overhead. Nicholas was startled by their sudden reappearance. As they rained down upon him, he watched not knowing what they were up to. They began to join together and formed a ball. As he watched silently, interested to see what they were getting up to, the ball of tiny bats then began to spin. Into the wall of ice, they moved, the exact spot where Nicholas himself had started to dig. As Nicholas watched in amazement, they began to create a tunnel into the snow. He sat back and watched in awe as they slowly made progress. Then as they disappeared from sight, Nicholas moved forward. He poked his head into the tunnel to see where they were and the tunnel rose upwards at a slow incline, but there was no sign of the bats. He decided to climb into the tunnel after them. It was just the right size for him to fit comfortably, and as he crawled along the tunnel, bright light suddenly burst through. *They must have made it out,* he thought to himself. This gave him renewed purpose and he crawled faster towards the light. As he clambered out of the hole, he realised just how much snow had fallen overnight. The tall tree that he had hidden beneath was half buried under snow. Some of the smaller trees had been completely buried. Whilst others had just the very top branches showing. The blizzard had stopped and just a few snowflakes were gently falling from the sky, the tiny silver wing bats were nowhere to be seen. Even though he was alone, he looked around for a more secluded spot. There were a couple of tall trees growing side-by-side. Nicholas hurried behind them so that he could pee.

Now he was on his own, he had to decide what he was going to do. It was an easy choice. He would head into the village. He knew it was early morning for the three suns had only just separated, and the rumbling in his stomach was telling him it was time for something to eat. He wasn't wearing his special shoes that allowed him to walk on the surface of the snow without sinking, and so each step he took, he sank knee deep which soon became exhausting. He stopped and sat on a treetop branch, to catch his breath. Nicholas' stomach was growing impatient for food and he was beginning to feel sick with hunger. He tore himself away from the treetop and headed hopefully in the direction that led towards the village.

The problem Nicholas found himself faced with was, after all the snow that had fallen overnight, everything looked completely different from before. As Nicholas trudged along with his feet sinking deep into the snow, he finally spotted rooftops in the distance. This gave him strength to carry on, but as he approached the buildings, it was disturbing to see, like the trees the houses were half buried beneath the snow.

At first sight of the half-buried village, Nicholas was worried. *Could anybody survive in such extreme conditions,* he thought, then Nicholas was taken by surprise. A tall upstairs window that sat just above the snow line swung open like a door in the house nearest to where he had stopped, and out stepped two people. They didn't seem distressed in anyway by the amount of snow that had engulfed their home, and once they had closed the window behind them, they headed off down the street.

Nicholas followed. Apart from the two people he was shadowing, he saw no one else. He thought of calling out for help as he passed between the houses hoping someone would hear and offer him something to eat, but he quickly put that thought out of his mind. Knowing that once he did that, Elvira would be informed of his whereabouts. He continued to walk down the snow-covered street. He could see the barn in the distance. He pulled the collar of his fur coat tight around his neck for the early morning air had a definite chill. It was eerily silent. Nicholas could not shake off a strange sensation he felt walking between the houses level with the upstairs windows. Some houses had their curtains open and as Nicholas walked past, he could see the occupants were still tucked up in bed.

The two people Nicholas had been following had reached the front of the barn. The doors completely buried beneath the snow. He watched as they approached the end of the barn and disappeared around the corner. He followed and tentatively looked around the corner, not wanting to be seen. As he watched from the corner, he could see the two people had reached a doorway set above the snowline, which they opened and then entered through. As the door closed, Nicholas made his way along the side of the barn. He was surprised to see when he reached the door that beyond was another door set even higher in the side of the barn, and beyond that, yet another door higher still. He then realised that they were obviously used to this level of snow, and were prepared if it became deeper yet.

When he finally pulled the barn door open, the smell of freshly baked bread escaped through the opening. It drifted its way to Nicholas' nostrils. The hunger in his stomach yearned for food. Nicholas' heart beat faster with excitement. He quickly ducked inside, pulling the door shut behind him once more. He found himself on a walkway high above the shops below. All of the barn was in darkness, but for one gleaming light coming from the bakery. His eyes adjusted to the level of light and he made his way along the walkway and down a set of stairs. With no one in sight, Nicholas made his way through the shadowed atmosphere, lured by the smell of freshly baked bread. Arriving at the shop, he peered through the window at the fabulous display of cakes and breads on show. His hunger seemed to grow stronger with every whiff of freshly baked bread that his nostrils drew in. With no one in the shop itself, he tried the door. It opened.

Luckily, for Nicholas, there was no bell on the door like there was on the glass shop, and he stealthily stepped inside. Once inside, he could hear at least three different voices coming from the back of the shop where the bread and cakes were baked.

Nicholas approached the glass covered counter to take a closer look. Most of the cakes on display were big enough for one person, some were round, some were square and others shaped like a pine tree, but all were covered in coloured icing. Just as he was about to sneak around behind the counter and help himself to one of the cakes, one of the bakers carrying a tray of loaves of bread entered the shop from the back room, whistling as he came through the door, warning Nicholas of his approach. Nicholas dropped to the floor and lay right up against the counter. He held his breath. The baker was placing the loaves on display, whistling as he worked. A distant voice called, "Come on, we've got loads more to do." As Nicholas lay perfectly still, listening, he heard footsteps and the whistling fade away. The baker had obviously gone out the back once more.

On his hands and knees, Nicholas crawled to the end of the counter. He slowly looked around the corner. From this position, he could not see into the back room. He would have to take a chance and just go for it. Luckily for Nicholas, sat upon a shelf right above his head was a stack of paper bags. He took three, then he slowly stood up so that he could reach what he desired. He quickly removed one of each cake. The icing was sticky and he kept licking his fingers. He placed them into one bag. Then he took two loaves of bread, one round, and one long and thin, placing each one into a separate bag. The voices in the back room were chattering merrily away as they worked. Nicholas had made it back to the door with his spoils and exited the shop. He felt a pang of guilt at stealing the food, but the hunger in his stomach was greater than his guilt, he slipped outside the bakery and into the dark, where he disappeared into the shadows to enjoy his spoils.

Nicholas sat in the dark and opened the bag of cakes. He placed his hand inside and his fingers met the soft sticky icing. He removed the round cake that was covered in white icing called a snow bomb. As he bit into it, cream from inside spurt out onto his cheek. He used his fingers to wipe the cream from the side of his face and left a smear of thin cream. He then tried to lick the cream from the inside of the cake so as not to waste any of it. By the time he had finished eating this one cake, he had cream on his nose, his chin and his cheek, and his fingers, covered in sticky icing felt as though they had been glued together. He decided not to try and eat anything else in the dark. Now all he was interested in was cleaning the sticky icing from his face and hands, even though he had licked his fingers in the dark and removed the icing the sticky feeling remained.

The side door high above that Nicholas had used to enter the barn suddenly opened. A mixture of male and female voices entered. The light that entered the barn as the door opened spread to within inches of where Nicholas was sat in the dark. He pulled his feet closer to his body as he sat with his knees bent. As the new arrivals descended the stairs, they dispersed towards various shops. Nicholas waited until they had passed him by, eventually getting to his feet and heading towards the door. He climbed the wooden stairs as quietly as possible. Just as Nicholas reached the door, it opened unexpectedly. Instinctively, he pushed past the person who stood holding the door open and raced off down the street. The woman left holding the door watched in stunned silence as the young child disappeared from sight. She entered into the barn to a commotion coming from the bakers.

Nicholas with his three paper bags clutched within his arms needed somewhere to hide. He had turned down a side street. He had never visited before. He slowed to a walk so as not to draw attention to himself. The wind had obviously blown in a favourable direction for the snow down this street was nowhere near as deep as the other one had been. A few people were heading in the opposite direction to the way he was going. He assumed they were heading towards the barn and its shops. Keeping his head down so that no one could recognise him, he came to the end of the street. As he passed the last of the houses, he ventured out into the countryside. Having completed his escape, he suddenly felt a lot happier. Taking one last look down the street, he was satisfied no one had followed thus far.

Moving into the forest that sprawled before him, Nicholas was aware of the trail he left behind. *If only it would start snowing again,* he thought, and suddenly, even before any clouds had formed overhead, the snow started to fall. He made his way deeper into the forest struggling with every step as he sank into the snow. He came across what looked like an abandoned cabin. There was no smoke coming from the pipe on the roof to indicate a fire was lit within, a wooden rail where horses would have been tethered was broken in half. He approached with caution. An old rusty water trough stood outside, completely frozen. As he got closer to the cabin, he was satisfied. No one seemed to be at home. He tried the door that was sitting ajar, and peered inside. It was obvious from the amount of dust and old cobwebs that covered everything that he had been right. No one had lived here for quite a while. He entered into the cabin. With his hands still feeling sticky, he placed the three paper bags onto the dusty table and found an old hammer leaning against the wall just besides the door. Having picked up an old piece of dusty cloth that was on the table, Nicholas left the cabin and made his way to the trough, where he began to repeatedly hit the ice with the hammer. Although there was a cracking sound after the first hit, it was only after a dozen or so hits the ice eventually shattered. Nicholas then put his right hand into the water to remove a piece of ice. The water was freezing against his bare skin.

"I wish this water was warm," he said to himself, and as he dipped the dusty old piece of cloth into the water, Nicholas was surprised to find the water was indeed warm. He didn't understand what was happening, but he wasn't about to complain. He used the cloth to wipe the stickiness from his fingers and then wiped all around his face, removing all traces of icing from his chin, nose and cheek.

When he had finished cleaning his hands and face, he decided to have a quick look around. He circled around the cabin. It stood alone amongst the forest of trees. There were no footprints in the snow. He went back inside the cabin and pushed the door shut. There was a bolt on the door that Nicholas slid into place to keep the door closed, more out of habit than anything else, but he could remember his father saying, you never can be sure of what might be lurking in the forest. Now that he felt secure inside the cabin, he started to have a proper look around. It didn't take long for the whole cabin was just the one room. It was pretty gloomy as there was only one small window that was so dirty hardly any light penetrated. In one corner covered in cobwebs like everything else, Nicholas discovered a stack of chopped wood already waiting to be burnt laid on the floor next to the fireplace. Nicholas placed four pieces of wood onto the remaining ashes left over from the last fire. *If only I could get this to light*, he thought, and instantly flames appeared. Startled, he stumbled backwards, as he watched the flames grow stronger and the warmth from the fire spread outwards into the cabin. Nicholas didn't know how it happened. First the water and now the fire, but he wasn't about to complain. He was just happy to be inside with the fire warming the cabin. He removed his fur coat which had kept him warm all day and the previous night. He retrieved the three paper bags from the table and took out the round loaf of bread. He ripped a piece off and started to eat. It was no longer warm but it still had that fresh just baked smell. Nicholas tore off a second piece and ate it heartily. When he had eaten enough, he wondered what to do next. He decided to have a go at cleaning the window so that he could look outside. With the now damp cloth that he had used to wash his hands and face, he started to rub away at the dirt on the glass, because it was only really dusty the dirt came off quite easily, and as Nicholas rubbed away, he had the shock of his life. For on the other side of the glass was a face staring at him through the window. He stumbled backwards in surprise and fell to the floor. When he regained his footing, he tentatively went back to the window wall. Looking out, all he saw were footprints heading off into the thickest part of the surrounding forest.

For two days, Nicholas stayed locked inside the cabin, fearful to leave in case the creature from the window had returned. Only when he had eaten all the food he had stolen did he think about leaving the cabin. In the two days he had been shut away, he had had time to think, time to think about Elvira and the white castle. Had it really been that bad, he had been safe, looked after, and well fed. It got a bit boring at times, but hadn't he been bored at times when living at home with his brother, Oliver, and his three sisters Alice, Dorothy and Mary.

Nicholas had hoped his great adventure would be as exciting as Oliver's had been, but it had not lived up to his expectations. He had wanted to return home, but he had no way of knowing where home was, and he was alone. He missed living at the white castle. He also admitted to himself, he missed Elvira and Eleanor. His mind was made up he was going home, to the white castle. Having looked out of the window and seeing no fresh footprints in the snow, he opened the cabin door and stepped outside. As he approached the trough however, he realised that there had been a visitor. Very large footprints surrounded the trough of water. Then he heard a noise coming from behind a tree. He froze on the spot as a large beast appeared. Walking upright on two legs, it had a rugged pink hairless face, with long straggly hair of blue that hung down from its head over its shoulders. The body of this creature was covered with white fur, as were its arms and legs. As Nicholas watched, it approached slowly. Cautiously, it seemed just as uncertain of Nicholas as he was of this strange creature, then without warning, two clawed feet plucked Nicholas from the snow and lifted him into the air. The strange, blue-haired creature retreated amongst the trees once more. Nicholas turned his head to look up to see who had plucked him from the ground. He was pleasantly surprised to see the giant white eagle once again. He looked down, hoping for a glimpse of the strange, blue-haired beast, but it had disappeared once more, hidden amongst the snow-laden forest.

Within a few minutes, the eagle had returned Nicholas to the courtyard of the white castle, having released him and flown off, Nicholas climbed the steps leading up to the castle. He called out, "Elvira I'm back," and when he reached the top of the stairs the doors opened, the tall, thin man in the blood-red suit stood waiting. As Nicholas passed through, the doors were abruptly closed behind him. Nicholas paused for a second startled by the slamming of the doors. Then without waiting for the tall, thin man to help him with his coat, he shrugged it from his shoulders and let it fall to the floor before racing off down the hallway, calling for Elvira.

When Nicholas finally found Elvira in her sitting room, he was shocked at how old she looked, as if all youth and vitality had been drained from her body. He had expected Elvira to be angry with him for running off the way he had, but he had never imagined this. She looked so frail. He ran over to where she was seated and took hold of her hand. She was sleeping, but the touch of his skin against hers sent a tingling sensation that coursed its way throughout her body and she awoke with a smile.

"Nicholas, you came back," said Elvira, as a tear left her eye and she squeezed his hand gently.

"I missed you so much," said Nicholas, "I'm never going to leave again." And he threw his arms around Elvira's waist and gave her a big hug. She gently stroked his hair as his head lay in her lap, and as she did, all signs of ageing on her hands faded away. The tingling sensation throughout her body continued, and when Nicholas finally lifted his head from Elvira's lap, she looked as youthful as ever.

Nicholas smiled to see Elvira looking the way she always had. "Where is Eleanor?" asked Nicholas eagerly.

"I will send for her," said Elvira, and instantly, a blink arrived at the doorway to Elvira's room. Without Elvira saying an audible word the blink turned and disappeared. Moments later Eleanor raced into the room and bent down to embrace Nicholas. They were all crying. Crying tears of joy for his safe return.

"I was so worried," said Eleanor, when she was finally able to speak, "where have you been?" she asked. Nicholas told them of the pine tree where he hid on that first night, and all the tiny silver wing bats that covered his coat.

Then he went on to explain how he managed to get into the barn. He was reluctant to say he stole some food from the bakery, but Elvira smiled and said, "We already know what happened at the bakery." He felt guilty at this point, but continued to tell them of the abandoned cabin he found in the forest, choosing to leave out how it had started to snow when there were no clouds in the sky. Just when he had wished for it to snow, and he didn't mention the water in the trough being freezing cold one second and warm the next, just as he had wished it was warm. These were secrets that for now he decided to keep to himself, and so he carried on with his tale and told them of the strange creature that had looked at him through the window.

Eleanor interrupted, "Did you see a blue-haired yeti?" she asked, sharing a worried glance with Elvira.

"I don't know what a yeti is," said Nicholas, "but what I saw definitely had long, blue hair."

Chapter 28
The Fight for Dante's Mind

Dante awoke in a soft bed of warmth and comfort, but he felt no comfort, only fear. With the covers pulled up tight under his chin, he lay motionless, rigid as a board, as if this would help keep him safe. Only his eyes moved as they searched the room. He heard a noise and turned his head towards the door as it slowly opened. His eyes widened with fear, gripping the bed covers even tighter around his body. He held his breath. Only when his sister Cressida appeared did he relax his grip slightly and breathe.

Her rainbow-coloured wings shimmered in the sunlight that permeated through the crystal walls. Somewhere in the depths of Dante's troubled mind, a glimmer of recognition showed in his eyes. As Cressida approached the bed, Dante sat up. She stretched out an arm to take hold of his hand, but he withdrew it under the covers once more. Cressida softly sat on the bed without saying a word, leaving Dante to make the first move.

Staring at Cressida's wings and brightly coloured dress, Dante removed one trembling hand from beneath the covers. He reached out and touched her gold and silver hair. Soft to touch and nonthreatening, he nervously smiled. She returned his smile reassuringly.

Then a knock on the door, Dante pulled his hand back under the covers, and gathered them tightly around his neck once more. He lay down, rigid as a piece of wood.

"Enter," called Cressida. As she rose from the bed to face the door, it was Aegeus the centaur who entered the room.

"Your Majesty," he said, "three of the younger centaur's did not return to the crystal palace." She looked at him uninterested by his news.

"Forget about them," said Cressida, "I need you to stay with Dante and keep him safe. Do not let him leave this room. I must find a way of bringing my brother back."

"As you wish, Your Majesty," said Aegeus. Cressida left Aegeus standing guard of the door, with Dante lying rigid beneath the covers, with his eyes firmly fixed on the centaur.

Beneath the crystal palace, in the chamber of magic, Cressida placed the crystal crown upon her head and called upon the magical powers contained within. "Show me how to retrieve my brother Dante from the curse of Helga, the one-eyed hag." After a short pause, the crown glowed softly and a shimmering light lit up the room. A haunting lyrical voice answered Cressida's plea.

"There is one who has the remedy to bring your brother back and free his mind."

"Who?" asked Cressida eagerly.

"You seek the one who has gained knowledge of all things magical, learnt over a thousand years."

"Yes," said Cressida, "but who is it? And where can I find him?"

"Not a him, dear child, for it is Saki you seek, mother of Percival, gatherer of knowledge, maker of potions."

Cressida's legs crumbled beneath her. She had heard the name Saki before, but only in stories of great magic. She had never believed it to be a real person. It was however learning the name of her son, Percival, that caused her to stumble. Surely not the Percival that she knew, she thought.

Cressida steadied herself and asked the question. "Is the son of Saki, known as Percival, the one who seeks Prince Nicholas?" She waited anxiously. After a short pause, the soft shimmering light lit up the room again. As the crown glowed, when the haunting lyrical voice spoke, it gave, a one, word answer.

"Yes."

Cressida wailed, as she struggled to comprehend what she had just learnt, for it was because of Percival, that Dante had been caught by the one-eyed hag in the first place, and now, she had to seek Percival's mother, Saki, in order to save her brother's mind. Cressida began pacing the room.

"Where can I find Saki?" she asked.

"She is in the frozen lands of Ice and Snow," sang the haunting, lyrical voice.

Cressida sought counsel with her most trusted advisers. Having sent three fairies to watch over Dante, Aegeus had been relieved of his guard duties, and summoned along with the fairy elders. Once everyone was present, Cressida seated high above them on her throne, asked, "How can we travel to the frozen lands of Ice and Snow?" The nine fairy elders, whose coloured wings had been diluted with age, and now looked a poor imitation of their former glory, gathered below Cressida huddled together, nervously talking quietly amongst themselves.

It was Aegeus who asked, "Your Majesty, may I be permitted to ask, why do you need to travel to the frozen lands of Ice and Snow?"

Looking down from above Cressida said, "I have learnt that the only one who can restore my brother Dante's mind, is in the frozen lands of Ice and Snow." At this news, the fairy elders parted from their huddle and faced Cressida.

"Who do you believe can restore your brother's mind?" asked the oldest looking fairy, as he leant on his walking staff, looking up at Cressida.

"Using the power of the crystal crown, I have gained knowledge that Saki is the one to save Dante," said Cressida. The fairy elders gathered together once more, as Cressida watched, growing impatient with every passing second.

When the elders parted for a second time, "Your Majesty, you must be mistaken, Saki died over a thousand years ago," said the oldest of the fairies, whilst all the elders surrounding him nodded in agreement.

Cressida rose from her throne, wings fully spread, the anger she was feeling was evident for everyone to see. Her beautiful rainbow-coloured wings were changing colour, turning scarlet before their very eyes.

"How dare you suggest I am mistaken," raged Cressida, heat radiated from her scarlet wings, and two of the fairy elders who were weak and frail, fell to the floor. Seeing them lying on the ground had an effect on Cressida and her rage abated.

They were helped back onto their feet. Cressida had briefly lost control in a way she never had before, as her temper had risen, but she had now come back to her senses, fearful of what she could have done, she told them all to leave except for Aegeus. The fairy elders backed towards the doors, bowed and then turned around and left Aegeus and Cressida alone.

"Your Majesty, what just happened?" asked Aegeus, showing concern.

"I'm not sure," said Cressida, "I think it has something to do with using the crystal crown."

Aegeus watched silently as Cressida floated to the floor and landed beside him. "Walk with me," she said, and so, they walked side by side and headed into the flower garden. Once she was sure they were alone, Cressida turned to

Aegeus, and said, "I have much to learn, about how to enhance the powerful magic of the crystal crown," she then admitted to Aegeus, "I have told no one this before, but when I use the crystal crown, it weakens me."

"But Your Majesty," said Aegeus, "you were not weakened this time; you turned bright red and radiated such heat as though you were on fire."

"Yes," said Cressida, "and that is the first time that has happened, and I don't know why."

"My observation, Your Majesty, is that you started to generate heat when you got angry."

"But that is no good to me if I cannot control it," said Cressida. She paused to sniff at a fragrant yellow rose, "I need you to travel to the frozen land of Ice and Snow," she said, "find Saki, and bring back a potion to restore Dante's mind, take as many centaurs with you as you need."

"But how will I find her, Your Majesty, it is a vast land and I have no idea what she looks like." Cressida held out her right hand. It was closed in a fist. As she unfurled her fingers, there sat in the palm of her hand was a small crystal.

"Take this," said Cressida, "I have cast a spell that will detect ancient magic. If it is true and she has knowledge of a thousand years, it will take you to her,"

"It shall be done, Your Majesty."

Chapter 29
Sleigh Ride

As Dorothy slept, she was sat dreamily before the glass bowl. She dreamt of her one true love, as the water in the glass bowl cleared and the image appeared, covered from head to toe in mud. The mud slowly began to slip away from the face of her one true love. She was feeling excited. Her heart was racing, at last to see his face, but as the mud slipped away, so did her excitement. For the face to be revealed was that of her brother Oliver. *Surely, it cannot be my own brother.* Confused, she shook her head in disbelief, then she stirred the water in the bowl and the lovebird eyes closed. As the water settled and the eyes opened a new image had appeared. Once more, covered in mud from head to toe, the mystery man approached. As the mud slid down his face to reveal the man of her dreams, standing before her was Joshua. *Surely, this cannot be right*, she thought. For she knew that Joshua liked her sister, Alice, and although she liked Joshua, she had no feelings for him in that way. Again, she shook her head in disbelief and gave the waters a stir. And once more, a new image formed, again covered from head to toe in mud. She was hopeful this time she would get to see her one true love. He had stepped clear of a pool of mud and was walking towards her. As he approached, the mud started to slip away, just as it had before on the two previous occasions. Dorothy's breathing became faster as excitement built inside her body. Her heart was racing. At last she was finally about to see her one true love. She knew it. He reached out a hand which she took eagerly, and using her other hand, she went to wipe away the mud from his face to reveal who was hidden. "Dorothy quickly, wake up," said Oliver, as he gave her a shake.

Dorothy woke so suddenly that for a moment, she forgot what she had been dreaming about. Then as Oliver left the room, she became aware of where she was, and the dream so rudely interrupted by her brother. She got dressed feeling disappointed, and when she left the bedroom, she found everyone was already sitting around Saki's large table eating breakfast. "What's all the fuss about?" she asked, directing her question at Oliver.

"The storm has cleared, and Saki has provided us with three sleighs for our journey," said Oliver.

"Oh, is that all?" replied Dorothy.

"What's the matter with you this morning?" asked Oliver, feeling annoyed with his sister's lack of interest.

"It's those lovebird eyes," said Joshua, giving Dorothy a cheeky wink.

"Oh no," said Oliver, "please tell me you're not still thinking about that?"

"What if I am," said Dorothy, "it's no concern of yours."

"Can someone please help," cried Oliver.

"Dreaming about it won't make it happen any quicker," said Saki, "and dreaming of who it might be can lead to disappointment, and confusion if it turns out to be someone different."

"Thank you," said Oliver. "Now will you please have something to eat, so that we can leave and continue our search for Nicholas?" Dorothy realised she was being foolish, for no dream ever came true, and Oliver's words about continuing to search for Nicholas had stung. He made it sound as if she didn't care, which was far from the truth. She joined everyone else at the table and Saki passed over a large bowl of warming porridge. Dorothy ate in silence.

"Before I let you go, there is a warning to give, a prophecy." They all stopped eating to listen, with all eyes focussed on Saki. She began, "One who gives birth to the power of five provides a force to take over a kingdom."

Looking bemused, Dorothy asked, "What does that mean?"

"Two things to remember," said Saki, "do not let Elvira know you have magic, and do not let her know you are five."

Once they had all finished eating, Saki led the way outside where three sleighs were lined up waiting for them. Each had two reindeer ready to pull the sleigh. "There is a pile of animal skin blankets to cover over your legs, for it is going to get even colder," said Saki, "and each reindeer has a bell attached to its antlers."

"What are they for?" asked Oliver.

"That is in case it starts to snow again, it will help you to stay together when you can no longer see each other," said Saki.

Oliver, Reif and Percival had taken charge of the reigns to each sleigh, Joshua had wanted to take control of one of the sleighs, but they had decided that considering how accident prone he could be, it would be better if he just went along for the ride as a passenger. Dorothy climbed aboard the sleigh with her brother, and pulled the animal skin blankets over their legs. Joshua went with Reif, who had control of the reigns, while Percival and the two remaining guards set off in front. Berwyn as usual strode alongside the sleigh Percival was driving.

As Dorothy tried to make herself comfortable, the sleigh jolted forward as the reindeer took off. "Sorry," said Oliver, as Dorothy was thrown sideways.

"I'm all right," she said, as she straightened herself once more. "So where are we heading?" she asked Oliver.

"Saki told Percival that Queen Elvira's castle is about four days travelling from here," said Oliver, "Saki believes there is a chance Elvira might be able to help us."

"You mean to say were going to visit our aunt?" asked Dorothy.

"Yes," said Oliver, "but remember Saki's warning, we cannot tell Elvira we have magic, and we must not let her know we are five."

As the three sleighs glided over the snow, the only sound was the tinkling noise made by the bells carried on the antlers of each reindeer. Dorothy marvelled at the beauty of the scenery, as the freshly fallen snow sparkled in the winter sun. Of course, they had snow back home in winter, but nothing that compared to this, deep snow sat upon the lower branches of the trees bending them so that they touched the ground. As they passed between trees, Dorothy reached out a hand and grabbed a handful of snow from one of the branches. She threw it at the back of Joshua's head who was seated in the sleigh in front of her and Oliver, who were bringing up the rear. "Ouch," cried Joshua, rubbing the back of his head, as the snowball had exploded on impact. He turned to see who had thrown the snowball and saw that Dorothy was laughing.

"I'll get you back later," shouted Joshua.

"You can try," said Dorothy.

Percival who was driving the sleigh up front with the guards for company suddenly screamed, "Ahhh." Along with the bells on the reindeer's antlers jingling madly, Berwyn howled. Having been laughing only a second before both Reif and Oliver pulled their reindeer to a halt. Dorothy looked frantically at her brother.

"Stay here," said Oliver. Reif and Joshua climbed down from their sleigh, as did Oliver, who he raced forward to join them. "Can you stay with Dorothy for me?" Oliver asked Joshua, although he felt a bit put out, for he wanted to know what had happened to Percival.

"Sure," he said, and so as Oliver and Reif moved beyond the sleigh to investigate where Percival had seemingly disappeared, Joshua climbed onboard the sleigh to sit with Dorothy.

"What's happening?" she asked, as Joshua made himself comfortable by her side.

"I don't know," said Joshua, "Oliver just asked me to keep you company."

"You mean he asked you to sit with me like a nanny with a small child. I want to know what's going on, don't you?" she asked indignantly, and before Joshua had time to answer, Dorothy had leapt from the sleigh and was heading towards Reif and Oliver.

Joshua called out, "Wait for me," as he also leapt down from the sleigh.

Oliver turned around as Dorothy approached, followed by Joshua. "I thought I asked you to stay with her in the sleigh," said Oliver.

"I don't need looking after," said Dorothy angrily, "so what happened, where's Percival?"

They were standing at the top of a slope. The only evidence Percival had been there were the tracks made by the reindeer's feet, the sleigh and on one side a wide pathway indicating where Berwyn had slid. With a look of astonishment etched on all their faces, it was Joshua who spoke first. "Are you thinking what I'm thinking?" he said.

"That depends on what you're thinking," said Oliver.

"Are we going to follow Percival?" asked Joshua. Oliver turned to look at Dorothy. She looked utterly terrified.

"Um," she said, not sure what to think.

"I think we need to make a decision and quick. Percival might need our help," said Oliver.

"But what if he is already dead," asked Dorothy, "we could risk losing our lives as well."

"I think we should take a vote," said Oliver, "majority wins." Dorothy reluctantly agreed. "All those in favour of following Percival raise your hand." Reif, Joshua and Oliver all raised their hands without hesitation. Only Dorothy didn't.

"All right," she conceded, "we follow Percival."

"You know he would do the same if it were one of us," said Oliver.

"I know," said Dorothy.

As Reif and Joshua's sleigh was in front, they approached the slope first. Dorothy and Oliver watched in silence. It happened so fast. One minute they were there and then in the blink of an eye, they were gone. The screams they left behind as they plummeted down the slope sent a chill down Dorothy's spine. Clinging to Oliver's arm, "I don't know if I can do this," she said.

"Just hold on tight," said Oliver reassuringly, with a broad smile across his face, "ready, here we go," said Oliver. And before Dorothy could answer she was ready, with a flick of the reigns, they edged forward. Suddenly, they were speeding down the slope. As she screamed, the sound trailed off behind them unheard. Trying to keep hold of Oliver's arm, they were jostled from side to side. Oliver held onto the reigns tightly but had no control over steering the reindeer. In front, they caught glimpses of Reif and Joshua as they sped ahead. One minute they were visible but then suddenly disappeared. Before Dorothy could gather her thoughts as to where they had gone, they found themselves in a tunnel passing beneath the snow. Then, just as suddenly, they were outside in the sunshine again, weaving their way between trees. Heading straight towards a fallen branch, with no hope of avoiding it, the slope dropped again taking them just inches below the branch. They dislodged a small amount of snow that showered down on them as they passed beneath. Dorothy screamed, "Ahh," and shuddered as the cold snow slipped down the back of her neck.

Everything was a blur, they were speeding so fast, Oliver was feeling sick, but still he clung onto the reigns. Dorothy had a tight grip on his left arm. Pins and needles were beginning to tingle in his left hand, and just when Dorothy thought she could take no more, to their surprise, they started to slow down. As their eyes became focussed once more, in the distance, they could see two sleighs. Dorothy's spirits rose. Hopeful everyone was all right. The sleigh had stopped sliding for the slope had ended. Now Oliver had control of the reindeers once more. The bells were jingling joyfully on their antlers, and as they finally came to a halt, Joshua came running over to their sleigh. "What a ride, did you enjoy it?" he asked, with a huge beaming smile across his whole face. Oliver turned to his right, leaning over the side of the sleigh, and threw up. "I guess not," said Joshua laughing. Reif had dashed forward and gone around the other side of the sleigh. He helped Dorothy as she tried to dismount from her seat upon the sleigh. She was happy for Reif's help. Her legs were shaking, and she tumbled in his arms, grateful for being caught. She also felt a little flustered.

Once more being so close to him, her heart skipped a beat as their eyes connected. *Could he be my one true love,* she thought.

"Ouch," she cried, Joshua had just thrown a snowball which had hit Dorothy on the side of the head, "I told you I would get you back."

Reif placed Dorothy on the ground. Standing side by side, they started throwing snowballs at Joshua, who was joined by the two guards. As the snowball fight ensued, Percival had made his way over to Oliver, who was still feeling the effects of the ride. "Here take a sip of this you will feel better." Oliver took the small bottle of green liquid without question and sipped. Instantly, he started to feel back to normal.

"Take no notice of Joshua," said Percival, "when Reif pulled his sleigh to a halt, Joshua had passed out, only when he was woken did he throw up." Oliver gave a weak smile, "Rest a while before we carry on," said Percival, "we still need to find our resting place for tonight."

After a short delay, Oliver announced he was ready to continue. Dorothy threw a snowball which caught one of the guards square on the forehead and he tumbled backwards into a snow drift, with only his feet visible. They all fell about laughing, Joshua and the other guard helped to pull the stricken guard from the deep snow, for without their assistance he was helpless, once he was clear they were ready to leave, Oliver was still feeling a little sick, so this time Dorothy took control of the reigns, they travelled without further incident passing through a snow-covered forest, it was late afternoon, when Percival came to a halt, "we have found our resting place for the night," called Percival. Percival had led them to a stone, built dwelling that sat in the middle of the forest, "how did you know this was here?" asked Dorothy, as Berwyn went on ahead and approached the house, sniffing the air as he went. "Saki gave me directions," said Percival, "she said we would reach safety before nightfall."

Next to the large, stone-built house stood a large wooden barn. Joshua jumped from his sleigh and called, "Is anyone going to help me move this bar?" The two guards who had been riding with Percival jumped from their sleigh and helped remove the bar that sat across the doorway keeping the barn doors shut. Once the doors were opened, the three sleighs were driven straight in. The reindeer were released from their harness, and found food at the back of the barn. A couple of horses stirred in their stalls but quickly settled as the doors to the barn were closed. When everyone had left the barn, Oliver and Reif put the bar back in place across the doors.

Percival and Dorothy approached the front of the house. Berwyn had laid on the front porch waiting. Percival tried the door and found it opened easily. He then stepped aside and allowed Berwyn to enter first, closely followed by himself and Dorothy.

Dorothy found herself standing in an elegant hallway. At the bottom of a wide staircase with dark wood bannisters on either side, leading up to a galleried landing, hanging above the hallway, a large candle chandelier which was alight. Dorothy turned to Percival and said, "Someone must be home," and without waiting for a response from Percival, Dorothy called, "hello, is anyone there?" As they quietly waited for a reply, the only sound they heard was the echo of Dorothy's voice calling. "If no one is home, why are the candles alight?" she asked Percival. Just then, Oliver, Reif and the others came bursting through the door.

"Wow," said Oliver, "what is this place?" He walked past Dorothy and Percival and started looking around. As he entered through a doorway to a room on the right of the hallway, the candles that sat in the candelabra that were strategically placed around the room all burst into flame. The whole of the room was illuminated. Then, as Oliver stepped further into the room, the large fireplace that sat dark and menacing suddenly came to life. Oliver, surprised by the sudden burst of flames, stopped in his tracks.

"Who on earth is that?" asked Reif, who had entered the room right behind Oliver. Hanging above the fireplace was a portrait of a large bear of a man with flaming red hair that reached his broad shoulders and beyond, and whose beard was as red as his hair. He had a triumphant look on his face, and looking down the painting, it revealed the man standing with one foot resting on the head of a large animal covered in white fur that was sprawled dead at his feet. A small label on the bottom of the painting read, Sir Cuthbert, yeti slayer.

As Oliver and Reif scoured the room, there was more evidence of Sir Cuthbert's achievements. At the opposite end of the room from which they entered was a large, wooden desk. Laid out on the floor in front of the desk was a large white fur skin, complete with the head of the yeti still attached, behind the desk were many shelves, stacked high with hundreds of books, and on the desk stood three mini statues. All depicting Sir Cuthbert in various poses, standing victorious, over the body of a slain yeti.

Dorothy entered alone the room Oliver and Reif were looking around, having left Percival and the others exploring the rest of the house. With the candles lit and the fire aglow at first glance, Dorothy thought the room felt warm and cosy. There were a couple of large sofas facing the fireplace, and comfortable looking chairs placed here and there. A sewing table sat in a corner illuminated, beneath a candelabra, where a piece of material with an embroidered picture unfinished lay. As Dorothy moved further into the room, she stood before the fireplace and looked at the picture of Sir Cuthbert. Standing over the yeti, a chill ran down her spine. As she moved away from the painting towards Oliver and Reif, she screamed, "Ahhh." Both boys had been studying the books on the shelves, most of which seemed to be about the exploits of Sir Cuthbert. Disturbed by Dorothy's scream, for they had been unaware of her presence until that point, Oliver and Reif turned around quickly, dropping books onto the floor. Dorothy stood transfixed, staring at the white skin displayed on the floor in front of the desk. Upon seeing that his sister was not hurt, but simply startled by the skin of the yeti, Oliver laughed.

"It can't hurt you, you know."

Regaining her composure, Dorothy replied, "Oh shut up," then asked, "what were you looking at?"

As Oliver retrieved his book from the floor, he said, "If you don't like the skin on the floor, then you are not going to like the books either." Walking around the skin, careful not to step upon it, Dorothy approached the desk to have a closer look at the three mini statues. When she realised what they were depicting, she felt nothing but disgust for this so called, Sir Cuthbert.

Percival appeared at the doorway. "We've found the kitchen," he said. Dorothy was glad of an excuse to get out of the room. As she hurriedly walked past the yeti skin sprawled over the floor, Oliver laughed at his sister's departure, but stayed with Reif as they continued to look through Sir Cuthbert's books, Dorothy ignored her brother's laughter.

Having followed Percival back across the hallway, she entered the kitchen. She could not believe her eyes. There was a large table laden with enough food for a huge party. Joshua and the two guards were standing next to the table smiling as she entered. On seeing the food, Dorothy suddenly realised just how hungry she felt. "There must be someone present in this house," said Dorothy.

"I have checked all the rooms downstairs," said Percival, "there is no one here."

"Then, they must be upstairs," said Dorothy.

"Should we go and look for them?" suggested Joshua. But Dorothy's hunger was overwhelming.

"I don't think anyone would begrudge us something to eat," said Dorothy. Percival, whose own hunger had reared its head at the sight of the food, was reluctant to give in to his desire to eat.

"Well, what are you waiting for?" said Dorothy.

"Shouldn't we wait for Oliver and Reif?" suggested Joshua.

"Oh, don't worry about them," said Dorothy, "they'll be along when they're ready, besides it's not like they're going to miss out." This was true. There was enough food for a party of a hundred people or more.

By the time Oliver and Reif tore themselves away from Sir Cuthbert's books and entered the kitchen, everyone else had finished eating. "Wow," said Oliver, looking at the vast amount of food on display.

"Tastes good as well," said Joshua, who puffed out his cheeks and expelled a huge sigh, his stomach fit to burst. "I can see you've had your fair share," said Oliver, speaking to Joshua, as he pulled out a chair and sat down.

"You never know when it's going to be your last meal," said Joshua, who was feeling so stuffed he was uncomfortable.

"Looking at how much you've put away, I think it might be the meal that finishes you off," said Reif. Everyone sat around the table laughed, including Joshua, but his stomach was so full. Laughing caused him even more discomfort.

Oliver decided he was not that hungry, and wanted to explore more of the house. He got to his feet and started to walk out of the kitchen. "Are you all right?" asked Dorothy.

"Yes, I'm fine," replied Oliver, "I just want to have a look around and check out the rest of the house."

"Do you want some company?" she asked.

"No, I'll be all right," replied Oliver.

"I think Berwyn should accompany you just in case," said Percival. And with that, Berwyn got to his feet and followed Oliver from the kitchen.

Standing at the bottom of the staircase wondering whether to go upstairs or not and have a look around, Oliver was not sure, but thought he could hear faint music being played. At first surprised because they had thought the house was empty, but then it occurred to him, the food had been hot, someone had to have cooked it and now there was music being played.

He eagerly started to ascend the stairs with Berwyn at his side. As the music got louder, excitement filled Oliver from within, and the hairs on his neck prickled with anticipated excitement. At the top of the stairs, he heard mingled with the music, laughter and voices talking. He paused briefly, listening intently to decide which direction the music and laughter was coming from. Once decided, he turned left. With Berwyn right by his side, he walked down a brightly lit hallway. Illuminated by many candles mounted on the walls, family portraits adorned the walls on either side, a large man with flaming red hair and beard stood in the centre of the largest portrait. A young blonde woman sat in a chair by his side. They were surrounded by seven children, one son with flaming red hair like his father, and six daughters as blonde as their mother.

As Oliver studied the picture, double doors at the end of the hallway suddenly burst open. Music and laughter escaped into the hallway. "Come on, let's go down to the kitchen and see what food there is to eat," said one of six blonde girls, who then raced passed. Oliver went to say hello, but as he did, he realised, they didn't even seem to notice he was there. As he stood in front of the portrait, Oliver watched the six young girls disappear as they descended the stairs. With Berwyn still by his side, he moved further along the hallway to where the music and laughter was coming from.

The six blonde girls reached the kitchen and entered in search of food, giggling and laughing merrily. Everyone seated at the table was surprised by their sudden appearance and stopped eating. As the six young girls approached the table, Percival and Reif immediately stood up and introduced themselves. "Good evening, ladies, my name is Percival and this is my young travelling companion and friend Reif." Joshua who was so full, having eaten too much, couldn't muster the energy needed to stand, and so nodded his head in acknowledgement of their arrival.

"I am sorry for the intrusion," said Reif, "we have travelled a fair distance by sleigh and were feeling hungry." The six blonde girls however approached the table and each one picked up a plate and started to load it with food, taking no notice of those seated at the table. Reif went to speak again, but it was Dorothy who spoke next.

"Good evening, ladies," she said, "how is the party?" But again the six blonde girls did not respond to being spoken to. Having loaded their plates with food, they simply left the room, laughing as merrily as when they had entered, leaving those sat at the table looking totally perplexed.

Turning to Percival, Dorothy asked, "What just happened, they didn't even see us?"

"I don't know what happened," said Percival, "but I think we should follow them and see if we can find out what is going on." With that, everyone but Joshua got up from the table and followed Percival as he raced after the six blonde girls.

"Are you coming?" asked Reif.

"No, I think I'd better stay here," said Joshua, with a look of discomfort on his face.

"All right," said Reif, "we'll be back shortly." And then, he turned and ran after the others. They were already halfway up the stairs when Reif spotted them, and so he quickly followed.

Oliver and Berwyn were in the ballroom where the party was taking place. As they mingled amongst the guests, no one seemed to be taking any notice of them, which made Oliver feel as though he and Berwyn were invisible. As the six blond girls re-entered the party, each carrying a plate loaded with food, a loud cheer went up from six dashing young gentlemen, all standing together next to a large bowl of punch. Oliver flinched slightly as he felt a hand grab his elbow. Expecting it to be one of his friends, he turned around. He gasped in surprise to see not one of his friends but a little old lady with blonde greying hair. "Come with me," she said softly. Holding on to Oliver's elbow for support as much as anything else, she guided Oliver to one end of the ballroom. On an elevated position overlooking the party were two high backed chairs. Seated in one was a large man with flaming red hair tinged with grey, and a red beard. Oliver immediately recognised him from the painting in the hallway. *Sir Cuthbert*, he thought. Then he turned to look at the blonde, grey-haired lady and recognised her as the woman seated in the chair surrounded by her children, and then lastly it dawned on him that the six blonde girls who were laughing and having such a good time, were in fact the six sisters. The blonde, grey-haired lady took her place by her husband's side, and introduced him.

"This is Sir Cuthbert Indio," she said, "and my name is Rebecca."

"I am Prince Oliver," said Oliver, "and this is one of my travelling companions, Berwyn." The giant white bear sat by his side and Rebecca smiled at them both.

"Pleased to meet you, Prince Oliver," said Rebecca, "and what brings you to my home?"

Before Oliver could answer, having followed the six blonde girls up the stairs, the rest of Oliver's companions stood in the doorway looking stunned. Dorothy called Oliver's name above the noise. Turning away from Rebecca, Oliver raised a hand and waved to his friends and sister. Percival spotted him first and pointed him out to Dorothy. They then weaved their way between the party guests.

"Excuse me," said Dorothy, as she ploughed her way through the crowded room, but just like the six blonde girls downstairs, no one seemed to notice that they were there. Eventually reaching Oliver and Berwyn who had laid down, at Rebecca's feet, Dorothy asked, "Who are all these people?"

"They are our guests," said Rebecca.

"Oh, I'm terribly sorry," said Dorothy, "I didn't mean to be rude, I didn't think you could see us."

"Only I can see you, my dear," said Rebecca.

"So what is happening here?" asked Dorothy, "if you don't mind my asking, that is."

"I don't mind at all," said Rebecca, "it makes a nice change to have someone to talk to after all these years."

"How long have you lived like this?" asked Percival.

"It is twenty-seven years since my son Cuthbert was taken from us," said Rebecca mournfully, "it was his eighth birthday, and so every year, we awaken on his birthday and celebrate."

"But everyone looks so young," said Oliver, "I mean his sisters look as though they are in their early teens."

"Ah, so you spotted them, did you?" said Rebecca. Dorothy looked at Oliver totally bewildered.

"Yes," said Oliver, "I was looking at the portrait in the hallway, the one where you are seated, surrounded by all your children."

"That's very observant of you," said Rebecca, "to recognise them, that was painted five years before my beloved Cuthbert was lost to us," she said.

"Lost, to you," asked Dorothy, "do you mean he died?"

"Oh no, my dear he is not dead, not as far as I know. He was taken by Elvira, the Winter Queen." Dorothy and Oliver glanced at each other quickly with a look of surprise on their faces. "Ah," said Rebecca, "I see you have heard of her."

Dorothy went to reply, but Oliver cut her off, worried she might tell Rebecca that Elvira was their aunt. "You asked me a little while ago," said Oliver, drawing

Rebecca's attention away from Dorothy, "what brings us to your home, well, we are searching for our younger brother."

"Who was snatched from our father's shoulders and carried off by a giant white eagle," said Dorothy, before Oliver could stop her a second time. The look of horror that spread across Rebecca's face was evident for all to see.

"So," said Rebecca, "you seek the Winter Queen?"

"What makes you say that?" asked Oliver.

"Because Cuthbert was carried away by a giant white eagle."

"But what has that got to do with the Winter Queen?" asked Dorothy.

"Why she was riding on its back," said Rebecca.

It was now Dorothy and Oliver who looked horrified. They had hoped that their aunt Elvira, known as the Winter Queen would be able to help them find Nicholas, now it seemed likely that she was the one who took him in the first place. "But why would she take your son?" asked Dorothy.

"No one knows for sure," said Rebecca, "oh, there are many stories I have heard over the years, some say she boils the children whilst still alive and then eats them; others say she puts them to work in her diamond mine. No one knows for sure, but she only ever steals away the young boys and girls, that much is true."

Chapter 30
Welcome Home Ball

With all thoughts of the blue-haired yeti put to the back of her mind for now, Elvira said, "we must throw a welcome home ball for Nicholas." Elvira was so happy to have Nicholas back at the white castle for he made her feel more alive than she had in years, and she needed him to be happy, so happy that he would never think of leaving again. She promised to throw a ball unlike anything she had done before.

Elvira made all the arrangements herself. She wanted it to be a surprise for Eleanor, as much as Nicholas. All week, Eleanor had kept Nicholas entertained at her mother's request, however, both had tried, on more than one occasion, to sneak a peek into the ballroom, and each time they had been thwarted, firstly by the tall, thin man in the blood-red suit, and on the second occasion, they had been hiding behind a giant blue and green decorated vase waiting for Elvira to leave, only to find the doors had been magically sealed.

Finally, the day of the ball had arrived. Nicholas was wearing a brand-new suit, of bright blue, with a gold-coloured shirt and shoes, which had been laid out on his bed while he was having a bath. He had been helped to get dressed by one of the blinks. Now he stood in front of the full-length mirror, he smiled at his reflection, happy with his new outfit. *This is going to be fun,* he thought.

A knock on his door alerted Nicholas that someone was about to enter. Beaming a huge smile that spread across his face, he turned to greet whoever it was.

Eleanor entered the room looking every inch a princess, gone was the dress covered in rubies, sapphires and emeralds. The gown she wore was purest white silk, delicately adorned with diamonds, and she wore a diamond necklace around her neck which complimented the dress without being too ostentatious.

"What do you think?" she asked Nicholas. Without saying a word, he raced across the room and flung his arms around Eleanor's waist. She was completely taken by surprise by his reaction.

"Now let me have a good look at you," she said. As Nicholas released Eleanor's waist and took a step back, "My, you do look handsome," she teased.

"And you look beautiful," he said.

"Why thank you, young prince," said Eleanor, as they both laughed.

Another gentle knock on the door was followed by the appearance of Elvira. Usually only ever seen wearing white, Elvira's appearance caused Eleanor to gasp. "Why mother, you look stunning." As she glided further into the room, the blood-red dress lightly decorated in diamonds sparkled beneath the candlelight chandelier.

"I thought I'd try a different colour, just for a change, what do you think?" asked Elvira. "Why mother, I think it's the most stunningly beautiful dress you have ever worn," said Eleanor.

"You know, I think your right," said Elvira, as she stood admiring her reflection in the full-length mirror.

"But, what about your dress?" asked Elvira, as she turned away from the mirror. Eleanor spun around to show off her dress.

"I love it, mother, thank you."

"And what about you, Nicholas, do you like your new suit?" asked Elvira.

"Yes, mother, thank you," said Nicholas, "I like it very much."

Without realising what he had said, Nicholas had filled Elvira with a joy she had not felt in a long time. To be called mother by Nicholas was so unexpected, a tear tickled down her cheek. Eleanor stepped forward to wipe the tear away from Elvira's face. "Why are you crying?" asked Nicholas, "What did I do wrong?" he asked.

"Oh no," said Elvira, "you've done nothing wrong, these are happy tears."

The guests for the ball had all arrived and were gathered on the dance floor awaiting the arrival of their host. Eleanor who had been sent on ahead by her mother was seated on her throne, wearing her white dress, the diamonds around her neck were causing quite a stir of jealousy amongst the female guests. Nicholas sat on a throne besides Eleanor's wearing his blue and gold outfit. Elvira's throne stood empty.

Eleanor and Nicholas looked down upon the guests who were all mingled together on the dance floor. The musicians burst into life unexpectedly, playing a fanfare, in a darkened corner a huge chandelier burst into flame. Everyone present turned towards the bright light, as a set of doors opened. Elvira wearing her bright-red dress rode in on a sleigh carved from ice being pulled by four ice sculpted reindeer. She was accompanied on the sleigh by a muscular, young man.

The guests on the dance floor parted, to allow the four reindeer to pass. Elvira was laughing as she circled the dance floor. Guests were frantically trying to evade the sleigh as it sped around the dance floor. As they approached the steps that led to Elvira's throne, the sleigh came to a halt and the muscular, young man lifted Elvira onto one shoulder and carried her with ease up the steps and placed her standing besides her throne. The music stopped. "Thank you, Ivan," said Elvira. He then made his way down the steps once more, climbed onto the sleigh and guided the four ice sculpted reindeer back through the open doors which closed behind them.

"That was quite some entrance," said Eleanor, to her mother.

"Did you like it?" asked Elvira smiling broadly. Once seated, the musicians started to play and the guests took to the dance floor. As always, Elvira led Nicholas to the floor first and when she danced herself tired, she returned to her throne, and Eleanor took over.

When Eleanor returned to her throne with Nicholas by her side, Elvira clapped her hands and the music stopped. "I promised you this ball would be like no other," said Elvira.

She descended the steps down to the dance floor. Once there, she called for the boxes to be bought in. Six blinks entered each carrying a small box. Ivan carried in one large box. Each box was placed on the floor in front of Elvira. Instructed by Elvira, all the boxes were opened simultaneously, anticipated excitement filled the room. A glow emanated from the dance floor, and as the glow got brighter, so the objects from the boxes grew. Then a final burst of bright light that caused everyone to look away, and when the light faded, floating a foot above the ground was a crystal slide, a hoop, a seesaw, a chair and a couple of miniature flying horses.

Everyone stood around in stunned silence not knowing what was happening. Elvira called to Nicholas who eagerly raced down the steps to join Elvira by the slide. "What do you think?" she asked.

"What it is for?" asked Nicholas, not understanding what was going on.

"It's for you," said Elvira. Taking Nicholas by the hand, she guided him towards the slide, but there were no steps to climb, only a tall cylinder. Elvira guided Nicholas so he stood beneath the cylinder and suddenly, he felt himself being sucked into the tube and floating up towards the top of the slide. It was a strange sensation, but more fun than frightening. Feeling totally weightless, he grinned at those watching below. Some of whom had a look of fear on their faces, but Nicholas felt no such fear. He knew this was going to be fun. When at the top of the cylinder, he floated forwards so that he was seated at the top of the slide. Thirty feet high, Elvira called up to Nicholas, "Let go." As he did, Nicholas plunged down the slide at great speed, feet first, gasps from the other guests went unheard by Nicholas as he screamed with delight. He shot off the end of the slide and flew straight through the hoop, also floating a foot above the ground and then he landed safely.

With a broad smile on his face and giggling, Nicholas asked, "Can I have another go?"

"Of course," said Elvira, "this is all for you." As he stood beneath the cylinder once more, he heard Elvira call to her guests. "Come, join in the fun." Then whoosh, he was sucked into the cylinder for the second time, and then flying down the slide once more, passing through the hoop and landing safely.

As Nicholas looked around at the other guests, joy swelled within his entire body. He smiled when he spotted Sir Cuthbert making his way onto the dance floor. "I'm not sure I'm going to fit inside that cylinder." Chuckled Sir Cuthbert.

"Of course you will," said Elvira, and just as Sir Cuthbert stood beneath the cylinder, he was sucked into the air. He felt the same strange weightless sensation as Nicholas and could not help but smile. It happened so fast. He didn't have time to doubt whether he would fit or not. Once seated at the top of the slide, he let go. As everyone watched on in stunned silence, an excited Sir Cuthbert flew off the end of the slide and shot through the hoop. Not knowing that Elvira had placed an enchantment on the hoop, Sir Cuthbert passed through and was instantly transformed back to when he was five years old.

Nicholas jumped for joy at the sight of Sir Cuthbert now only a few inches taller than he was, and minus the beard. They raced back to the slide together for yet another go and were quickly followed by many of the other guests. Having been down the slide for the third time, Nicholas was ready to try out the seesaw, but had no idea how to use it. As he approached, Ivan and his wife Priscilla appeared. Priscilla told Nicholas to stand on one end, which then sank to the floor. She then sat on the chair that had appeared the same time as the slide and

Ivan lifted it into the air. He then mounted onto a box so that Priscilla was ten feet above the seesaw.

"Ready," she called to Nicholas. As she then stood on the chair and launched herself down onto the opposite end of the seesaw, Nicholas, was sent soaring through the air, did a somersault and was caught by Ivan in the chair.

Lowering Nicholas to the floor, Ivan asked, "Did you enjoy that?"

"It was brilliant," replied Nicholas.

Sir Cuthbert asked, "Can I have a go?"

"Of course," said Ivan, and so Priscilla climbed onto the chair once more as Sir Cuthbert climbed onto the seesaw.

Again, she called, "Ready," and she launched herself down onto the seesaw. Sir Cuthbert had never experienced anything like it. Flying through the air, he screamed as those watching from below became a blur, then he was caught by Ivan in the chair.

"Enjoy that?" asked Ivan.

"That was the best thing ever." Laughed Sir Cuthbert.

Nicholas and the five-year-old Sir Cuthbert then raced over to the two miniature flying horses. Waiting to help them climb onto their backs were Eleanor and Elvira. "What do you think of the ball?" Elvira asked Nicholas.

"It's the best ever," said Nicholas. Once the two boys were seated on their flying horses, Elvira spoke to both of them.

"Do not worry, you cannot fall off," she said, and with that, the two tiny horses took to the air, circling high above the ballroom. Then swooping down to pass beneath the thirty-foot-tall slide, as more party guests flew down the slide and through the hoop, all transformed into their younger selves.

Only a handful of adult guests did not join in the fun. Elvira had noted who they were but was not about to spoil the party. She would deal with them another day. All those that had been changed back into their younger selves had the best time ever, but eventually the evening had to come to an end, as the enchantment wore off and the adults returned to normal size. Sir Cuthbert returned to normal whilst sat upon the miniature flying horse just as it landed. For a split second, he looked ridiculous as he towered over the tiny animal standing between his massive legs. Then the slide, seesaw and miniature flying horses all disappeared.

"Thank you all for coming and making this such a special night, and good night," said Elvira. Many of the guests were still laughing as they left the ballroom. Nicholas was feeling tired and was sat upon Eleanor's lap, as they watched them leave.

"That was the best party ever," said Nicholas, and then he yawned and fell asleep.

Chapter 31
Elvira's Greatest Shock

At midnight, all the party guests at Rebecca's had fallen asleep for yet another year. Rebecca had told Oliver and his friends they were welcome to stay the night, but there were no available beds. "We will be fine on the floor," said Oliver, "thank you."

Next morning when they all awoke with stiff joints, and aching limbs, Rebecca greeted them with a hot drink. "Here, drink this and I promise you will feel much better," she said. Joshua was the closest to Rebecca and so the first to try the drink offered.

"Well, here it goes," said Joshua, "can't feel any worse than I do right now." The drink was bright red and thick, almost like a syrup. Joshua was not convinced by its appearance, but when it passed over Joshua's lips and he drank it down, he was pleasantly surprised by the sweet taste and instant relief from all pain. "Wow, that is amazing," he said. Pretty soon, everyone had followed Joshua's lead, and all were feeling totally pain free.

"That is quite some potion," said Percival.

"It was passed on down to me by my mother," said Rebecca.

"I would very much appreciate the recipe," said Percival.

"I will write it down for you," said Rebecca. Having procured the list of ingredients and information on how to make Rebecca's pain-free potion, Percival bade her good morning. The others already waiting by the sleighs were eager to get going. Rebecca pointed them in the right direction, heading for Elvira's white castle. "If you see my son Cuthbert, will you tell him, I love him?" she asked.

"Of course," said Dorothy, "and thank you."

Rebecca watched as they drove away, the bells ringing joyfully on the reindeer's antlers. She felt consumed with a mixed feeling of joy and sadness, but hopeful they would find her son alive and be able to pass on her message of love.

Having lost their multi-coloured hair, they were grateful for the fur coats Saki had provided. There was a definite chill in the air. Travelling at great speed on their sleighs, they covered a lot of ground without any incident. By late afternoon just as Rebecca had said, the white castle belonging to Elvira came into view. They stopped and looked upon the white castle. With its stunning mountain backdrop, Oliver said, "So that is the castle belonging to Elvira, the Winter Queen."

Dorothy smiled broadly at the sight of the white castle as her excitement swelled from within. "What are we waiting for?" she asked.

"I think it best we show caution," said Percival, "we don't know if we will be welcome."

"Oh come on," said Dorothy, "she's our aunt. Once she realises who we are, surely everything will be all right."

"Do not forget Saki's warning," said Percival, "you must not tell her of your magic, and you must not let her know you are five. Please promise me this," said Percival. Dorothy looked at Oliver and smiled.

"We promise not to reveal our magic," said Oliver.

"And remember you must not reveal you are five," said Percival. They both nodded in agreement.

Oliver understood why Percival wanted to show caution, but like his sister believed that once Elvira knew who they were, there would be no problem. Besides, it was getting close to nightfall and he didn't want to spend a night sleeping outside, even though they had plenty of blankets and their fur coats for warmth. Percival reluctantly agreed, knowing that they needed shelter, but told Berwyn to stay out of sight. And so they approached the white castle, leaving Berwyn behind. Surprisingly, the gates to the castle were open and so they drove their sleighs straight into an empty courtyard. Oliver and Dorothy had entered through the gates first and came to a halt. The only sound was that of the bells ringing on the reindeer's antlers, and muffled footsteps because of the snow that covered the stone courtyard floor. When the other two sleighs came to a halt, Oliver found himself whispering, "Where is everyone?"

Suddenly, without warning, burning torches approached from all sides as doors were flung open. Surrounded, Oliver recognised those holding the torches as blinks.

As Dorothy clung to Oliver's arm, "What are they?" she asked, looking alarmed, her voice shaky with fear, staring at their strange appearance. "They don't seem to have a mouth, nose or ears," she said.

"That's because they don't," said Oliver.

"But how do they communicate?" asked Dorothy.

"They communicate to their master what they see by blinking," said Oliver.

Before Dorothy could ask any more questions however, a tall, thin man with long, blonde hair and wearing a blood-red suit approached. "I am sorry if their appearance disturbed you," he said looking at Dorothy, "but let me assure you, they are quite harmless, merely servants, that is all." Oliver knew from previous experience that they might seem harmless, but when needed by Eleanor, they had proved themselves to be determined and accomplished fighters.

"Please follow me," said the tall, thin man. As they ascended the steps towards the main castle entrance, the doors opened. The tall, thin man stepped to one side to allow them to enter, followed closely by the blinks. Although Dorothy had been eager to meet Elvira, now that she was standing in the white castle, surrounded by blinks, she suddenly felt quite fearful. A prickly sensation seemed to crawl over her skin and she clung to Oliver's arm for support as she looked around the large entrance hall. The blinks carrying their torches walked on by either side of Oliver and Dorothy. She watched as they disappeared into the darkest corner of the long hallway, the flames of their torches extinguished as if by magic, and they were gone.

A loud thud as the door closed behind them made Dorothy jump. She looked behind her to see the tall, thin man smiling at them. As he walked past, he said, "Follow me." Percival followed his lead. Dorothy's legs didn't seem to want to work properly and she stumbled. Only because she still had hold of Oliver's arm did she not fall to the ground. Reif took hold of Dorothy's other arm, and so she was escorted down the long hallway. Joshua and the guards followed at the rear.

Giant candle chandeliers lit the way, hanging from the ceiling high above. The white walls were bare, void of any pictures. As Dorothy glanced through the windows, night had fallen and the sky was black, snow had started to gently fall.

Silently, they followed the tall, thin man. At the end of the hallway were a set of double doors. He pushed them open and as before, stepped to one side to allow them to enter.

The room was full of exquisite white furniture. Dorothy looked around, to one side, stood a round table with a glass top, placed in the centre of the table, a clear glass vase of white flowers, with four ornately carved white chairs seated on the floor, perfectly positioned around the table. Then her eyes fell upon a pair of identical small white tables, each with a different sculpture, on one a dragon made from white marble, whilst on the other a white marble unicorn.

As her confidence grew, Dorothy released Oliver's arm and stepped further into the room. The door closed silently, leaving them alone. A large white sofa and four matching chairs stood before a white marble fireplace. The only colour in the room was provided by the blue flames of the fire, and a portrait of an elegant lady, wearing a white dress, with ruby red lips and long, blonde hair. The picture was hung above the fireplace, a small printed label read, Elvira, The Winter Queen.

"So, this is our aunt," whispered Dorothy turning to Oliver, who stepped forward to have a closer look, reading the label for himself. Quite unexpectedly, the double doors clicked open behind them. They all turned around not knowing what to expect, and found themselves face to face with Elvira.

Recognising her from the portrait, Oliver approached and introduced himself, "Your Majesty, my name is Prince Oliver." She seemed surprised by his greeting, but offered her hand and as he took it in his, she felt a tingling sensation, when he then kissed the back of her hand. It was like an elixir that coursed through her veins, even stronger than what she felt from Nicholas. As he took a step back, she revelled in the glorious sensation. "May I introduce my sister Princess Dorothy," said Oliver.

Elvira had greeted Oliver with a warm smile, and her spirits had soared at his touch, but as Dorothy approached, Elvira gasped in shock, and stumbled. Her legs giving way as if they had been made of snow and suddenly she had found herself standing in front of a raging fire, only preventing herself from collapsing onto the floor by placing a hand on the glass topped table. Oliver rushed forward and took hold of Elvira's arm to steady her while Reif pulled out one of the four chairs so Elvira could sit down. She was pale and visibly shaken. Dorothy approached and asked, "Are you all right, is there anything we can get you?" But Elvira looked at Dorothy as if she had seen a ghost. The resemblance between Dorothy and her mother Elizabeth was so great that Elvira sat looking at her younger sister once more. Unable to speak, feebly she raised a hand to touch Dorothy's face, at which Dorothy pulled away, but looking into Elvira's eyes, she saw only sadness and so leant forward to allow Elvira to reach out and touch her face. Elvira gasped and took a deep breath as a tingling sensation spread from her fingertips and coursed its way throughout her body, just as it had done moments before when Oliver kissed her hand.

"What is wrong with her?" asked Dorothy.

"It seems your appearance has caused our host to suffer a terrible shock," said Percival, as he checked Elvira's pulse.

"But why should my appearance cause such a reaction?" asked Dorothy.

"Because of your resemblance to your mother," said Percival.

Just then, a musical voice that Oliver immediately recognised as that of Eleanor, called, "Mother, what are you doing in here?" Dorothy and Oliver looked at each other, as Eleanor stopped in her tracks. Her eyes quickly swept around the room, until she spotted Elvira slumped in the chair at the glass-topped table. "What have you done to my mother?" she asked, as she raced across the room. Kneeling in front of Elvira, Eleanor spoke to her mother. "Mother, are you all right, what did they do to you?" she asked. The only response Elvira gave was to raise a trembling right hand and point at Dorothy. Puzzled by Elvira's reaction, and deeming that it was Dorothy who had done this to her mother, Eleanor stood. She towered over Dorothy. "What have you done to my mother?" Her voice so cool and calm, yet menacingly demanding, it sent a shiver down Dorothy's spine. It felt as if the fire and warmth of the room had been extinguished. Dorothy stood terrified, not knowing what to say, she backed away from Eleanor's gaze. It was Percival who intervened, as Eleanor took a step forwards, towards Dorothy.

"She has done nothing to your mother," said Percival, "it seems your mother has suffered a terrible shock."

As Eleanor continued to glower at Dorothy, Elvira had recovered some of her composure. Standing up shakily, she called to Eleanor, "The girl has done nothing wrong." Upon hearing her mother's voice, Eleanor turned and saw that she was standing. Eleanor crossed the room to help her mother, who indicated she wanted to sit on the sofa in front of the fire. When she was seated and comfortable, she finally greeted Dorothy with the same warmth she had shown Oliver. She invited Oliver and Dorothy to join her on the sofa, indicating for the others to be seated.

Percival was watching Elvira intensively, for he did not trust her, carefully listening to every word she said. "So, what brings you to my castle?" asked Elvira.

"We are searching for our younger brother, Your Majesty," said Dorothy.

"A younger brother you say," said Elvira.

"Yes, Your Majesty, his name is Nicholas." Eleanor sat silently watching, for she knew Oliver to be Nicholas' older brother, but she had been unaware of a sister.

"You remember, mother, I told you when we found Nicholas in the courtyard, he had a brother called Oliver."

"Oh yes, that's right, I remember now," said Elvira.

"So, he is here, can we see him?" asked Dorothy.

"He is here," said Elvira, "but I'm afraid he is not very well."

"What do you mean, not very well."

The look of horror on Dorothy's face prompted Eleanor to quickly say, "Oh, do not worry, it is nothing serious, just a cold. I've given him something to help and he is sleeping, but you can see him tomorrow." Dorothy let out a great sigh of relief as she turned to Oliver.

"Did you hear that, Nicholas is here," she said, as she flung her arms around Oliver's neck, her heart pounding with excitement.

"Yes, I heard," said Oliver, who had not expected it to be that easy.

"You must be tired after your journey, are you hungry?" asked Elvira.

"I'm not hungry," said Percival, as he looked at the others, who all agreed.

"But I am feeling tired," said Dorothy.

"Follow me," said Eleanor. She led them down a pictureless white hallway, the only colour, the orange yellow flames of the burning candles, and the contrasting blackness beyond the windows, looking out into the night.

Having climbed a surprisingly narrow staircase which meant they had to follow in single file, Eleanor came to a halt. Standing before them were four doors leading to separate bedrooms. "I think you should take this one," said Eleanor, indicating to Dorothy the door to the far right.

"Thank you," said Dorothy, "well goodnight." And as she opened the bedroom door, she heard Oliver and Reif agree to share one bedroom, while Joshua would go with Percival leaving the two guards to share the fourth.

Dorothy woke the next day. As she pulled open the curtains, she was greeted with a weak sun and a flurry of light snow. Her window looked out onto the snow-covered grounds. Without any idea of the time, she climbed back in bed, and made herself comfortable. She lay there for a few minutes of sheer luxurious warmth before she remembered where she was. "Nicholas," she screamed, as she sat bolt upright in bed.

Having dressed quickly, she dashed across the room to the door. Turning the handle, to her utter amazement, she found the door locked. Pounding on the door, demanding to be let out, she couldn't have cared if she woke the whole castle.

A door behind her opened and Oliver entered from a connected room. "I see you're awake at last," he said.

Dorothy jumped with fright at the unexpected voice behind her, but was so angry at finding herself locked in, she turned to face the intruder, standing besides her bed were Oliver and Reif. "I thought you was never going to wake up," said Oliver, smiling. Dorothy's mind was in a state of confusion. The door to the hallway was locked and yet here stood Oliver and Reif.

Recognising his sisters confused expression. "Oh, there's a connecting door by the fireplace." Indicated Oliver. As her eyes scanned the room, they passed over Reif who was still in the process of putting on his shirt, evidently only just having woken himself.

Regaining her thoughts, Dorothy asked, "Is your door locked as well?" immediately realising this was a stupid question to ask.

"Yes, it is," said Oliver, "and although our rooms are connected, I cannot find a hidden door leading to Percival and Joshua."

"Why do you think they have locked us in," asked Dorothy, but before Oliver could answer, "listen," said Dorothy, "I can hear footsteps." She pressed her ear against the door. Rightly enough, footsteps were approaching the other side of the door, and then stopped suddenly. A loud click filled the room, as the door was unlocked, her heartbeat with anxious excitement and she took a step backwards away from the door allowing it to be opened. As she was joined by Oliver and Reif, the door was flung open and in raced Nicholas, followed closely by Eleanor and Elvira.

Upon having Nicholas in her arms once more, she cried the happiest of tears. All thoughts of annoyance and anger at being locked in evaporated from Dorothy's mind, as quickly as morning dew on a hot summer's day.

Having been released by Dorothy, Nicholas jumped into the open arms of his brother Oliver, and Dorothy hugged them both. As Eleanor and Elvira watched this happy scene, they were joined by Percival, Joshua and the two guards whose doors had also been unlocked. Smiles were on everyone's faces at this joyous reunion, everyone that is except Percival, who although happy, had his gaze firmly focussed on Elvira, wondering what she was up to.

After they had eaten breakfast, they were all gathered in one of Elvira's sitting rooms. Eleanor was questioning Percival, asking how they had managed to find their way to the white castle.

Percival answered carefully, not wanting them to know he had seen his mother Saki, nor did he want them to know they had been given directions by Sir Cuthbert's mother, Rebecca.

"We were lucky," answered Percival, "we saw a giant white eagle like the one that took Nicholas, and followed it, taking a chance it may have been the same one." Eleanor shot a glance at her mother, who apparently wasn't listening, all her focus and attention was on Dorothy. "And it led us here," finished Percival.

Nicholas was happily sat between Dorothy and Oliver, recounting all the things that had happened whilst at the white castle.

"There was a ball with a three headed dog," said Nicholas, Dorothy gasped.

"I stroked him," said Nicholas, as if this was the most normal thing in the world to do, "then there was Favonious, the flying horse, I got to ride him, and we flew out over the countryside, oh, and there was a kitten," said Nicholas. Oliver could not help but laugh.

"You have been busy," said Oliver, but Dorothy had turned white. If the three-headed dog hadn't been a shock, the thought of a flying horse, yet Nicholas had taken it all in his stride.

Oliver's expression did change however when Nicholas told them of his sleigh ride with the snowman at night. "As the wolves closed in the snowman split into four and surrounded me, then mother came flying through the air on a blue dragon and rescued me," said Nicholas.

Dorothy was gazing at Nicholas with a bewildered expression on her face. "Who did you say rescued you?" asked Dorothy.

"Why mother did," said Nicholas. Dorothy's eyes sparkled with excitement and her heart skipped a beat. With thoughts running through her mind, our mother is alive, but then, how could this be possible. She turned her gaze from Nicholas towards Oliver. Her body trembled with unparalleled joy.

"Did you hear that, Oliver?" she asked. Oliver, with no joy upon his face sat looking first at Dorothy who could not understand why Oliver was not as excited as she was.

He turned away from her happy face and asked Nicholas, "And where is your mother now?"

"There," said Nicholas, pointing straight at Elvira.

Dorothy's joy disappeared in the blink of an eye. She had turned quickly to see where her mother was standing ready to run and give her a hug. Happy tears were streaking down her face, but as she turned, there was no one standing behind her. Only Elvira seated as before smiling across at Nicholas. A sudden realisation hit Dorothy as if an arrow had pierced her heart. No longer crying tears of joy, she got to her feet and fled the room. Reif went to follow. "Let me," said Oliver. As Reif sat back down, all talking had ceased, and all eyes followed Oliver as he left the room dashing after his sister. The only audible sound was that of Dorothy crying on the other side of the door, and comforting words from Oliver.

"How did you know," asked Dorothy between sobs.

"He wouldn't have recognised our mother," said Oliver, "she died when he was only three days old."

"But there is the portrait of our mother," said Dorothy.

"True," said Oliver, "but for Nicholas, it's just a picture, have you not noticed how Elvira looks at him, and Nicholas at her."

Dorothy had stopped crying and with Oliver by her side, they re-entered the sitting room. Straight away, Dorothy noticed Nicholas was now sat upon Elvira's lap cradled in her arms like any child needing reassurance by their mother. "How are you, my dear?" asked Elvira, seeing Dorothy enter the room with red, teary eyes.

"I'm fine," said Dorothy, struggling to hold back more tears, "it was just a bit of a shock, you see our mother is dead."

As Percival sat watching Elvira's reaction closely, he noticed the faintest of flickers in her eyes as she heard the news of her sister's death. Percival then asked, "Will you be able to help us return all three children safely to their father King Richard?" Elvira turned to face Percival, having composed herself before answering.

"Of course, nothing would give me greater joy than to reunite a father and his children, but there is a ball tomorrow, surely you can stay for that?"

Nicholas leapt off Elvira's lap and stood before Dorothy, smiling. Nicholas took hold of her hands and asked, "Please, can we stay for the ball?" Dorothy and Oliver looked at each other and smiled.

"Yes," said Dorothy, "I don't think delaying our departure until after the ball is a going to make any difference." Nicholas was so happy. Letting go of Dorothy's hands, he raced over and jumped into Oliver's arms.

"You wait, tomorrow will be the best ball you've ever been to," said Nicholas excitedly.

Dorothy sat with a smile etched on her face, but her thoughts were with her mother. She had thought for one brief, moment that she would see her again, feel the warmth of her embrace and the tender loving care that was always given. It had been five years since her passing, five years to get used to her not being there, and yet in that one joyous, exhilarating moment, she would have given anything for one more embrace.

The tall, thin man in the blood-red suit appeared in the open doorway. "Your Majesty, lunch is ready to be served."

"Follow me," said Elvira, and she led the way to the dining room. "Please be seated," said Elvira. She took her place at the head of the table. Eleanor sat at the opposite and, Dorothy sat closest to Elvira, whilst Nicholas sat between his brother and sister, Reif sat closest to Eleanor, then Percival, Joshua and the guards sat the other side of the table.

"You talk of your father, but say you mother has died," asked Elvira, talking to Dorothy.

Dorothy looked down at the bowl that had just been placed in front of her. "What is this?" she asked.

"It is a delicacy we have, when we have honoured guests, spiced parsnip and red lentil soup," said Elvira. Dorothy watched as the steam spiralled upwards, gathering her thoughts before answering, then choking back the tears that seemed determined to escape once more.

"She died three days after giving birth to Nicholas," said Dorothy.

Elvira dropped her spoon which clattered into her bowl of spiced soup, sending copious amounts of hot liquid flying in all directions. "Sorry to hear that," said Elvira. As all eyes had turned in her direction, she cleaned up the mess with a wave of her hand.

Percival was still watching Elvira closely.

"What was your mother's name?" asked Elvira, hoping she was mistaken by Dorothy's resemblance to her sister.

"Elizabeth," replied Dorothy.

A flash of recognition emanated from Elvira's eyes. The news was like a dagger to the heart. So her sister was dead, but here sat her daughter. Moving swiftly, she had taken everyone by surprise, even Percival, grabbing hold of Dorothy by the hand. "Come with me," she commanded.

Dorothy had no choice but to follow, the grip was firm, as she was led away. Oliver went to stand, pushing his chair away from the table. "Stay where you are," said Elvira, and he found himself unable to rise from his chair.

Turning to face Eleanor, he demanded, "What is going on, where is she taking Dorothy, and why can't I get out of my chair?"

Eleanor was laughing at Oliver. "All will be revealed in time," she said, and she stood up and walked towards Nicholas.

"Leave my brother alone," shouted Oliver.

Taking no notice of Oliver and the rest, as they struggled to stand, Eleanor offered her hand to Nicholas. He took hold and stood from his chair without resistance. Then without another word being spoken, Eleanor and Nicholas left the room, neither looking back as Oliver, screaming in frustration called, "Why are you doing this?"

Elvira was leading Dorothy down a narrow staircase that took them beneath the white castle, the only source of light, pale blue flames, provided by the wall mounted candles that flickered and danced casting strange shadows as they passed.

Having reached the bottom of the stairs, the blue-flamed candles on the walls illuminated a distant door. If ghosts existed, Dorothy imagined they would be the colour of that door, white with a hint of blue that seemed to emanate from within. The door stood veiled in a fine mist, then as Elvira moved forward, the tiled floor gave off a luminescent glow with every step she took. All these things increased the sense of dread within Dorothy, but she found herself unable to resist.

Filled with curiosity and fear, Dorothy stumbled as they approached the door. The glow from within seemed to get brighter the closer they got. Accompanied by a chill that stung the lungs with each breath, Dorothy's throat seemed to be constricting, as she struggled to breathe.

Elvira stopped in front of the door. Dorothy, held firm in Elvira's grasp, also stopped. A piercing blue eye appeared in the door. Dorothy gasped. Elvira leant forward placing her eye close to the eye in the door. The process of recognition took a matter of seconds. Then a voice filled the passageway.

"Welcome, my queen." And as Elvira straightened up, the door swung inwards allowing entry.

Dorothy found to her great delight that once they had entered over the threshold, breathing became normal once more. Elvira finally released Dorothy's hand without saying a word. It was a few seconds before Dorothy even realised this. Only when Elvira moved away leaving Dorothy standing alone did she look down at her hand, then as she looked up again, she started looking for Elvira who seemed to have vanished.

As Dorothy moved around the room, wall-mounted candles burst into blue flame, firstly revealing a collection of children's toys. She picked up a small bear and a vision of two young girls playing appeared in her mind. She dropped the toy. Startled, she looked around the room calling for Elvira. "Where are you?" Dorothy moved further into the room. Elvira did not answer. Further candles burst into flame. This time, children's clothes were highlighted, then adult dresses. She moved on, under a glass dome. Jewellery was laid out on a table neatly arranged, and again, Dorothy called, "Elvira, why am I here?" Stepping from the shadows, wall mounted candles burst into flame either side of a full-size portrait.

"I wanted you to see this," said Elvira.

As Dorothy's gaze moved from Elvira to the painting, she suddenly realised what she had been looking at. "Are these my mother's possessions?" asked Dorothy.

"Yes," said Elvira. The portrait standing before Dorothy showed Elizabeth when she was about the same age as Dorothy. The clothes were different, but the facial features and hair were identical. Dorothy was used to being told she resembled her mother, but the only portrait they had seen before was of Elizabeth as an adult, now it felt as though she was looking at herself, reflected in a mirror.

Dorothy raised a hand to touch her face, half expecting the portrait to do the same. It remained motionless. With no knowledge of how long she had stood there staring into those familiar eyes, she was bought back to reality when Elvira asked, "Was she happy?"

Dorothy began to cry, and turned away from the picture. "Yes," she said in answer to Elvira's question. With trembling fingers, she lifted the glass dome and ran her fingers across what had been her mother's jewellery, but she did not pick it up. It felt wrong to disturb it.

As Elvira watched, she asked, "Did your mother ever perform magic?" Caught up in the moment of high emotion, Dorothy hadn't heard the question properly. Staring at the jewellery Dorothy gently replaced the dome.

"Sorry, what was that you just asked?" said Dorothy.

"I asked, did your mother ever perform magic?" said Elvira.

Dorothy laughed between sobs. "Heavens no," she said, "why would you ask that?"

"Because I can," said Elvira, and there Dorothy stood, surrounded by her mother's possessions, in the glow of the blue flamed candles as snow gently fell around them. She tilted her head back to look up as the snowflakes fluttered down onto her eyelashes. Brushing against her skin the gentle caress of each flake tickled. Then Elvira asked the one question Dorothy knew she had been dying to ask. "Can you perform magic?" asked Elvira.

"Why no," said Dorothy, "I mean, how do you do it?"

"I can make things happen with just a thought," said Elvira.

"Oh really," said Dorothy, remembering how she had made the guard float up in the air and saved him from the yetis, when she had no idea how she had achieved it. A glimpse of recognition had flashed in Dorothy's eyes, noticed by Elvira, but she chose not to question Dorothy any further. The snow stopped falling and Dorothy moved back towards the toys. Again Dorothy picked up the bear, and more images of Elizabeth and Elvira playing danced in her mind. Turning to Elvira who was also crying silent tears, Dorothy asked, "May I have this?"

"Of course," said Elvira, wiping away the tears.

As they left the room, the candles expired, and the door sealed behind them. Dorothy turned towards Elvira. "Why did you bring me down here alone?"

"I knew you would appreciate seeing your mother's things alone," said Elvira. Dorothy considered these words and smiled. She was grateful she had had the chance to be alone with her mother's possessions.

By the time Elvira and Dorothy arrived back at the dining room, Oliver's anger had abated. Under careful guidance from Percival, they had already finished eating their spiced soup and were enjoying a hot drink of, blackberry mulled wine.

As Elvira and Dorothy resumed their seats, Elvira asked, "Where are Eleanor and Nicholas?"

"We are here, mother," said Eleanor, as she led Nicholas back to the table and sat down.

"I am sorry," said Elvira, as she looked down the table and addressed Oliver, "I did not mean to upset you in anyway, there was just something I needed to show Dorothy alone, please forgive me."

Under Percival's watchful gaze and remembering to stay calm, Oliver replied, "I am sorry I got so angry, please forgive me."

"There is nothing to forgive," said Elvira.

Once lunch was over, Elvira offered to give a tour of the castle and asked if anyone would care for a sleigh ride down to the village. Nicholas was eager for Oliver and Dorothy to see the shops. "Please come for a ride, I want to show you Sir Cuthbert's glass shop." At the mention of Sir Cuthbert, Dorothy and Oliver looked at each other.

Remembering Rebecca's request, "We would love to join you for a sleigh ride down to the village," said Dorothy.

Elvira gave the tall, thin man in the blood-red suit instructions to arrange for three sleighs to be made ready to travel down to the village. Percival apologised, he was still feeling tired and asked if he could be permitted to stay behind and rest. Elvira saw no reason to deny the request, and so as the others set off, Percival watched from the bedroom he had been allocated.

The master of the carriages was driving the horses that pulled the sleigh containing Elvira and Nicholas. She had requested Dorothy to ride them. Percival hoped and prayed that Dorothy remembered what he had told her, not to reveal your magic or that you are five. The second sleigh carried Eleanor, who was joined by Oliver and Reif, being driven by the tall, thin man in the blood-red suit. The third sleigh was driven by a blink, Joshua faced forwards and the remaining two guards rode side by side going backwards. Percival, standing next to the window, watched until they were out of sight.

Chapter 32
Elvira's Secret Discovered

Percival had left his room as soon as the sleighs had disappeared from view. He wanted to explore the white castle alone. Blinks were busy doing chores. As he moved from room to room, they seemed to take no notice. He had descended the narrow staircase from the bedrooms and had already looked around the sitting room that contained the exquisite white furniture and the portrait of Elvira.

Opening a set of double doors, he found himself entering the ballroom. Suspended high above the dance floor, candle chandeliers burst into flame. At first startled, Percival descended the blue marble staircase. Standing in the middle of the floor, he slowly spun around taking in every detail. The two thrones sat side by side, and to their right, seats where the musicians sat and played. Way back in one corner, Percival noticed a set of doors. He crossed the ballroom floor. His footsteps echoed all around him, bouncing off the walls and high ceiling. It was as if he had twenty men accompanying him. He approached the doors. There was no handle or lock, but when he tried to open the doors, they would not budge.

What a strange set of doors, thought Percival, if they had been locked, he would have thought no more of it, but magically sealed doors meant there was something to hide. He was determined to see what was beyond.

Percival placed the palm of each hand on the surface of the doors. He could feel the ripple of magic which held the doors sealed. He smiled to himself, a simple enough spell to break if you knew how. The harder one pushed, the more the doors would resist. Percival removed his hands and with one finger lightly touched the door. They opened instantly to reveal a steep set of stairs leading down into darkness.

As Percival stepped between the open doors, they gently closed behind him, sealed in darkness so complete that Percival could not see his fingers even when he touched his nose. He reached into one of his many pockets to find the orb that had lit their way through the mountain. With the orb held in his hand, it shone brightly. Although the bottom of the stairs remained contained in darkness, Percival made his way down the steep stairs.

Counting each step he took, he stopped at 377. He turned to look back. The doors, even with the light from the orb were no longer visible. He gave up counting as he looked towards the bottom of the stairs, which were still shrouded in darkness.

Percival had lost all sense of time, travelling through the dark, and when the last step finally appeared, he felt relieved. He had been concentrating so much on not falling whilst descending the steep stairs he had not noticed the chill in the air. Now on level ground, he followed the tunnel. Without his fur coat to keep him warm, the cold air grasped at his limbs. He ponderously moved forward down the tunnel.

Quite unexpectedly appearing out of the dark, Percival found himself standing in front of a dark wooden door. A metal grill made up the top half of the door. As Percival stopped in front of the door, he could see a faint glow in the distance. He covered the orb with a handkerchief to reduce the brightness, then tried the door. It opened.

Elvira was obviously confident no one would get beyond her magically sealed door. He passed through the open door, and this time it stayed open. He slowly moved towards the glow ahead. The shrouded orb giving just enough light fort Percival to see where he was placing his feet.

Percival stopped abruptly. Voices, he was sure of it. He stood motionless listening, nothing, but his senses told him otherwise. Something lay ahead, or was his mind beginning to play tricks on him, he wondered, but as he was about to move forwards again, more voices, shrieking and laughter. This time he was certain, and they were the voices of children. Percival moved forward at a faster pace, eager to discover what lay ahead.

To his astonishment and surprise, he stepped out from the dark tunnel into a garden filled with rainbow coloured trees. For a moment, he thought he had returned to Cressida's rainbow forest, but when he turned around to look behind him, the dark entrance to the tunnel was still there. Turning back once more to look upon the garden, it was flooded with sunlight, without a hint of snow. A dozen or more young children were cheerfully playing on swings and slides. Some were climbing trees that stood no taller than ten feet. As Percival watched one small child, a girl, she fell to the ground. Percival's first instinct was to run over to the child to see it she was injured, but she simply bounced on the grass, got to her feet and ran off with her friends.

Puzzled, Percival moved further into the garden. The children continued to play, as if he wasn't even there. As he walked past one of the trees, a voice called, "Hello, who are you?" He turned around to see a young girl sitting with her back resting against the tree. She looked about the same age as Dorothy, with blonde hair that hung in ringlets down beyond her shoulders. Her face was freckled and lightly tanned. She had large, round eyes a milky bluish colour, that resembled the colour of opals, that shimmered in the sunlight. She wore a plain, green dress with short sleeves and round neckline, and when she stood, it hung just below her knees. Her feet were bare.

"My name is Percival," he said, in answer to the young girl's question, "but, what is this place?" he asked. She gave him a bewildered look.

"Why, this is the garden of youth," said the young girl.

As Percival walked around the garden, the young girl fell in step beside him. "My name is Hebe," she said.

"A pleasure to meet you, Hebe," said Percival. They walked side by side, "Can you tell me about this place?" asked Percival.

"What would you like to know," said Hebe.

"Does it have a purpose?" asked Percival.

"I'm not sure what you mean," said Hebe.

"What is it used for?" asked Percival. Hebe laughed, and now it was Percival who looked bewildered.

"You are silly," she said.

"Why is that?" asked Percival.

"The garden of youth is where you come if you want to stay young and beautiful," said Hebe, "and I am its guardian. As long as there are young children happily playing here and the Winter Queen visits at least once a week, she can stay youthful forever. Every so often, she brings a new child for my collection."

"What happens when the children grow older?" asked Percival.

"Why, she sends them back to their parents," said Hebe.

"Are you certain of this?" asked Percival. Hebe stood silently looking at Percival.

"Who are you?" she asked, growing agitated.

"Why, I am Percival," he said.

"How did you get down here?" she asked, but before Percival could answer, Hebe stood, staring at Percival and blinked, and before he could retreat back into the dark tunnel, he found himself surrounded by blinks. He knew it was futile to struggle and so let himself be escorted from the garden. H was taken to a doorway that was hidden behind a multi-coloured weeping willow tree that stood in one corner. As they stepped through the door, they entered into the sitting room with the exquisite white furniture from there Percival was led to his bedroom. As the door closed, he heard it lock.

Chapter 33
And So, There Are Five

As the master of the carriages drove his sleigh towards the village, Elvira spoke to Dorothy. "I see you came prepared for the cold weather." Admiring Dorothy's fur coat. "How was your journey to the winter castle?" she asked.

"Extremely pleasant," said Dorothy, "I love the snow, and the scenery is stunning."

"Did you manage to get here without any trouble?" asked Elvira.

"We did see a small avalanche," said Dorothy, "but it was way off in the distance, and caused us no trouble."

"You were very lucky," said Elvira. "Tell me, how is it that you and Oliver are here searching for Nicholas and not your father?" asked Elvira.

"Our father was taken ill," said Dorothy, "and so was not able to make the journey." She squeezed her brother's hand gently and they looked at each other and smiled, Elvira smiled also.

"I hope he has someone to look after him," said Elvira.

"The court physician will look after him," said Dorothy.

"And Alice and Mary," said Nicholas. Dorothy turned to look at Nicholas with an expression of horror on her face.

"Who are Alice and Mary?" asked Elvira.

"Our sisters," said Nicholas, with a huge grin on his face.

"So, how many brothers and sisters do you have?" asked Elvira. She was looking directly at Dorothy, who was biting her lip. She didn't want to answer, but Nicholas had already ruined everything. She had no choice but to answer.

"There are five of us," said Dorothy.

The look on Elvira's face was impossible for Dorothy to read, was it fear or excitement, whatever it was, it was fleeting, and the questioning stopped. Elvira spent the rest of the journey into the village talking about the forest and the lakes and how beautiful they were. Dorothy listened, but her mind was elsewhere. She had let Percival down. Elvira knew they were five, but at least Elvira didn't know that she could do magic.

Nicholas got excited as the barn came into view. He pointed it out to Dorothy and then called to Oliver. "Look, there's the barn," he shouted.

Oliver waved a hand and called to Nicholas, "I cannot wait to see Sir Cuthbert's shop." The sleighs pulled up outside the double doors and they all dismounted. As the doors opened, the cacophony that greeted them was as welcoming as the warmth from within.

They hurried inside and closed the doors to keep the cold air out. Dorothy tried to get to Oliver to tell him what had happened, but Elvira called her back. Nicholas grabbed hold of Oliver's hand and headed off towards Sir Cuthbert's glass shop.

Dorothy was left behind with Elvira, while Eleanor, Reif, Joshua and the two guards followed Nicholas and Oliver. "How old are you?" asked Elvira.

"I am twelve," said Dorothy.

"And your brother and sisters?" asked Elvira. Dorothy didn't know whether to tell the truth or not, but in the end decided she would. After all, what difference could it make? Elvira already knew they were five.

"My sisters and I share the same birthday, along with Oliver," said Dorothy. "So, the four of you were born on the same day," said Elvira, "how interesting, have any of your siblings ever performed magic," she asked.

"No," said Dorothy. Trying to keep her voice as normal as possible, but she was feeling under pressure, and felt sure her voice would betray her.

Nicholas and Oliver had reached the glass shop owned by Sir Cuthbert. As they entered the shop, the bell above the door rang, announcing the arrival of customers. The shop was empty, but within seconds of their arrival, a tall man with flaming red hair and broad shoulders appeared from the back of the shop wearing his protective clothing. He removed his face shield.

Oliver needed no introduction. There was no mistaking the man stood before him. He was the spitting image of his father, from the portrait. "Sir Cuthbert," said Oliver, "I am Nicholas' brother, Oliver." He offered his hand to shake, which Sir Cuthbert grasped enthusiastically and shook.

"Welcome to my shop," said Sir Cuthbert. Oliver was about to pass on the message from Sir Cuthbert's mother Rebecca, when the bell above the door rang once again, and in walked Dorothy, followed by Elvira. Eleanor and the others waited outside. The shop was hardly big enough to hold them all.

"Your Majesty," said Sir Cuthbert, as Elvira entered the shop. She did not even glance in his direction, but simply made her way to the cabinet that held the brooches. Dorothy took her chance and grabbed Oliver by the arm pulling him to the other side of the shop, leaving Nicholas to look at the brooches with Elvira.

"She knows we are five," said Dorothy.

"How did that happen?" asked Oliver in an angry whisper.

"It was Nicholas," said Dorothy, "Elvira was asking questions about who was looking after our father. I said the court physician, and Nicholas mentioned Alice and Mary, I couldn't stop him. She also asked again if any of us have performed magic. I told her no, but I don't know if she believes me or not."

"Thanks for the warning," said Oliver.

Elvira wasted no time in choosing the brooch for the ball the next day with the help of Nicholas. As Sir Cuthbert wrapped the brooch, Elvira turned to see where Oliver and Dorothy were. "Oh there you are," she said, "is everything all right?"

"Yes, we were just admiring the workmanship that has gone into this piece of glass, I have never seen anything like it before," said Dorothy.

Sir Cuthbert handed the wrapped brooch to Elvira. "I think it's time we headed back," she said. Oliver told Dorothy to go with Elvira and he would catch them up. As they left the shop, Oliver waited until the door had closed, only then did he speak, he moved closer to Sir Cuthbert, and in a whisper.

"We have seen your mother," he said to Sir Cuthbert. Visibly shaken, Sir Cuthbert sat down.

"How is she?" he asked.

"She is tired," said Oliver. "Your mother has no idea whether you are dead or alive, and yet each birthday she holds a party for you, hoping one day for your return."

"And my sisters?"

"No one has aged since you were taken, except for your mother. On the stroke of midnight, she puts all the guests to sleep for another year. Only she remains awake, praying for your return. Only your mother knows you were carried off by the giant white eagle, ridden by Elvira," said Oliver.

As Oliver watched Sir Cuthbert struggling with his emotions, "She said to let you know that she loves you," said Oliver. Sir Cuthbert sat with his head buried in his large hands. "Why do you stay?" asked Oliver.

"She has my children," said Sir Cuthbert, "I cannot leave without them. She says I can have them back when she no longer has a need for them." A wry smile appeared across Sir Cuthbert's face. "You have no idea what she is capable of," he said. Oliver left the shop feeling anxious after Sir Cuthbert's remark. "Until tomorrow," called Sir Cuthbert, "for I shall see you at the ball."

Oliver caught up with Dorothy back at the sleigh. "Is everything all right?" she asked.

"Yes, of course," said Oliver, fully aware Elvira was listening. She smiled broadly, but there was menace in her eyes. Oliver returned her smile with a broad grin of his own. She continued to watch as Oliver climbed aboard the sleigh and made himself comfortable next to Eleanor, with Reif seated opposite. Once everyone was settled, they were off, heading back towards the white castle, however, they took the more scenic route.

Elvira pointed out one of the frozen lakes to their left. Oliver turned his head to look. It reminded him of 'dead man's lake' back home. Completely covered in snow, it was invisible to the unwary. He commented on this. "Is it not dangerous to travel so close to the lake?"

"See those shrubs covered in snow, they form the boundary of the lake," said Elvira, "look closely and you can see the difference." Oliver looked again. Looking carefully, he realised, leading up to the shrubs, the snow lay uneven, where shrubs and bushes were partially buried, but beyond, the snow lay as smooth and flat as a white marble floor. "It's easy to spot when you know what you're looking for," said Elvira. As Oliver turned to face forward once more, a collection of pine trees stood tall to the right, covered from top to bottom in snow. They sparkled in the daylight.

Without any warning, a large blue dragon appeared from beyond the trees. It flew towards the sleigh that carried Elvira, Dorothy and Nicholas. Elvira did nothing, and Nicholas who had been saved by the blue dragon before sat smiling at its magnificence. Dorothy however reacted on instinct. As the blue dragon swooped down from a cloudless sky overhead, Dorothy raised her hands as if to shield her face, a wall of impenetrable snow rose from the ground between the sleigh and the dragon, blocking its path.

Witnessed by the others from their sleighs, Oliver looked on horrified and screamed, "No." Both Oliver and Reif had made a move to leap from the sleigh, to race over to Dorothy. Both were grabbed by Eleanor, who held them tight. "Stay seated," she said, and both Reif and Oliver found themselves unable to break free. Joshua and the two guards sat helpless. Without weapons, there was nothing they could do. Then the large, blue dragon turned and disappeared as quickly as it came, and the defensive wall of snow collapsed. Dorothy was visibly shaken. Exhausted by the effort needed to stop the blue dragon, she slumped onto the seat beside Nicholas. Elvira looked triumphant, as she stared down at Dorothy and Nicholas. Then turning to look at Oliver sat besides Eleanor, her grin grew wider.

Oliver looked at Elvira with fury in his eyes. He was certain she had set this up to see if they had magic, and Dorothy had played right into her hands, but he did not blame Dorothy. He knew full well that he would have used magic to stop the blue dragon had it attacked his sleigh.

Oliver's concern now was for Dorothy, as she lay slumped, unmoving on the seat next to Nicholas, who was anxiously trying to wake his sister. Elvira's sleigh was leading the way back to the white castle, followed by the sleigh that carried, Eleanor, Oliver and Reif. Oliver struggled against Eleanor's grip, which seemed to tighten the more he fought. "Please, let me go," begged Oliver, as he looked directly into Eleanor's eyes. Unexpectedly, Eleanor relaxed her grip.

"How did she do that?" she asked.

"How did she do what?" said Oliver, rubbing his sore wrist, where red finger marks were visible from Eleanor's vice like grip.

"Stop the blue dragon," said Eleanor. Oliver shrugged his shoulders.

"I don't know," said Oliver, "we've only just discovered that we can perform magic."

"So you can perform magic as well?" asked Eleanor.

There seemed no point in lying now and so Oliver answered, "Yes."

The rest of the ride back to the white castle was made in silence. Oliver was annoyed with himself. There had been two things that Percival had warned them not to tell. Firstly, that they were five, and secondly that they could perform magic. They had failed him on both counts.

The question now was, what would Elvira do next.

Chapter 34
Centaurs, Ice and Snow

Sent by Cressida to seek out Saki and find a cure for her brother Dante, Aegeus and half a dozen centaurs had been travelling for many days heading north, leaving the rainbow forest behind. They had successfully managed to pass through the land of ogres without any conflict. Onwards further north they travelled, the warmth of the rainbow forest they were used to had been left far behind, the winds that blew unrelentingly day and night carried a chill like the centaurs had never experienced before. The ground underfoot was frozen solid, and as night fell, so did the wind. Frost descended upon them like a frozen blanket. They lit a fire for warmth, but it provided little relief against the night chill. When dawn finally arrived after a restless night of trying to sleep, no bird song greeted Aegeus and his companions. Only the distant cry of a snow eagle on its early morning hunt. Grey clouds were gathering, quickly blocking out the small amount of sunlight, turning early morning back to night. Aegeus had the crystal that Cressida had given him in a pouch that hung around his neck. He tipped the crystal into the palm of his left hand, hoping for a sign of magic; there was no glow. Placing the crystal back into the pouch, "We must keep heading north," said Aegeus.

Not used to the freezing conditions, Aegeus and his companions felt the cold in their stiff joints and frozen limbs; a feeling they did not enjoy. "How much more of this cold are we expected to endure?" asked one of the centaurs.

"We will keep going until we find Saki and the cure for Dante," answered Aegeus. Disgruntled noises came from the group. "Cressida will not be happy if we return without the cure," said Aegeus. More murmuring of discontent, but as Aegeus led the way, the other centaurs followed in single file. Frost had covered the ground where they had slept, but the further north they travelled, the frost covered ground gave way to snow. At first, patches of light snow here and there was evident on the ground, and on the north facing side of the trees, indicating the snow had come from that direction, but by afternoon, they were walking through snow that was four inches deep. Passing through a valley, a river sat frozen at the edge, where water plants stood encased in ice. Only the deeper water in the middle of the river lay unfrozen, slowly travelling on its way. It glistened black against the edge of white ice. Hills on either side were dotted with human dwellings. Those at the bottom had barely a covering of snow, but those nearer the top of the hill were half buried. Smoke escaping from chimneys indicated they were occupied. Aegeus removed the crystal again to see if it was glowing, but it was as clear as ever. "We need to keep moving," said Aegeus.

As they passed through the valley, they were being watched by the humans, peering from behind their shuttered windows. One of the younger centaurs moved alongside Aegeus. "They're watching us," he said.

"I know," said Aegeus, "they've probably never seen the like of us before." This thought provided little comfort. Humans were known to be aggressive when faced with the unknown.

Grateful when the human dwellings were finally left behind. The hillside grew wilder, a forest of trees stood tall and strong, a dense growth of bushes and brambles grew intertwined, forcing them to follow but a single pathway, peppered with footprints of various animals. As the day wore on, the wind had increased once more. Howling, as it passed between the trees. Snow began to fall, then, the crisp snap of a branch, and a low grumbling noise made them realise they were not alone. "Be alert, everyone," warned Aegeus, as he removed his bow from over one shoulder and gathered up an arrow from its quiver. Following his lead, the other centaurs did the same. As they stood with arrows ready to shoot, the low grumbling noise increased, moving ever closer, as the snapping of snow-covered branches and twigs circled around them. Snow crashed to the ground causing more confusion. The centaurs turned their heads from left to right and back again, trying to see where the danger was coming from. Suddenly, a gang of large hairy pig like creatures burst through the bushes. With a bony plate that extended beyond their long snout, they shovelled away the snow that covered the ground, searching for food. They had short pointed ears that stood upright, sturdy short legs, and solid fat bodies. They were covered in long, white, shaggy hair, grunting aggressively as they appeared on the pathway one of the centaurs fired an arrow and missed. "Here, what do you think you're playing at?" roared a human voice. Then a large human figure appeared, with long, dark hair that hung down beyond his shoulders, he had piercing blue eyes and a rugged complexion. He was wearing clothing of white shaggy hair and he carried a long staff gripped in strong muscular hands. A second centaur fired an arrow at the large human. The arrow embedded in the staff, the human roared again. "What the hell are you doing here?" As he moved closer, he was flanked by two large dogs with thick fur coats of white, snarling at the centaur, as he reloaded his bow with yet another arrow.

Aegeus ordered the centaurs not to fire another arrow as the human approached. Realising that Aegeus was in charge, the large human ordered the two dogs to stay. They obeyed and lay on the ground. Their eyes firmly fixed on the centaur that had fired an arrow at their master, who then pushed his way past the pig like creatures that had stopped moving forward and were using their snouts to rummage for food beneath the snow. He addressed Aegeus. "Who are you, and what are you doing here?" asked the human.

"My name is Aegeus, and we are on a mission to find an elderly woman called Saki." The human studied Aegeus for a while before speaking.

"My name is Ragnor, and I have lived in this valley all my life, never before have I heard the name Saki."

"Thank you for your assistance," said Aegeus, "and sorry for the shots fired, but if Saki is not here, we must be on our way." Ragnor laughed.

"Just as well they missed, or my dogs would have attacked." As Aegeus started to walk away.

"Why do you seek this Saki?" asked Ragnor. Aegeus stopped, he saw no reason not to tell the truth, and turned back to face Ragnor.

"We have been sent by Cressida the rainbow fairy queen to seek Saki, our queen is hopeful that Saki can help her brother who is ill." Leaning on his staff, Ragnor studied Aegeus with his piercing blue eyes.

"Follow me," he said.

With a flick of his staff on the rump of one of the snow hogs, they moved on down the path snorting as they went. "Come," Ragnor called, and the two large white dogs followed on after the hogs. Aegeus fell in line behind Ragnor with the rest of the centaurs following. "I know everyone in this valley," said Ragnor, "and the name means nothing to me, but I can point you in the direction of the next village."

"That would be most helpful," said Aegeus. "But first you will need some winter clothing for it will be much colder where you are heading," said Ragnor.

One of the younger centaurs complained, "We do not wear clothing like you weak humans."

Ragnor laughed. "It makes no difference to me whether you wear them or not, young centaur, but if you wish to survive rather than freeze to death, I would accept the offer if I were you." The young centaur snorted in disgust, but Aegeus said they would appreciate any clothing Ragnor could provide.

Having returned to the dwelling where Ragnor lived, he introduced Aegeus and the centaurs to his brother Abner. Abner had been feeling unwell and was sprawled across a large metal framed bed covered in snow hog skins of long white shaggy hair. He pushed himself so that he was sitting upright. "How are you feeling?" asked Ragnor.

"Better," answered Abner, as he looked curiously at the centaurs. "What is going on?" Abner asked.

"Do not worry, brother," said Ragnor, "I am just looking for some skins that no longer fit you. Ah, here they are," said Ragnor.

From a pile of snow hog skins that were stacked in a corner, Ragnor selected seven. He tossed one to each centaur. "Try these," he said. The young centaur who had complained earlier about not needing clothing sniffed the skin he had been given.

"This stinks of pig," he moaned, "I shall not wear this."

"As I said before," said Ragnor, "it is your choice, whether you choose to wear these or not, but it is going to get a lot colder where you are heading."

The skins had been cut and stitched together to form a jacket. Each of the centaurs tried them on, all except the young complainer. "They are water resistant and the wind does not pass through," said Ragnor, "they will keep you dry and warm."

"Thank you," said Aegeus. The young centaur still looked upon the jacket with disgust, but eventually tried it on. It dwarfed him and hung to the ground.

Ragnor could not help but laugh at the sight, as Abner said, "He looks like an overgrown snow hog." Infuriated, the young centaur removed the hog skin and threw it across the floor.

"My apologies," said Ragnor, and he selected a smaller jacket from the pile. "Here, try this one," said Ragnor. The second jacket fit perfectly, but it still had the stench of pig.

Abner lay down once again as Ragnor said, "I will be back within the hour."

"Farewell, centaurs," said Abner, as they headed out into the cold once more. The snow hogs had been placed in a holding pen whilst the two large dogs were left inside the dwelling with Abner.

Twenty minutes after leaving Ragnor's dwelling, they passed beyond a coppice of trees, and found themselves at the entrance to a narrow pathway between what looked like a mountain split in half. The walls either side were sheer and covered in ice. "This is as far as I go," said Ragnor.

"You expect us to go in there?" asked the young centaur angrily.

"You have two choices," said Ragnor, "you can go around the mountain which can take up to a month, or you can take your chance and get through this day."

"Thank you for all your help," said Aegeus, "we will go through."

"Farewell, my friend," said Ragnor, "tread carefully." As Ragnor turned away, he could hear the young centaur complaining yet again. Grateful he would not have to listen to him anymore, he headed home. Aegeus gave the command to move forward and although the young centaur was not happy, he fell in line. The ground was frozen underfoot and slippery to walk on as it was covered in ice, with a layer of snow on top, the ice covered, wall on one side sparkled golden reflecting the sunlight, whilst the wall in shadow appeared silvery grey.

To the left of the pathway they followed, evidence of a frozen river ran alongside. The pathway twisted and turned, ascended and descended, as the river ran parallel, then as they turned a corner, they passed beneath a large piece of rock that lay covered in ice forming a frozen archway. As they moved further on, frozen waterfalls hung in the air as if caught by magic, and the coldness of the air was evident with each breath, with each centaur's head shrouded in mist.

A howling echo bounced off the sheer walls of ice, and encompassed the centaurs. Aegeus at the front of the line froze, listening intently and looking up, the following centaurs came to a halt. "What was that?" asked the young centaur nervously. As a second howl broke through the silence, louder than the first, a flurry of snow fell from the ice-covered wall as a crack appeared in the ice.

Aegeus did not answer, but moved on slowly, encouraging the others to follow, fully aware of the nervousness that had spread through the group like a rampant disease. "We must keep moving if we are to get through this before nightfall," said Aegeus. Aegeus himself was nervous but knew he must not show fear to the others if he expected them to follow his lead.

Aegeus let out a sigh of relief as they reached the end of the pathway that had led them between the ice-covered walls. Stepping away from the mountain, he realised Ragnor had been right. The air was much colder than before. Grateful for the snow hog jackets, Aegeus took time to pause. The snowy landscape was stunning in its beauty. An expanse of snow lay before them, with a forest of frozen trees to their right that sparkled golden in the sunlight. As he stood surveying the vista that awaited them, he noticed smoke spiralling up above the trees from an invisible fire. Aegeus then removed the crystal from the pouch around his neck. As it sat in the palm of his left hand, it glowed. Filled with joy, Aegeus called to the other centaurs. As the centaurs moved forward to gather around, the young centaur spotted something in the snow. A fresh set of large footprints. On closer inspection, the front of the footprint revealed four large indents in the snow, with four smaller holes in front, to the rear was one larger indent.

"Look at these," he called. It was the last thing he ever said, for at that very moment, a giant snow leopard sprang from its hiding place, camouflaged against the snow with its pure white coat. Grabbing the young centaur by the throat and crushing its windpipe, death was swift.

Caught unaware by its sudden appearance, the centaurs reached for their bows but by the time they had removed an arrow from its quiver, the giant snow leopard had retreated back into its snow hole, dragging the body of the young centaur with it, leaving behind a trail of blood in the snow.

"There is nothing we can do for him now," said Aegeus. Holding up the crystal for all to see, "Magic is near," he said, "we will head towards the smoke," pointing towards the frozen forest where the smoke was floating away above the trees.

Aegeus led the way and instructed everyone, "Keep your bow in hand loaded with an arrow, we don't want to get caught out like that again." Each centaur carried out the order, following Aegeus in single file. Nervously looking from side to side, they entered the frozen forest. The trees that sparkled were not covered in frost or snow, but were encased in ice. As they passed between the trees, their reflections accompanied them. This only added to their fear, for reflected movement from the trees was distorted and so as fear turned to panic. One of the centaurs fired an arrow at his own reflection only for the ice on the tree to crack and fall to the ground, narrowly missing two of his companions. An argument broke out between the three centaurs. Aegeus stopped. "Calm yourselves," he said, softly, and then turned to carry on. Holding the crystal in his left hand, he checked to see if it was still glowing. It was brighter than ever. He knew they were close. The reflected images however continued to cause fear. One centaur thought he saw something large and white reflected in the ice standing behind him. But when he turned, there was nothing there. No footprints were visible in the snow that lay undisturbed. Turning around once more, he realised he had been left behind. Following in the footsteps of those that had gone before he raced to catch up, was it his imagination or was there something keeping pace with him. He couldn't be sure, reflected images were more blurred than before because of the speed he was travelling. How could he have been so stupid, he thought to himself, allowing them to get so far ahead. When he finally caught them up, he was out of breath, his heart pounding in his chest.

The further they travelled through frozen forest, the trees thinned, and a cabin appeared in a small clearing. Grey-white smoke billowing from the roof of the cabin told them someone was home. Aegeus stopped and removed the crystal from the pouch around his neck. It glowed too bright to look at. "I believe we have found the place," he said.

The door to the cabin opened and a voice called to them, "Welcome, won't you come inside?" Aegeus led the centaurs towards the cabin. As they approached, an old lady appeared. Her skin was deeply wrinkled and she moved slowly as if time itself had slowed, but the emerald eyes were sparkling and youthful. "Come in, come in," she said welcoming them, standing to one side as they entered, then closing the door as the last passed into the cabin. Aegeus went to introduce himself to the old woman.

"My name is—"

"Yes, yes," said the old woman, "I know who you are and what you seek."

"Then I assume you are Saki?" said Aegeus.

"Yes, yes," she said again.

"Can you help us?" asked Aegeus.

"Of course I can," said Saki, "but tell me, why should I?"

"I have been instructed to promise you anything," said Aegeus. Saki studied him with her emerald eyes, contemplating, saying nothing. The rest of the centaurs felt uneasy, but Aegeus stood tall and proud.

"I wish to return with you to the rainbow forest, so that I can give Cressida what she needs in person. Pull my sleigh for me and I will protect you from harm."

The angry response from the centaurs was not unexpected. "We are not work horses," said one particularly aggressive looking centaur, as the others jeered in agreement. Saki simply sat down at the large dining table without saying a word and watched. It was Aegeus who spoke next, turning to face his companions.

"We have been ordered to promise Saki anything she asks," he said.

"I will not pull a sleigh," said the large, grey centaur, flaring his nostrils angrily and stomping the floor.

Saki spoke softly. "That is your choice," she said, "but I cannot protect you from harm if you are not prepared to help me."

Aegeus pleaded with the large, grey centaur, "Rufus, I beg of you, is it so terrible to pull a sleigh."

"I would rather die a thousand deaths than allow myself to be used like a common horse."

"And the rest of you?" asked Aegeus. "Will you help me pull Saki's sleigh?" Each and every one of the centaurs avoided Aegeus' gaze choosing instead to look at the floor.

"It seems I am the only one willing to pull your sleigh," said Aegeus.

"Then so be it," said Saki.

"Come, I am ready to leave." Aegeus was taken by surprise, as were all the centaurs.

"We are leaving straight away?" asked Aegeus.

"I see no reason to wait any longer, do you?" asked Saki. Opening the cabin door, she stepped outside. There ready and waiting was a bright-red sleigh, with a harness for one centaur.

"How did you know that only one of us would pull your sleigh?" asked Aegeus.

"I know everything," answered Saki, but they had to be given the choice. Aegeus walked to the front of the sleigh and the harness magically attached itself to his body. Saki then climbed onboard. The grey centaur watched on resentfully. "Well, goodbye then," said Saki with a wave of her hand. "Onwards and upwards," she called to Aegeus, who took his first step and was shocked to feel the ground disappear from beneath his feet. He found the sleigh weightless as he continued to walk forwards. Leaving the ground behind was a strange sensation, but he somehow knew this was meant to happen. Then the sleigh began to rise higher and higher clearing the trees. Rufus and the remaining centaurs watched on in awe. Only when the sleigh had disappeared from their sight did they lower their gaze, but too late, they had been surrounded by a group of white, long-haired yetis, and before they could react, the attack was launched, and swiftly over.

Chapter 35
Hebe in the Garden of Youth

On returning to the white castle, Elvira had instructed that Prince Oliver and Princess Dorothy and their friends should be escorted to their bedrooms, where they would stay until further notice. Although Oliver objected at first, when he and Reif were shown to their room, they unexpectedly found Percival waiting there. Oliver waited until they were left alone, listening besides the door as the lock clicked into place and he heard footsteps walking away. "She knows everything," said Oliver, as he crossed the room and sat beside Percival.

"How did that happen?" asked Percival.

"It was Nicholas," said Oliver, "Elvira was asking Dorothy questions, who was trying to answer carefully without letting anything slip and Nicholas mentioned Alice and Mary, and then Elvira set a trap. A winged blue dragon flew towards the sleigh carrying Nicholas and Dorothy and Dorothy created a wall of snow to halt the dragon."

Percival sat thinking without saying a word. "Did you not hear me," said Oliver, "she knows we are five, and that we have magic, she knows everything you told us to hide from her."

"That cannot be helped," said Percival, "it is done."

Lowering his voice to a whisper, "I have discovered something while you were away," said Percival.

"What is it, what did you find?" asked Oliver.

"I found a room full of children playing in a rainbow-coloured garden beneath the white castle," said Percival. Oliver and Reif looked at him disbelief. "In there, I met a young girl who said her name was Hebe. She said the garden is called, the garden of youth, and as long as Elvira visits once a week, she will stay youthful, young and beautiful." Oliver and Reif looked at Percival in awe. Then just as Oliver was about to speak, a click from the door alerted Percival and

Oliver that a key in the lock was being turned. They stopped talking. As the door opened, Dorothy entered the room first. She seemed nervous and raced across the room into the arms of Reif, then in walked Elvira accompanied by Eleanor and Nicholas.

"I see you have been exploring my castle while we were out," said Elvira, addressing Percival.

"Yes, Your Majesty," said Percival.

"Did you find anything of interest?" asked Elvira.

"I found the garden of youth," said Percival, watching Elvira's reaction closely. Elvira laughed.

"Did you speak to Hebe?" she asked.

"I did," said Percival.

"Poor child," said Elvira, "she is under the illusion that I use the room to stay youthful, which is why she calls it the garden of youth."

"So, what is the purpose of the room?" asked Percival.

"Why it is for the young children of course. I provide them with somewhere to play safely while their immune systems grow strong enough to cope with the freezing cold temperatures they will have to endure living here. Would you like to visit there again?" she asked.

"I would," said Dorothy.

"Follow me," said Elvira. She led them to the room of exquisite white furniture, and as she crossed the room, a wall panel disappeared revealing a well, lit staircase. Leading the way, Elvira started to descend. Dorothy, Oliver and Reif followed, with Eleanor and Nicholas bringing up the rear. The journey down to the garden of youth was much quicker this way than Percival's previous route. When the door opened, Elvira stood to one side allowing Dorothy to enter first. Her eyes widened in wonder at the rainbow-coloured trees. Even though she had seen pictures Stephen had painted, nothing compared to the real thing. She approached the nearest tree and reached up to touch the pink and purple leaves that sat on the lowest branch.

"They feel so real," she said.

"They are real," said Elvira. Walking below the branches, Dorothy was amazed at how many different colours there were. Even the trunk of the tree was multi-coloured.

"This is amazing," said Dorothy. Oliver, Reif and Percival followed as she moved further into the garden.

As they passed the tree at the centre of the garden, a voice called. "Hello again," said Hebe, as Percival passed by the tree where she was seated once more upon the ground.

"Hello, Hebe," said Percival, "these are my friends, Dorothy, Oliver and Reif." As Hebe studied each in turn, her eyes settled on Dorothy.

"Hello, Dorothy, do you like my garden?" she asked.

"It is very beautiful," replied Dorothy.

Two little blonde-haired girls were playing with a little red-haired boy. All dressed alike from head to toe in white. As Dorothy watched, the ball they were playing with ended up rolling across the green grass and resting against her left ankle. As she bent down to pick up the ball, the little red-haired boy asked, "May I have my ball, please?" Dorothy smiled.

"There you go," she said, as she handed it back. When she straightened up, Elvira who had followed her into the room was standing right by her side.

"As you can see," said Elvira, "they are all perfectly happy. If you don't believe me, why don't you ask them why they are here?"

"Okay," said Dorothy, "I will." Looking around at all the children, Dorothy decided to ask Hebe as she felt the others were all too young. "Hello, Hebe," said Dorothy, crouching down beside her so as not to tower over her, "can you tell me why you are here?"

"I am here to look after the children," said Hebe, as Dorothy doubted whether Elvira had been telling the truth, Hebe continued, "they are not yet strong enough to live in the cold above."

"Thank you," said Dorothy.

"You see, I told you," said Elvira, "there is nothing going on here except a young child's wild imagination."

"I think it is time we went back upstairs," said Elvira, "you will want to have a bath and change your clothes before tonight's ball."

"I had forgotten about the ball," said Dorothy, "I have nothing to wear."

"You need not worry about that," said Elvira, "you will find new clothes laid out on your beds. I guarantee they will fit."

Dorothy practically ran up the stairs leading the way, so eager to have a warm bath and put on a new dress for the ball. Elvira stood holding the door to the garden of youth open. Percival was the last to leave. She gave him a satisfied smile, and he nodded his head without making comment. As he started to climb the stairs, Elvira closed the door and followed.

Bathed and ready to get dressed, Dorothy found laid out on her bed a pale pink dress. A blink was in attendance and helped Dorothy to slip the dress on and then button up the back. A pair of shoes in matching colour were sat upon a velvet cushion on the bedside table. Dorothy placed the shoes on the floor and slipped her feet into the shoes which were a perfect fit. She danced her way across the room to stand in front of the full-length mirror. On the right-hand side of her dress starting from the neckline all the way down to the hem were tiny embroidered flowers of the palest shade of blue. Her hair had been washed and brushed and as she stood looking at her reflection, she thought she looked more like her mother than ever before.

A knock on her door. "Come in," she called. As the door swung open, Oliver dressed in a black suit with white shirt entered. Dorothy was still facing the mirror. As she turned, Oliver stopped in his tracks. Momentarily, they stood looking at each other smiling, when Oliver finally spoke.

"I have never seen you look more like our mother," he said. Dorothy blushed a little as Reif entered the room, followed by Eleanor holding Nicholas by the hand.

"It is time," said Eleanor. She then turned and led Nicholas from the room. Using his free hand, Nicholas beckoned for the others to follow.

They entered the ballroom to whispers, greeted by the tall, thin man in the blood-red suit. He called for silence. The candle chandeliers were lit, and the room was full of party guests. The tall, thin man in the blood-red suit introduced each of them in turn. "Your Majesty, may I present Princess Dorothy and Prince Oliver, and their esteemed friends, Reif and Percival." Eleanor who was wearing a pale green dress decorated with diamonds, led them down the blue marble staircase. Still holding Nicholas by the hand, like his brother Oliver, he was dressed in black. Whispers from amongst the party guests started up again, as they crossed the ballroom floor. Who are they, was the question that followed them, where did they come from. When they finally arrived at the steps that led to Elvira's throne, she rose and greeted them.

"Welcome to the ball."

The music began to play and Elvira made her way down the steps to the dance floor. Wearing a white dress decorated with diamonds, she sparkled beneath the chandeliers as she took Nicholas by the hand and danced around the room. As party guests joined in, Reif asked Dorothy if she would care to join him on the dance floor, and she accepted. Oliver asked Eleanor to dance and she duly obliged, leaving Percival alone. He found a seat and sat down, keeping a watchful eye on everyone.

The party had been in full swing for at least an hour, when Elvira decided she had danced enough. Taking Nicholas by the hand, she left the dance floor and made her way up the steps to her throne. Once there, she clapped her hands and the musicians ceased playing. All eyes turned towards Elvira.

Dorothy, Reif and Oliver had no idea what was happening, as the party guests hurriedly left the floor. Eleanor told them to stay there, as she left them in the middle of the dance floor, and stepped away. Elvira made her way down to the ballroom floor once more. "We have a little surprise for you," she said. As she approached, everyone around the dance floor held their breath wondering what was about to happen. Elvira bent down and placed a small glass brooch on the floor. They watched in wonder as she stepped away. The brooch began to pulse a soft glow. Dorothy glanced at Oliver excitedly, still holding Reif's hand. As the glow grew brighter, the brooch began to grow. A golden horned head appeared first. Then as the body grew, wings unfolded, and in a bright flash of light, they all turned away. Only when the light had dimmed did they turn to look again at the creature before them. It had the golden face of a lion, but with a red mane and horns. The wings stood vertical from its back at least eight feet high, the body of the beast was multi-coloured and sparkling, as were the wings, and to finish off this strangest of animals, it had the segmented tail of a red scorpion, including its sting.

Percival was on his feet and quickly made his way onto the dance floor. It seemed as if the creature was still waking up as Percival passed, turning its head from side to side. Percival reached Oliver, Dorothy and Reif just as it screamed a terrifying roar. "What is that?" asked Dorothy, no longer enjoying the spectacle.

"It is a Manticore," said Percival.

"A what?" asked Oliver.

"It is a Manticore," repeated Percival, "a relentless hunter with a taste for humans that will eat not just flesh but will consume all bones as well, leaving nothing."

"What can we do?" asked Oliver.

"Stand perfectly still," said Percival, "the worst thing you can do is run." Just at that moment, the two guards travelling with Oliver raced onto the dance floor before anyone could stop them. The Manticore didn't hesitate to attack, grasping one in its powerful jaws the crunching of bones echoed around the room. The second guard stumbled and fell to the floor. Before he could get back to his feet, he found himself lifted into the air impaled by the Manticore's sting. Dorothy screamed along with many of the guests. She looked away, shocked by what had happened and fearful for their lives. "Don't worry, Elvira won't let it harm you," said Percival, "it's a test, trying to force you into using magic." The Manticore finished devouring the guard caught within its jaws, and with the second guard impaled on its sting, suspended high above its back it moved closer.

Oliver didn't know why he did it, but he drew in a deep breath and then blew it out. A wall of windows behind them flew open and in rushed a gale force wind that halted the Manticore in its tracks. More screams from the party guests mingled with the howling of the wind. Snow carried in on the wind now lay as a covering on the dance floor where it had frozen turning to ice. The Manticore took a step closer. This time, it was Dorothy who acted. Raising her arms out in front of her, fragments of ice were lifted from the floor. Then pushing her hands away, the splinters of ice shot at the Manticore. On impact, the ice shattered as did the Manticore, and laid out across the ballroom floor was nothing more than coloured glass, and the body of the dead guard.

Dorothy cried a mixture of tears, tears of happiness that the ordeal was over, but tears of sadness for the loss of the two guards. Elvira looked down upon them with a smile of sheer happiness. Oliver glared back. His dislike for Elvira plain for everyone to see. As they stared at each other, party guests were already fleeing from the castle ballroom before Elvira called, without taking her eyes off Oliver, "Party's over."

Oliver, Dorothy, Reif and Percival were left standing alone in the centre of the dance floor as the ballroom emptied. Dorothy clung to Reif for support with her head resting against his chest.

Elvira waited for the last of the guests to exit. Only then did she speak. "Thank you," she said, "for the wonderful display of your talents."

"Why did you have to kill them?" asked Dorothy.

"Why I didn't kill them," said Elvira, "they just got in the way of the Manticore."

"You knew what you were doing when you set it upon us though, didn't you?" said Oliver.

"Well, I had to find out for myself what talents you have," said Elvira.

Before another word was said, Oliver, Dorothy, Reif and Percival found themselves surrounded by blinks. "Do not be alarmed," said Elvira, "they are only here to escort you back to your rooms."

"And what if we don't wish to go?" asked Oliver.

"I have ways of making people do what I want," said Elvira. Oliver went to argue some more, but it was Dorothy who stopped him.

"Look," she whispered, "she has Nicholas." Oliver lowered his eyes from Elvira's and only then noticed how closely she held Nicholas. As anger rose within his body, he remembered a warning Saki had given about evil witches using loved ones as a hostage to control another.

"Why go to all this trouble when you could have just asked us about our magic?" said Oliver.

"Because you would have lied, and anyway, this was much more fun," said Elvira.

"So, what do you want from us?" asked Dorothy, trying to stay calm.

"I want Oliver to take Eleanor back to your castle so that you can collect your sisters and bring them to me," said Elvira.

"Are you mad?" said Oliver. "Why would I do that?"

"You will do as I ask if you want your brother and sister to live," said Elvira, whose tone of voice had changed from sickly sweet too harsh.

Dorothy and Oliver looked at each other. "You can't do this," pleaded Dorothy, "you can't bring Alice and Mary here."

"I don't see how I have a choice," said Oliver, "I can't just let you and Nicholas die, can I?" Turning to face Elvira. "All right, I agree to take Eleanor to our home, but I don't know how to leave your kingdom," said Oliver.

"I will provide an exit from my kingdom," said Elvira, "you just make sure you keep to your side of the bargain and return with your sisters."

Chapter 36
Saki Saves Dante's Mind

Aegeus and Saki had completed the journey across the sky, travelling throughout the night by the light of the purple moon, arriving at Cressida's crystal palace at dawn as the three suns were drifting apart, the crystal palace sparkled the colours of a rainbow as light was reflected from the three suns. As Saki dismounted from the sleigh, it immediately disappeared. "Your sleigh," said Aegeus.

"Oh, I won't be needing that anymore," said Saki, "lead the way."

As they approached the front entrance to the crystal palace, the doors opened. A guard of honour appeared to escort them inside. Passing through the crystal palace, many brightly coloured fairies had come to get a look at Saki, believing her only to be a myth. She moved slowly as if time itself had slowed but took no notice of the inquisitive stares that she had aroused. Whispers followed as she passed from room to room. The guard of honour led Aegeus and Saki all the way to the throne room where Cressida sat awaiting their arrival. Cressida was sat upon her throne high above where Aegeus and Saki stopped. Saki lowered her head. "Greetings," said Cressida, as Saki raised her head Cressida opened her rainbow-coloured wings and elegantly floated to the ground and gently landed in front of Saki.

"Your Majesty," said Saki. "Where is your brother Dante, it is imperative that I heal him as quickly as possible."

Cressida was at first stunned by the lack of courtesies shown by Saki but realised the eagerness in the question. "This way," she said, and she led the way from the throne room and up the large staircase, Saki followed at a much slower pace. On more than one occasion, Cressida had to stop and wait for Saki to catch up. Finally having reached the room where Dante was resting, Saki asked to be allowed to go inside alone. Cressida was reluctant at first to agree but under the gaze from Saki finally gave permission, and so the doors were opened for Saki to enter alone.

Dante was awake but in bed with the covers pulled up tightly around his neck. Laying on his side, he watched as the door opened. When Saki walked in, there was a sudden intake of breath and his eyes opened wide with fear. He began to tremble as she approached the bed. "There, there," she said to him as she got closer, in a soft and soothing voice. Immediately, the trembling ceased and the wild staring eyes relaxed. "Everything is going to be all right." Without hesitation, Saki walked all the way across the room and sat on the edge of Dante's bed. He flinched slightly as she sat down, but otherwise made no movement or sound. She had been wearing a green woollen shawl around her shoulders that matched the colour of her eyes, which she now removed. Hanging on a single thread of gold around her neck was a small glass bottle. Inside were two small pink leeches. Dante spotted the leeches and the fear in his eyes returned, along with the trembling. "There is no need to worry," said Saki soothingly once more, and once again, he lay still. As Saki gently tipped the leeches into the palm of her left hand, Dante's eyes followed. She moved her hand up alongside his head, so he was now looking out of the corner of his eyes. With her right hand, she placed one of the pink leeches onto his right temple and then the other on his left. As the leeches burrowed into his skin, Saki gave the command. "Only remove the fear inflicted by Helga the one-eyed hag." She repeated the command over and over. At first, Dante's body had gone rigid, but as the seconds ticked by, he became more relaxed and within a couple of minutes, the once pink leeches were now re-emerging from his temples, having absorbed the evil, and in doing so, turned black.

Saki gently lifted the leeches from Dante's face and placed them back in the glass bottle that hung around her neck. She then replaced her shawl. "You may come in now," called Saki. Hesitantly, Cressida entered the room, not sure of what to expect. She was overwhelmed with joy to see Dante sitting upright in bed and beaming a huge smile.

"How can I ever thank you," said Cressida.

"Do you know of the prophecy, of the one who gives birth to five who combined will have the power to overthrow a kingdom?" asked Saki.

"Yes, or course," said Cressida, "but why are you asking me this?"

"Because they are here," said Saki, "well three of them are." Saki was watching Dante's expression, waiting for him to realise who she was referring to.

"I know who they are," said Dante. "But how?"

"Their mother was Elizabeth, sister of Elvira," said Saki.

"So, what can we do?" asked Cressida.

"There is only one thing I can do," said Dante, "get the last two of Elizabeth's children and bring them here."

"You realise you will not be alone in your attempt to bring Elizabeth's children here," said Saki.

"Then let the race commence," said Dante.